P9-ARQ-327

"BARNETT LITERALLY PULLS
OUT THE BIG GUNS....
Strong, multidimensional characters,
simultaneous love stories,
and enlightening historical detail
add up to a breakout novel
destined to extend her audience."
—*Booklist*

"An unforgettable novel that brings
to life the Greatest Generation."
—Susan Elizabeth Phillips

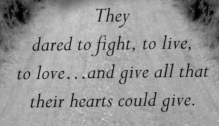

*They
dared to fight, to live,
to love…and give all that
their hearts could give.*

"More than a love story, *SENTIMENTAL JOURNEY* is a rich tale of men and women whose lives intersect in a time of war and desperation, passion and pleasure. Intensely poignant, unforgettably compelling!"

—Christina Dodd

"A RIVETING, MULTILAYERED MAINSTREAM NOVEL OF HEROISM, LOVE, AND PERSONAL GROWTH set against the emotionally charged backdrop of World War II. Fast-paced and turbulent, her story sweeps a quintet of compelling characters from their diverse and separate lives and brings them together in adventure and tragedy, linking them forever in ways they could never have predicted. Witty dialog, a refreshing sprinkle of humor, and well-chosen details of the 1940s lighten this poignant, emotionally involving novel that is definitely mainstream but still spins a series of love stories with enough romantic appeal to please even the most die-hard romance fan."

—*Library Journal*

"AN EPIC, ROMANTIC STORY. . . . Not only has Jill Barnett managed to write a book that reminds us of the classic sagas, but she has written a loving tribute to our parents and grandparents, explaining why they are known as 'The Greatest Generation.' Her characters leap from the pages as do the heartstopping flight scenes and emotionally moving love scenes. Readers looking for that old-fashioned 'big read' will find it here in a masterful story."

—*Romantic Times*

"A FASCINATING STORY that will hold your interest from start to finish."

—*The Old Book Barn Gazette*

"A POWERFUL AND MOVING NOVEL ABOUT LOVE, HONOR, COURAGE AND REVENGE. The story is set against the background of World War II with action ranging from the American West to the battlefields of Europe. The characters are vividly drawn men and women whose lives are woven together then forever changed by the onset of world conflict. . . . Barnett has excelled in her first hardcover novel with a tale filled with remarkable and memorable men and women tempered by a war that at times seems to be tearing the world apart at the seams. It is a tribute to everyday people who in times of trial and stress became authentic heroes and heroines."

—*Abilene Reporter-News*

"A PAGE-TURNER AND MUST READ. All the fine attributes defined by the 'Greatest Generation' and more can be found within the pages of Barnett's *SENTIMENTAL JOURNEY.*"

—Barnesandnoble.com

"COMPELLING . . . . Readers will not want to miss *SENTIMENTAL JOURNEY.* Barnett weaves together five characters in a tale that spans three continents. . . . Extremely well-written."

—America Online Romance Fiction Forum

Books by Jill Barnett

Surrender a Dream
Just a Kiss Away
Bewitching
Heart's Haven
Dreaming
Imagine
Carried Away
Wonderful
Wild
Wicked
Sentimental Journey

Published by POCKET BOOKS

JILL
BARNETT

SENTIMENTAL
JOURNEY

A Novel

POCKET **STAR** BOOKS

New York   London   Toronto   Sydney   Singapore

This book is a work of fiction. Names, characters, places and incidents are products of the author's imagination or are used fictitiously. Any resemblance to actual events or locales or persons, living or dead, is entirely coincidental.

 A Pocket Star Book published by
POCKET BOOKS, a division of Simon & Schuster, Inc.
1230 Avenue of the Americas, New York, NY 10020

Copyright © 2001 by Jill Barnett Stadler

Originally published in hardcover in 2001 by Pocket Books

ISBN: 0-671-03534-7

First Pocket Books paperback printing March 2002

10 9 8 7 6 5 4 3 2 1

POCKET STAR BOOKS and colophon are registered trademarks of Simon & Schuster, Inc.

For information regarding special discounts for bulk purchases, please contact Simon & Schuster Special Sales at 1-800-456-6798 or business@simonandschuster.com

Front cover illustration by Robert Hunt
Tip-in art photo illustration by Lisa Litwack

Printed in the U.S.A.

I grew up at the knee of one of the finest storytellers ever born in Texas, and that's saying something because most Texans can surely tell one hell of a good tale. Guy Barnett was a tall, red-haired devil, a veteran of World War II, a damn fine Big Band musician, and a man who loved to fly planes.

He was one of those rare people who talked to strangers, and rarer still, he listened to what they had to say. He could walk into a room full of people and two hours later tell you something interesting and personal about each and every person there. He was my father, and part of a fading generation of patriots who believed in their country, in the American flag and what it stood for.

His stories of the war were my bedtime tales, the lush sweet notes of his muted trumpet were my lullabies. Long before a woman ever burned a bra, he taught me I was his equal, and it was by his example that I learned what a good man was.

This book is for him and his courageous generation—the men and women of World War II who were willing to risk their lives for honor and for their country, so their children, like me, could have the freedom to write about it.

NORTH AFRICA

1942

LIBYAN DESERT

OCTOBER 11

There's no rhyme or reason as to how the mind of a soldier works in battle. Men holed up in a farmhouse will cook dinner in the middle of a sniper attack, setting the table with a checkered cloth and folded napkins, a platter of sliced fruit and cheese sitting in the center, like they were chefs in some Italian joint back home. You find that you don't think they're nuts for longer than that first stunned moment, that one second of rational thought in a place where hell's a-popping and nothing makes sense.

If there's no guarantee of a tomorrow, you need normalcy to ground you. And it's then you realize that maybe those cookin' fools have got a helluva good idea. You sit yourself down with them and stuff your face, while the whole damn war is going on around you.

You see a soldier fall into a ditch of mud and dead men, then come crawling out more worried about the photographs in his wallet than about cleaning his rifle. It sounds insane, but when you have the chance to, you squat behind a tree, bullets flying around you, and there, behind that tree, for just one second, you pull out your own wallet and flip open the pictures.

In a bar or at a canteen dance, when some dame finds

out you've been in combat, she asks questions like, "Before a battle, do you think about heaven?"

No.

"Do you think about dying?"

No. You're too damn afraid to. You might jinx yourself. You decide early on that no matter how much the enemy shoots at you, you'll be damned if you're going to get hit.

Kitty asked one night, "Don't you ever get scared?"

Everyone gets scared. Fear keeps you alive. But once you see the enemy, you don't have much time to be afraid. Or to think about it. The truth is, it's fear of the unknown that really gets you.

She understood. She lived with that kind of fear every waking minute. Maybe that was the night they fell in love, when they were alone, spilling their guts to each other, thinking life made no sense because they were damn near freezing to death in the middle of the Sahara Desert.

Just like now.

He was back in North Africa, in the desert again just before dawn, where it was still and quiet. The sand was hard and bare and so cold it was like lying on snow.

Through a perimeter of wooden crossed-stakes and entangled wire stood his objective—a bowl of Axis trouble hollowed out of an endless range of sand dunes in the Libyan desert. Dim lights downlit the corners of the buildings and the northeast side of the compound, where a convoy of trucks and tanks were lined up for fueling at first light.

From here it looked like a movie set, the type of place Gary Cooper stormed in *Beau Geste*. But this was 1942, a different time, a different war. This was real.

In less than ten minutes, Allied mission Foxfire would begin. Their job: to infiltrate Rommel's compound. Ten minutes after that, they would blow everything sky-high: the compound, the largest Deutsches Afrika Korps supply dump in the desert, and the Jadgwaffe's airfield.

He checked his watch ... every few minutes.

Time moved at glacial speed. Seconds and minutes—measurements of a lifetime that have little meaning by themselves.

He waited. Tense. Edgy. Until 0400.

This was it.

He clipped a hole in the wire and moved forward, shimmying down a dune and up over another like some kind of desert viper.

"Halt!"

He froze at the edge of the dunes, half afraid to look up because he didn't know if he would be staring into the barrel of a Kar98k or if the voice he'd heard had carried up from below.

Lt. Colonel J.R. Cassidy raised his head slowly to find he was alone in the dunes.

But below and from out of nowhere, a troop of armed soldiers ran all over the compound. Spotlights sliced through darkness, sudden and glaring. The place lit up like a ball field in October.

Rommel's men had been waiting for them.

U.S. Army Air Force Captain Red Walker set the last charge on the supply bunker, grabbed his munitions pack and rifle, then slung each over a shoulder. He moved quietly along the concrete edges of the supply building. At the east corner, he stopped before making a cold run for it. He'd seen men lay their charges, then act like jackrabbits and get their fool heads shot off.

A hundred feet of open space stood between him and the cover from a stack of Nazi oil drums. He had four minutes to get to the airfield before everything blew. Four minutes that could feel like a lifetime, or an instant.

A German officer stood in the middle of the yard, between him and those barrels. Red could try to take him out, but that was chancy. The guy was standing in the middle of the compound.

Red pulled back and checked the time, then leaned his head against the building and waited. Overhead was a clear night sky that sucked all the day's heat from the loose desert sand. The air was cold as ice. Twenty-two degrees had been predicted at the final briefing. Yet here he was sweating.

Nothing made much sense anymore. War changed things. Everything. The whole goddamn world felt upside-down, sideways, and jackass-backwards. For years all he'd wanted was to get out of Acme, Texas. But here he was in the middle of the desert, blowing up the compound of a man he'd never seen, an enemy from a place as far away from Wilbarger County as a rattlesnake was from the North Pole.

He waited a few more minutes, then stared out past the perimeter at the desert beyond and mile after mile of nothing but sand dunes.

Hell . . . and people said West Texas was an armpit.

He checked his watch again, then wiped away the sweat that trickled into his eyes. His mouth was drier than week-old bread. For just an instant, he thought

about a big old Texas-sized glass of tea, sweetened with
a handful of white sugar and poured over two handfuls
of ice . . . about bluebonnets growing beside the road
and the clean smell of a woman who washed her hair
with lemon.

He shook his head and shifted, then looked around
the corner.

The officer hadn't moved.

Three minutes.

Should he run? He eased back, chewed it over. He'd
wait. Once his charges blew, it wouldn't matter if he had
to fire his rifle. It wouldn't matter if he fired a two-ton
ack-ack. It would be too late. The den of the Fox would
be on fire.

Cassidy had been on a dozen of these missions. He
claimed the difference between living and dying was in
the timing. He'd said it to Red and others over and over.
Time it exactly. If you rush, you die. If you wait too
long, someone else dies.

Instinct screamed inside Red's head, *Go, go, go! Get out
of there!* He asked himself how much of that instinct was
fueled by panic. Panic could kill you or make you a hero,
depending on how the chips fell. But thinking clearly,
well, Cassidy said that was what saved your sweet ass.

The soldier in him checked his watch again.

Thirty seconds more.

He began to mentally count it off.

Twenty-eight . . .

Twenty-five . . .

Twenty-two . . .

Twenty seconds.

"Halt!"

Sweet Jesus. . . .

The order was distant, as if it came from the truck depot. But sound carried in the desert like it did over water.

Compound spotlights came on as white and blinding as the Texas sun in July. Enemy soldiers ran out from the shadows. One of them was heading right toward him.

Next to the compound, a German bomber, a Junkers 88P, taxied down the narrow desert airstrip past a line of burning Messerschmitts, ME 109s. A smoking Panzer tank blocked the end of the runway. Two more planes blew up, Stukas, now nothing but flames flaring into the air.

The JU turned sharply; it was the only aircraft on the field left in one piece, and it was moving toward the compound.

An armored car marked with the Deutsches Afrika Korps palm tree and mounted with a machine gun came speeding in from the road and raced by the plane, the soldiers inside the vehicle motioning to the pilot to follow them.

The car careened in front of the bomber, leading the way, so the pilot slowed the plane a notch and moved in directly behind the machine gunner; they both headed for an Allied half-track stalled a few hundred feet away.

The Junkers's nose guns swiveled, sighting a target.

Too high.

The pilot shoved forward on the yoke, hit the brakes, and powered the tail; then he pressed down on the trigger and fired so many deadly rounds there was a gaping hole in the Korps vehicle where the palm tree and swastika had once been.

British Royal Air Force Pilot Commander George "Skip" Inskip released the trigger button and reduced power. The tail of the plane dropped back to the ground with a jar that would have rattled his teeth if they hadn't been clenched so damned tight. He looked ahead of him and taxied the plane closer toward the fence, on solid ground between the airfield and the supply dump.

There was chaos in the compound. Smoke and fire.

Am I the only one left?

That was a balmy thought, and not bloody likely. Along for the ride today were the Long Range Desert Group, those Desert Rats who gave Rommel hell; the SIG, experts who made successes of suicide missions; and the Yanks, two of them, commando-trained and specially picked by the OSS. Cassidy was a miracle-working scrounger who had a reputation for doing the impossible, and Walker, an ex-Air Corps pilot, sharpshooter, and demolitions expert, a tall, quiet Texan who hated Skip with everything he had in him.

Perhaps Walker had already corked it.

On some level, Skip understood Walker's hatred of him. He just didn't care. Charley would say he had to feel something deep down inside, but then Charley still believed he was square and aboveboard.

Skip looked ahead. The compound was burning, the fuel depot destroyed. And they had a dog's chance of getting out.

A moment later a man burst through an orange wall of fire and smoke. The soldier disappeared under the plane's wing before Skip could get a look at him.

The belly door of the JU suddenly opened. Hot air and smoke blew into the cockpit.

Hell....

Skip pulled his revolver, an Enfield No.2MK, and turned, one hand still on the controls.

"Don't shoot, you limey son of a bitch, or you'll have to explain to Charley that you were the one who killed me." Red Walker pulled himself up and inside, then rolled into the cockpit and strapped into the copilot's seat.

Skip shoved the gun back into his holster. "Where's Cassidy?"

"Last time I spotted him he was crawling down into the bunker. But that was before the whole thing SNAFU'd." Walker paused, looking around them. "Where are you taking this thing? The airfield is back that way."

"Tanks are blocking the runway. The place is lit up like a parade ground. I'm heading for the macadam," Skip said. "The airfield's useless." He gave the plane too much power and hit the road too fast. Beast of a machine was heavier than the fighters he was used to.

"Stop!" Walker was half turned in his seat looking out the glass. "I see Cassidy! He lost his helmet. I can see his blond head!"

"Most of the bloody Afrika Korps have blond heads."

"It was him."

"Did you plant the charges to blow both bunkers?" Skip kept going.

"Yes."

"Did the command bunker blow?"

"Yes."

"Did you see Cassidy get out?"

"No, but I was a little busy with about half a platoon of mad-as-hell Jerries. Cassidy got out. He always gets out."

Skip checked the time and kept going. "We were supposed to be out of here five minutes ago. Cassidy isn't here. The bunker's gone. This mission has had it." It looked like hell was coming up to meet them. Everything was burning. "Look!"

Walker glanced back out the window.

"We've done what damage we can to this place. I'm taking this plane up now." Skip reached for the throttle switch.

A pistol cocked next to his temple, the cold ring of the barrel pressed into his skin.

"No," Walker said quietly. "You're going to wait."

"I could kill you for this."

"By golly, you sure could."

"If I report your actions, your army would have you court-martialed."

Walker shrugged. "I could pull this trigger and there wouldn't be a report or a court-martial."

Skip laughed bitterly. "Just a mess in the cockpit, right?"

"Right . . . as you Brits always say . . . a bloody mess." Walker checked his watch. Tension hung between them, second after second after second. He looked out the window, but apparently saw no one, because he checked his watch again. He faced Skip but didn't move the gun. "Three minutes more. If Cassidy isn't here, you can hit the throttle for all she's worth."

Skip braked, then sat there, arms resting on the yoke, waiting.

Walker didn't drop the gun.

"I'll give Cassidy three minutes, but pull the gun away from my head."

"I was pretty darn young when my granddaddy taught me not to walk around the backside of a pissed-off mule, least not 'less I want to get my marbles kicked to hell and back. I'll just keep this gun right where it is for now."

From the compound, the sound of gunfire echoed back at them, ticking off time in sputtering rounds of ammo shells. It was quite amusing, really, him sitting there next to Red Walker, allies in spirit and duty, but enemies at heart, the barrel of a .32 caliber pistol against his head and the trigger held by the one man who truly wanted him dead.

He glanced at Walker, who wasn't smiling, but then the Yanks and the British didn't share the same sense of humor. Walker kept watching out the window for Cassidy. So Skip sat there, the smell of fuel and the taste of fire seeping slowly inside the cockpit until it was in every breath he took and his lungs felt tight and full.

He checked his watch. "Time's up."

Red swore one of those off-colored Texas colloquialisms, but he kept his word and holstered the pistol.

"These bloody gauges are unreadable." Skip moved the JU forward. He looked at the short strip of road ahead, the only level spot before the road humped up and down the dunes too deeply for a takeoff. He didn't have time to think. He just powered up and went for it.

"Goddammit, Inskip!" Red was leaning out the window. "Shitfire and hell! There's Cassidy! He's running just behind us!" He pulled his head back inside and glared at Skip. "Look for yourself!"

The engine noise was so loud Skip could barely hear him.

"Look, Inskip! It's Cassidy!" Red turned back. "Run, Colonel! Run!"

"If I stop now, we won't make it!" Skip saw Red turn and look at the gauges, then up at the road ahead. Red was a pilot. He could see the short length of level road.

Swearing, Red unbuckled, crawled out of his seat, and slid down into the belly of the plane.

A second later Skip heard the belly door drop open and a blast of air hit the back of his head.

J.R. jumped the fence, picked up an MP40, and fired. He had seen Walker hanging out the cockpit of the bomber, shouting, but J.R. kept firing until there was nothing to fire at. Inskip had to be behind the controls of that plane.

Damn. . . . He was late. Those two should have left already.

J.R. spun around. Smoke and fire were everywhere. He turned eastward, weapon poised and ready. But there were no enemy troops, just the British Desert Rats in an armored car, hanging on to their seats, guns firing as they sped away and disappeared over the dunes as if they had been a mirage.

He turned again.

No one was coming at him. Hell, he might just make it. He looked back. The bomber was moving down the blacktop road, its Jumo engines roaring to life. J.R. took off after it.

Running . . . running . . . running.

He was close, then closer.

He pumped his arms and legs.

"Run, Colonel! Run!" Walker was hanging out the plane door. He gripped the side of the plane and extended his hand.

He was still a few feet away.

Faster! Faster! Faster! I can make it! I can!

Bullets suddenly ate the ground behind him.

Pop! Pop! Pop! Pop! Pop!

The bullets sounded like popcorn. Firecrackers. Cap guns. They never sounded real. They never sounded like they could kill you.

RABAT, MOROCCO

1941

"I WONDER WHAT'S
BECOME OF SALLY"

S omeone was following her.
She'd been listening to those footsteps for a while, a cadence that was resolute and determined—the way men walked. Along the restless edges of the market district, the streets were a terrain of silent sandals, soft-soled babouches and dusty bare feet. His hard leather boots sounded heavy and bellicose.

To test him, she shifted left.

He shifted left.

She sped up, so did he.

She passed a vendor's booth where the air was filled with the acrid scent of tannin. A leather seller with newly dyed goods from Fez.

She stopped suddenly, turned back as if something had caught her eye.

His footsteps stopped, too, a silent echo of her motion that was a mere second off. She turned and stepped out of the cool morning shadows of the buildings along the Rue Souika. She forced herself to walk casually while still weaving in and out of the growing crowd.

Under the shadow of a mosque, a wall fountain at the Attarine spilled into a copper basin that made a deep tonal sound like water spilling into a sea cave. About a hundred feet away the newer dirt street changed to old flat stone paving, and once there, she moved between people, walking faster than anyone around her, moving farther into the center of the crowd.

The moment the man stepped from the dirt street to the stone paving, she heard him. His feet slipped; the sound was gritty, a scraping, chalkboard noise, the kind you felt in the back of your teeth.

She couldn't seem to shake him. She sped up, but from behind her came the sharp, angry voices of those he shoved aside. Her fear grew cold and chilly, a live thing. It did more than scare her silly. It did more than send eerie sensations down her arms and spine. Fear made her suddenly aware that she had done a stupid thing.

Fool . . . fool . . . fool . . . You weren't free until the plane was in the air. Until the boat was on the sea. Until the train crossed the border. You weren't home until you walked through the door.

She did not look back. It would do no good. At the corner she turned onto a narrow street. Slatted awnings hung protectively over the fruit-and-vegetable sellers and cast shade down on her head. With each breath she took she could smell the ripe casaba melons displayed on wooden tables made of old crates. It was like running through a sweet, invisible fog.

The crowd moved in the same direction, toward an open area where the harsh tropical sun once again beat down from overhead. Within moments she was hot and sweaty and running past the fragrant strawberry trees, into the zenana of the henna souk: the women's domain, where they chattered like desert larks. Here, antimony sulfide from eye kohl filled the hot, dry air, along with the stench of ghassoul from bath soap made of clay.

From nearby came the nasal voice of a woman singing a song about a lost nightingale. A goat brayed. She wanted to cry out for help herself. But the women here were worse than the men. No one in the women's souk would help the foolish American who was not wearing the anonymity of a haik.

Because she was finally going home, because the papers she carried would finally give her freedom, she wore a smart felt hat over her black hair, a hat she hadn't worn in months. A frivolous thing, wearing the hat, wearing her hair down. Just that morning she had finger-waved it, then rolled it under into a pageboy, a style that brushed her shoulders and made her feel feminine in a place where femininity was hidden away as if it were shameful to be a woman.

Her arrogant, self-important intention to prove a point for all of womankind seemed inconsequential to her now. Grandstanding for the female sex in a land where life had stayed the same for thousands of years? Kathryn Kincaid: some modern Joan of Arc, an icon to Middle Eastern womanhood, facing danger for the sake of an ideal in a place and time where only avarice or power changed the ways of men, and no amount of money changed anything for women.

She could disappear. Women often did. How utterly ironic that on the day she was to leave, she had forgotten the first thing she'd learned when she came here almost two years before. She could hear her friend Susan saying, "Kitty, you're brain wise and street stupid."

She kept moving, trying to hide from the man as she ran down one narrow street after another. Blood began to pound loudly in her ears; it made a hollow, beating sound that reminded her she was very much alive, but that soon she might not be.

The last remaining odors in the air were suddenly, inexplicably gone. It was as if that blazing sun overhead had just up and melted them away, leaving nothing behind but the scent of the chase.

She turned right and ran between two stone buildings, ran like crazy into another square. A wagon was coming through. She ducked down, grabbed hold of the side of the wagon and used it for cover. She reached up and unpinned her hat. She tossed it under the cart wheels, then jerked the thin, ivory chiffon scarf from her neck and wrapped it around and around her hair, frantically tucking in the ends as she moved alongside the wagon.

The market voices grew distant. The wagon picked up speed. She needed to half run to keep up.

A moment later the shadow of an alleyway cooled the right side of her face. She listened for a second, then quickly turned away from the wagon, still bent down as she ran down the alley, past a group of young boys playing a game of ball.

Their shouts and laughter were all around her. She heard the dull sounds of the ball bouncing against the sandstone walls, before it sped past her, rolling, rolling over the constant layer of sand that seemed to coat everything in this exotic land.

She stumbled. Her hand hit the warm stone bricks of the alley wall.

She couldn't hear the man's boots anymore.

Somewhere ahead of her dogs were barking, sharp, distant, but growing louder as she ran. Another animal brayed; for one instant it sounded like a scream.

She smelled lamb roasting over a fire pit. She knew the food sellers were on the western edge of Rue des Souks, where the city wall ran along one side. The booths were open there and staggered in a square surrounded by streets that were too wide to fill with people and were patrolled by the Vichy police.

And the police would not ignore her scream.

His soles clapped rapidly on the stone.

From behind her the children in the alley shouted again. Not at her this time, but at the man chasing her.

She stayed to the right side, dragging her hand along the sandy stones of the wall so she would not stumble again. The dry desert wind kept coming at her and was making a set of brass tent bells ring like wind chimes. A sweet sound, as if safety were right there.

He was running now, too. Closer.

Oh, God. . . .

Before her was nothing but a blur. Tears of fear swelled in her eyes, spilled onto her cheeks, and streamed back into her hair. She felt them drip down behind her ears. She heard him gasp for breath. The sound was so close to her she wasn't sure if it was the dry desert wind or his breath that brushed her ear. She tightened her fists and pumped her arms, picking up speed and running faster than she'd ever run in her life.

The dogs barked louder. Louder. Louder.

She stumbled again and fell down. For just a moment she was confused. Her sense of direction was gone, but she got up, afraid to stop running. But now she didn't know if she was running away from him or toward him.

Ahead of her she heard the shift of heavy transmission gears. An armored car? A truck? She ran toward it.

Sunshine, sudden, hot, and intense, hit her face. She was outside the alley, in the open and running over dust and hard-packed dirt.

Someone called out, *"Vite, vite, l'Américaine. Dépêche!"*

She heard the truck suddenly bearing down on her. She heard the engine noise and the rattle of its axles as it bounced over the pocked dirt streets.

She couldn't run any faster.

Beside her came the squealing scream of truck brakes. Inches away.

She stopped, afraid of running into its path.

Dust flew everywhere, into her nose, into her mouth. She stood in a cloud of it and waited for the impact, her eyes tightly shut . . . so ludicrous.

She would die on the day she was free.

Time stopped the way she'd always heard it did at moments like this.

She continued to stand there, waiting, shaking, unable to move, her chest burning for a real breath. Against her legs she could feel the undulating heat from the truck engine.

The truck tailgate opened with a junky rattle.

She opened her eyes. The sun was so bright there was no shadow, no silhouette, nothing before her eyes. Breathing was impossible. She bent down and placed her hands on her knees, disoriented still, trying to catch a breath that was out of reach.

Men jumped down out of the truck. She smelled male sweat, desert dust, and something else—the slightly burnt odor of starched and ironed twill. The smell of uniforms. The men wearing them surrounded her; their shadows blocked out the hot sun.

She felt an incredible sense of relief. The Vichy could protect her from the man who chased her. She took one more shallow breath. *"Aide. S'il vous plaît. Un homme me chasse."*

They said nothing. The Vichy had never given her any trouble other than the political quagmire that made her and others like her have to wait for exit papers. But that was all over now. She was going home.

She straightened. *"Pouvez-vous m'aider?"* Will you help me?"

The only answer she got was the click of a rifle. Then another, and another, all around her, *click . . . click . . . click . . .* like doors of escape locking closed.

"Qu'est ce que vous-voulez?" she said more forcefully.

A man grabbed her shoulder. His hand was hot and sweaty. He was panting. It was her pursuer.

Couscous. An inane thought. He had eaten couscous? What did that matter? She could feel the edges of hysteria: a laugh that was rising from her gut.

He jerked the scarf from her head.

Her laugh came out as a cry, small and final; the same pitiful noise the rabbits made when market butchers chopped their back feet off so they couldn't run away.

For just a moment she thought she might faint. She wobbled slightly, head down. Her loose hair fell into her face; it was damp and stringy and smelled of the Breck shampoo she'd used that morning.

He grabbed her hair in a tight fist, then twisted it hard and jerked her head up and around so she faced him. The bright sun behind him made everything look white.

She smelled that same frighteningly distinctive odor she'd first encountered years ago when she was just a kid, standing in front of a cage full of leopards at the zoo; it was the metallic, bloody smell of a predator, the kind of smell you never forgot. Now it was all around her, emanating from this man who was a good foot taller than she was.

He twisted her hair again even harder.

It hurt so badly she cried out.

He laughed.

She kicked him.

He spun her by her hair so her back was against his chest, his other arm clamped hard across her ribs.

"Someone help me!" she shouted. "Oh, God . . . Please! Help me!" she screamed it in English, in French, then in Italian.

He let her go, then kicked her feet out from under her.

She fell to her knees. Small, sharp pieces of gravel cut through her stockings. He stepped behind her and twisted her head back until her neck was exposed.

Oh, God. . . .

He was going to slit her throat.

She screamed as loud as she could.

He laughed. The sound was cruel. He thought her fear was funny.

She reached up and dug her nails into the bastard's wrists.

He released her. "Bitch!"

She stood up quickly, but she couldn't run because

the men surrounded her; their guns poked into her back and her ribs.

She faced him, then, defiant. If she was going to die, she wouldn't do it begging for her life.

She took a deep breath and stood there, ready to kick or claw again in an instant.

Two men grabbed her arms. She fought them. She punched and kicked, screaming and trying to make a scene that she hoped someone would remember for the right price.

She tried to pull her arms back and away. She kicked. They pinned her between the two of them, their hands clamped hard around her upper arms. These men smelled like the dust from the desert, like leather and sweat, except one of them had drunk a beer. Uniform buttons pressed into her forearms, then pistol holsters ground into her sides, and the rifle butts hit her back.

She fought, but the soldiers only tightened their grips on her arms and dragged her away kicking and screaming. She twisted hard and grabbed one man's rifle butt . . . jerked it downward as hard as she could. The thick leather shoulder strap held, but she could feel it dig into his shoulder.

He cursed violently.

The words she heard made her freeze for just one instant, and in that single moment, the men lifted her up and shoved her inside the back of the truck.

She fell hard against the riveted metal of the truck bed; it was covered with some old, vile-smelling straw. She lay there stunned.

She pushed up onto her elbows and turned toward

the outside light, toward the warmth of sunlight that was coming into the back of the truck.

The light disappeared as the canvas flapped closed.

Panicked, she scrambled toward it, pushed at the canvas flap, but the men had already securely tied it down to the tailgate. She hit it with her fists, her shoulders and head, grunting she hit it so hard. She felt like a trapped bird, butting against the cage again and again.

She sobbed, cried for help, her hands still beating on the canvas, because even though it was useless she couldn't just give up.

She began to scream. Again and again. If she made enough noise. If someone were to ask after her. Her father. Her brothers. Surely some man in this souk, unlike the women, would gladly speak about the foolish American for the right amount of francs.

She gripped the tailgate. No matter how hard she pushed, it wouldn't budge. She kicked at it, sat back and hammered it with her feet. It was locked in place.

Finally she fell backward, exhausted, panting, her throat raw.

The air in the truck had the musty scent of sun-baked canvas, stale hay, and the sweet flavor of the Evening in Paris perfume she had dabbed at her pulse points that morning, as if she were home and it was just another warm, sunny day in California.

The door to the truck cab opened, then slammed shut. It rattled the whole vehicle.

A man settled inside.

There was a long moment of silence.

"We have her," he said. His words were in German.

NARRAGANSETT
BAY, RHODE
ISLAND

"BOOGIE WOOGIE BUGLE BOY"

A sleek and low, boat-tailed Auburn used its eight supercharged cylinders to speed right past a road sign that said:

> This is God's country,
> So don't drive through it like hell!

The car was a bright electric blue. So was the summer sky overhead. And when that blue convertible flew past a dusty old Model-T truck full of chicken feed, farmer Melvin Johnson actually thought the sky was falling.

But the sky didn't fall around J.R. Cassidy; women fell. Hard. James Raleigh Cassidy III was to women what a Betty Grable pinup was to enlisted men—sweet, dreamy candy for the eyes.

It was a curse, or perhaps a blessing, to those Cassidy men, men whose blond good looks could make you believe they were created on God's best day. J.R. looked so much like his father and his grandfather that the women of the family just shrugged. If they gave birth to a boy, they knew never to look for a nose, a chin, eyes, or even a dim feature that bore any resemblance to their own ancestors. All that would be staring back at them was a face that was pure Cassidy.

J.R. was six foot two, with thick, wavy dark-blond hair that shone gold with a dab of Brylcreem and would streak almost platinum after two days of sailing his racing sloop in Rhode Island Sound. His smile was quick and white. He had the kind of smile that could melt a mother's heart . . . and usually did.

His eyebrows were dark, a sharp contrast to his blond hair and something that drew attention to him, as if God and the genetics that created man were showing off. He had green eyes the exact color of the two imported olives that Jonesy the bartender at the Officer's Club speared with a wooden toothpick and dipped into J.R.'s usual—a double shot of smooth, hundred-proof imported vodka . . . on the rocks.

There were creases in the corners of J.R.'s eyes from a life spent outdoors and from a hint of wry humor that said he could and did laugh at himself. When he shaved with a new Gillette blade, a five-o'clock shadow still smudged his jaw, which was square and hard and reflected the stubbornness of the Cassidy men.

His grandfather had been a mercenary soldier, one who fought in Angola, fought again in the Philippines prior to the Spanish-American War, during which he finally joined the U.S. Army in an official capacity and used his reputation and skill for a cause more patriotic than mercenary avarice.

Of course by the time that first Jim Cassidy had joined Roosevelt's Rough Riders, he had earned enough money for himself, for his son, and even for his future grandchildren to live out their lifetimes like Rockefellers.

Jim Sr. had been known as *the Scavenger,* a man who by hook, by crook, or by steel balls could do the impossible. When Colonel Teddy Roosevelt had his favorite mount shot out from under him the day before his heroic charge up San Juan Hill, Jim Sr. had crept behind Spanish lines and stolen General De Vega's horse, a prime Arab that the very next day carried Roosevelt into the history books.

As the story went, while Jim Sr. was filching that horse, he also stole half the Spanish Army's Mauser ammunition.

His years in the regular Army had earned Jim much more than mercenary gold and a reputation for skilled thievery; he earned a Medal of Honor and a general's silver stars.

His son, Jim Jr., carried on in his father's wily footsteps when he stole a German biplane—a contraption he swore to this day was made of little more than rags and wood. Still, he flew himself and a buddy out of captivity in France during the First World War.

Now Jim Sr.'s grandson, U.S. Army Captain J.R. Cassidy, was earning the same reputation, not as *the Scavenger,* but as *the Scrounger.*

Earlier in the year in conjunction with Special Services, he had been involved in a rescue mission for three important diplomats from a detention camp in Nazi-occupied Poland. While he was there, he stole a code book, two Panzer tanks—one that was towing a Messerschmitt—a German fuel truck stocked full, four prisoners of his own, and Generalmajor Ernst Weber's wallet, his PO8 Lüger, and his Knight's Cross.

According to the latest scuttlebutt, information and German machinery weren't all J.R. had recently commandeered. It was rumored Adele Langdon, the base commander's pretty young wife, was with the captain at his place in Newport for a very long and clandestine weekend hot enough to melt the seams in her last pair of stockings.

But of course this was only gossip. Gossip seemed to chase after the Cassidy men, the same way women did.

But on this bright morning, J.R. wasn't concerned with gossip as he drove along in the warm sunlight in his Auburn with its tan top crushed down and the wind blowing carelessly past him. He made a left turn and came up to the gates of his base. He paused long enough to toss a bottle of single-malt scotch to the corporal at the guardhouse; then he put his foot to the pedal and sped off, swerving around two lumbering troop trucks, a tall pyramid of rusted gasoline barrels, and a crusty old Army bus unloading a group of recruits so green you could put French dressing on them and serve them up in the mess hall.

J.R. spun the steering wheel in a hard right. The speedster fishtailed under a magic motion of 150 hp and 4000 rpm, then whipped like blue lightning between two Quonset huts. The rear whitewalls sent a spit of gravel through one hut's open transom windows and up over the edge of the corrugated tin roof, where they sounded like machine gun fire.

Less than a minute later the car skidded to a stop in front of the Officer's Club, a small wooden wing attached to the "T," a long, sterile building that housed the officers' quarters and sat between an old sea wall and the camp bakery. In the middle of the night, when the salty breeze off Narragansett Bay came in, it carried the scent of baking bread dough to the nose of every man who left his window open. By dawn you would wake up craving cinnamon raisin bread with your coffee and nigh on hungry enough to eat a whole loaf all by yourself.

J.R. hopped over the car's low-slung door. He tossed the silver keys in the air, then pocketed them with a jangle and took off his hat. He drove a quick hand through his hair a couple of times, then rubbed the heel of his fist over the twin silver bars on his cap and set it back on his head at a cocked angle. He jogged up the wooden steps in the loose-legged way he did everything: walking, running, or dancing the lindy at the Starlight Room. He shoved open the door and headed straight for the bar.

The long and lazy sweet notes of Glenn Miller's "Tuxedo Junction" swung from the radio in the corner where a group of young Gene Krupa wanna-bes were jiving and drumming on a nearby tabletop. A few feet away, a lieutenant sat in a wooden chair balanced carelessly on its two back legs, his feet propped against an Army-green wall. He nursed a foamy beer while staring at a swell pinup of Rita Hayworth in black lace so skimpy you could see all the full curves of her.

"Hey, man! Look at this!"

J.R. turned, knowing that whatever "this" was, it wasn't Rita.

His buddy Mich was crossing the room, waving something in one hand. "Michigan" Mark Roberts was from Detroit, and he must have been born in a bookie joint. That crazy cat would bet on anything from the number of flies in the latrine to which brunette lost her virginity after the Junior League canteen dance on Friday the 13th.

Mich stopped waving and shoved a piece of cardboard under J.R.'s nose.

J.R. glanced at it. It was a baseball pool, for the Series, which was weeks away. He laughed. "You don't think this is a little early?"

"Nah. I'm giving five to one odds if you place your bet now."

J.R. stuck his hand in his pocket and pulled out a handful of silver dollars left over from a good night at a poker hall. "I'll take Detroit." He dropped the money on the counter behind them.

Mich grinned and clapped him on the shoulder. He turned toward the room. "Now *here's* a man who knows a sure thing!"

There were moans and groans from everyone who'd had to listen to Mich and his love of the Detroit Tigers.

"To hell with you, Roberts. I'll take the Cubs!"

"The Cubs? Who you kidding, Jawolski? It's gonna be the Yankees! No one else can beat 'em."

"We're gonna skin those Tigers of yours. When Boston's through with 'em, they'll be nothing but a rug for us to rest our ruby red socks on . . ."

The club grew noisier, each man talking up his home ball team with the same sense of loyalty and patriotism that made these men join up, ready to show Hitler a thing or two for bombing England, for swarming on Europe and its people like a carnivore, for actually thinking Americans would stand by passively while his U-boats canvassed their Atlantic shores. The U.S. might not be in the war yet, but Americans didn't scare easily.

J.R. rested his arms on the smudged brass rail of the bar. Soon the baseball banter had died down, replaced by quiet talk and the whiskey-soft tones of Ella Fitzgerald singing about a brown-and-yellow basket. Jonesy began to whistle along as he dropped two olives in a highball glass, set it on a cocktail napkin that was stamped with the U.S. Army insignia. He slid that drink toward J.R.

"Thanks." J.R. took a swig, then cupped the cool, damp glass in two hands and stared at the milky flecks in the ice cubes, his mind on everything, and on nothing. He was just reaching for the olives when the door swung open and a corporal from Colonel Langdon's office came inside.

The room grew tellingly quiet as the kid walked up to J.R. and gave a quick salute.

J.R. used the toothpick with the olives to stir the drink, never taking his eyes off the kid.

"Captain Cassidy, sir, the colonel wants to see you. He said on the double, sir."

J.R. didn't say anything. It was obvious from the quiet around him that the gossip about Langdon's wife had spread fast. He dropped the toothpick and raised the glass to his mouth, then took a long, slow drink and licked his lips. He leaned back slightly, crossing his feet as he rested his elbows on the counter behind him, the drink still in one tanned hand.

The aide was rocking from one foot to the other, looking like a little kid in trouble.

What the hell . . . J.R. figured it wasn't the kid's fault that he was assigned to the biggest horse's ass in the Army. He took another drink and straightened, then used his glass to gesture toward the door. "After you, Corporal."

The kid was out the door in a instant. J.R. glanced over at Mich, who looked worried. J.R. shrugged, took a swig of his cocktail, then moseyed out the door, his drink still in his hand.

Once outside, he jogged down the steps and walked over to a brand-new vehicle—a prototype Ford GP with a white star freshly painted on its Army-green door. He crawled into the shotgun seat, his drink still in one hand. The melting ice cubes rattled as he settled his long legs past the emergency fire extinguisher and out onto the riveted floorboard. He slung an arm over the back of the seat and turned to the kid, who had his finger on the starter, but was just sitting there, his other arm resting on the steering wheel as he eyed J.R.'s vodka with an uncomfortable look.

"You gonna take that drink with you, sir?"

J.R. looked at the drink. "I sure am. Do you have a problem with that, Corporal?"

"No, sir. But . . ." He swallowed his words.

"Go on."

"You know how the colonel feels about protocol, sir."

"Yes, I do. But I have a feeling I'll be needing this drink." He swallowed a mouthful of clear, smooth vodka, leaned back against the seat cushion, and gestured toward the road with his highball glass. "Let's go, Corporal. Our commander awaits."

The kid pushed the starter, jammed into gear, and the jeep took off toward headquarters, with J.R. sucking on an olive.

"SOMEONE TO WATCH OVER ME"

Camp headquarters was in a clapboard building with a green roof and thin, veinlike cracks in its many layers of government-issue white paint. There was a hollow sound to the front steps when your shoes hit them, and the railing had splintered wood on its underside that stuck into your palm if you made the mistake of using the damn thing.

The tall, narrow front door was painted the color of a boiled lobster. Someone once joked that the door was a warning—the first sign of all the red tape you'd have to put up with if you ever wanted to get anything done.

The camp commander, Colonel Langdon, wasn't from that old school of officers who'd been commissioned on the battlefield in the trenches of Belgium and France during World War I, the ones who'd worn gas masks that made them look like bottle-eyed elephants as they dodged mortar shells and faced the snarling teeth of German machine guns firing thirty rounds per minute. Those were the men who had learned initiative and leadership the hard way.

But not Langdon. He was a rule man. A by-the-book officer. He had used the rule book to earn his way to a colonel's silver eagle, and by God, he was going to run his little piece of the Army by that same book, whether it made sense or not.

J.R. believed that Langdon was one of those officers who could easily send the men under his command to their deaths while following his damned book. He had all the flexibility of a cement block, a cunning ability to lay claim to the successes of those he commanded—which accounted for his rank—and a need for supreme power that made him all too dangerous. He was a man who talked the game of fighting, but hadn't done much of it.

Langdon had made it clear early on that he did not like J.R. After being reassigned last spring from Special Services, J.R. had driven into camp and reported to the colonel. Langdon had thumbed through J.R.'s impressive file, then tossed it on his desk and said, "I don't like your reputation, Captain. Or your tactics. While you are serving under me, you *will* play by the rules. You *will* follow instructions to the letter. You *will* do exactly as I tell you. Is that understood?"

J.R. had understood; his success was a threat to Langdon.

General Marshall had thought he'd been giving J.R. a break when he came back from his assignment in Poland. The general had stationed him to a base close to home. J.R. had grown up in Newport, where his family owned an English Tudor mansion on Ocean Drive— one of those ostentatiously gilded fifty-room summer "cottages" with a dozen chimneys on the roof and a thousand rhododendron bushes in the garden. He'd spent his idyllic youth sailing in the Sound or walking on narrow white beaches, where more starfish washed ashore than pebbles. During summers home from West

Point, he'd played baseball with his buddies at Cardines Field, drunk cold beer and eaten fried oysters in pubs with names like the *Tides In* and *Blue Moon Saloon,* places where you could sit on a red leather barstool and look down on Sayer's Wharf and the old New York Yacht Club, and whenever a door opened you breathed in a little bit of the Atlantic.

Colonel Langdon had all but eaten J.R. alive for the first few months he was stationed here. He'd learned to make the best of it till he could draw a new assignment. Until then, he was just a typical victim of Army-issue SNAFU.

The screen on the front door rattled closed behind him. Here, inside camp headquarters, the rooms were small and hot. Whirring slowly overhead was a ceiling fan, and in a distant office a phone rang as loudly as an old tin alarm clock. A battle line of gray metal filing cabinets stood along the wall.

Another of the colonel's aides, a second lieu, with a broken stub of yellow pencil stuck behind one big ear, was sitting at a desk hunched over an old Royal typewriter, pounding away on the keys as if he were Count Basie.

The kid finally looked up, then bolted to attention. "Captain Cassidy, sir."

J.R. returned the salute. "At ease."

The kid turned and looked nervously at the colonel's door.

J.R. hitched his hip on the cluttered corner of the desk, finished off his last olive, and set his empty highball glass on a stack of mustard yellow supply forms. He chewed on the toothpick for a moment, then slid it to the corner of his mouth. "From your look, Lieutenant, I'd say that the colonel's his usual pleasant self."

"Worse," the kid mumbled on a half groan. "He said to send you right in, sir. On—"

"I know . . . I know. . . ." J.R. held up his hand. "On the double." He stood and strolled toward the back offices.

"He's not alone, Captain."

J.R. stopped and turned.

"Lt. Colonel Harrington from HQ is with him. . . ."

Great. Two horses' asses together in one room. He threw the toothpick into a metal ashtray and wondered what was up. If it was his lucky day, then he'd be getting an assignment. Out of there. Finally.

If it wasn't his lucky day, well, he could be doing anything from touring some congressman around the batteries to representing the U.S. Army as a hog judge at the nearest country fair.

There was, however, one job he knew he wouldn't be doing again. Based on camp scuttlebutt, Langdon wouldn't order J.R. to escort his lush young wife, Adele, again any time soon.

J.R. gave the door a firm knock. Langdon's voice came through the door, a command to enter. J.R. walked inside.

The colonel's office smelled of old coffee, cigar smoke, and dogmatism.

Langdon looked up, his face unreadable. He stubbed out his cigar, and they went through the routine, J.R. saluting two men he did not respect. Oh, he supposed Harrington was all right, if you could stand a pansy-assed, stiff-necked boot-licker of the first order.

Langdon gave J.R. an icy look.

J.R. returned it unflinchingly.

The colonel was about five inches shorter than he was, had light brown, graying hair and a deeply receding hairline. When you looked at his forehead, you saw that hairline formed an *M,* which made you think he had joined the wrong branch of service. He should have been a leatherneck.

"Sit down, Captain."

The instant he sat down Langdon rose. It was a calculated move; now Langdon could look down at him. J.R. watched his commander walk over to the west window, his back to the room and his hands clasped behind him as he stood there—the little shit—milking the moment.

A fly buzzed around J.R.'s head. He ignored it, but looked up—a search for hebetude. The old metal ceiling fan spun lazily overhead and ticked like a timing device counting off tension in seconds. Outside the door, you could still hear the aide's frenetic typing, then the sharp, final ring of the typewriter bell. Less than a second later the carriage return slammed over to the left side of the machine with a plangent rattle.

Langdon waited a long time before he faced him again.

J.R. counted six more rings of that typewriter bell. He knew this game. The colonel had played it often enough for J.R. to wonder if it was in the goddamn rule book.

"It seems that the State Department has a little problem, Captain, and according to a staff memo Lt. Col. Harrington bought down from HQ, your name keeps popping up as the man they want to handle it."

He was getting an assignment from HQ. Something from over Langdon's head.

Thank God and GHO!

"You've heard of Arnan Kincaid?"

"The genius who heads the scientific research at Wynberg-Kincaid Labs?"

"That's the one," Lt. Col. Harrington piped in.

J.R. just looked at him. Harrington was an annoying weasel, like the one in that nursery rhyme, the one who popped his head up from a bush every few minutes. Harrington did it just to make sure you remembered he was there.

"Rumor has it Kincaid's working for the government." J.R. aimed his comment to Langdon just to piss off Harrington. "But as far as I can tell, no one wants to confirm that information."

"Consider it confirmed." Harrington's voice was smug in the way of those who liked it when they knew things others didn't. He was a surefire security risk, the kind of man whose ego wouldn't let him keep his mouth shut.

Langdon shot Harrington a sharp look, then turned back to J.R. "Kincaid is working on a top secret project. But he's not the problem."

"What is?"

"Not *what*. Who." Langdon crossed back over to the desk and sat down. "Kincaid has a daughter. Kathryn. She disappeared almost two weeks ago." The colonel held out a hand toward Harrington, who flipped open a briefcase, riffled through some papers, then handed him a photograph.

Langdon slid it in front of J.R.

The woman who stared back at him from that eight-by-ten was one helluva dish. She had flawless features and fine bones, a square but soft jawline, a broad smile with perfectly straight teeth and full lips that bowed in the center. Her skin looked pale in the gray tones of the photo. She had a long, elegant neck strung with a single strand of perfectly graduated pearls, the kind debs wore for their coming out balls. Her dark hair was thick, parted on one side, and waved down along her face in that sexy, starlet way, before it curled under at her shoulders.

Her head was tilted slightly, as if she were thinking. Thick, dark lashes framed her eyes. Her eyebrows looked natural, thickly winged with a slight arch, instead of tweezed off and drawn on with thin pencil like so many girls did nowadays. He never understood the theory behind that style. It made them look continually surprised . . . and a little stupid.

This babe looked anything but stupid.

"The last time she was seen, she was heading for the marketplace in Rabat."

J.R. looked up. "Rabat? What the hell was she doing in North Africa?"

"She's been there for a long time, since thirty-nine."

"Doesn't she know there's a war on?"

"According to Kincaid, she made up her mind to go to work with the family of a college friend. He said she had something important to prove."

Prove? What? That she was stupid? J.R. wasn't sure who was more foolish. The girl for staying there or the father for not dragging her sweet butt home, where she belonged. He stared at the gorgeous image in the photo a moment longer. Foolish, but a real looker. "It always amazes me when civilians do nothing to get out of harm's way." He dropped the photo back on the colonel's desk and leaned back in his chair. "Why was she there in the first place?"

"That's not your problem, Captain," Langdon said sharply.

Ah, J.R. thought. He doesn't know either. "Then just what is my problem, Colonel?"

Langdon's expression grew grim. "I'm not certain I agree with HQ, Captain. You don't seem to me to be the kind of man for this assignment."

Harrington popped up again, neck straining. "But, sir—"

Langdon cut Harrington off with the quick raise of his hand. This assignment was eating at Langdon. HQ had ordered Langdon, J.R.'s superior officer, to give him this assignment, and it was driving the bastard nuts.

Good.

"The name 'Cassidy' seems to be like 'God' around HQ." Langdon looked at him.

J.R. didn't respond.

But the colonel was waiting with an officious smile, as if he thought J.R. was stupid and hot-tempered enough to fall for that crap.

Harrington coughed in the silence, then cleared his throat.

Langdon continued, "Her friend's family obtained their exit papers a few months ago. Kincaid was supposed to fly back to the States. But Pétain signed the armistice with Germany. The borders closed quickly. She was caught and unable to get the papers she needed to leave. Her father has been putting pressure on his friends in high places. Someone in the State Department had just made a deal with the Vichy to get her out. She disappeared the day before she was scheduled to leave."

"How convenient." J.R. glanced at the photograph again.

"Kincaid was contacted last Sunday night by an operative near his home in California. His daughter's now in the hands of the German Occupancy officials."

"Another bogus name for one of Hitler's agencies," Harrington added as if J.R. had been born yesterday.

"She's now their leverage against Kincaid. They want him to cooperate, to give them information in exchange for her continued safety. He was savvy enough to have a close friend contact the State Department immediately."

Langdon reached over, pulled a packet from Harrington's briefcase, and added the photo, along with some files from his desktop. He came around the desk and stood in front of J.R. He handed him the packet, then glanced at his wristwatch. "You're flying out for Gibraltar at fourteen hundred."

"That's only two hours." J.R. paused. "Sir."

"I know."

"The airfield is almost two hours from here." J.R. looked at Langdon.

"Then I suggest you leave right away, Captain."

J.R. had opened the envelope and quickly scanned the information. "According to this, she's being held outside Ouarzazate. In Tizi." They had confirmed she was in an old medieval Kasbah-type fortress that dominated one of the sheer crags almost six thousand feet up in the Atlas Mountains. It was one of those places ingeniously built hundreds of years before and a hundred years from now would still be difficult to infiltrate.

"That's right, Captain." Langdon leaned casually back against his desk and gave J.R. a snide look that said he liked this part of it. "And it's your job to get her out of there."

"THE BIRTH OF THE BLUES"

Less than five minutes later U.S. Army Colonel Robert Langdon, Commander, Camp Endicott, stood at the west window of his office and watched Cassidy drive off in the direction of the base officers' quarters, hoping he would never see him again, and then . . . neither would Adele.

"You didn't tell him."

"Tell him what, Harrington?" Langdon didn't move from his spot. A fly was trapped by the closed window and kept batting into the glass, then falling down on the sill, where it buzzed frantically and beat its wings.

"You didn't tell him about the girl. The memo specifically said that Cassidy was to be apprised of the problem."

"I didn't?" Langdon rubbed a finger against his lip, his back to that toadying Harrington, who he knew was only worried about his own ass if HQ found out. "Hmmmm. That's odd. I thought I did tell him. I was certain I did." Langdon watched the jeep with Cassidy in it disappear between a maze of old buildings in a cloud of dry dust. He stood there enjoying the moment: Cassidy disappearing.

He smiled to himself for a full minute, before he

turned and faced Harrington. "Are you certain I didn't tell him?"

"Yes, Colonel."

Langdon waited long enough for Cassidy to pack up. Meanwhile he could hear Harrington squirming in his chair. Langdon enjoyed that, so he stood at that window, until all the flies inside the room had died.

He watched the jeep with Cassidy and his camp bag in it drive out through the camp gates and speed off in the direction of the airfield. Langdon turned then and walked back to his chair, where he sat down and lit himself an imported cigar. He puffed on it for a second or two, then watched the smoke curl up toward the ceiling fan and dissipate. He leaned back in his chair and looked at the cigar tip glowing in his right hand. "Are you sure I didn't tell him?"

"Yes, Colonel. I'm sure," Harrington said dryly. He'd finally caught on.

"Hmmm, that is a shame. You know I think it's too late now. He's already left the base." Langdon paused, then took a long hit off the cigar. "HQ's fair-haired Captain Cassidy is just going to have to find out that bit of information *all* by himself."

"ME AND MY SHADOW"

The walls around her were made of stone, and when she rubbed her hands over them, fine sand coated her damp palms. She didn't know where she was, but she knew they had taken her into the mountains. The truck had shifted gears and the turns had been hairpin for the last two hours. The road had turned steep and the air had grown cooler and thinner, the way it did when you rose in altitude. She'd clocked the drive time. She was five hours and twenty-two minutes from the outskirts of Rabat.

For Kitty time passed by her heartbeat, by the feel and taste of the air, which changed constantly; it felt different against the sensitive hairs on her skin, tasted different when she breathed it in.

Her cell was a fifteen-by-ten-foot stone room. There was a metal cot against a wall at nine o'clock. On the twelve o'clock wall was a high, narrow window that she couldn't reach even when she'd stood on the furniture. A dry sink sat at three o'clock, and there was a pot for a toilet that was discreetly placed behind a deeply carved wooden screen.

Each morning her guard—a man she dubbed Adolf— brought her warm wash water, fruit, goat cheese, and flatbread along with a pot of strong African coffee with too much sugar. Around ten A.M. she was taken outside to walk in circles in a courtyard with a stone birdbath in its center—set in gravel that crunched underfoot—and framed with a line of cedar trees that made the air smell like the sweater drawer in her bureau back home.

When she came back to her cell, there were clean towels, a pitcher of fresh water, and the pot had been emptied and disinfected with something that smelled like camphor. In the evenings, Adolf brought her a hot meal of lamb and bulgur that was usually too much for her to eat.

On one occasion, he brought her two extra woolen blankets. It had been shortly after the wind had begun to howl outside and the temperature dropped a good thirty degrees.

For ten long nights and eleven days, that routine had been her existence.

She heard distant footsteps on the stairs.

Heil! Adolf was coming. But at the wrong time.

He came down a narrow hall that made the sound of his boot heels echo until they stopped abruptly right outside her room. The lock on the door clicked. She felt a wave of cool air when the door opened. There was a moment's pause.

"You will come with me, *Fräulein.*"

"A late walk, Adolf?"

"I told you my name is not Adolf."

"But you refuse to tell me your name, so, I must improvise. You don't like being nicknamed after your *Führer?*"

"What is this . . . 'nickname'?"

"It's an endearment like *Liebchen.* If you don't like

Adolf, you might prefer Hermann. Although you don't seem like a Hermann. Perhaps Heinrich?"

He said nothing, just grabbed her hand and pulled her up.

"What about Karl?"

"Come."

She let him guide her to the door. She could smell the musty wool of his clothes. "The seasons must be changing. You are wearing a wool uniform today."

That stopped him for a moment. She liked to confuse him, which wasn't too difficult. She suspected Adolf's IQ was equivalent to his belt size.

They had expected her to act hysterical. Once the truck left Rabat, she didn't. Any one of her brothers would tell these men that she seldom did what people expected.

"Come."

This time she jerked her arm from his grasp and faced him. "Come where?"

"You will not be harmed." He took her arm again. "Unless you do not cooperate. If you kick me again, I have orders to chain your feet together."

"I had no plans to kick you," she lied and held her head up.

They went out the door, his gloved hand tightly gripping her upper arm and his other hand clamped onto her waist.

"Halt." He grabbed her shoulder to stop her. "The stairs are here."

She knew there were exactly twenty-seven even footsteps from her room to the staircase. Forty-two small stone steps went down in a circle and passed by five narrow windows that sent cool cedar-scented air into the passageway. She was being held in some kind of old tower.

They reached the bottom and turned right for the usual fifteen steps. She started to turn left.

Adolf pulled her back. "No. Turn right."

She acted as if it did not bother her that they were going someplace new, but a small amount of perspiration broke out in her hairline.

They went down two more hallways, each about twenty feet long. The second one was carpeted. One left turn and they were in a corridor where fatty-smelling tallow candles burned somewhere above her head.

Ten steps and he stopped. He rapped three times on a door, then opened it, not with the turn of a doorknob, but the hard rasp of an iron latch.

He drew her inside.

"Ah, Miss Kincaid." The voice belonged to her nemesis, her shadow from the marketplace; it was a voice she had not heard since they'd first brought her here. "You look well this morning."

It was afternoon, not morning. Close to three o'clock, but she chose to keep her knowledge to herself. This man did frighten her. He was no dumb Adolf. "Why am I here? Who are you? And what do you want?"

"Show the *Fräulein* where the chair is, *Leutnant*."

Adolf was a lieutenant? How nice to know the Third Reich had such a high caliber of junior officer.

It was barely five steps to a stiff wooden chair. Kitty sat down easily, her chin up the whole time, facing the man who held her captive. "You haven't answered my questions."

"I know."

"The U.S. State Department made arrangements for

me to go home. Kidnapping is illegal, even here, under the Vichy. My government will not be happy."

"Let's not exchange threats, Miss Kincaid. It's a waste of our time."

"Our time? Why, I have plenty of spare time." She leaned back against the chair and crossed her legs.

The silence dragged on as she could feel him watching her. It was one of those spider-and-the-fly kind of moments. "Who are you?"

"My name is Werner Von Heidelmann, agent for the German Occupancy Department."

To those in the Vichy his title might be that innocuous, but she knew by instinct he was something else altogether. There were rumors of secret police, of Hitler's special forces and agents whose true agenda was nothing like what their titles implied.

"You have an opportunity to gain your release."

"And what opportunity might that be?"

"Your father is a very important man."

Her father's work, of course. He'd been in *Life* magazine and the topic of countless newspaper articles. She knew he'd been working on some kind of rocket, but no one would find that out from her.

She sat there silently. Let Herr Von Heidelmann make of it what he would.

"Your father has chosen to do nothing to aid in your release."

Oh, God. . . . They've contacted Dad.

"It seems, Miss Kincaid, that you, his only daughter, are not terribly important to him." He paused then, and she could feel him gauging her reaction, so she gave him none.

"You have six brothers, do you not?"

"And your point is?"

"It must be very difficult for a young woman to grow up in a home full of men, one where her own father does not care for her. Where the sons are more important than daughters."

Kitty knew her father loved her. But she also knew Arnan Kincaid was no traitor, and not even for her safety would he betray his country. Her father was also well aware that she knew where his allegiance was, which Kitty hoped gave him the power to find some alternate method to save her. He must have acted as if he didn't give a damn about her, which is exactly what she would have done.

"Not so difficult as you believe, Herr Von Heidelmann." She shrugged. "We women have learned to accept our lesser value in this man's world." Her brothers would be rolling on the floor if they'd heard her.

"Perhaps in your country, Miss Kincaid. The *Führer* values the women who work for him. Under the Third Reich, women are equal to men. Whether they are engineers or mothers. It does not matter to us."

She laughed then. "Are you really asking me to believe that it doesn't matter to the Third Reich whether, say, a woman designs an airplane that can fly thousands of miles or makes a mean sauerkraut and wiener schnitzel? You want me to believe that they are equally as important to you?"

"Soldiers must be fed, Miss Kincaid."

She only laughed.

"Women are vital to the Fatherland. They are its backbone. We have women working in every facet of our government. There are women who are respected and given many opportunities that your government keeps strictly for men. It is a man's world only in the United States."

"Do you honestly believe if your *Führer* had a daughter that he would care more about her than about, say . . . Poland?"

"You equate the importance of your father's research with our occupation of Poland? Poland will be much stronger under German Occupation.

"Tell us what your father is working on and then you may choose to go home or to work in a high position of the Third Reich. We can offer you the opportunity to be part of the future. Unlike in the United States, you will be important in Germany."

"No, thank you. I know nothing about what my father is doing. I've not been home for over two years. "

There was a long moment of silence.

She sat there, unmoving.

"My advice is that you should think about this. If you choose to cooperate, you will have the chance to be on the winning side of this war."

"I have nothing to tell you. I don't know anything about my father's work. You can keep me locked up here until your Führer has gray hair." She stood up. "Now you are wasting my time and your own."

"Take Miss Kincaid back to her room, *Leutnant*. Let her contemplate which is the bigger waste of time: talking to me or being locked in that room."

Adolf crossed the room and took her arm, but Kitty didn't move because she had one more thing to say. "You forget something important, Herr Von Heidelmann. I am a U.S. citizen. We are not in your war."

"And you forget that you are not safely tucked away in your home in the U.S. Your country has been shipping aid, aircraft, food, and arms to Britain, and has been for months. Your president meets regularly with Britain's Churchill. Our U-boats are already in place to patrol your Atlantic coast in the same way we patrol and blockade the Channel. It is only a small matter of time.

"We *will* take Great Britain, Miss Kincaid, and there will be nothing between the United States and Germany except the Atlantic Ocean. A little water will not protect you. Before long the Luftwaffe will be bombing the U.S. every day in the same way we are bombing England. Imagine New York, Washington, D.C., Atlanta, Chicago, and before long, your hometown in California, all under the control of the Third Reich. Technically, you are correct. Your country is not in the war. But trust me, it will be."

"JEEPERS CREEPERS"

SIXTEEN THOUSAND FEET OVER THE DROP ZONE:
THE DRAA VALLEY,
MOROCCO, NORTH AFRICA

The only thing J.R. hated about his choice of career was jumping out of a goddamn airplane. It wasn't just that he was afraid. He was smart enough to know fear was a healthy thing in a soldier. It was fear that kept men alive.

He'd had a discussion with his granddad about it one time. When you weren't scared, well, that was when bad things happened. A sniper's bullet in a vital organ. A land mine under your boot. A mortar shell with your name on it.

Being scared sharpened your senses. You paid attention. You listened. You looked. Your sense of self-preservation was at its highest point.

Fear was an emotion, and emotions were just things you felt in your gut. If you let an emotion get into your head or, worse yet, into your heart, then you were a dead man.

So it wasn't the fear that made him hate this part of his job. For all he knew, his phobia could have dated back to jump training in the wilds of Georgia, a surefire hell he didn't want to relive again in this lifetime or any other.

During jumps they had landed in watermelon fields, in pine trees, and at night, between electrical and telephone poles, where the wires squeezed the shroud lines together and pushed the air from the canopy, something that sent you to the ground so fast and so blasted hard that anything in your jumpsuit pockets tore right though the bottom seams. On one hard, bone-ringing landing, J.R. had actually lost a filling from his back molar.

Another time they'd landed in a huge and muddy hog farm, where one five-hundred-pounder took offense when a lieutenant from Mississippi who never wore socks landed on the animal's hairy back. The hog rolled over and broke the lieutenant's leg, sending him to the local hospital where, while he recovered, he could contemplate the joy of going through jump-training hell all over again, after his leg healed.

From then on, whenever someone was busted up on a landing, the men called it "boarfooting."

At night in the barracks, the men all made bets on

whether the Army scouted out the worst possible places for them to land, then made those spots a required jump target.

One night before a graded jump, the instructor—a grizzled World War I sergeant and expert paratrooper plucked from the 501st Parachute Battalion, who according to rumor had grown up in Hell's Kitchen—caught J.R. leaning on a wall, talking and joking with some buddies when they were all supposed to be packing their chutes.

Every single one of them was an officer, some of them fresh out of the Point, like J.R. But the fact remained that every one of them outranked a sergeant. However, jump training was run by sergeants and Sergeant Wilford Rufus Huxley had the final word.

He was it.

He was god.

He was the be-all and end-all.

So J.R., a second lieu at the time, learned a hard lesson that night, when it was raining like a sonofabitch. With a nine-and-a-half-pound Garand caliber .30 M1 rifle in his hands, his chest and back strapped heavily with ammo magazines, and packing full gear, J.R. ran double-time around the parachute packing shed singing:

> *"Sergeant Huxley is on the ball,*
> *He caught me leaning against the wall."*

Every so often Huxley would stick his shiny bald head out of the shed and yell, "I can't hear you, Cassidy!"

J.R. was screaming at the top of his lungs.

When it was over, he was hoarse for days, and no one else spoke a word to each other outside the barracks for a full week. From that day forward J.R. was the first one done packing his chute, then he would stand there, silent as a rock.

The disturbing thing about jumping was: It wasn't normal human behavior to throw yourself out of a plane. Hell . . . you stood there, the door off the plane, being blasted by engine and wind noise and flying so high the air could never be anything but so icy cold you swore your balls were turning blue. The wind force was so strong it flattened your skin against your face bones until you looked like an old cow skull someone dug up in the desert.

You were stuck there, standing at that open plane door, chute buckled around your chest and waist and strapped around your precious nuts, with land thousands of feet below you and nothing between the two of you but clouds and air and enemy fire if they saw you.

No, this was not his favorite outdoor sport.

On his last assignment, he could still remember jumping out into the air and feeling like one of those metal ducks they had in the shooting galleries, one with a huge white silk canopy over his head that said, "Look! I'm dumber than dirt. I'm jumping out of a plane. Shoot here."

And now he was back here once again, some sixteen thousand feet in the air, standing at the door of a USAAC C-33 transport, engine noise wailing back at him from its twin Pratt-Whitney Hornets, ready to jump out and drop to the earth below with his expertly self-packed, U.S. Army–issue parachute that better damn-well open.

He looked down at the targeted drop zone and felt his eyes tear from the wind. To cheer up, he told himself there would be no hog farms in North Africa.

The copilot leaned out and shouted, "Two minutes, sir!"

J.R. pulled down his goggles, then gripped the metal casing of the door opening. At least the flight was smooth. When there was turbulence, it was real hell. He looked down again at the approaching drop zone. To the north were the Atlas Mountains. Below him was nothing but miles and miles of rippling mounds he figured was sand.

The drop zone was the south side of the mountains, near nothing. He was to meet an operative who would take him the back way into the mountains, and from there, he was to infiltrate the Kasbah so he could play good guy and save Kincaid's dishy daughter—the one who didn't have the sense to go home.

He looked up again, then shifted his gaze to the red and green jump lights.

Nothing.

He waited.

A good four minutes had passed by.

The copilot stuck his head out and was frowning at him with a "you're still here" expression. He turned back and hit a few switches. His head poked back out and he cupped a hand around his mouth and hollered, "The lights aren't working, Captain! Jump!" He gave him the thumbs-up sign.

J.R. turned back. His right foot was already over the

threshold, and he slid his hands outside and put his palms against the outside of the plane.

He looked down, then took one deep breath. "Ah, what the hell . . ."

He threw himself out of the plane.

A second later he was sailing into the air, arms crossed over his chest, and he began to count. "One one thousand . . ." *Somebody's got to come up with a better way of getting from a plane to earth.*

"Two one thousand." *Soon . . . real soon.*

"Three one thousand." *Hail Mary, Mother of God . . .*

"Four one thousand." *Open, open, open . . .*

"Five one thousand . . ." He pulled the rip cord—his favorite part—and got the crap jerked out of him by the chute, which was far better than watching the canopy collapse above him as he fell to earth at a few thousand feet a minute.

He spun for a moment or two as his risers unwound; then he floated in that great silence, the one that always followed the chute's opening jerk.

He gripped the lines and looked above him.

Off in the distance, the plane had banked to the northeast and was moving away. Back to base. For the briefest of moments it looked like a metal crucifix hanging sideways in the sky.

By the time the plane was nothing but a flea speck in the distance, J.R. was floating through the air above the desert, some four minutes, at the very least, and God-knew-how-many-odd seconds outside the designated drop zone.

'PAPER DOLL'

Another five days had gone by, and every single one of them had been more difficult than the last. The morning after her cheery little talk with Von Heidelmann, Adolf got her up early and took her outside to walk in the courtyard.

It had been raining. She was soaked to the bone, but instead of taking her back to her room afterward, he took her directly to Von Heidelmann, who talked to her for hours. All she could do was sit in that hard wooden chair and tell herself it didn't matter that she was wet and cold and miserable.

At first she tuned Von Heidelmann out the way she had tuned out her brothers when they would pester her to death. She answered only when she wanted to. But some nights she swore she could hear him in her sleep, that trapped inside her head was a constant drone of Nazi jargon.

A few days ago she had started her period in the middle of the night and had to tear strips from her one towel to use as menstrual rags. She tried to hide the rags. But there was no place to hide anything in her room. When she was at her weakest point, cramping and tired and drained, Von Heidelmann had battered her with propaganda all night long.

Some days there had been no dinner. Some days there

had been too much food like before, but when they piled the food high on her plate, it turned out to be something that she couldn't wrap in a napkin and save under her cot for later; it was always a type of food that would spoil easily.

Some nights, when she was sound asleep, they came and got her up, making her rush down to Von Heidelmann's office, dazed, barefooted, and half asleep, only to spend the rest of the night listening to him drone on. He would ask her questions. She would only sit there and cry. She understood the psychological games he was playing.

She played the role of fragile female.

Let Von Heidelmann think he was winning.

She heard those familiar footsteps. A second later she was deep under the blankets and feigning sleep.

Adolf came inside. "Wake up, *Fräulein*." He shoved at her shoulder repeatedly. When she opened her eyes, he pulled her up. "You come with me now." He took her by the arm but didn't yank on it. She had noticed he was less gruff with her and did not jerk her around as he had before. Perhaps Adolf was half-human after all.

"You must come now." His voice was quieter, his actions softened, like her brothers' response when they felt bad about something they had done to her.

She hated pity . . . had fought it like crazy for years. But this time, she took advantage of his pity and stood there for a moment. She pretended to shake out her clothes, then brushed her tangled hair out of her face. She faced him. "Let me venture a wild guess, Adolf. Herr Von Heidelmann wants to talk with me."

"HELL'S BELLS"

He landed in a fucking palm tree.

When J.R. looked down, he was hanging some fifty feet off the ground—which was conveniently riddled with what appeared to be knife-sharp rocks. It was good to know some things never changed. Mr. Murphy came along for the ride.

He checked the position of his chute; it was secure, or securely stuck, depending upon your outlook—optimist or pessimist.

Apparently that single Hail Mary had done some good. Otherwise he might just haul down on the shroud lines and suddenly go *smash!* Right down on those rocks.

He jerked the lines. Palm dust, dates, and other palm tree crap rained down on him. He swore, then brushed the dust off his face while a few more dates hit his shoulders and head.

He gripped the lines tightly and kicked out, so he began to swing back and forth. He had the darkly amusing thought that he ought to hum carousel music.

Back and forth he swung, building momentum, dodging dates and dust and more dates. A few more good swings and he was close enough to the tree trunk to clamp his legs and one arm around it.

The damn thing was prickly as hell.

He reached up with his free arm and released his chute.

A second later he was swearing a blue streak and sliding down the rough tree trunk with all the finesse and comfort of a fireman sliding down a pole made of pineapples.

As landings went, it wasn't his best. He hit hard and bit his tongue. He could taste the saltiness of blood in his mouth. He spit, then pulled himself up and checked his gear. Mosquitoes buzzed and swarmed around his head and bit him on the neck. He slapped it and pulled his hand away. He counted a dozen dead mosquitoes on his palm. They were everywhere. He waved them away, then gave up and let the little mothers bite him. He did the routine—patted his chest, his wrist, his crotch, and his pockets as he murmured, "Compass, watch . . . testicles, spectacles."

Yep, all the important stuff's here.

He took a swig from his canteen, then swiped at his mouth with his sleeve and checked out the area's perimeter. He was in some kind of oasis—a cluster of palm trees, rocks, every single mosquito in the continent of North Africa, and a stone well off to the west where some vegetation grew and a few ugly white flowers were poking out of a patch of swordlike weeds.

He refastened the canteen to his belt, shoved aside his rope-and-toggle hook, then unsnapped his jacket pocket. He pulled out his compass and his maps. He scanned them, then looked around him.

The mountains were to the southeast. That was good. That's where they were supposed to be.

He knew he'd overshot the drop zone, but he didn't know by how far. He studied the map for a minute or two. From what he could calculate, he was about fifteen klicks northwest of his rendezvous, if this spot was the well marked on his map as *Robinet*.

The sun was late in the sky; it was still hotter than hell. He checked his watch, then turned and took off toward the southeast at an even run.

He had only two hours to rendezvous.

"DEUTSCHLAND, DEUTSCHLAND ÜBER ALLES"

The sand dunes rippled across the horizon, endless and golden like thousands of tanned backs bent down to hide from the hundred-and-twenty-degree sun. Standing in his armored halftrack SdKfz 250 Greif, Feldleutnant Frederick Rheinholdt took out his 6 ×30 binoculars and searched that immutable horizon for a cloud of dust or a flealike speck in the distance. He searched for some sign of the 105th Panzer Regiment coming from the west, for reconnaissance, or the unit from the 900th Engineers Battalion.

He checked his watch, a futile motion because time did not matter in the desert. Hours and minutes seemed as unchanging as the horizon. He took off his field cap and the British anti-dust goggles he'd captured at Halfaya Pass. He wiped the grit and sweat off his forehead with the dusty rolled cuff on his sweat-drenched tunic, then used the hem of his tunic to clean the dust and grime off the goggles.

One of the first things you learned on the desert front

was that sand was your constant comrade. It got into everything. You ate it. You drank it. You breathed it. And when you looked ahead, it was always there before you, inevitable, uncontrollable, like your destiny.

He glanced down at his driver, Obergefreiter Veith, who had finally rid himself of the ridiculous army-issue tropical pith helmet some idiot in Berlin thought necessary if you were anywhere near the equator. It might have been fine for hunting elephant on the plains of Africa at the turn of the century, but in the desert it was impractical and uncomfortable.

Veith was finally wearing the lighter, cooler field cap as Rheinholdt had suggested when they had been two hours into the desert. Callow and young, the corporal was too much of a neuling yet to veer far from military convention. He had been assigned as his driver only a week before, just days after fresh troops had landed in Tripoli, the newest divisions and regiments assigned to the Deutsches Afrika Korps.

Rheinholdt had been with the DAK for a year, yet when he looked at Veith, he felt like it had been ten. The young blond soldier was staring at a map and sipping water from the aluminum cup of a new-issue brown felt canteen, his legs still in breeches and high boots, but stretched out into the depths of the floorboards. He looked for all the world as if he were sitting in a sidewalk cafe on Kurfürstendamm in Berlin, eating Kuchen, reading *Signal,* and sipping on coffee. Rheinholdt wondered how long it would take him to realize that the cup he was using was worthless in the desert because it would fill with sand and dust that turned the already vile-tasting, salty water to mud.

Rheinholdt put his cap back on, then unclipped his own canteen and took a drink.

"Can you find our location on the map?"

Veith did not answer right away. He was frowning into his canteen cup.

Rheinholdt smiled, then asked again.

"Thirty kilometers, Herr Leutnant."

"Good. We have close to two hours until sunset." Rheinholdt turned, signaled the rest of the motorized unit forward, slid on the British goggles, and sat down. "Keep heading southwest."

"CLING TO ME"

Kitty awoke the moment a man's hand clamped over her mouth. She struggled against him, drew back her left fist, and punched out at him as hard as she could.

Three rapid knuckle-punches that she felt hit square in his face.

"Jesus-Fucking-Christ!"

She stopped mid-punch. Good old American male swearing. The sweetest sound she'd ever heard. A small groan of relief slipped out from her mouth against his callused hand, muffled. Her throat grew tight with sudden emotion. "Thank God . . ." she murmured.

"Quiet. Don't make a sound, Kincaid," he said into her ear.

She could feel tears of relief fill her eyes, and she

inhaled deeply through her nose. There was a small catch in her throat as if she'd hiccupped. To her horror she was going to cry.

"Don't start crying," came a hissed order.

She nodded.

His arm and shoulder were across her. He was heavy. She could feel his warm breath as she lay there listening to see if anyone had heard.

From his stillness, she could tell he was listening, too.

No footsteps came down the hallway or up the stairs. There was nothing but silence. He hardly made a sound; his breathing was shallow, very evenly controlled. As she lay there on the cot in the room that had been her prison for seventeen days, she took short, sharp breaths that gave her little oxygen and wished he would take away his hand. She wasn't stupid. She wasn't going to make a sound.

He smelled of the desert, an odor of dry sand and even drier dust, mixed with musky male sweat, like he'd been running.

She moved her right hand slightly and touched his chest. There were metal zippers on his clothes and thick seams on a flap pocket that snapped closed.

He pinned her hand back onto the cot.

She could feel him shake his head at her before he turned to look back toward the door. She lay there on the cot, him half-crouched next to her, his upper body pinning her where she was.

Time crawled by.

"Okay," he whispered into her ear. "I don't think they heard anything. I'm U.S. Army Captain James Cassidy, and I'm here to get you out of here. Understand?"

She nodded.

"Good. I'm going to take my hand away. *Do not talk.*"

She nodded again.

He took his hand away.

She took a good long breath. It was the small hours of the morning. She could tell by the temperature of the air.

"Get dressed."

She'd slept in her slip, so she swung her legs over the side of the iron cot and grabbed her dress from the end of the bed. She slid her feet into it and stood, shimmied into it, then reached under the hem and jerked down her bunched-up slip. She started with the top buttons and worked her way down. The belt hung loosely from the belt loops at the waist, and she pulled it together and buckled it, then reached for her cotton stockings and girdle.

She wiggled into the girdle, sat down and rolled the stockings into her hands, then slid them over her foot and up her leg. She attached the garters, front and back. Less than a minute later she was done.

He was standing next to her the whole time. She could feel him watching her.

She didn't care. She just wanted out of here. She bent down over the edge of the cot and grabbed her scarf, then stuffed it down the neckline of her dress into her brassiere.

"Let's go," he whispered, then grabbed her upper arm in his hand and took a step. "Quietly."

She froze, pulled her arm back, and shook her head. "My shoes."

He stopped moving.

"Get them. Hurry!"

They were under the table at two o'clock, seven steps

from the bed. She took two steps, then another. Her foot hit something soft. A cloth duffel or pack.

She stumbled forward.

He grabbed her shoulders from behind in a hard grip, then pulled her upright and steadied her, her back against his chest.

Her breath came fast. It scared her, almost falling like that. It made her feel lost and out of control when that happened.

He spun her around so she faced him.

She could feel him looking at her.

He released one shoulder. She heard his pocket flap snap; then he was digging around inside it.

A moment later a lighter clicked.

He held it up between them.

She could smell the lighter fluid before she saw the blurred light from its flame pass in front of her eyes.

For just a moment there was nothing in the air but a sense of dawning realization.

He swore viciously under his breath and said, "You're blind."

'I KNOW NOW'

J.R. flicked the lighter closed with a snap. He had the sudden urge to bust the chops of a certain colonel. There was no way HQ would not have informed him that Kathryn Kincaid was blind. This little piece of info was what had been behind Langdon's snide smile.

J.R. crossed over to the table, picked up her shoes and put them in her hand. "There, you've got your shoes." He slid on his gloves.

"No one told you I'm blind." She put on one shoe, then the other.

"It doesn't matter. Getting out of here does." He took her hand. "Let's go."

He moved toward the window.

She moved toward the door.

"Not that way." He pulled her with him. "We go out the way I came in. Through the window," he whispered. "Listen closely. There's a rope hanging out here. I'm going to climb out the window, grab the rope, and brace myself on the tower. When I say to, you'll climb out, grab a hold of the rope, and clamp your legs around it, so it's between your legs, and grip it tightly with both hands and slide down so you're in front of me. I'll be behind you the whole time." He paused for a fraction of a second, then said, "Guess I don't have to warn you not to look down."

"No. You don't."

"Then you need to let go of the rope, put your arms around my neck, and I'll take you down to the ground." He paused. "Understand?"

"I think so."

"Repeat it quietly."

She did. Verbatim.

"Good."

He slipped out the window, took the rope, swung out, and secured it, taut, then braced his boots against the stone tower.

He looked up.

She had already crawled out onto the stone ledge, her back to him. She was sitting there, waiting.

It was a good thing she couldn't see the drop down. This old fortress was situated on a tall and rugged cliff high above the road. Going down it was going to be like rappelling the sheer face of a mountain.

"I'm ready," he whispered. "Grab the rope with both hands."

She waved her arm a little in the air. He realized she was feeling around for the rope.

He should have put it in her hand. He started to climb back inside but saw that her hand found the rope and she gripped it tightly, then pulled it between her knees.

"Cross your feet together around it."

She did.

He moved up the rope. "Put your arms around my neck." He took one hand to show her where his shoulder was. She locked her arms around his neck.

"Hang on, Kincaid." He pulled her off the ledge.

"There is no way I'm not hanging on, Captain."

"Good. Then here we go." He began to slide down, a few feet at a time. It took time, tense minutes because they were in plain sight, with only the darkness in their favor.

"You're doing fine." With their combined weight, it wasn't easy to take it slowly, to slide only a few feet at a time. He could feel the strain in his arms, shoulders, and back.

"Someone's walking below," she hissed into his ear. "To the west."

He froze. He'd just heard the footsteps, too. How the hell did she know it was west? He scanned the area and saw a man at the far edge of the lower wall. He was facing away from them as he lit a cigarette.

It's three in the morning and this guy wants a smoke.

J.R. watched the small orange cigarette glow brightly in the guard's mouth before the man exhaled a foggy cloud, then rested his arms on the wall.

Great.

If the guard turned this way, he could see them, hanging by the rope about halfway down the stone tower.

J.R. looked down. He needed an out. Fast.

He had a hunch the guy was going to turn around any second.

What the hell. . . .

He shoved off from the wall with about a hundred and thirty pounds of Kincaid's blind daughter clinging to his neck.

They slid like a lit fuse down the rope. A good seventy feet. Friction from the rope burned right through his gloves.

He used the rope to brake their descent. They jerked to a stop, and hung there, now low enough to be partially hidden by some trees growing inside a stone wall that surrounded the central courtyard. With *Lalla Luck* on his side, the crowns of those trees blocked them from view.

J.R. looked down. The place was situated on a sheer cliff. They still had a long way to go.

He didn't dare take them on down. He couldn't take the chance that the guy would see the rope move. So they just dangled there. Someday, J.R. figured, he would joke to his buddies that he came out of this assignment well hung.

He had to give her credit. It had been a helluva drop and she hadn't made a sound. She was so still she made his job easier.

Her right ear was near his mouth so he whispered, "Now you know how a yo-yo feels."

She didn't say anything. No sense of the ridiculous.

After a minute more she asked, "How long do we wait?"

"Till he leaves. The trees are in the way, so I can't see him."

"Me either."

She did have a sense of humor. Good. They were both going to need it.

Her breathing was soft and even.

It was quiet in these mountains. Not much in the way of sounds. Noise always carried in the dead of night. You learned to take your voice down real low when your life was on the line. She was a smart cookie. She always placed her mouth very close to his ear when she spoke and her whispers were barely a breath of sound. He figured she'd taken her cue from him and he gave her points for that.

"He's leaving."

J.R. couldn't hear anything.

A moment later, a door closed.

He waited. There were no more sounds. "Okay. Here we go again. Hang on. . . ."

Her arms tightened around him, and he took them down, five feet at time, to the road below.

"CHEEK TO CHEEK"

The truck bounced so hard over a rut in the road that Kitty hit her head on the roof of the cab. She flinched, reached up and rubbed her head, but kept quiet because Cassidy did. She was wedged in between him and the driver, a man he only called Sabri, who smelled of garlic, turmeric, and sweaty cotton baked by the sun. Cassidy was sitting on her right and had a crumpled map spread open on the dash.

They had been on this road a long time. It was not the road she'd come in on. The grade was too steep and there were more hairpin turns. Without any warning they careened around a turn so sharp that she had to brace both hands on the roof to keep from falling into the driver. It felt like they'd turned on only the left two wheels.

There was a horrible pause, the kind that precedes imminent disaster. She waited for the truck to roll over.

The truck slammed down on the road so hard she felt it clear into her back teeth.

But no one said a word.

Sabri downshifted the gears a second later—the warning of another steep turn.

She slid right, into Cassidy's arm. The map he was holding crackled. He just shook it out before they hit another rut and she flew off the seat again.

She hit her head so hard only a mute could have kept quiet.

"You say something, Kincaid?" he asked.

She could tell he wasn't looking at her. His voice was directed toward the map. "I said forget the yo-yo. Now I know how a martini feels."

He laughed quietly just as Sabri downshifted again into another turn.

She made a quick grab for the seat and got Cassidy's thigh. She held on anyway, but as soon as they straightened she let go of his leg.

He wasn't looking at that map anymore. She could feel

him looking at her for a very long time. When he didn't turn away, she asked, "Are you a betting man, Cassidy?"

"Sometimes. Why?"

"Twenty bucks says you were just grinning."

"Still am, sweetheart. But don't worry. If you want to cop a feel, I won't stop you."

"Don't get your hopes up. My hands aren't that small."

He paused. "You're pretty quick, Kincaid . . . for a blind broad."

"You're pretty obnoxious, Cassidy . . . for an officer."

The truck rattled over a rut and almost drowned out his laughter.

She braced her palms on the cab roof.

"Here, this should help." He dropped his bulky canvas pack on her lap.

It weighed a ton. "What's in here?"

"A few necessities."

"Oh." She nodded knowingly. "A tank."

She heard him fold the map, then felt him shift and tuck it in his pocket.

"We won't be needing a tank to get out, sweetheart. By tomorrow we'll be in Gibraltar, and before you know it, you'll be home again."

"You're wrong, Captain. I'm not your sweetheart. I'm not anyone's sweetheart."

Sabri shifted the gears into overdrive. The truck screeched too fast into another turn. She leaned her head back against the cab and whispered, "I just hope that's the only thing you're wrong about."

TEXAS

'WITH PLENTY OF MONEY
AND YOU'

Red Walker lay in the brown stubble of a wheat field, his hands clasped behind his head and his bare feet in the warm dirt. He sucked on a couple of Sen-Sens and stared up at a big, blue Texas sky.

Everything was big in Texas.

His granddaddy Ross told him that a good hundred times.

"Everything's big in Texas," he would say in a booming voice that always ended with a crooked white grin that was bigger than any other Red had ever seen. He had a knobby, tanned, old farmer's face; it was a face that was much kinder, but butt-ugly when you compared it to his daughter's. Red's mama, Dina Rae, was a real beauty.

His granddaddy told Red a farmer's story, about how years before, in the days when you still dug a well with sweat and a shovel and a prayer, you could ride through the fields on horseback and that dadgummed wheat was shoulder-high.

Now it was the absolute Bible-swearin' truth that most Texans could tell a tale as tall as a silo. They sort of figured any fool could tell the truth, but it took some sense to tell a good lie. His granddaddy was no exception, so Red never knew whether to believe him or not. If someone pulled your leg that often, well then, you'd better not believe them 'less you want to spend most of your life walking funny.

A few years later his granddaddy died on a soft summer morning, the kind of day that made you believe the angels just came right down from heaven and lifted him up there, like he'd always said they would.

In a will hand-scrawled on the back of an old wheat contract, he left a small wooden box to Red. Inside it were mother-of-pearl cuff links, a pocket knife with a real bone handle, and a few old photographs. Nestled into the south corner was a knuckle-sized hunk of real turquoise his granddaddy had carried in his pocket for some fifty-odd years, rubbing it with his fingers so "it took the worry right out of your head." That worrying stone was smooth as spit.

After that day, on the wall above Red's narrow bed, just where the last coat of green paint was chipping through to thirty-year-old yellow, was a small, square, jagged-edged photograph of his granddaddy. He was wearing that big old straw hat he wore every single day but Sunday for as long as anyone could remember, and he was riding good old Pete—a brute of a Morgan—through a golden field of wheat that was as tall as God.

Everything's big in Texas.

That old man was right as rain, Red thought, lying there in the field and glancing at everything around him. Out back of his own daddy's filling station, just past the big round sign with its red Texaco star, there stood a row of pecan trees nigh on thirty feet high. In July, when the

110-degree Texas sun beat down and burned the breath clean out of your mouth, those trees were the only slip of shade for ten square miles.

You could see their thick green crowns all the way from the front steps of Christ Baptist Church, and those rugged trunks were harder than hell to climb barefoot. But a single one of those fourth-generation trees could throw down enough sunburnt nuts to feed icebox cookies and pecan pie to half of Wilbarger County.

Red took out a thin red-paper Sen-Sen packet from the patched pocket of his denim overalls, flicked open the flap with one thumb in the city-slick way he'd seen a young fellow from Fort Worth do; then he held it up and shook a few of them onto his dry tongue. They tasted like a mix of licorice and his mama's Camay soap, the kind she'd used to wash his mouth out when he repeated one of her curse words.

He'd first tried Sen-Sen to cover up the smell of the two Chesterfield cigarettes he'd smoked behind the old wooden water tower when he was eight. But now, four years later, he'd grown to like the way they made his mouth feel. They were cheaper than one of those blue packages of Clove gum and lasted longer. You got your few pennies' worth out of a Sen-Sen pack.

He closed his eyes, figuring he'd sleep a bit. But he opened his eyes and cocked his head when he heard a distinct and distant hum in the air. He propped up on his bare elbows and looked eastward.

There, in that blue sky, was an airplane, flying right toward him.

He'd seen planes a couple of times, once up real close, when a barnstormer buzzed into Quannah on a Saturday in May a few years back and gave rides to whoever could afford to pay a dollar for one. His daddy took Nettie and him over so's they could see that biplane in person. It wasn't hard to figure out that his daddy had wanted to get his nose into the engine as badly as Red wanted to ride in the thing.

But they didn't have dollars to waste on plane rides, so Red had just walked around it over and over again, spinning the propeller, sliding his hand along the bi-wings and the tail, trying to imagine what it would be like to get into that bucket of a seat, to put goggles over his eyes and fly right out of Acme, Texas, away from the bootlegged beer bottles that filled the kitchen trash can every day, away from the chipped supper plates that weren't good enough to give away with a gasoline fill-up and the jelly-jar glasses they used for meals, away from the hollering that echoed in their lopsided old house out back of the gas station, hollering that came from his mama's restlessness and his daddy's confusion.

Red stood up, shaded a hand over his eyes, and watched.

The biplane flew overhead; it rocked its wings at him and circled once. He waved back at the pilot, then ran through the field after that plane, still waving, ran and ran and ran, until his arms were spread out like wings and his face was turned up toward the sun and the sky and tomorrow.

"Billy Joe!"

Red stumbled and fell on his knees, his palms skidding into a warm furrow of dirt. He knelt there in that rust-colored Texas farm field while the plane kept on flying away, until it was only an arrow in the distant sky that was as unreachable as a dream.

He stood, dusted himself off, then shoved his hands in the deep pockets of his overalls, where a hunk of smooth turquoise slipped right into his fingers as if it were meant to be there. He looked toward the house and the female voice that called him.

The sun caught his mama's bright red hair, a burst of shining color against the weathered wood of their scrappy gray house, which was really little more than a three-room shack that leaned like a Saturday night drunk and sat under an old wooden water tower with a narrow platform that was a favorite spot of his. That water tower was branded with cigarette burns along the back rail, and he could sit there on that small platform for hours, wishing, dreaming, and looking out to the west where there was nothing but the flat Texas horizon for as far as his eyes could see.

"Billy Joe!"

It must be after four o'clock. She never got up before four o'clock, and that was just because she had to get ready for work. Six nights a week she played honky-tonk piano at a club just across the Oklahoma border called *The Afterthought,* where the Harmon County law enforcement turned a blind eye to the drinking and gambling because the governor's brother owned half the place.

Red's older sister, Onetta, said she heard the church ladies laughing about Mama's job. They said it was pretty far-sighted of Dina Rae to be working in a club called *The Afterthought*.

He didn't exactly understand what that meant, until Nettie explained.

Dina Rae Ross Walker had been known to drink enough beer between dusk and dawn to try to forget she had a husband whose hands and fingernails were never clean and who reeked of oil and grease and the small town she'd always wanted to leave far behind her.

"Billll-eeee Jooooooooe!"

His mama called him Billy Joe, or if she was real mad, William Joseph. His daddy just called him Red. Just Red, after his full head of wavy red hair—a gift from some Ross relative, a Scot who settled here after the Clearances.

Billy Joe or Red. What they each called him pretty much typified his folks' marriage. That, and what they called each other when they were yelling late at night. He wondered sometimes how those two ever got together in the first place.

"William Joseph Walker!"

He cupped his hands over his mouth. "Coming!"

She raised the long-necked brown beer bottle in her right hand. A gesture that looked like a toast.

He ran toward her.

She stood in the open doorway, her long slim arm propped casually on the splintered, crooked frame of the screen door. She was taking a good draw off that beer.

She'd started early today.

"Didn't you hear me calling you?"

"Sorry, Mama." He was out of breath and the words came out in a stutter.

"Your daddy had to run out to the Miller place. Old Cora Miller's DeSoto won't start. Probably because she took a good, long gander under the hood and the engine just upped and died. Lord knows she's got a face that'd kill a weed." She tossed her head, then swiped a wave of hair out of her right eye. "He wants you to watch the pumps, hon, till he gets back."

"Yes, ma'am." He wedged his way into the doorway.

She stopped him with a soft hand on his shoulder. She smelled clean, like soap and the cherry-almond hand cream she always used.

He looked up at her.

At that moment he thought he might have just understood why his daddy put up with her. It was the same reason Red did whatever she asked him to do, the same reason he wanted to make her happy. He'd remembered his granddaddy saying there wasn't a man alive who after taking one good look at his Dina Rae wouldn't give her the moon.

She brushed the hair off of his forehead with a tender touch of her hand. "You need a haircut."

"Aw, Mama."

She laughed. "Don't you 'aw, Mama' me. I'll cut it on Saturday."

"Yes, ma'am," he muttered. He liked his hair over his ears because they looked too big for his head. Although lately he thought he might be growing into them like his daddy said he would. But he still liked his hair longer. She always cut it too short.

"I think we have time for one song. You want to sing with me?" She gave him a wink.

"Sure."

"Go look outside that window, hon, and see if there's anyone out front."

The filling station was empty, the gas pumps standing there tall as Injuns. "Ain't no one out there."

She gave him a narrow-eyed look. "There's no such word as 'ain't.'"

"But, Mama, everyone says 'ain't.'"

"No, everyone doesn't. And if everyone shot their dog and their daddy, too, would you do it?"

He stuck his hands in his pockets and mumbled, "I don't have a dog."

"You want people to treat you with respect, Billy Joe, then you can't talk like some old farm boy."

His granddaddy had been a farmer, and he was the best and the smartest man Red had ever known.

"You remember what I tell you, now." She walked into the house. "You use the sense God gave you and good English. You hear me?"

"Yes, ma'am."

"Good." She patted the spot next to her on a feeble, short-legged bench. "You come here and sit by your mama."

He crossed the room and sat down next to her in front of an old cabinet piano made of some kind of dark wood the deep color of Texas farmland. It had belonged to her grandmother Chisholm, who was nothing more to Red than an old image in a photo—a small woman with a silly-looking calico bonnet and a sagging chest.

His mama flexed her hands.

He looked down at the piano. Over the past thirty-odd years, the keys had turned as yellow as an old man's teeth, and there were white rings melted into the wood from the beer bottles she had set on top of it.

She didn't need any sheet music. She carried all the notes in her head. She could play anything. You just named a song, and she could sit right there and pound out the sweetest melodies.

A second later her hands flew over the keys in a rousing rendition of "Ain't She Sweet."

He knew she played that song on purpose. He'd asked her once if "ain't" wasn't a word, then why was it in a song title? Didn't make sense to him and he said as much.

She told him that if he was looking for things to make sense in life, he might as well give up right now. That was his mama. Like her daddy, she said things he remembered.

Her foot tapped and pumped the brass piano pedals, drawing out those sugar notes. It was always the same for Red, sitting there beside her on that wobbling bench, tapping his fingers on his patched knees in time to the music. Suddenly the cracked paint, the beat-up old wood floor that slanted south, and that worn-out blue divan in the corner didn't matter.

Oh, Lord, the sound she could lure from that piano was enough to make an angel cry and the devil dance.

A car horn blared from out front.

She stopped playing suddenly and swore one of those raunchy, mouth-washing words. She took a deep breath and let it out slowly. "Better see who it is." She was reaching for her beer bottle.

Red got up and ran out the front door. He shoved the screen open so hard it banged on the outside wall, then rattled against the frame when it snapped closed.

He stopped running halfway down the front steps and stood there frozen.

Sitting right in front of the tall, glass-topped ethyl pump was what looked to be a brand-new Ford-blue cabriolet with its canvas top crushed down. It had sparkling whitewall tires. The hubcaps were polished steel, and the background of the V-8 emblem was painted in the same glossy Ford-blue as the chassis.

Red let out a soft whistle. It was some automobile. He ran toward the driver, a tall man in an expensive suit and a Panama hat who was leaning against the spare tire in the rear and puffing on a cigar that smelled like black walnuts.

"Is this a real V-8?"

"Sure is."

His daddy was going to be mad as cats in a sack. A real V-8 engine and he wasn't there to see it.

"Fill her up for me, son."

"Sure." Red went over to the pump and began to fill the car. As far as he knew no one had filled up their gas tank in a good six months. It was always a dollar's worth here or fifty cents' worth there. "Is that carpet on the floor?"

"Yep."

Red craned his neck a bit. "In the back, too?"

"Yep."

He shook his head and just stared at that beauty of a car, holding the gas nozzle in the tank on the right rear fender.

The man grinned at him from around his cigar.

With the rag top and windows down, the car was the sportiest thing Red had ever seen. The bench seat was russet brown leather, and it smelled just like new shoes, although it had been so long since he'd had a pair you'd think he would have forgotten the smell by now.

Even the rumble seat was covered in leather.

"Well, my, oh, my, will you look at that."

Red pulled his gaze away from the dream car and

watched his mama saunter toward them, over the warm blacktop driveway in a pair of fancy red high heels he'd never seen.

The man straightened up like he'd just been starched. He whipped off his hat. "Ma'am."

She was wearing lipstick the color of a vine tomato. It made her lips look fuller and her skin look as perfect as fresh cream. She had a flowered comb pulling up one side of her shoulder-length, wavy hair. The comb matched her best blue-and-red dress, which was not the one she'd been wearing a few minutes ago, but now skimmed her long, bare legs.

She ran her hand along the car in the same tender way she'd brushed the hair off of Red's forehead.

He got a sick kind of feeling in his stomach—the kind you got when someone played a joke on you and you hadn't seen it coming.

"Why, I think this is the prettiest car I have *ever* seen."

"Thank you, ma'am."

"My name's Dina Rae." She held out her hand and looked straight at the man in the same way Red looked at his teacher when he wanted her to believe that he hadn't let those big old spiders loose in the girls' washroom.

"It makes me feel like an old woman when people call me 'ma'am'," she said.

That was news to Red. He was brought up to say "ma'am" out of respect. If he hadn't, he would have gotten one hell of a licking with his daddy's belt or his granddaddy's razor strop. He knew that for sure because he'd made the mistake of testing it once.

"Roland Stiles." The man took her hand in his.

Red's knuckles tightened on the gasoline nozzle.

She smiled, then pulled her hand away and walked slowly along the car, dragging a finger along the shiny paint until she was standing in front of it. She stepped back a foot or so and put her hands on her hips.

Roland Stiles was looking at his mama the way a hungry dog looked at a ham bone.

Red was watching them so closely that he lost track of things and pumped gasoline all over the fender.

Shitfire!

He snatched an old rag from his back pocket and hunkered down, trying to wipe the gas off as fast as he could. When he looked up again, embarrassed, and ready to hear about what he'd done, he saw that they hadn't even noticed.

". . . No," Mr. Roland Stiles was saying. "I'm from Jackson. Not Jackson County, but Jackson, Mississippi."

"I figured as much. I don't think you can buy a brand-new Ford in Altus." She grinned up at him, then shaded her eyes with a hand as she cast a quick glance up at the late afternoon sun. She turned back and began to fan herself. "It's hot enough out here to wither a fence post. Why don't you come along inside. I'll get you a nice cold Dr. Pepper and you can tell me all about Jackson, Mississippi." She threaded her arm though his and then turned back to Red. "You take good care of Mr. Stiles's car, now, Billy Joe. Wash that windshield real good."

He just stared at her.

"Did you hear me?"

"Yes, *ma'am*." He looked away. He couldn't watch as they walked toward the small station building where bottles of Dr. Pepper, Bireley's, and Creme Soda were kept inside a white-and-red porcelain cooler that looked like a washing machine.

Once, a long, long time ago, he remembered his mama taking his daddy's arm like that and walking and talking with him. At least he thought he remembered it. It was back in the days when they all went to church on Sundays, those days when she made shirts for his daddy and him, and dresses for his sister.

But that was before his granddaddy died and before Mama got her night job. It was when his mama still talked to the church ladies, like Cora Miller and Ida Mae Dodd, talked to them instead of about them. He couldn't remember a time in the last five years when she'd been close enough to his daddy to even touch his arm.

Red rubbed hard on the windshield, scouring off the crusted, yellow bugs. He finished and began to polish the single side mirror, then stepped back. It was shining like a new nickel. He swiped at his dripping forehead with his bare arm. He was hot. *He* wanted a Dr. Pepper. He stuffed the rag in his back pocket and marched toward the station.

Inside, they were standing side by side, both leaning against the wooden counter and talking about the seventeen thousand World War I veterans camped out in Washington, D.C., trying to get their service bonuses just so they could survive.

Red leaned over and grabbed a warm Dr. Pepper from a crate in the corner. He slid it into the slot in the top of the cooler and a cold bottle came out the opposite side. He stuck the bottle top into the opener, popped off the metal cap, then pulled off the cork liner to see if he'd won a prize.

"Did you win?" Stiles was watching him.

Red shook his head. "I never win anything. I'm the only person I know who got a Cracker Jack box with no prize inside."

Stiles laughed.

"I'm not lucky," Red said.

"You have to make your own luck, Billy Joe."

He just looked at his mama.

She smiled and tossed him a slim pack of Planters peanuts she'd torn from the blue-and-white cardboard display next to her. He didn't smile back—to punish her—but he took a long few gulps of his cold drink, then tore open the peanuts with his teeth and poured them into the Dr. Pepper bottle.

He looked up to find them both looking into each other's eyes in a dumb way that made him angry. He tapped Stiles on the shoulder with a stiff finger. "Your car's ready."

Stiles pulled his attention away from his mama and looked at him. "How much do I owe you?"

"Five dollars and thirty cents."

Stiles stuck his hand in his pants pocket and pulled out a monogrammed silver money clip that was a good two inches thick.

Red had never seen that much money in his whole life.

Stiles peeled off a twenty-dollar bill and handed it to him.

They didn't have that much in the whole cash drawer. He just stood there staring at the twenty-dollar bill. "I don't think we have change."

"I don't need any change, son. Keep it."

Red glanced up at his mama. She had a funny expression on her face, one he'd never seen before.

The money began to burn his fingers.

She shoved away from the counter and said, "Oh, my Lord! What time is it?"

Stiles flexed out his left arm. His pearl-linked cuff drew back to reveal a large gold wristwatch. "Five-fifteen."

"I'm going to be late for work." She crossed over to the window, placed her hands on the sill and looked outside. "Where is your daddy?"

His daddy? She made it sound like it was all Red's fault that she would be late.

"I'll take you, Miz Walker."

She cast a soft glance over her shoulder at Stiles. She gave him the kind of smile that made you think you were the only person in the world. "That's right kind of you, but I don't want to put you to any trouble."

"How could it be trouble when I would be driving the prettiest woman this side of the Mississippi?"

"Lord, how sweet you are. . . . Let me get my things. I'll be just a few minutes." She left the station and walked toward the house.

They both stood there, staring at the empty doorway. After a minute the screen door on the house rattled closed.

"My daddy will back any minute."

"It's no trouble, son. I'm going that way." Stiles finished the last of his soda and tossed the empty bottle in a trash bin next to the counter.

After a long moment of tense silence Red reached out and dug into the trash and picked up the bottle. He turned and put it into the wooden bottle crate in the corner, along with the other empties. They were worth a penny apiece.

"I'm ready!" His mama was waving at them from outside. She stood by that shiny new Ford in her blue-and-red dress.

Red followed Stiles outside, but stopped in the doorway underneath a double-sided flange sign that advertised the Firestone Tire slogan: *They'll Get You Where You Want to Go.*

Stiles opened the car door for his mama, then leaned in as he closed it and said something to her that made her laugh. He walked around the car without a look at Red. He got in and started it up.

His mama turned and waved at him as they drove off down a long, lonely strip of blacktop. The highway was a good five miles to the west.

As he watched them shrink smaller and smaller, his mama's bright red hair whipping in the wind from the speed of the V-8, he thought for just one second that she looked as if she belonged in that car.

His mama must have thought so, too, because they never saw her again.

"TOOT, TOOT, TOOTSIE, GOO'BYE"

His daddy sat them down a few nights later, when he knew for sure she'd run off. He said it was his fault. That he couldn't live in a city like she wanted. He couldn't breathe in a place where there were so many people stealing the air from your lungs.

He had been a towering, black-haired man with light blue eyes and ears that were too big for his head. He was so tall that he had to duck when he came into a room or he would bump his head on the doorjamb.

In Texas, men walked tall, but for as long as Red could remember his daddy walked with a slight stoop to his shoulders as if he were carrying the weight of all the wrong choices he'd made.

Dina Rae sent Red and Nettie a postcard from Dallas with a picture of an oil well on it. She signed it *Love, Mama.*

Their daddy got a fat yellow envelope from some fancy divorce attorney in Jackson.

His daddy wasn't the same after that. He stayed in the old gas station with its chipped sign that swung back and forth, back and forth, waving good-bye to everything that might have been. He stayed there between the wood walls that seemed to turn suddenly gray like his hair had. And it was there, with that unending Texas sky above him, that he spent his days and his nights with his head hidden under the hoods of countless cars the way an ostrich hides its head in the sand.

Red and his sister came to accept the myth that their daddy never came to Red's basketball games or to see Nettie in the school play because he had to work late on Jimmy Jessup's delivery truck or Homer Wilbarger's John Deere tractor.

Some nights Red would look at him, bent over their kitchen table and working on some engine part. Every once in a while his daddy's eyes would go blank, as if he had gone someplace else, someplace hopeless. Later, he would stand at the sink in the kitchen for the longest time and scrub his hands so hard that by morning they would crack and bleed. He never could get that grease out from under his fingernails.

Two years to the day that she'd left, Red woke up and found his daddy slumped over a carburetor he'd taken apart the night before.

The doctor said his heart just gave out.

"No. It broke," Red told him. "It just, plain broke."

He quit school at fourteen and took over the station. Nettie married a nice boy named Louie Lee and they set up house in Vernon.

Red worked hard enough to pay the bank without much left over. He didn't need much. But every once in a while, as he was walking inside the station door, wiping the grease off his hands with a rag he still kept in his back pocket, he would stop and look up at the Firestone Tire sign and wonder if his mama got where she wanted to go.

"DEEP IN THE HEART OF TEXAS"

MAY, 1938

Charley Morrison looked down from the cockpit of the bright yellow Piper Cub for the hundredth time in the last two hours and searched for some kind of distinguishing mark on the land below.

A futile effort.

There was no mountain, not even a hill beneath the broad Texas sky. Just flat land with an occasional clump of green or a gray strip of road that didn't look like any kind of highway, and came and went as often as a sailor. There was nothing below, and there had been nothing below for most of the afternoon, nothing but brick-red faceless land and mesquite the color of a biscuit.

Over the last half hour, a few scattered farms and a small town had appeared, but not a single building among any of them had a roof that looked sturdy enough to paint an airmark on it.

A group of five experienced pilots with a minimum of over two hundred flight hours had been hired by the federal government to air-map the U.S. It was their job to fly over the nation—sixteen thousand or so towns and cities—looking for rooftops where a mark would be visible from the air as a navigational aid for pilots.

Charley was one of the five.

At six foot one, Charley was tall enough to see easily from the cockpit of the small plane, although that height didn't help much now, when there was nothing to airmark but tumbleweeds.

There was no choice but to turn back and head for the last marking spot between here—wherever here was—and Lubbock. Plainly speaking, nothing left to do but start all over again after wasting almost a full day flying around for nothing.

But airmarking was a job, and a good one, at a time when jobs were hard to find. A person was lucky to have a regular paycheck, even luckier to have a government check. Both were rare for a pilot in these pinched times when the economy had gone bad so fast and no one but the very wealthy had money for flying lessons and joyrides.

It had been a long and dismal nine years since the Stock Market had crashed and sent the country into a tailspin, one that left little prosperity and a lot of people who were hungry, homeless, and out of work.

Charley was one of those lucky five pilots who, for the last four months, had flown from state to state, city to city, town to town, mapping America from thousands of feet above the land.

Almost nine years ago to the week, another lucky pilot called Lindy had set down in Paris in the dead of night after flying alone for thirty-three hours and thirty-nine minutes across the unpredictable Atlantic. Who'd have thought then that man would have discovered a whole new wilderness, that he would have a new perspective of his place in the world—from the air high above it.

The five airmarking pilots covered different regions of the country. There was one in the North, three in the middle and one in the deep South. Charley was one of the three in the middle. Although today, it looked like this particular section of the middle was not the place to be. At least not in a plane.

It hadn't been clear weather this morning, but high clouds seldom stopped a plane from taking off. By early afternoon, those clouds had changed into a heavy, gray sky, the kind that happens just before the weather turns real ugly.

Now the wind had picked up, too.

A savvy pilot understood that the air could change

quicker than the weather; it happened that way often in the Midwest, especially in Oklahoma and Texas, where the weather was as wild and woolly as the region's history.

The Cub dropped suddenly, slapped down from the sky by the mighty hand of the elements. Charley took the plane lower, downstairs, then scanned the skies all around. Off toward the south was a front of dark clouds, rolling in fast and looking like God on Judgment Day.

The temperature changed quickly. The air grew thicker, then cold. The sudden, dark storm looked massive, bearing down in a huge hurry. Flying got rougher and controlling the plane was more difficult. The weather tossed it up and down, up and down, until the Cub was flying so low you could almost see the whites of the cows' eyes.

The plane bounced around like a rubber ball.

This way.

That way.

Then, a long straight strip of road appeared off to the left. A blacktop lifeline, wide enough for a landing. Charley gripped the stick in two hands and banked the plane, heading for that thread of blacktop.

A pilot learned quickly to sit evenly, so you could tell if you were banking at the right speed. You could literally feel the turn in your butt. Flying by the seat of your pants wasn't just a quippy saying.

A crosscurrent hit hard. Feet on the rudder pedals, Charley fought to keep the stick steady, fought the air and the drafts that wanted to knock the plane around.

The road grew larger. The ground rose up as if it were swelling.

Closer . . .

Closer . . .

The Cub's wheels hit it hard: a sharp thud and a rubbery screech. The plane bounced and wobbled, then rolled ducklike down the road, heading straight for a small, clobbered-looking Texaco station.

The red star in the middle of the Texaco sign grew bigger and bigger. On the side of the building, painted in stark white and red letters was a huge advertisement for drinking Dr. Pepper at 10, 2, and 4.

Charley hit the brakes, which didn't stop the plane, just made it roll slower.

A gust whipped the plane starboard.

Now it was headed straight for the gasoline pumps.

Whoa, baby, whoa. . . . Come on. . . .

A tall, lanky young fellow with a crop of bright red-orange hair stepped out from the shadow of the station building. He stood there as if his feet were frozen to the spot, but he was waving his arms like crazy.

The plane rolled to a stop about ten feet shy of those pumps. Charley revved the engine up a bit, turned the plane, and taxied into the lee of a ramshackle building that sat beneath a crippled-looking water tower with the thick line of trees growing behind it.

The tree line would give the plane some protection from the buffeting wind. The storm was moving in quickly, and the clouds were getting blacker and higher, looking as if they filled the whole sky.

A flick of the switches and the engine was off. The propeller slowed its spinning rotation until you could see the blades, then their outline, then the looped shape of each one.

Charley took a deep breath of sticky, storm-heavy air that tasted like wet hay and smelled like country.

The young man was all legs and reminded Charley of a greyhound, moving with that seemingly never-ending, limber-legged gait. He was stuffing a faded red rag in the back pocket of his old, grease-stained work coveralls. "I thought for sure you were going to hit those pumps and send us both to Kingdom Come."

The two gas pumps were ten foot tall cylinders with round glass globes on top of them that looked as if they'd been cracked by BBs.

He had a smile as wide as the Texas horizon.

Charley jumped down to the ground with a thud.

Close up, he was just a kid, really. Maybe seventeen, give or take a year or so. His red hair and freckled face made him look young, despite his height.

But then it could have been his expression that made him look younger, the way he was looking at the plane with such awe.

He took a step closer and stuck out a big, freckled hand. "I'm Red Walker."

Charley took his hand, and shook it, then slipped off the goggles and the leather helmet. "Charley Morrison."

"Christ on a crutch!" He frowned. "You're a woman!" His hand went slack in hers. After a second he glanced down at their hands and pulled his back, then quickly shoved both deep in his pockets.

It amazed her that even with newspapers and air races, with cinema newsreels and the swiftly changing times, even with the fast-rising fame of women flyers, there were still a lot of people who never imagined a woman could fly an airplane.

Most of those people were men.

"Yes, I'm a woman and you're a man. So now that we've settled that, how about you help me get this plane secured?"

A gust of wind hit the Cub and rocked it in a wild way that worried her. She scanned the area. Next to the station was a work garage that leaned eastward and had a wide wooden door held open with three-foot stacks of old black rubber tires. Inside was a rusted Ford pickup truck, that had once been black. The building was high enough and the doors wide enough to take the Cub, if she angled it in right and could fit the wing around that truck bed.

She gave a nod in the direction of the clouds. "That storm's coming right at us, and I don't want it taking this plane and my income along with it."

"Your income? You mean someone pays you to fly a plane?"

She turned away before she said something that she'd regret. Something about boys too wet behind the ears to understand that women had the same intelligence and drive that men did.

She took a second to stick her headgear inside the zipper of the flight suit, then felt she could face him and not say something ugly. "Ever heard of Amelia Earhart?"

He gave a snort of laughter. "You're not Amelia Earhart. She disappeared last year."

"I didn't say I was. But she flew planes."

"I know who she was and what she did. I've seen her picture in the newspaper."

"I bet you have. I bet you look at all the pictures in the newspaper."

He gave her the once over. "You from California?"

"No. Why?"

"You know what they say."

"No, I'm not certain I do."

"Well, that women from California do all kinds of stupid things."

"What does that mean? That men from California never do anything stupid?"

He didn't say anything, but looked away for a moment, his hands deep in his pockets, and he rocked on his heels.

"Maybe you meant that only people from California do stupid things?"

"Well . . ." He paused, then nodded. "I suppose so. They make movies there. It's a made-up world in California. You know what I mean. This isn't California. This is Texas."

She crossed her arms and nodded slowly. "You know, I think I do understand what you're saying. Because they make movies in California and movies aren't real, people there do stupid things, yet people in Texas never do stupid things."

He said nothing, just looked at her.

"So that would mean . . . logically speaking . . . that people everywhere outside of California never do stupid things, unless of course they make a movie. Then suddenly the cameras and actors arrive and the whole state goes off half-cocked doing all kinds of stupid things. Like letting women out of the kitchen."

She had him now. "It's really funny, the way we can be so small-minded. Like it comes to us naturally." She tapped a finger on her temple. "From somewhere inside our heads. We don't want to take risks. And it's our willingness to accept the ordinary that keeps us from reaching for our dreams."

Let him think about that. She turned away. She couldn't stand people who were too afraid to be different. They tried to make the world more difficult for those who weren't. It was a fact that if you chose the harder road, people threw boulders in your way instead of waving you on.

He still wasn't talking, this kid who was throwing his own rocks.

The wind was blowing hard. She needed to push the plane into that garage. She was annoyed enough to push a whole train clear to Dallas. She placed one hand on the fuselage, then the other on the wing, near where they joined.

Luckily for Redneck Walker, she cast a quick glance over her shoulder before she gave it the old heave-ho.

He was standing in front of the left wing, staring at the Cub, lost in thought and oblivious to the fact that he was in the way.

"Look, that wind is whipping up like crazy. If you're not going to help me, then get out of my way."

"IT'S AN OLD SOUTHERN CUSTOM"

They barely made it inside the house before the hail fell. Balls of ice the size of your fist hammered the roof and hit the ground so hard they bounced up as if they were made by Firestone Rubber.

Red had his back to her. He stood at the kitchen sink washing his hands.

"My God...," she said. "Would you look at that hail?"

He didn't need to look at the hail. He was born here, right under that water tower with the word *Acme* painted on it. He knew the Texas weather by the sound and the feel of it. If you lived here, you could even taste a storm before it hit. It tasted like the crops the local farmers were growing: wheat, alfalfa, hay, or maize. And the air always got thicker than potato soup.

He turned back around, leaning back on the counter and drying his hands on a dish towel.

She stood at the front window, her back to him, her hands braced palm-down on the sill. He took a gander at her figure, which from the way she was standing, you'd have to be blind to miss.

From this angle he could tell she was lush and curvy and all woman even in the zippered jumpsuit and clunky boots she wore. Too bad she hadn't bent over the plane that way. He'd never have thought she was a man.

He tossed the towel aside, then cast a quick glance over his shoulder and out the back window. The storm clouds were getting so black that it grew darker inside and made the place look even more dreary than it was.

Red flipped on the black wall switch for the overhead light, hoping it might brighten the place up a bit. It was like hoping for the sun to rise in the kitchen sink. The single fixture hung off-center from the middle of the ceiling and the light from its cracked and dusty bowl of frosted glass dimmed and flickered when the power generator surged.

He stared up at it, hope gone.

There were black specks in the basin, dead bugs and flies he hadn't noticed before. It spread bright light down on the kitchen table, where a dismantled carburetor, a set of pistons and barrels, a manifold, and a distributor were spread out like Sunday chicken dinner.

His pride made him suddenly want to make the whole place just disappear.

"No one could possibly fly in that mess of weather out there." She still didn't look at him, so he didn't know if she was talking to him or to herself.

Most people hereabouts believed that only the very old or the very crazy talked to themselves. He was nineteen, yet he'd been talking to himself for years.

The wind whistled down the walls, through the old window frames, and rattled the glass, then over the roof and through the eaves, making them shudder slightly. It was a loud, howling wind.

She straightened suddenly and turned around, leaned back against the windowsill and stared up at the ceiling as if she expected it to fall in.

"Your plane should be safe enough inside the garage. It might look like the roof could cave in, but it won't."

"I've never seen hail like this. It's huge."

"Then you haven't been in Texas long."

She pushed away from the window looking as out of place in the shabby, small room as a silver dollar in a handful of plug nickels. She was so tall she could look him in the eye. He'd never seen a woman that tall before . . . well, at least not a pretty woman.

"I was in Lubbock last night and had planned to be in Wichita Falls by this afternoon. Instead I'm in . . ." She paused, then looked at him, frowning. "Just where am I?"

"Acme, Texas."

"Oh."

"A hundred miles west of Wichita Falls."

For a second the only sound in the place was the hammering of the hailstones from outside. He went to hitch his hip on the corner of the kitchen table and sat down instead on the distributor. He felt his face flush hot and red, so he turned and tried to push the parts aside.

He sort of wished she would keep talking. The silence made him feel naked. He said all the wrong things to this fly-gal. He'd just never expected a female pilot to land in his gas station. Who would? But she made him feel like he was dumber than toast.

It was strange, the way she jumped to the conclusion that he thought she couldn't make a living at being a pilot because she was a woman. All he'd been surprised at was that anyone could be paid for something as fantastic as flying an airplane.

He might have set her straight, but somehow he figured there was a big argument in that, at least when she was still mad as hens at him for something he didn't really say.

He was a little rusty at talking to women, except for Nettie, his sister, and Ruth Wendell, Pastor Wendell's wife, who invited him for beef dinner the first Sunday of every month. He talked to female customers once in a while, but most of them were older than Eve. They had known his granddaddy as well as his daddy, had white hair, and remembered the day Red got his first tooth and his first haircut.

She wasn't looking at him, but around the room.

He wondered what she thought when she looked at the place. All he ever saw was the emptiness of it. It wasn't much different from how it had looked when his mama left, except for the three-year-old Kadette radio on the kitchen counter, and the barren windows with only five-and-dime store roller shades wedged into the top of the window frames.

On the day his daddy died he'd finally taken down those old, rotting lace curtains his mama made. Nettie wanted to take them down before, when they'd gotten the postcard from Dallas. But their daddy had always said no. Perhaps they reminded him of another time, when Red's mama hadn't wanted to run away, when she had been a woman who sewed for her man and her children, and made the place a home.

"What's this you're working on?" She had crossed to the table and was staring down at the engine parts.

His mama had always gone on and on about greasy auto parts on the kitchen table. She and his daddy had fought about it.

Charley Morrison picked up a piston and turned it this way and that, completely ignoring the grease all over it. She set it down and casually wiped her hand on her jumpsuit as she studied everything on the table. "Pistons, barrels, carburetor . . ."

She knew what they were.

He almost said something stupid like, *Well, I'll be damned*. Hell, with that chip on her shoulder a comment like that might get him slapped.

"I'd say by the look on your face that you think women don't know about engines." She sounded exasperated with him.

What was it about his face that told this woman something he was surely not thinking?

"Is that what you think?"

Finally he just laughed and raised his hands in the air. "Not me. I'm no fool. I'm not thinking anything except what you want me to think."

"You're a fast learner, Red Walker."

They stood there, neither of them saying anything.

"Your turn," she finally said.

"My turn for what?"

"To ask me a question. I ask you a question, then you ask me a question. It's called conversation."

"Well, okay . . . Right now I'm trying to figure out if I should ask you where you learned what a piston looked like."

"Afraid I'm going to bite your head off?"

"Something like that."

She sat back and gave him a direct look, then crossed her arms and one leg over a knee. "My pop told me a long time ago that if you're going to fly a plane, you'd better know how it works, especially when you're running it thousands of feet in the air."

"I suppose that makes sense."

The hail had stopped. Now it sounded like regular rain pounding down on the roof.

She shifted her weight to one side, unzipped a pocket, and stuck her hand inside it, rummaging around for something. "Look. Can I get something to drink?" She set some change on the table. "I saw the soda pop advertisement on the building, so I figure you must sell them, right?"

"I'll get you one." He stood up so fast he hit a knee on

the table and wanted to swear. "Stay put," he said, walking for the door. "The cooler's in the station."

"Wait! Here's some money."

"I'll get it." He was already half outside. The screen rattled closed behind him. He went inside the station and got a couple of bottles of soda, stuffed some bags of peanuts into his pockets; then he stepped back outside.

The wind had stopped. Now it was quiet, that empty kind of quiet that preceded something just the opposite, the kind of silence that made you stop and pay attention.

He walked toward the open side of the station and stood there a minute, holding the cold Dr. Pepper bottles by their long, damp necks.

Off toward the south, the clouds were black as iron and rolling over and over, down and sideways, twisting and moving toward the ground. A narrow outline of thin black was spinning like thread from the bottom of those heavy clouds.

He turned and ran to the house.

She met him at the door, standing with the screen propped open against her back.

"Here's your drink." He shoved it at her, then kept walking past. After a second he called back, "Come on."

"Come on where? Where are you going?"

"This way!" He made straight for the tower. "Out back!"

He heard her run down the steps. "What's going on?"

He turned around, but continued trotting backwards. "That's tornado weather off toward the south. Look! There's a funnel cloud!"

Not only did she have a name like a man. She swore like one.

'LEANING ON THE
OLD TOP RAIL'

Charley froze where she was, the word *shit* still hanging in the air. High in the sky were clouds as black as coal dust. Two long, dark, spiral clouds were joined together by a thin thread and were hanging down from the storm like some kind of uneven jump rope that moved constantly.

She ran after him, around the corner of the old wooden building that was the base of the water tower.

He had disappeared.

She looked around on the ground for the doors to a cellar or storm shelter of some kind.

There was nothing.

She scanned the area and saw nothing but a freshly combined wheat field and a dark sky.

"The view's better from up here."

She looked up.

Red Walker was leaning on a wooden railing, looking down at her from a narrow platform that ran around the tower.

"What are you doing up there?"

"Watching the tornado. You coming up?"

"Up? Don't you think we should go someplace safer?"

"Like where?"

"In a cellar or storm shelter. Underground. Far away?"

He laughed. "Why?"

"So we don't die."

"We're not going to die. It's only a tornado."

Charley looked off toward the clouds.

Only a tornado. That's like saying only an airplane crash.

She could see a funnel beginning to form beneath the roiling storm clouds. She looked back at him. "Are you crazy?"

He shrugged. "If you're scared, don't come up, but that seems a little strange to me."

"What seems strange? That I'm afraid of a tornado cloud? Pilots have to fly around them, Red. Planes can't fly as high as that cloud."

"Have you ever seen a tornado?"

"Not up close, thank you."

"Well, that's interesting."

"Interesting? Why?"

"You claim we shouldn't accept the ordinary, but here you have a chance to do something out of the ordinary and you won't do it."

She gave him what she hoped was a look as dark as those clouds, then she turned on her heel and climbed up the ladder. She crawled through the ladder hole and onto the platform.

He was sitting down with his back to the splintered wood of the tower, his long legs dangling freely over the edge.

He faced her and patted the platform. "Sit."

She shifted into the same position he was and

watched the clouds warily. She began to fidget. She wanted to be someplace belowground, not high above it. It was humid and warm and sticky. She unsnapped the cuffs on her flight suit and shoved the sleeves back to her elbows.

He just sat there, calm as a toad in the sun.

She realized there was suddenly no sound outside. No birds. No wind. Nothing. Just strange, empty air. "How come there's no siren blowing?"

"They have warning sirens in town. This is farm country. Out here we don't have any sirens, and if we did, they wouldn't do a lick of good. Most farms are a few hundred acres."

"If that's supposed to reassure me, it doesn't. I can't believe I'm just sitting here calmly—"

He laughed. "Calmly?"

"All right, sitting here hysterically and watching weather that could easily kill us."

"These storms don't move that fast."

"Who said?"

"I just know."

"Did you ever think that you just might not have *seen* one that moves fast?"

"You understand weather when you live in it all your life."

"Okay." She eyed the storm uneasily. It was still far enough away to make her not want to run screaming from the tower. "How long have you been doing this crazy thing?"

"Probably longer than you've been flying a plane."

"That long?"

"Since I could climb the tower, I guess. These marks

here in the wood are for the tornadoes I've seen go by." He took out a pocket knife with a bone handle and made a mark on the rim of the platform. There were at least five long rows of marks. "The number isn't true. I didn't start marking them here until I had a pocket knife, after my granddaddy died. Then I started cutting a notch in the wood for every tornado that went by."

"There must be nearly a hundred marks there."

"Yep."

"You've never had a tornado come straight through here?"

"Nope. One came close enough to pull the leaves off that pecan tree over there, but that was about it. The twister dropped down for only a second or two, then went right back up into the sky."

"And you were sitting here when that one hit?"

"I sure was. Hell . . . when you live in Texas, you see tornadoes come down and take the feathers right off of the chickens."

She stared at him, then laughed. "You're teasing me."

He shook his head and, with a perfectly straight face, said, "It's true. Afterward the chickens will be just standing in the yard, pecking away, but they're as bald as the head on a turkey buzzard."

"And just where are all these bald chickens?"

"I ate 'em."

She laughed. "I'm not swallowing that."

"I swallowed 'em and they were right good, too. Fried 'em up for Sunday dinner. Didn't even have to pluck 'em."

"I think you're telling one of those tall Texas tales I've heard so much about."

"That's only because you've never seen a bald chicken."

He was clowning with her. The funny thing was, you couldn't tell he was joking from his straight face. He was maybe two or three years younger than she was. She thought about him sitting here, as a young boy, and wondered what would have happened if a tornado had turned and headed for him. "Didn't your mother worry about you sitting up here all alone in such dangerous weather?"

He snapped the pocket knife closed, leaned forward a bit, and stuck it back in his pocket as he looked off at something somewhere in the distance, his expression as wooden as the platform they were sitting on. "My mama was gone."

She wanted to ask him where his mother had gone. If she was gone as in "she left," or if she was gone as in "gone to heaven."

His expression told her to leave it alone.

She could see the funnel cloud was still some distance away and off toward the southwest. The cone was getting wider and deeper in color. There was a long black column coming up from the ground like it was being sucked clean up into those clouds.

He shifted and brought one leg up, then rested his hand on it. "I always sort of figured if I had to, I could outrun a twister."

"Let's hope we don't have to test that theory today."

"My bet is it'll pass south of us."

"What's that black spot there? See?" She pointed.

"The funnel cloud is touching down. Watch that tail, the one that looks like a kite tail. It'll whip down. See?"

"Look at that!" She watched it spin, strangely—spinning like crazy yet seeming to move toward them molasses-slow. "Look. It's growing. I heard once that they can be miles wide."

She knew tornado clouds could be over thirty thousand feet high. You never tried to fly over one. "It's so huge. . . ."

"Yep. Everything's big in Texas."

She looked at him then.

He grinned at her. "My granddaddy used to say that." He gestured at the soda bottle still in her hand. "You gonna drink that?"

She held it up. "The cap's still on."

He took it from her and leaned forward, placed the cap on the edge of the rail, and slammed his fist down on it. The cap flew off. He handed it back to her.

All along the railing she noticed little teeth marks, like bites—a hundred or more bottle caps had made their marks along that wooden rail. The history of Red Walker.

He opened his soda bottle and took a long swig, then pulled a package of peanuts from his pocket, tore it open with his teeth, and emptied the peanuts into the Dr. Pepper. He crumpled up the empty bag and stuffed it in his pocket.

A second later he raised the bottle to his mouth and swallowed Dr. Pepper and peanuts.

"And you think people from California are nuts."

"If I had made that kind of bad pun, I'd bet you'd have had something snippy to say." He pulled another package of peanuts from his coveralls and handed it to her. "Here. You try it."

She stared at the peanut bag.

"Go on. Try it. It'll give us something new we can argue about."

He had a good sense of humor.

She opened the bag, but only put three of the peanuts in the bottle, one at a time.

He was staring straight ahead, as if he hadn't been watching her. But he said quietly, "No guts."

"Weak stomach," she said without looking back.

So they sat there like that, as the tornado swirled in the distance, pulling up so much red Texas dirt that the funnel looked rusted.

The storm was traveling northeast, and as it moved, there was a distant hollow kind of sound, the kind that comes from deep inside a drum. The sound grew deeper, louder, more hollow sounding, until it was like some unearthly being screaming.

The wind whipped violently even in the storm's perimeter, and the tower, well, the tower just quivered like a coward.

The air felt electric. Charley looked down, and the fine hair on her forearms was standing on end from the static. The heavy surrounding air tasted of dirt and rain and destruction.

The tornado whirled through a fallow farm field, kicking up a mess. The wind blew so hard that sitting there, even from a good distance away, it was like flying in an open cockpit. Her hair flew straight back, her eyes teared, and she had to close her lips because the force of the wind hurt her front teeth.

It passed by as he had predicted, and she realized she was sitting there, hugging her knees tightly, and smiling.

It was the very same feeling she'd had the first time she ever flew. She just looked at that tornado blowing across the flat land and said, "Wow!"

"I'd say that about says it all."

The funnel cloud was spinning along the road, before

she finally relaxed and leaned back against the tower again. Still half-turned, she watched it slowly disappear.

It was the strangest thing. It just wound down as if it were just getting tired of spinning. One moment the cone was there, and the next it looked like it had been swallowed up by the clouds. Gone.

The dark and heavy clouds were thinning. They faded from black to gray, and a shot of clear golden sunlight streamed through the eastern side of the storm front and cast purple shadows on the ground, where debris lay sprawled over the remnants of the field.

A large tree had been pulled from the ground and lay there; its roots looked like clawing fingers that had tried to hold on. Whole bushes, weathered and splintered boards, and an old tire were tossed there, stolen from only God knew where.

"See? You had nothing to worry about. It didn't even come close." Red killed off the last of his soda and was chewing on the peanuts.

She wasn't certain what she felt. She'd sat out a tornado on an old water tower with this wild kid drinking Dr. Pepper and peanuts. "You know, I've heard people call flying a plane sheer craziness. They say it's nothing but a danger-seeking thrill."

"You like it."

"And you like facing down tornadoes." She paused. "Or are there other dangerous things you like to face down?"

"Snippy female pilots?"

She faced him.

"Should I duck?"

"No. I'm not dangerous. Yet."

He laughed and stretched back a bit, folding his hands behind his head. "I watch tornadoes because there's not much else exciting to do around here."

"You're saying it's dull here in Acme, Texas?"

He shrugged. "I'd bet being a pilot isn't dull."

"It's not."

"What exactly does it take to be a pilot?"

She was drinking from her soda. She swallowed and faced him. "Lessons."

He laughed. "I'm serious."

"It takes a love of flying, Red. A fascination with aeronautics. A deep and abiding desire to be up in the air, to look down on the world that exists, instead of looking up at a world you can only imagine."

He seemed to understand that. She could see in his eyes that he wanted to fly. He had all the signs, signs she knew only too well. "If that plane wasn't filled with equipment, I'd take you up."

He turned and looked at her then.

"You could take flying lessons."

"How much do lessons cost?"

"Enough hours to get licensed?" She added it up in her head. "I'd say maybe five hundred dollars."

He whistled and shook his head. "That's a *lot* of money. Guess I'd have to strike oil in the garage to be able to learn to fly."

"Maybe you could work out a trade. Exchange engine work for flying lessons."

"Don't know much about airplane engines. I could learn, but it would take me a while."

"I meant car engines. You could trade auto repair and maintenance for flying lessons."

He seemed to think about that.

"Wouldn't hurt to go to the nearest field and give it a try. All they can do is say no." She set the bottle down on the platform and watched the sun burn the clouds away. There was a deep red-and-blue sunset starting west of them. "When I finish this job, I'm going to get my instructor's license."

"So you can teach other women to fly or so you can earn a fortune and retire rich?"

She glared at him. "So I can teach *anyone* to fly, even pigheaded young Texans."

"You are all too easy to get a rise out of."

"The truth is," she said, "if you want to get rich, flying isn't the way to do it. Especially if you're a woman."

"Is that why you use a man's name?"

"No. It's been my nickname for as long as I can remember. My real name is Charlotte. Pop called me Charley because he said it fit me better. My mother's mother was a Charlotte and I was named after her. Charlotte Evangeline Morrison. Pop said it was the stuffy name of a bunch of European queens and not so great for his daughter. So he called me Charley. It stuck. I don't know if I would even answer to 'Charlotte' anymore." She faced him. "My name did get me entered in my first air race. When I filled out the forms, they thought I was a man."

"What happened when they found out you weren't?"

"They took the prize money and the trophy away."

"You won?"

"You don't need to sound so surprised."

"I wasn't surprised."

"You were, too. I'll have you know I'm very good at what I do."

"Unless you're headed for my gas pumps."

She punched him in the arm.

"Ouch!" He grabbed her hand and held it up. "Look at those bony knuckles. You ought to be a prizefighter."

"Very funny."

They had quietly settled into an easy camaraderie. Two hours ago she was ready to clobber him. Now she supposed she would have to admit she liked him.

His smile faded, and he was looking at her with an odd expression; then he was quiet. He turned away, pensive, looking like he had nothing to say.

So they sat there quietly, and it was odd, because Charley didn't feel as if she needed to say something to fill the void. The moment wasn't awkward, so it didn't need filling with nervous words.

She turned toward him.

He was staring at the soda bottle and the almost full package of peanuts in her lap. "So, Charley Morrison, you can win an air race against a bunch of men, but you won't put more than a few measly peanuts in a soda bottle."

"You don't give up, do you?"

"Nope."

She dumped the rest of the package into the bottle and then drank a few sips, chewing on the peanuts. It wasn't bad, but she wouldn't admit that to him. A girl had to have some secrets.

"Where'd you learn to fly?"

"Pop taught me. He was a barnstormer and bought his first plane when I was four. By then there was only the two of us. Mom had died, so we spent a lot of years flying all over the place. I grew up in a plane. We'd fly over a town, and he'd pump the throttle to make a lot of noise, then circle round and round and land in a field somewhere just outside the town boundaries."

"What about school?"

"I went to school in different places. He'd make deals for me to study in the county we were in at the time. He traded rides for favors."

"Tell me what it feels like up there in that plane. Tell me what it was like the first time."

She thought about it for a minute, shifted on the hard boards, and stretched her legs out. "Well, you feel light, as if you weigh no more than a feather. That was the first thing I can remember. In those days, all the cockpits were open, so the wind would blow in your face and through your hair. The air tastes different up there, cleaner, cooler. It's like drinking a big cool glass of water."

"How long have you been flying?"

She gave him her usual evasive answer. "I got my license when I was sixteen."

He turned to her and said, "That wasn't what I asked."

"Okay," she said with a laugh. "You caught me. The truth is, Pop taught me to fly as soon as I could reach the rudder pedals and see over the rim of the cockpit."

"He waited that long, huh?"

"Well, I guess there were a couple pillows under my bottom. Legally, however, I couldn't get my license until I was sixteen." She faced him then and leaned back against the tower wall, crossed her arms, and asked sweetly, "When did you drive your first automobile?"

"When I was ten. No pillows, though."

"I soloed when I was eleven. I was as tall as a sixteen-year-old then. Pop trusted me, said if I hadn't learned it all by now, I never would. So up I went."

"Is he still flying?"

She nodded. "He has a ranch outside of Santa Fe with a landing strip and a hangar. That's where I learned about engines and pistons."

"He works on planes?"

"Yes." She laughed a little. She didn't want to embarrass him and tell him that her father wasn't just a pilot who understood the mechanics of airplanes. He was Lilienthal Aircraft, a company whose modified planes won most of the air races in existence.

"What's so funny."

"Nothing really. Pop's a great pilot and he taught me so much. I had to learn all about planes, how they run, the concept behind flight and the mechanics. He wouldn't settle for me to learn only how to take off and fly. He made me into a good pilot. Taught me a skill level that is pretty high."

"In what way?"

"Well, as an example; he wouldn't let me just land anywhere. I had to land precisely in the center of the landing strip. He would make me do it again and again. Up and touch down in the center. Up and touch down. Perfect landings. Until he bragged that I could land on top of the hangar if I had to."

"Is that true?"

"He was exaggerating. But he never treated me any differently because I was a girl. Pop taught me to reach for my dreams, by example, because he reached for his and didn't let anything stop him. I never thought I couldn't fly just because I was a woman. I've never felt as if there was a job I couldn't do if I set my mind to it. I suppose that's why I'm doing what I'm doing today. Because of him."

"What exactly is it that you're getting paid to do?"

"Airmarking. I work for the government. We fly over certain parts of the country, looking for roofs and buildings to place marks you can see from the air as directional points for pilots. We're mapping the country from the air."

"You know, I never thought about that, about how a pilot would be able to tell where he was going."

"Maps don't work if there are no navigational points of reference you can see."

He nodded. "Makes sense. Flying with no points of reference must be like driving and hitting a fork in the road during a sandstorm."

She agreed. "Planes have opened up a whole new world. It's pretty amazing when you think about it."

He looked at her for the longest time. "Yeah, I guess it is a different world. One day out of the clear blue a plane just up and lands on the road, almost takes out the station pumps—"

"I did *not* almost hit the gas pumps."

He grinned. "You came awfully close. But then, that didn't surprise me half as much as when you pulled off that helmet."

"You need to broaden your horizons, Red Walker. Women are as capable as men are and perhaps more capable in some things."

"Yeah, I can't cook worth a darn."

She gave him a narrow-eyed look and crossed her arms over her chest, the half-full Dr. Pepper bottle still in her hand.

He nodded at the soda bottle. "If you're not going to finish those peanuts, then give them to me and I'll empty them over the side."

She looked at the bottle, then raised it to her lips and drank down the flat, salty Dr. Pepper and soggy peanuts.

"THE WAY YOU LOOK TONIGHT"

That evening they ate thick, melted cheese sandwiches and Campbell's alphabet vegetable soup on blue-and-white speckled enamelware. As the moon crawled up the night sky and a thousand stars began to glitter, they were sitting peacefully at the time-scarred kitchen table with a Ford distributor between their dishes, while the Bakelite radio in the corner was tuned to CBS and playing the last of The Johnson's Wax Program:

"We're not going anyplace, Fibber McGee, if I can't get this suitcase open pretty quick."

"Bang it on the floor, Molly. That's the way they come open for the bellboys."

Red leaned back in the hard ladder-back chair and rested an ankle on one knee while he sipped his coffee and watched Charley laugh. She had a great laugh. Not loud or giggly, but free and easy. Like their conversations.

She reminded him of Irene Dunne. The two shared that same pecan-colored hair, nice skin, and wide smile, but it was something more. They had something about them that made you like them.

He looked at her sitting across from him, her face turned to the radio as if she could hear it better if she looked at it. He wondered why people did that, huddled around the radio like it was a stage.

Another sip of coffee and he stared at her over the rim of his coffee mug. She was a good six foot one or two if she was an inch. He liked that she could look him in the eye. He liked that he didn't have to hunch down to talk to her like he did with the little old ladies who brought him their cars or the few town girls who were small as birds and just as flighty.

For Red, looking at Charley Morrison was sort of like seeing a sleek modern skyscraper standing smack dab in the middle of his flat ordinary world. He didn't think he could ever get tired of looking at a woman like her. To top it all off, she was living his dream.

He put the coffee mug down and got up to clear the table. His chair scraped the floor.

She turned back around, saw him reaching for her plate, and stood quickly and grabbed the plate, too. "I can do that."

"No. You sit there. Listen to the show."

"It's over. See?" She waved her free hand in the direction of the radio. "They're playing the finale."

They were both standing there, holding the same plate.

He didn't let go.

She didn't let go.

He looked from it, to her. "This going to be another argument, isn't it?"

"Probably." She laughed.

At that moment he almost gave in and let go of the plate. Almost.

"Let me help you, Red. It's the least I can do to repay you for giving me a place to stay tonight."

"Nettie's old room is empty. It wouldn't be very hospitable of me to make you sleep in the garage." He pulled the plate from her hand. "Come on. We'll do them together."

By the time they finished the dishes and walked away from the sink, the radio was playing the soft, silky tones of the Tommy Dorsey Orchestra.

"I love this song." She stopped and stood there, swaying a little to the music.

He paused and listened.

"'I'm Getting Sentimental Over You,'" she said dreamily, eyes closed.

"Must be my Texas charm."

She stopped and looked at him, then burst out laughing. "That's the song title, and you know it." She looked past him, over his right shoulder. "What's that over there?"

He turned as she moved toward the piano behind an old, faded screen with bamboo painted on it.

He felt his smile melt away.

She faced him. "Do you play?"

"No."

The radio announcer marked off the time, and there was a commercial for Ovaltine.

He was quiet. It was one of those awkward silences where you thought you should say something but, for the life of you, you couldn't think of a thing to say that wouldn't sound as if you were reaching for something to say.

She sighed and bent down to pick up a green canvas flight bag she'd brought in earlier from the plane. Straightening, she said, "I should turn in now, and let you get some sleep. Me, too, I guess. I'll need to get an early start tomorrow."

"Follow me, then." He moved toward the small narrow hallway. "You know where the bathroom is." He went past it to the two doors at the other end. He opened the one on the right and flipped a switch.

There were two small beds in the room, both built into the wooden walls. Each bed had a thin, blue-and-gray ticking mattress on it and a feather pillow. Years before, he and Nettie both had slept in here. Once his daddy had passed on, Red moved into the other room with the double bed. Nettie refused to sleep in a bed that her mother had slept in . . . ever.

It hadn't been easy for Red, caught in between Nettie's anger at their mother and his father's crushing, defeated sense of hurt. When one person feels so strongly one way, and another the opposite, it's difficult to be in the middle. You're afraid to feel anything because you might be like them; you might take it too far. So you don't let yourself feel at all.

He stepped into the room and she followed him inside. "It's not much——"

"It's fine. Really."

He looked levelly into her eyes and warned, "It's a short bed."

"Don't you find at our height everything is too short? Especially beds?"

"Yep, that's true."

"It doesn't matter," she said casually, standing so close to him he could smell her hair. It smelled like lemon. "I sleep all curled up anyway."

He took a step backward, into the doorway, where there was only the old wooden doorjamb next to him. No tall, sassy woman who smelled too good to be true. "The bed's not made up, but there are sheets and blankets in the dresser."

She sat down on the edge of the bunk. "Great. Thanks again." She was sitting on his old bed.

"Sure." He turned, feeling bigger than the door he walked through. He went straight into the kitchen, drank three glasses of tap water, then leaned against the counter and wiped his mouth with a sleeve, while the water sloshed around uncomfortably in his belly. A few deep breaths and he set the glass down, then switched off the light.

The soft and wavy moan of a muted trumpet playing the blues came from the radio. Cab Calloway began to sing.

Red turned off the radio with a sharp flick. He managed to get about four steps into the dark, narrow hallway before he stopped.

She was humming the song.

The door to his old room was half open, and the light cast her silhouette on the door. Her shadow moved provocatively while the sound of her humming drifted all around him.

He couldn't move, not for a few moments. Instead, like some kind of Peeping Tom, he watched the shadow get undressed. She moved out of the light.

He rushed past. But at his door, he took one last look over his shoulder.

The silhouette was gone. She stopped humming. A second later she turned out the light, leaving nothing but silence and a hollow feeling that he knew too well.

He closed the bedroom door behind him, stripped, and got into bed. The sheets were scratchy and stiff from drying on the line out back. He lay there in the dark, staring at the door.

Tomorrow she would be gone, flying off to do her job.

Tomorrow he had to fix the Baptist minister's oil leak and take new tires out to the Streit farm.

Everything would be the same old, same old. He would eat alone and listen to the radio alone, and life would be normal and dull and familiar. He closed his eyes for a second, but all he could see was the silhouette of a tall woman, humming the blues. He jerked the sheets up to his neck and felt his feet slip out the end of the bed. He lay there on his side staring at the door again.

I sleep all curled up anyway.

He was nuts. Too many bags of peanuts. He turned away angrily, his bony bare feet sticking out of the bed. But he didn't give a hoot. He punched his pillow a few times.

He'd been living alone for too damn long.

"SHOO FLY PIE
AND APPLE PAN DOWDY"

The next morning Charley paused in the doorway of the living room, where Red was sitting at the table, absorbed in reading a newspaper. In front of him was a pastry in a pie tin and a pot of coffee. They both smelled wonderful.

"Good morning," she said.

The newspaper crackled when he dropped it on the table. He stood up quickly. "Morning." His voice was gruff and deep and had that soft touch of a Texas twang. He looked lanky tall. He wasn't wearing old coveralls, but a pair of brown pants, a tooled leather belt with a silver buckle, and a cotton shirt with small blue and brown checks on it and pearl buttons on the pockets. There were creases ironed sharply into the sleeves, and the collar points were pressed and starched. His hair was combed back, slick and gleaming, and as she came closer, she could smell the scent of Vitalis.

She helped herself to the coffee and waved at him. "Sit." She thought it was sweet, the way he'd dressed up for her.

He bent his long frame back into the chair, resting an ankle easily on his knee. "I was thinking about you just before you walked in."

She sat down across from him and rested her elbows

on the table, cupping the mug in her palms. "So, why was I on your mind . . . or shouldn't I ask?"

"There's an article about a pilot here in the paper."

She looked at it. It was open to the comics. "Moon Mullins or Joe Palooka?"

He folded the page back. "No. Here on the front page. Some guy flew his plane to Ireland."

She frowned. "Why is flying a plane to Ireland enough to put the article on the front page? Did he crash?"

"I guess he landed there by mistake."

"Where was he going?"

"California."

"You're kidding?"

"Nope. Look." He handed her the paper.

She scanned the article and laughed a little under her breath, half embarrassed for the guy. "The poor man. They're calling him Wrong-way Corrigan."

"Yeah."

She handed him back the paper. "You wouldn't be implying that he and I have anything in common, would you?"

He shook his head. "Not me. No sir-ee. Might end up with that chip of yours embedded in my head. Then everyone would say, you know, that Red Walker was a handsome devil until the day Charley Morrison hammered that ugly chip into his head so he looks like Boris Karloff, and it all started when that gal almost landed her plane right into his Texaco gas pumps . . ."

"I give!" She laughed, holding up both hands. "I admit it. I almost hit your gas pumps."

He just grinned at her.

She looked down at the pastry. "I thought you said you weren't very good in the kitchen."

"I'm not. I change the oil and tune up Cora Miller's DeSoto and she brings me the best baked goods in the county. Fresh bread, cakes, and pies."

She took a bite. "This is wonderful." While she was eating the pie, he reached out and poured more coffee in her cup. He sat there watching her in a way she wished he wouldn't.

She drank some more coffee, then shifted a little sideways in her chair, and picked up the paper. She tried to read it.

The silence grew more and more awkward, nothing but the sound of the newspaper when one of them turned a page. She quickly downed the rest of her coffee and stood. "Thanks for the great breakfast." She checked her watch. "I have to get going. It's late."

He stood up. His expression said he didn't want her to go.

She turned and left the room in a hurry. She didn't want to see the look on his face.

"ALONE AT A TABLE FOR TWO"

Red was leaning against one of the gas pumps when the plane buzzed low over the filling station for the second time, then rocked its wings at him and flew east, off toward Wichita Falls.

He had the sudden urge to run after it. To go out into

that field behind the station and just run and run with his arms out to his sides, and maybe some miracle would happen and he would take wing and fly far, far away, away from the ordinary.

It was hot, almost a hundred degrees according to the Oilzum thermometer in the garage. He changed out of his good clothes, back into a clean set of overalls, and as he walked back outside, he stuffed that old red rag into his back pocket.

It was almost ten. Already heat rose from the blacktop in waves, the kind that could boil the breath clean out of your mouth. He stood on that blacktop and could look around him in all four directions. There was nothing but flat Texas horizon for more miles than the human eye could see.

He shoved his hands in his deep pockets and went into the garage and began to drain the oil in Reverend Bailey's pride, a Tudor DeLuxe five-window coupe with mohair interior and dual sun visors.

That evening he went to his sister's for supper and told her and Louie Lee about the plane landing there and about Charley Morrison.

Nettie listened all through dinner; then she looked at him for a long time over dessert, last summer's canned peaches and vanilla ice cream that he and Louie Lee had cranked out of the wooden ice cream maker.

She shook her head and said, "You're just like Mama."

"Why do you say that?"

"You want out of here so badly, Red. You always have. When the cars and the trucks stopped at the station, you always went on all night about where they were coming from and where they were going. You used to look up in the sky whenever one of those barnstormers flew over, and anyone with half a brain could see that you wanted to fly away. That's why Daddy took us to see that plane. He knew you were like Mama."

He stared at the ice cream melting in the bowl. "I'm like Daddy. I like working on cars."

"Do you?"

"Yep," he answered stubbornly, but he couldn't look her in the eye.

It was still hot at nine o'clock when he went home. The breakfast dishes were sitting on the table, crumbs scattered around them, and a couple of flies were on the last of the shoofly pie. He cleared the dishes, two mugs, two plates, two forks, washed them and put them away in the drawer and open shelf above the counter, where there were six plates and six mugs and six bowls. In the drawer there was plenty of gasoline giveaway silverware with mother-of-pearl handles. If you opened a kitchen drawer or looked at that shelf of dishes, you would think that a whole houseful of people lived there. A big boisterous family where they all talked at once and they didn't need the radio on for company.

He looked at those stacks of dishes and began to move things, an earthenware bowl with blue stripes went on the open shelf next to the plates; then he exchanged pans for dishes, dish towels for silverware, mugs for jelly-jar glasses, rearranging everything in that small room, but in the end, not changing a thing.

LONDON

1940

"HURRAY HOME"

H e was going home.

Pilot Officer George Agar Inskip was one of the Brylcreem boys, those glorious, adventuresome flyers of the British Royal Air Force whose images stared back at you from hair oil ads postered all over London. Since May, however, when the Allies suffered a humiliating defeat, that golden-boy shine had quickly tarnished.

There had been long weeks of what-ifs and whys, of army scorn and rampant public criticism of the RAF and their actions in the Battle of France. Those same weeks had been equally long for the pilot officers and crews with No. 77 Fighter Squadron at Wellingham, Essex, a fighter station less than forty miles from London proper, where low morale, a grounding sense of failure, and the no-leave restrictions had made the men tense and edgy.

It had been sheer hell for Skip, who was married scarcely six months and had not even had the opportunity to be one of the pilots involved. Instead of confronting the Luftwaffe over France or evacuating Allied soldiers from Dunkirk, Skip had been relegated to testing aerocraft at Biddington Airfield until a chap named Cunningham finally came in and replaced him.

He sat solemnly in the back of a black cab as it wound its way through a silver maze of London streets thoroughly soaked by the foul weather. Since he'd last been in town, sandbags had been stacked to cover the wide windows of street shops and quaint restaurants. Through rain-beaded cab windows he could make out the hard shells of concrete pillboxes scattered along the Thames. They sat there like giant grey tortoises at the entrances to the bridges and along the low river walls.

The kerbs, trees, and lampposts were painted white at their bases so one could see them on blacked-out nights, when even the light from a match was forbidden on the city's streets. Civilians in damp raincoats walked down the roads with canvas gas-mask satchels slung casually over their shoulders and helmets dangling from their arms as if they were merely holiday purchases.

People sidestepped the corrugated steel roofs of Anderson shelters that stuck out from the ground at the corners of parks and greens where colorful flower beds had once grown. Home Guardsmen, with their bayoneted rifles, sped through the streets on roller skates, so if a German paratrooper ever landed nearby, they could be there waiting for him before his Nazi boots ever touched British soil.

This was Britain in the high summer of 1940.

It had been some time since that Sunday morning last September when at a quarter after eleven Prime Minister Neville Chamberlain's quiet and disheartened voice came over the wireless to tell the nation that Britain was at war.

But to everyone's surprise the months following had been anticlimactic. So little had happened that people began to call it the phony war. There had been no invasion as prophesied by the overeager news-press, no gassing or bombing as was direly forewarned in print and on the wireless every single day before Germany invaded Poland.

After the PM's broadcast, the nation had rushed to paint bus and train windows dark blue, to mask headlamps on taxis and cars, and to swiftly gather up and hide road markers and signposts to confuse any invaders. The people of Britain hung blackout material over their windows, and that same night they huddled deep in their homes, ears sharp and sweat beading on their foreheads, as they waited for the drone of German war planes, for the whistling scream of Nazi bombs, for the hammering sound of distant gun battles echoing from the sea.

But the Luftwaffe never came.

Instead there had been nothing but a few distant skirmishes over the Channel, some frequent buzzing by German planes along the south coast, and an Axis blockade in the Channel that forced more rationing. An easy belief began to spread throughout the country that war was really much further away than anyone ever thought.

Then came the Battle of France and with it a horrid loss of life, of pride, and loss of the belief that their Royal Air Force could protect the soldiers of Britain.

It was an ugly time.

Skip, like so many others, needed to go home. The men needed to remember what they were fighting for, to be with their families and to believe in themselves again.

At least one squadron had been kept in permanent readiness twenty-four hours a day, and officers were confined to camp for long stretches of dead time. However, now the RAF was relaxing its restrictions for the sake of its men's abominably low morale. Leave was once again available.

He sat in the backseat of a taxi with little pretense of patience. The cabbie, a chap with his cap on sideways and an empty pipe between his teeth, had said little to him except to point out that "the RAF had made a bloody hash of it at Dunkirk." The taxi made the final turn onto a quiet square near Hyde Park and stopped in front of a familiar Georgian townhouse with tall white columns at the front door—which was painted a glossy black and bore the number twenty-seven in brightly polished brass.

Skip paid the cabbie too much and stuffed a roll of pound notes back into his pocket, then turned, his head down to the bucketting rain, and made for a low, wrought-iron gate and the front steps. A few moments later he stood on a bloodred Aubusson carpet in the warm, dry foyer of the London townhouse he'd known for most of his twenty-four years.

He carelessly shook off the rainwater like a hunting spaniel and tossed his leather gloves and peaked cap on the hall table, a gilt-gesso George II monstrosity with snarling golden dragon heads for feet and an intricate mother-of-pearl inlaid top. The table had been a gift from some royal personage to the first earl of Chittendon. Skip hated the thing. Always had. It had been in his family for enough years to give beastly nightmares to seven generations' worth of Inskip offspring.

But his wife adored it. And he was so bloody in love with her that denying her anything was out of the question. He decided long ago that he would teach his future children to have loud fits of temper whenever they looked at the ghastly thing. Perhaps the little mites' tears would send the bloody table to the darkest corner of the fifth floor attic once and for all.

He looked around him for a moment, soaking up what was familiar but didn't quite feel familiar, until the warmth and smell of home began to permeate his memory. While he took great pride in his position with the British Royal Air Force, while he loved flying and planes, at that particular moment, Skip thought it was a damn fine thing to be home.

For the next few days his mind and body would not belong to his country. He would not have to think about the advantages of Hurricanes and Spitfires, of learning to identify enemy aircraft, of flight schedules or meteorology or why they had lost in France. He would not think about Goering's Luftwaffe or Nazi Germany or the fact that his country was ashamed of the RAF. He wanted, and perhaps needed, nothing more than to concentrate his efforts on his wife and on making that newest generation of Inskip children.

He draped his heavy, government-issue greatcoat on a nearby coat-stand and glanced in the giltwood mirror above the grim table. His dress blues fit him well and were clean and neat. Some officers had been hit with mud and dirt clods by rowdy soldiers and angry citizens who had spotted the pilots at the train station near the airfield.

He ran a quick hand through his black hair, raised his chin to straighten the knot in his dark tie, then tugged down twice on his uniform jacket before he turned and took the marble stairs two at a time.

"Greer?"

"Skip? You're home? I'm up here, darling!"

She met him at the top of the stairs, running towards him in the vibrant way she had. She was laughing a joyous and wonderful laugh—all because he'd come home.

Suddenly nothing else in this wild and war-torn world mattered.

Her long, slim arms wrapped around his neck, her hands drove through his hair, and her lips were on his. She smelled like Greer, like Ma Griffe and the lemon water and vinegar she used to rinse her hair, scents that reminded him of everything that was vital in the world.

She pulled her lips from his, looked at his face as if she were trying to memorize it, then drew her fingers over his mouth, rubbing slightly. "Red lipstick," she explained.

"Tastes good."

"It's called Cherry Bomb."

"You taste good."

Her smile was familiar, and still could make him lose his thoughts. Then she gave him a long erotic kiss that rocked his gravity and hit him as if he were greying out at four G's. "Welcome home, my darling husband."

"God . . . but I missed you." He brushed his hands along her wavy blonde hair. Her body against his was finer than in his dreams, softer than his memory. Just the pressure of her breasts made him so hard he felt like he could fuck for a week. He slipped his tongue into her mouth, then slid his hands slowly down her back, along her spine, and gripped her bottom.

Her body was slim and tight from years of riding, from jumping, hunting, and dressage, at which she was more than accomplished; she was a master in haute école.

And he was glad of it, especially late at night when she was on top of him, when his cock was so hard it ached like it was bruised, until that single, final moment when he was finally buried deep inside of her, where she was hot and wet and only his. He loved her naked, her pale skin glistening with sweat from a night of long, slow, drawn-out fucking, the kind where you both were so together you made it last without a single word, without a challenge. Those were the times when her tight thighs—those of a superb equestrian—flexed and gripped his hips hard as she rode him. And it was then when he thanked God, King, and Country that he'd married such a fine horsewoman, particularly one who knew not to rush her fences.

"I'M STEPPING OUT WITH A MEMORY TONIGHT"

The next afternoon Skip stared down at his notes on the desk and tried to think of anything else he needed to include in his report.

> *The Defiant tested out pleasantly enough, handled well and without any vices. Its Merlin engine with increased boost pressure from 6 to 12 psi for short periods is as fine as it is in the Hurricane or the Spitfire.*

The possibility of a two-seater, pilot and gunner, is admirable, but therein also lies the basic flaw of this aeroplane. While an original concept, the massive four-gun turret set in the fuselage behind the cockpit creates a distinct division between the pilot maneuvering the aircraft and the gunner trying to line a sight. The pilot must anticipate the gunner's needs—an impossibility. With no fixed forward-firing armament, the craft has a blind spot and is vulnerable to an enemy attacking beneath the tail . . . .

He replaced his pen into the silver inkwell, and put his report in an envelope for the post. One thing was certain, the Defiant was no Spitfire. He'd flown his first Spit about eight months before the war began, when his squadron had received the new planes.

The Spitfire was a monoplane, designed with a new concept: cantilever construction. In a biplane you could look out and see the lines that held the wings together. The monoplane's construction was hidden and didn't seem at all plausible. The first time he took her up, he kept looking at the wings, expecting them to fly off at any moment, especially when he took her speed to full force.

But he and the other pilots found that the Spitfire was just what her name implied, an aeroplane that soared as elegantly as an eagle and handled as if you were flying a dream. She could reach an unprecedented four hundred miles per hour in level flight, easily carried a total of eight Browning machine guns, and was so maneuverable that she could outdive and outclimb any other British aerocraft. She was sleek. She handled beautifully. And she looked fast.

There was an old saying that if an automobile looked good, then it was good. The same proved true for planes, and no plane looked better than a Spitfire.

The doors to the third floor library suddenly swung open with a clatter.

Skip looked up.

Greer stood there beaming at him.

Yes, if something looked that good, it was that good.

She was wearing some kind of filmy, flowered frock that clung to her figure and floated near her bare calves. She had told him once that the thing she missed most since the war began was her silk stockings.

But he loved her legs without those stockings. He would walk into their dressing room and see her in her lace slip, bent over a stool as she creamed her bare legs with almond oil that made the narrow room smell of Christmas marzipan. He loved that he could sweep his hand over her bare leg and feel her, not some sheer fabric.

"Look here!"

He pulled his gaze away from her long, sleek legs and looked up at her.

Her face was flushed, as if she had run all the way home, and she proudly held up two fresh brown eggs, something so precious and scarce that the egg produce of British chickens could have rivaled that from the House of Fabergé.

"No powdered eggs for us tomorrow morning." She danced in a small, silly circle like one of those American comediennes at the cinema, only she held an egg in each pale hand.

He stood quickly and stepped around the desk while her back was to him, her hips moving seductively to the catchy Latin band music playing from the wireless in the corner. She finished dancing in a circle and he was waiting for her, swept her into his arms, then danced her about the carpet in a smooth rumba.

"Watch the eggs!" She frowned and stepped out of his arms.

"Married scarcely half a year and my wife is already pulling away and scowling at me. The next thing you know we'll be sleeping in twin beds, then separate rooms, next on separate floors, and within a few years, separate houses. You will be in Devonshire and I shall be holed up in a garret in London, my pain spilling from a brush onto an oil canvas and me a bitter soul who can do nothing but mourn what might have been."

"You bitter? Mourning? And an artist?" She laughed. "Never, darling. Besides which, as I recall, you do not paint, not even the dressing room walls, which you were supposed to do before we married."

She never let him get away with anything. She had known him since he was a gawky lad from a neighboring estate, one who used to climb elm trees to sneak a peek into the maids' bathing room, and who taught her to throw chestnuts at the hares in the woods whenever they happened to move too near an iron trap. The two of them together had saved hundreds of hares that summer when she was eight and he was ten.

"If you knew what I had to go through to get these eggs. The queues took hours this morning, and you know how much I dislike waiting in lines."

"You have no patience. Your family spoiled you terribly."

"I'm not spoilt. I only find queues a waste of time,

especially when I could be with you. I must tolerate them for the war effort."

"You must tolerate them because you have no choice in the matter."

"That too." She grinned. "But listen. Fortune was with me this morning. I saw Aunt Jane's cousin and I was able to barter for these two lovely and wonderful eggs."

"If fortune is with me, you will have bartered away that dragon of a table that haunts the foyer."

"I love that table." Her voice turned indignant and she gave him a mock glare. "It's priceless."

"It's a nightmare."

With a sidelong look she stepped closer, lowering her voice the way she did whenever she truly wanted to have her own way. "I wonder how you would feel about that same table, darling, if we were to make love on it?"

He slid one hand down over her bottom and pressed her hips against him. "I wouldn't take the chance, love. If you conceived, the child might be born with a long forked tail, gilt teeth, and breathing fire from its mouth."

She pulled back and searched his face for a moment. "What's wrong?"

"Nothing." She smiled softly. "Perhaps I might be the one who breathes fire."

He moved his hands up to her breasts.

She swatted them away. "Now stop trying to seduce me and listen."

He wanted to ask who was seducing whom, but instead he stepped back, hitched a hip on the desk, and crossed his arms. He could wait and hear her out.

"Along with Loretta, was—"

"Who's Loretta?"

"Aunt Jane's cousin. Oh, I suppose she is removed a few times, but she was at our wedding. You remember her."

"Five hundred people were at our wedding."

"I know you would recognize her if you saw her. Now, as I was saying, her very own good friend, a Mrs. Woodleigh, whose husband, Edmund, is a farmer and who has had no cigars for all too long a time—"

"Mrs. Woodleigh smokes cigars?"

"No. Her husband, Edmund. Now stop that! Do you want to hear my tale or not?"

"I'm not certain."

"Now, Skip darling, you know how very much I dislike your cigars."

With a sick feeling he leaned back and lifted the humidor lid.

It was empty.

"I made a marvelous trade."

"You gave someone my last five imported cigars in exchange for two . . . eggs?"

"Rid yourself of that frown. I also left with three pounds of fresh butter, a side of pork, a huge hank of beef, green beans, lettuce, *and* tomatoes!"

"All that for the last few cigars of the war," he said wryly.

"Now, darling, you know very well that cigar smoke makes me ill. Those odorous things reek up the house. Anything that smells that horrid cannot possibly be good for you."

He stood, then pulled her close and began to slowly dance with her again. To hell with the cigars.

"Wait! The eggs!" She leaned over his arm and placed those precious eggs of hers in a blue Chinese bowl on the corner of an end table; then she turned easily back into his arms, slid hers about his neck and her fingers into the hair at his collar while their bodies moved slowly and easily to a Vera Lynn love ballad that crackled from the wireless.

She rested her head against his shoulder and hummed along for a moment, then she said casually, "You know, darling, if you truly wish to trounce my toes, we should go to the Savoy tonight, where you can cripple me to a live band. It's so much more elegant that way."

"You are a cheeky thing. First you give away all my cigars, then you insult my dancing skills and now you want me to reward you and take you out on the town."

"Um-hummmm."

"Tonight?"

She leaned back in his arms, her expression suddenly serious. "Would you mind terribly? I know you only have five days this leave."

"I would hate it." He pulled her back against him and looked over her head. "What sane soldier, especially one who has been away from home for over a month, would want to spend the evening with his wife's body slithering against his?"

She laughed softly, then grabbed the knot on his tie and pulled his face down close to hers. "I slither well, flyboy."

"Yes. You do."

She kissed him then for a long, long time, before she broke away and looked up at him. "Then you will take me dancing?"

"I'd rather take you to bed," he whispered against her ear.

"Why, George Agar Inskip. You are becoming dull and predictable."

"Dull? Watch it, wife!" He grinned and reached out to give her a soft swat on the bum.

She scampered away towards the doorway while he was laughing at her.

"Wear the red frock tonight, my love."

She grasped the doorjamb in both hands, then swung out and away from it like Katharine Hepburn playing a ditzy American debutante. She cast him a seductive glance, grasped the fabric of her skirt, and slowly raised it halfway up her thigh. "The red gown with the slit up the leg?"

"Yes." He smiled when she stuck her long leg out like some pinup girl. "*That* red gown."

"Sure thing, flyboy." She winked and disappeared around the corner.

'STOMPIN' AT THE SAVOY'

They were in the ballroom at the Savoy, dancing slowly to the last song when the music suddenly stopped. The bandleader stepped up to his microphone. "We have just received word that all leaves have been cancelled immediately. Every member of the military is to report to their bases by midnight."

In less than five minutes the darkened hotel entrance was crowded with couples vying for lampless cabs and cars that had to make their way awkwardly in the dark to the narrow entrance. Skip and Greer stood under the awning, while five taxis ignored his signal.

"Must be the uniform," he muttered, then decided he'd had his fill and stepped out into the middle of the street.

"Skip!"

He turned to Greer and held up a hand. "Stay there."

He walked between the cars towards an empty cab two cars back. The driver looked at him, then hammered his horn as he wrenched the wheel right and the cab darted into a suddenly empty lane. The cabbie floored the gas pedal and whipped past Skip, who slammed a hard fist on the bonnet of the cab as it sped past him. "Damn bloody fool!"

Frustrated, he looked down. His uniform cap had fallen into the street. He stared at it a moment, then picked it up and walked over to the kerb. He stared down at the cap in his hands; it was spotted and muddy, like the RAF's reputation. He felt such mixed emotions: anger, shame, confusion.

Greer took the cap from him and cleaned it on her coat, then stood on her toes and placed it on his head. "There." She threaded her arm through his. "Let's walk home, darling."

"It's raining. You'll be soaked."

"I don't care."

He looked up. A cabdriver on the opposite corner pointed and waved him over.

Skip looked behind him, thinking the cabbie was waving at someone else. He turned back. The cabbie was still pointing at him.

"Come, love! Quickly!" He grabbed Greer's hand and pulled her with him out into the traffic-jammed street, then led their way through three lanes of cars. He quickly opened the taxi door, half expecting it to be a prank.

"You and the missus going to number twenty-seven again?" It was the driver he'd overpaid the day before.

"Yes. There first." He turned to Greer. "Get in, love."

Skip crawled inside after her and closed the door.

The cabbie was half-turned in the seat. He looked from him to his wife and back at him again. "From the sound of those sirens, I'd say we're going to need you boys again."

"He's the best pilot in the force," Greer said with pointed pride and a distinctive, stubborn tone Skip knew all too well.

"My wife's somewhat biased."

"Don't listen to him. He is the best."

The cabbie didn't comment, but turned, shifted into gear, and they moved down the street.

Greer leaned closer. "You are the best at everything you do, and I love you for it."

He held her hand as they drove along the dark streets at a restricted speed of just under twenty miles per hour. He didn't feel like the best at anything right then, even though his blood was pumping faster at the promise of air combat and his palms itched to hold the stick of his Spit.

The trouble was, at the same time he felt strangely ill, like he had the first time he'd ever flown aerobatics, that memorable moment when he was upside-down, scared shitless, and so bloody damned excited that he couldn't wait to do it again. He was ready for war, God knew he was ready, but there was this sense of the unknown battling inside of him, along with the risk and wanting so badly to show the Germans that the British could be a fierce adversary.

This was the RAF's chance to show the world they were the best, now that war was on their own shores. The buggers had taken Guernsey and blocked the Channel. Poland and France were gone. It was enough.

Greer rested a hand on his arm.

He smiled down at her. Sitting there next to him was his reason—multiple reasons—for risking his life. At dinner she had told him they were "expecting a child." It had happened in early May on his last leave.

In the darkness in the back of the cab, he could only make out her silhouette, her features came only from his mind's eye. But he could see the white skin of her leg and thigh reflected against the darker fabric of her red gown. He loved her in red.

He lifted his gaze; her belly was as flat as always. While they were dancing he had held her against him, pressed his hand on the low part of her back. He'd thought he might feel the life inside of her.

But there was no change. A miracle they had made together was going on inside of his wife, yet he couldn't see it. He was on the outside looking in. He wanted to see his child growing in her. He needed to see the miracle on some elemental level that he couldn't explain. He just did.

"Skip?"

"What, love?"

"Shouldn't you go back to your field immediately? I can get home on my own, darling."

"There's time." He slipped his hand into hers.

She rested her head on his shoulder.

The cabbie made a tight turn and ran over a kerb.

She crushed the hell out of his hand. She was frightened and trying not to show it.

"Sorry!" the cabbie called back over a shoulder, then jerked the gearshift into reverse and backed the tyres down a few feet until they slammed back onto the road. "Can't see a buggering thing in the dark."

Skip put an arm around her and held her tightly. He didn't blame the man, driving through the dark streets, while the air-raid sirens were blaring and the devil coming from across the Channel was bent on only God knew what kind of terror.

He checked his watch and then wondered if he could make the next train. After a moment's thought he leaned forward. "I say there, I need to get to the airfield at Wellingham, and the trains are likely to be a tangle. Are you up to giving it a go?"

"Wouldn't let you get there any other way. You shoot down one of those ruddy Nazi buggers for me."

"Be happy to." Skip glanced down. Greer was trying to be brave, but she was worried. "I'll be fine, love. We've been training for this. They aren't going to get us. Not this time. We won't let them. I'll be home before you know it."

She smiled up at him and nodded, but her look was distant, so he said nothing because he couldn't change things.

Within a few minutes the cab came to a halt in front of No. 27. Skip slid out and opened the door for her, then helped her stand. He bent down, his head level with the window of the taxi. "I'll be only a minute."

He straightened then and took her cold hands into his. For the briefest of moments they stood on the pavement, facing each other in the long, rectangular shadows of the surrounding townhouses. The air was thick with the plaintive sounds of distant air-raid sirens and what was to come.

The rain had stopped. The taxi's engine was running; there was a slight ticking and pinging noise, and warm exhaust brushed against Skip's leather dress shoes and trousers; it made Greer's hemline flutter against his legs, and a couple of leaves brushed by.

Even in the darkness he could see her features, tense and strained, her skin taut and pale over the fine bones of that face he loved. The siren pealed over and over, sounding faraway and yet so near, unreal but real. It felt as if the war were on the other side of an invisible glass wall, another dimension away from the two of them.

He could taste her breath between them. She'd been sipping on a crème de menthe before they'd left the Savoy. It was a strange thought, mundane in a moment that was anything but.

Then he saw that she was crying. "Greer . . ."

Her hands tightly gripped the fabric of his coat. "I'm being a goose, I know." Her voice was wet.

"You need to go inside, love, and promise me you will go immediately down into the wine cellar until those sirens signal it's clear. Go into the room we set up. You'll be safe there."

"I will."

He was leaving her, but this time there was an urgency that had not been there since war was declared. She was carrying their child. He knew women felt differently then, had heard that pregnant women were more emotional. "Would you rather have me take you to the shelter on the corner? It will be crowded, but you won't be alone."

She shook her head, but she was looking down at his shirt, not at him. "No. I want to stay in our home. It will seem as if you aren't gone at all."

He slid his hands into her hair and tilted her face up so he could look at her. "You're certain?"

"I'll feel closer to you if I stay here. I might not wonder, then, if it's your plane I hear."

He didn't know what to say to her. She must have understood because she took a deep breath and raised her chin, then slid her hands down to his forearms to grip his hands in hers. "I will go directly inside, where I will put those eggs away and save them for when you come home. I promise to make you a cheddar-and-tomato omelet that will be so much better than any old cigar ever could be."

The kiss they shared was everything neither one of them could say. When they broke apart, the only words that came from his mouth were, "I love you."

"I know." She smiled weakly, then pushed him away. "You go. I'm fine. Truly." She swiped once at her eyes, looked up and ran her fingers over his mouth the way she always did. "Watch your tail, flyboy."

He kissed her fingertips. "Always."

She turned and ran up the steps, then disappeared inside the door.

"I'M SHOOTING HIGH"

One was on his tail. A Messerschmitt 109.

Skip hauled back on the stick so hard he felt it in his belly. The Spit, bless her, climbed fast, and he could feel the G-force pressing his spine against the seat. His blood sped through his body like strong gin, burning at first, then making him high. Through the cockpit canopy he saw nothing ahead of him or over him but the clear blue sky.

He turned hard to the right—God, but this sweet little fighter could turn—and headed for cloud cover.

He burst through white cotton.

Within seconds the sun cracked through the cover in a gold-and-yellow glow from overhead. He banked again, saw that the aileron angled down, nice and sweet and smooth, just like she should; then he was diving, down ... down ... diving deeply as the needle hit 400 mph, fast and at a perfect angle for attack with the sun above and behind him.

Below and flying ahead he could see a group of bombers, Junkers, 88As with full bomb loads. They were in formation but bouncing in the air from antiaircraft guns that bellowed black bursts of flack into the sky from navy ships below. These Luftwaffe bombers would drop their bombs on his country, on ships, factories, and airfields.

His jaw was tight, his hand gripping the stick so hard that it shook. He could see that same 109 below him, could see the black crosses on the wings, and watched the pilot's head turning this way and that, looking for him.

"Up here! In your blind spot and heading straight for your Nazi tail!"

He pressed his thumb down on the gun trigger. Tracers shot through the air between the two planes in streaks of smoking light. He could feel the bullets fire, could feel the static vibrations of rapid repeating shots.

The 109 pilot turned to escape.

Skip turned with him, even tighter, came in from starboard, and let loose another long burst of fire. The 109 began to waltz from side to side, trying to evade a fixed sight. Skip caught the same rhythm, still firing and coming at the other plane so fast he could see the rivets on the hull.

A second later the 109 pulled up.

He followed it, climbing right with him. *Don't stall, don't stall . . .* He was on the 109, firing, his thumb never leaving the button until he saw the tail stream with smoke.

"Got 'im!" Skip banked away, came back around, and saw the German pilot bail before the plane began to spiral in a smoky trail down towards the Channel, which was misty grey with smoke and haze from the battle in air and sea.

Clean and done. His first hit. He backed off the throttle and slowed her down. He was panting hard, as if he'd run for miles. He took a couple of long breaths and leaned to his port side. He spotted the German's parachute mushrooming beneath him; then he dove and flew past the lad, giving him a cocky wave as the German flyer floated down, where someone would pick him up from the Channel waters.

Skip sent the Spit up to full speed and headed for the rear bomber. He could see the Junkers ahead, but he needed to come in on them from behind and from high up to blind the German gunner in the rear cockpit.

He shot up, then turned, his belly rolling with the motion of the fighter. Two minutes, maybe three and he levelled out, then eased the throttle to reduce closing speed. Two miles ahead. Collision course.

Get a bead on them . . .

Not yet . . .

Not yet . . .

Tracers whipped past the cockpit.

Skip jerked his head around, then swore.

Two bandits were coming at him.

He made a hard turn, tighter than both of them, then dove, because he knew he couldn't outclimb them. He held on to the dive.

From the corner of his eye he saw another Spit go after one of the bandits.

Hemmings.

There was still one on his own tail; he turned again and slid under the other plane so closely, for an instant he thought he'd had it. He came back around from behind at the 109, but missed getting a sight when the German looped back the way Skip had and tried to get onto his tail again. The same maneuver.

They kept it up, one trying to outfly the other, turning, diving, climbing, and weaving.

This flyer is good.

Skip tried every trick, every turn. He came out of a cloud and saw the German bombers just ahead. He dove towards them, keeping with the dive until he got his bead, closer, closer . . . He fired.

Streams of ammo spit towards the bombers. He flew between them, right through their formation—an evasive maneuver so fine he was grinning. The JU gunners pivoted their machine guns around, but too late. All they could do was pelt his wings with bullets. The 109 pulled off his bum. The German had to or he'd shoot his own planes.

The Spit was faster in a dive. Skip pushed the stick downwards, then levelled and flew beneath them, out of gunner range. He took a few deep breaths. Sweat poured off his head and down his face. He turned and shot up through them in a fast climb, looped, and came back close, firing on the last bomber, closer and closer, never taking his thumb from the trigger, almost trancelike, until he was so close to the Junkers he could see the gunner's face staring at him through his sight as they both fired.

Skip was on him. He had him! He had him. . . .

Flames and smoke burst from the bomber. Skip pushed the stick forward. The Spit shot downward in a steep dive. Dust and muck flew up from the cockpit floor. His head cracked up into the canopy with a thud, and his stomach jumped into his throat under the force of negative G.

Then he levelled off again, slowly. His belly was still somewhere near his throat; his heart pounded against his chest.

Below him, the crew of the JU 88 was bailing out. Where was the bandit?

Skip looked about him.

Nothing.

The next thing he knew the 109 shot up from beneath his line of vision, levelled off. For just one brief instant the two pilots looked at each other. Then the German looped up and back and began to fire on him.

Skip turned.

The 109 turned.

Skip dove.

The German stayed with him.

He took a hit in the tail and swore, felt the control stick loosen.

Don't let him get me . . . . God, don't let him get me.

By sheer instinct he let off the throttle, an evasive maneuver that rapidly slowed the Spit down.

The Messerschmitt shot past him. Too late.

Skip fired.

Smoke burst from the tail of the 109, and the plane rocked. He could see the pilot trying to get the canopy open.

"Jump, man, jump!"

Skip realised then that the canopy wouldn't open. In a moment that hung there like a year, he saw the pilot— not as an inanimate object he only viewed through his sight—but a man just like himself. The pilot pressed his hands to the glass that trapped him.

When you've fired the shot that kills, there isn't a bloody damn thing you can do to change it.

He looked at Skip.

A second later flames engulfed the cockpit.

He watched in sick horror as the plane spun out of control; it smoked with fire, then twisted downwards, burning one last streak of grey life into the sky.

The plane crashed into the water and disappeared.

He sat frozen in the seat. Bile rose to his throat. He started to gag, then coughed and forced it back down.

He'd killed a man.

Until that very moment the whole battle had been like some sport—rugby at the Academy. They had talked a good game of war, of flying, of shooting, of showing the Germans who was better.

The truth was, in war, you killed people. He killed people.

In that minute of morality, he questioned what he was. Somehow shooting at the planes had been acceptable when the enemy had parachuted out.

But the best pilot of the lot hadn't bailed. He was dead.

Skip's squadron leader came on his wing, looked over, and gave him a thumbs-up, then signalled him back to base. He nodded but felt numb and concentrated on flying the plane. After a moment he glanced around, cold to the point of shivering, his hands and knees shaking as he looked left, then right, then overhead, watching for some enemy to dart out from behind him and shoot him down. Death was no longer just a five-letter word.

He felt an insanely panicked need to get back to the base. He was scared. He looked about him. There was nothing but his own squadron there in a loose formation behind their leader. He hadn't even realised that the Germans had turned back.

He returned to base, flying on nothing but instinct. He could see some of the others, perhaps a dozen with him, and watched them landing before him, one after another like black insects lighting on the grass field below. Then it was his turn, he made for the green grass. His wheels hit the ground. Dust and grass flew up as he slowed, then taxied in. He hit the brakes too hard and the nose dipped but tilted back when he let off.

The ground crews ran out of the hangars like swarming ants to meet the incoming No. 77 Squadron.

Goggles up. He tore at the seat buckle. He couldn't get out of that plane fast enough.

He threw back the canopy before a crewman could get to him, jumped onto the wing, and down to the ground, where he stumbled on rubber knees and hollow legs. He knelt there in the grass, seeing nothing but that flyer on fire—an image so real he could almost smell it.

Then he vomited his belly dry.

"I'M GONNA SIT RIGHT DOWN AND WRITE MYSELF A LETTER"

Wellingham Airfield, Essex
25 July, 1940

My dearest Greer,
It seems as if I have not seen you for years. I miss you every hour of every day. Has it been barely three weeks since I left? I do receive your letters. Although you write them every day, mostly I receive them in bundles. The Post is having as much trouble as we are getting information through with everything happening—the air raids, bombings, and the Channel battles.

As I told you when I rang you up the other day, Goering's Luftwaffe is certainly keeping us busy. We have as many as six sorties a day, remember those are missions not night parties as you thought when I first used the word. I am smiling, my love, at the memory of that. You delight me.

Things have been heating up here since the first week. No one can call this a phony war any longer. The war is real now.

I hope that what you say is true, and that you are well most of the time despite your morning illnesses. And yes, I like the name Phillip. Regarding my mother and her opinion on the baby's name, I don't care if Uncle Archie is earl and my mother's favorite cousin, put Archibald off the list.

As a note, in the future, do not listen to my mother, dear.

Your loving husband,

Skip

27 Berkeley Court, London
7 August, 1940

My dear Skip,
Your mother found your last letter sitting open on my desk. She is not pleased with you. Watch for a letter from her. It might have smoke trailing from it. She felt quite hard done by it. So, my love, on your behalf I pretended to faint. It was rather well done of me, I must say. I wobbled slightly, braced myself on the end table—the one with the charming French legs?—pulled out my lace handkerchief and lifted it to my mouth.

Since I do this every morning at the first sight of food, it is a gesture with which your dear mother is vastly familiar. With a suitably weak moan, I pressed the back of my hand to my brow and sank divinely into that lovely chintz-covered chaise in our bedroom. Your mother has not since brought up the name Archibald.

We are going to Knightsbridge this afternoon to work with the Red Cross. Last week we handed out sewing kits, cartons of cigarettes, hot tea, and fresh biscuits to the boys of the infantry who were off to man the batteries on the south coast. Some of them looked so young, as if they ought to still play with tin soldiers instead of being one. One boy named Johnny was a charmer. I could not imagine him firing a huge antiaircraft gun. I am twenty-two and yet I felt like his mother.

Perhaps that is because motherhood is so very much on my mind. I must end this all too soon. With every breath I take I miss you, my darling. Keep safe and come home to us.

Until I am in your arms,

Greer

P.S. I have put the eggs in the icebox to save them for your return. I ate the tomatoes. Did you know your mother snores?

Wellingham Airfield, Essex
10 August, 1940

Greer, my love,
These days somehow get away from me. No telephone calls allowed. We have been up three times today and had two rousing air battles. It is barely noon. I'm holding up on

strong tea and a bit of cherry cake brought us by the ladies of the village of Brookings.

If you think Mother snores, my dearest, you should be here. We sleep in snatches, an hour or two here and there, in the dispersal hut on an iron cot or in a folding chair waiting for the call to scramble. Some lads sleep so loudly that if you weren't so tired yourself you'd think to smother them. One chap walked over and had a wickedly long conversation with the flight lieutenant. No one realised he was sleepwalking until he called lieutenant "Mum."

I received my mother's letter—hallo, Mother—and she claims that you are pale. She blames me for not marrying you before "that horrid little man Hitler became such a world nuisance." Had I married you sooner, she reasoned, you would have had a child or two by now and been used to the rigors of motherhood. I have written to her. Perhaps she will share the letter with you, love. It should make you smile.

She also tells me that you lost your ration book on the way to the Red Cross station in Knightsbridge. Fortunately, she does not blame me for that. Enclosed is my ration book, which I had meant to leave behind. Use it, dearest. We do not want for much here.

I carry your picture in the pocket of my jumpsuit for luck. It is the one with you standing in the barge on the Thames. Remember? I bought you violets. I wish there were violets nearby so I could pick one and put it under my pillow and feel closer to you. Until then I have your photograph as close to my heart as I can.

I love you,

Skip

27 Berkeley Court, London
14 August, 1940

   My darling husband,
   I wish I could feel your arms about me. Your mother is good company, but every time I look at her I see your wonderful blue eyes in her face and I want to cry because I miss you so terribly. We rolled bandages this week at the Red Cross station. Oh, my darling, but that was so difficult, sitting there knowing those bandages could be used on you. I worry that you are not sleeping enough to fight well. Can they not relieve your squadron soon?
   I came into the library one afternoon and found your mother sitting at your desk, holding our wedding photograph and crying. She is frightened, too, my darling. We held each other—we do that so often now—and pray for you, for everyone, for the country. She told me that when she travelled to town, there were wire towers situated on the outskirts of small towns and people had driven their automobiles into fields and parked them in lines so invasion planes could not land.
   The BBC predicts the fighting will only get worse. In the last few days they have put up barrage balloons in the parks and squares all through town.
   I must take this to the Post. I love your letters, my dearest darling man. They are my strength. I have enclosed a small gift for you. Put it under your pillow and think of me. I have taken to sleeping in your shirt.

                 You are in my dreams,

                 Your loving wife

Wellingham Airfield, Essex
23 August, 1940

Dearest Wife,
Firstly I must thank you for the dried violets. I had not known that you pressed them in your journal. You may trust that they are quite happy in their new home beneath my pillow. Sleep in any item of my clothing, but make certain you write to me about it in great detail. The image of you in nothing but my shirt was certainly a welcome one.

We had heard from HQ that the target date for a German invasion was 15 August. But the day has come and gone. I suspect the BBC, as they did before the war, is trying its best to provide information to the people in the hope that they will save lives.

All the squadrons from Fighter Command have had much success of late. We are holding our own against wave after wave of attacks. New aeroplanes are coming every week, thanks to Lord Beaverbrook's efforts. Remember the day when you gathered our aluminum cookware and took it to the salvage trucks for the war effort? The Spitfire I am flying could be made from our very own pots and pans.

Now, please read this carefully, my dearest one. You asked if it was not dangerous for us, so many missions per day, every single day. A fighter pilot would never fall asleep in the cockpit. You can be so fagged you feel as if you cannot bear to stand. Then the call comes and you're out the door, fastening gear as you run for the plane. There is no time to think. No time to be tired. There is little time for anything but doing your job.

*I cannot tell you when we'll be relieved. But the moment
we are, I shall come straight to you, love. You owe me a
cheese omelet in lieu of my fine cigars. I love you, Greer.*

Until then, yours forever,

Skip

27 Berkeley Court, London
8 September, 1940

My darling husband,
*They bombed London yesterday. It seemed to go on for-
ever. By evening the sky towards the east was nothing but a
glow from the fires at the docks and warehouses there. You
are not to worry because we went down to the room in the
cellar. All was fine. The small wireless you settled down
there works wonderfully, and the candles lit the place
rather well. Rest assured that we did not come up until the
sirens sounded the all clear. I think that now that both your
mother and I have been through a bombing raid we are less
frightened than before.*
*This morning Mrs. Lindsay came by to bring your
mother an invitation to a luncheon for the war fund, and
she said they were in a shelter near St Paul's last evening
and the incendiaries were raining down as if it were the end
of the world.*
*Your mother is very put out by this whole incident.
When we were in the cellar room, all bundled up, sipping
tea and listening to the bombs whistle, then explode, she
declared, quite indignantly, that she will never again see
another Marlene Dietrich film.*

I expect that you are smiling now. I do so love your mother, darling. I am thinking that perhaps she and I should go to the country when things let up a bit. What keeps me here is that I am so very afraid that I will not be able to see you when you get relieved. I know it would only be for a day or two, but I couldn't bear it if you were given a forty-eight and I couldn't see you.

Know that I love you with all my heart, my darling, and I miss you as always, but trust, too, that I know you are up there flying the skies and protecting us. While I worry about you, I know you are the very best at everything you do and that you will come back to me when this is all done.

I keep you in my heart.

Greer

"SEPTEMBER IN THE RAIN"

Wellingham Airfield, Essex
10 September, 1940

My lovely Greer,
Rumor is that we are to have relief sometime in the next week. I have heard this for a while, but was hesitant to tell you until the time was growing close and until I could make certain the rumor appeared to be not merely wishful gossip. Our flight commander has said leave is most likely to happen

very soon, and since he is never one to spread idle rumors, I would say it is so.

While common sense tells me that certainly I would prefer to have you tucked safely away in Keighley, I know, too, that I would not be able to see you there with a mere forty-eight-hour leave. I want you to remember that I think you and my mother are very brave. I am proud of both of my ladies.

Mother's comment about Dietrich was quite fun, and knowing Mother as I do, I suspect she will soon write the poor actress a pointed letter condemning her for having the audacity to be born in Germany.

I shall end this brief letter by reiterating that I adore you and miss you terribly. I shall see you soon, my dearest and sweetest wife.

All my love forever,

Skip

He leaned back in a hard wooden chair as he sealed the letter; then he set it on the small desk in the corner of the dispersal hut and penned the address on the front of the envelope. He stood and crossed the room, then placed the letter in the mailbox and tossed a penny for the Post in a can that sat next to it.

There was a blackboard above the table where they marked hits. It was the ace board for the squadron. He had seven hits.

He turned away from the board and braced one hand on the wall, then pulled a packet of Craven "A"s from his pocket, stuck the cigarette between his dry lips, and lit it. He stood there and watched the smoke curl.

The hut was filled with smoke, because there was little else for them to do between missions. Sit there in readiness, smoke, drink black tea and coffee. Eat some of the tomato and cheese sandwiches or local-made cakes that were stacked on the food table between a beat-up old icebox with a motor that chucked loudly and a wooden trash bin filled with crumpled cigarette packs, snuff tins, gum and chocolate wrappers. There was as much raw tension in the air as there was cigarette smoke.

A quiet game of whist passed the time for some flyers across the room, their Mae West life vests stacked in a corner and their chutes piled beneath each man's spindled chair. Others were reading, slouched on sofas, in deep chairs, or on skeletal cots with the news or a book.

Skip couldn't concentrate enough to read a book. He had no focus when he was outside the cockpit. So he wrote letters and paced the room like a caged cat. And like the others, he waited.

He hadn't told Greer about his deepest fears. At first he told himself it was because she was carrying their child and he didn't want to worry her. But perhaps he was too ashamed to tell her. She did think he was the "best pilot in the RAF"—the best pilot in the RAF who vomited his belly out whenever he landed.

This was much on his mind of late, and he remembered something similar happening to him when he was just a lad. He had wandered into a field where his father and some other chaps were trapshooting at clay pigeons. A flock of rooks flew overhead, and one of the men swung his gun around and picked off a bird.

It hit the ground and a moment later the flock turned back, cawing and circling over the dead bird for the longest time. Skip remembered being very ill. He'd emptied his stomach of the pot-beef and cheese sandwich there in front of all, so the men stopped shooting and went back to the house. His father forced him along ahead of him, but did not speak of it. To this day Skip never knew what his father had thought.

Before the sun had gone down, Skip had walked back to the small meadow and sat there cross-legged in the grass, holding his tight belly and watching the flock as it still circled the dead bird. It had been hours. Finally, as if the funeral were done, the birds began to fly away, one, then two, then more. When the sun was completely down and the air was growing chilled, there was only one bird left, cawing in the half dark and circling over its lost mate.

When Skip was flying his Spit and saw someone killed, a comrade or the enemy, he felt like that lone bird, circling high in the sky, still alive but understanding that someone else just like him no longer lived. He never told Greer how he was so very relieved whenever he saw an enemy parachute. He didn't tell anyone. He didn't tell her that when he made a kill, he inevitably flew back to base and emptied his stomach the moment his feet hit solid ground.

He saw that other flyers came back with a dulled look on their faces. The energetic, anxious, and bright glow they'd had before all this started had promptly disappeared from their eyes as surely as if someone had killed it. The Brylcreem boys weren't so bright and glossy anymore.

War did that to a man, changed you whether you

were on the right side or not. Your basic beliefs were tested. You did what you had to do, but war played havoc with your values and your internal barometres of morality, with what was right, and what was wrong. War turned everything on its ear. He could see that in all the men of No. 77 Squadron. Innocence lost to the fact that they had to kill or be killed.

There were long nights when he would lie in his cot in the barracks and think that he wanted to turn in his wings and walk away. Duty and pride wouldn't let him. There was immense irony in the fact that all he really ever wanted to do was fly a plane. He had thought in his youthful naivete that the Royal Air Force was his path to glory. When they plotted and planned and flew maneuvers, they used the term "kills" and talked about "aces" and "dogfights." But that was only talk, words with no experience attached to them.

Now he was shooting men out of the sky, because he had no choice.

"Look here!" Hemmings waved a newspaper at the room in general.

"Hold the bloody thing still so we can see it." Mallory tried to grab the paper.

Hemmings stopped waving it, folded it back, and held it up.

There was a huge cartoon that covered the entire page; it was of a giant RAF pilot standing in the clouds, pulling Luftwaffe planes out of the air like King Kong. Beneath was the caption: HORATIUS OF THE SKIES.

A cheer went up in the room.

"There's a quote here from the PM," Hemmings added.

"Read it!"

Hemmings looked down and read, "Today Churchill voiced what the nation is feeling at the heroism and valor of the British Royal Air Force. Said the PM, 'Never in the field of human conflict was so much owed by so many . . . to so few.' "

There was a long moment of silence as the PM's words and meaning hit every single man in the room.

Mallory took a hit off his fag and said casually, "He must be talking about our pub bills."

At that, everyone laughed. It felt damn good to laugh. And for some flyers the joke was true. A noggin or two of beer, a gin or a scotch or single malt was the only way they could find the courage to go up again the next day, day in and day out, week after bloody week, facing repeated waves of the Luftwaffe. Others needed to drink themselves to sleep, to knock back shot after shot of hard liquor until they were numb enough to sleep.

The door to the dispersal hut opened and the flight commander came inside. Skip waited for the inevitable words, "Scramble men! Scramble!"

But there was no panicked order, just a long, drawn-out pause from their squadron leader.

"No. 55 just came in by truck to relieve you. No. 77 has a forty-eight effective at fifteen hundred."

The clock on the wall said eleven hundred. The official start of leave was still four hours away.

The others turned away from the clock and began to grumble and mutter. Some cursed. Even Mallory, who seldom showed anything close to a human emotion, threw his cards down on the table. One chap in the corner stood up, clearly ready to go at it with whomever he could find.

The CO began to laugh. "You should leave now, unless some of you are dead keen on waiting four lousy hours."

Books slammed closed. Newspapers drifted to the ground. Chair legs scraped the floor. Someone tossed a king of hearts into the air, the pool of fifty pounds quickly abandoned. It wasn't long before most of No. 77 Squadron had gathered around the train station near Wellingham, talking, smoking, and waiting for the trains. The men were off in different directions: some into the arms of a sweetheart, some towards a huge serving of Mum's flaky pastry and a good night's sleep in their own feather beds, while others went to Piccadilly and more rackety entertainment, the kind that came in the form of noisy pubs, London's Follies Bergere, or the Windmill Theatre with its tall and buxom girls who wore military hats and little else.

Not a single man who stood there was aware that at the exact same moment the next train squealed its way into the small, rural station, air-raid sirens in a crumbled and smoldering London began to sound the all clear.

"HEAVEN CAN WAIT"

"Mrs. Inskip, can you hear me?"
Someone was calling her. The words dragged out slowly and were indistinguishable, as if they were

coming from a broken gramophone. She didn't know who it was. She couldn't understand them. She wanted to ask, "What?" She could think the word, but she couldn't speak it. There was something in her throat. She could not speak around it. When she tried to take a breath, everything smelled charred, like the autumn air of Keighley the morning after the October bonfires.

"Mrs. Inskip? Can you hear me?"

Of course I can hear you!

"If you can hear me, raise your hand or your foot. Give us a signal."

She tried. She couldn't move them, because she couldn't feel them. She couldn't feel much of anything. The edges of her world were as misty as the Thames in winter.

Raise my hand. He said to raise my hand.

She raised her hand.

"Still nothing," the man said on a half sigh.

I'm lifting my hand. Look!

"There is no sign from her. She cannot hear me."

I can hear you!

She lifted her hand again.

Blast it all! Why did they not see it? Pay attention!

Someone tapped her on the bottom of her foot.

I feel it! I can feel it!

"There is still no response."

Yes, there is, you damned fool!

She could hear the scratching sound of someone scribbling with a pen on paper, then a woman's voice. "Such a shame."

What is a shame?

"I'll come back this evening and check on her, nurse.

Keep her as comfortable as possible. I've reduced the morphine."

Morphine? My God . . .

"Perhaps lowering the medication will bring her around. Let me know if there's any change."

"They're bringing in more injured, Dr. Falconer." A new voice, a woman's voice, came from a distance.

"I'll be along momentarily."

Wait! Wait! I can hear you!

She heard his footsteps going away, the tap-tap-tap of his shoes.

Come back! I am here! I can hear you! See my hand? Aren't I lifting my hand? I can feel it! Come back! Don't leave. Please don't leave me . . . .

She could feel tears slide from the corners of her eyes and curl behind her ears as if they were only the reading spectacles she put on every day and not the frustration and pain that was spilling out of her. She tried to move, tried to sit up, but something sharp and jagged shot like fiery knives through her whole skull. It hurt so much the world disappeared into nothing but black, hollow silence.

"MAKE BELIEVE ISLAND"

There were no taxis, so Skip had to go on foot from the train station. He didn't walk. He ran, sidestepping the bricks, wood, debris, and broken glass in the streets, alleys, and walks. His musette bag was slung over a shoulder, where it bounced heavily on his upper back like some huge hand that was shoving him towards home. He took a shortcut through the park, which wasn't crowded. Silver barrage balloons flew like toy dirigibles over the greens. Soot coated everything from the grass to the hedgerows, and a fog of smoke lingered in the lower branches of the old trees.

There was a huge black hole in the ground where a park bench and fountain used to be. Pieces of shattered marble and cement peppered the neighboring ground. Nearby shade trees, once wide and broad, had been splintered by the blast of the same German bomb.

Skip came out of the park running, scared by what he saw and more afraid of what he might see. He skirted the knot of fire trucks that were busy pumping water where incendiaries had fallen and spread fire in random, destructive patches for a whole city block.

His heart racing, he turned onto a street a few blocks from his house and stopped suddenly.

There was no damage here. It was postcard perfect—giving a surreal sense of walking into another dimension. The trees planted leisurely along the walks still wore their yellowed leaves. The townhouses themselves bore not even a fingerprint of the war. Not a cracked window. Nothing.

He looked back over his shoulder, wondering for an instant if he'd had so much combat that he looked for destruction and danger when there was none.

He was so much relieved he could feel his eyes tearing as he walked briskly toward home. He took deep breaths as he walked. Experience had taught him that breathing helped to stop the crying. There were moments in his plane when he escaped a near hit or a chase that he would realise there were tears streaming from his eyes.

It was a fact of war: men were frightened and men cried.

He rounded the street corner. He was running again, searching for No. 27.

And there it was. The iron grate at the base of the steps. The lacquered black door. The polished brass numbers. Two. Seven. Unharmed.

He stopped he was so relieved, a hand over his damp eyes.

All was untouched. All was perfect.

He took a few more breaths. A sparrow was chirping loudly from above. He would have to get the nest from the eaves or the little buggers would wake him at a ghastly early hour.

He looked up.

The top three floors and the roof of No. 27 were blown completely away.

"FOOLS RUSH IN"

It was sheer chaos at the entrance to the hospital. Everyone was talking at once. There was only a narrow set of doors where people were sandwiched together, trying to wedge inside. Skip ran around to an alley entrance where an ambulance was wheeling in someone. He walked up to the front desk.

A nurse was thumbing through a stack of papers and clipboards.

"Please." Skip could hardly speak he was so out of breath. "I'm looking for a Mrs. Inskip." He braced his hands on the desk in front of him, hung his head, panting. "The Home Guard sent me here. My wife was brought in about three, perhaps four hours ago."

The nurse at the small desk began checking a list. She picked up a second list and looked up. "I'm sorry. We have so few come in with names. The casualties have been flooding the place for three days now. But today is the worst of it. The good news is they just found a girl who had been buried under rubble for almost a hundred hours. A hundred hours. Can you imagine?" She shook her head in disbelief and went back to scanning the list. "Here she is. Inskip. Ward three, second floor. Take those stairs."

He took the stairs two at a time, then pushed open a door that led into a corridor busy with hospital staff and doctors. He passed three wards until he reached the one with the number three painted on the hall wall. There was a nurse coming out of the doors and she blocked him.

"I'm looking for Mrs. Inskip. I'm George Inskip."

Her face was kind but serious. "She's in the fourth bed on the right. Still unconscious. We cannot get any response from her, but perhaps hearing your voice will help. Come." She pushed open the door.

He followed her inside to a long, narrow, and sterile room that smelled of alcohol, camphor, and soot, then followed the nurse over to a bed, his heart hammering like machine gun fire.

She stopped at a bed and moved out of his line of sight.

"Greer?" He took a step towards the bed, then froze. He stood there as though in some kind of strange nightmare. It wasn't his wife's lovely blond hair he saw, but black hair. It was his mother.

He turned without a word to the nurse and left the

room, shoving open the door with a straight arm, and then he stood there in the hallway, disoriented, somehow lost. His mother. He hadn't once thought about his mother. He had forgotten her. The floor seemed to swell up towards him. He stepped back to the wall for support. Greer? His mother?

The nurse came out. She placed her arm on his. "Perhaps it's a good thing that she is still unconscious. Such injuries are difficult to see in someone you love."

Injuries?

He hadn't even noticed anything about his mother but the shock of seeing her familiar black hair. He'd seen that it wasn't Greer's, and he'd left.

"My wife . . ." he explained quietly. "I thought she was my wife. She's my mother. I never thought to ask about my mother. They were together." He looked back at the ward door.

"She's unconscious. I have a duplicate set of lists over at the nurses' desk. Come. We'll find your wife."

He followed her blindly. He was numb all over.

"Mrs. Inskip? Is that correct?"

He nodded. "Yes, Inskip."

She looked down the list.

Greer. Greer. . . . He reached out to the nurse and touched her arm. "Mrs. George A. Inskip. Of Berkeley Court."

She nodded and went back to the list.

It felt as if a month had passed by as she turned the last page. Then she picked up another clipboard and flipped through it. She stopped reading. "Her name is here."

"Where? Which ward?"

She held out the clipboard.

The heading at the top of the page read: "Morgue." He vaguely heard the nurse say, "I'm sorry." All the names blurred into a jumble of letters. All the names but one:

"Mrs. G.A. Inskip. Berkeley Ct. Time of death—3:50 P.M."

'I'LL NEVER SMILE AGAIN'

It's been said that the essence of real human love is the one shared between mother and child, where a mother feels the presence of her child even inside the grown man. A basic human instinct? All she knew was that her son was in the hospital room.

"George?" Odd that her voice sounded like someone else's. They had taken the breathing tube from her mouth that very morning. Deep inside her throat it burned when she tried to make a sound; her words came out charred around the edges.

"I'm here, Mother."

A metal chair scraped across the floor; then she felt the touch of his hand on her arm, the one with the tube stuck into her vein. In her mind's eye she could see her son's hands: the flat nails, the tanned skin, the strength in them.

Almost a quarter of a century ago in the bedroom at Keighley, after hours and hours of labor during which she thought she was going to die, she looked down at her newborn son for the very first time, counted his fingers and toes, and saw a small version of his father.

"I knew it was you. You were in the doorway only a

few moments ago. It wasn't the first time. Weren't you here before? Yesterday? Last night?"

He said nothing.

"Am I wrong? Perhaps it was the medication and I dreamed it."

"Are you in much pain?" He grasped her hand.

"Sometimes it feels tight. My arm hurts." She searched for the words and thoughts to describe what she was feeling and came up empty-handed. "I must look a fright."

He did not reply.

"I don't suppose it matters, since I cannot see."

"Mother . . ."

"I always did so despise all those huge bloody mirrors at Keighley. Every room you walked into. I used to tell your father that he must have been descended from Narcissus. There are even mirrors hung about the library, for God's sake, as if someone would want to look at themselves as they were reading. Now I shan't be bothered by them any longer."

"You don't have to do this for me."

"Do what?"

"Pretend."

"Don't." She held up the hand with the tube taped to it and winced. "If you love me at all, don't say anything. I want to revel in my pity for a few days." She tried to sound flip, but failed even to her own ears.

There was nothing from him, no words for the longest time. "She's dead," he said quietly. "The baby's dead."

"George . . ." she whispered his name. His hand was clammy and felt cold. *Oh, he's so young for this.*

"Why?"

"I tried to keep her from going back upstairs."

"She went upstairs?" The chair creaked as he stiffened in it.

"She said something; then she stood up and ran from the cellar room."

"In the name of God, *what* could have possibly been that important?" His tone was icy hard, his voice was hoarse, as if he had been screaming at God and Heaven and the world.

"The bombs were so loud this time. They were closer than ever before. Then it was the oddest thing. The bombing had stopped with an eerie kind of suddenness. We were sitting there in the silence. I believe she thought she was safe. The candles were burning. She was talking about you and a promise she'd made you. She had been reading one of your letters aloud; then she stood and bolted for the stairs. I followed her, calling out for her to wait for the all-clear siren. But by the time I was up into the foyer she was already up the staircase to the second floor. I followed her. I tried to stop her." What was left of her voice disappeared momentarily, as if she had swallowed it along with the bitter pill of war and reality. She saw the image of her son's lovely, animated wife rushing into the kitchen just before everything suddenly disappeared in a ball of hot light.

Now she began to cry. It went on for a long time, and the worst of it was crying didn't make her feel one whit better. It made her feel weak and out of control. And it hurt her face.

"I know, Mother. I know," was all he said. His grip on her hand did not change. He was sitting so still.

She wanted to see his face, but the doctor had told her that very morning that her eyes were burned, along with half of her face. They could not guarantee she would ever see again. She laughed without any humor. "My eyes can still cry these foolish tears, but they cannot see a thing. I cannot even open them."

"You will, Mother. The doctor said they have to heal before you can open them again."

"What good will that do me?" She did not want to cry. She was not a weak woman.

She turned towards the sound of his breathing. "I'm sorry." For just a moment she asked herself if she truly did want to see again, to see what losing Greer and their unborn child had done to her son.

"I stayed in the house last night." His tone sounded distracted, surreal, as if he had left his soul somewhere far, far away.

Sometimes there were grand loves in the world, the kind that were apparent to anyone who had even half a heart and half a brain. She knew this because her marriage had not been a great love affair. It had been comfortable, tender, secure, like two parallel lines moving side by side.

But it had not been profound and unassailable, not the kind of love that George and Greer had, one that was a complete circle rolling through life in one single continuous perfectly formed shape—a shape that protected what was within that circle: George and Greer, Greer and George, two hearts, two souls, one love.

On a summer day almost fifteen years ago, a ten-year-old boy with a quiet intelligence and a gentle heart met a golden-haired girl who had wit and charm and was his other, more spirited half. And that was it.

"I slept in the front bedroom." The sound of his voice

came from above her. He was standing by the bed. "It looked unchanged, not a window broken, not a sign that anything had happened at all. Nothing even out of place. How could that be when the third floor and the entire back of the house is gone, Mother? How could that be?"

"I don't know. I ran after her," she whispered. George was speaking, but she didn't really hear him. She was reliving the scene in her memory. Running up the staircase. The sound of her feet on the carpet. Down the hallway.

Greer! Greer! A slip of a floral dress disappearing around the edge of the kitchen doorway.

Then came that terrifying whistling from overhead, that ominous shriek of a noise that made her stop and listen, made breathing and thinking impossible; it kept her frozen to the sound when she knew she should run away.

So many times they had heard the whistle, then breathed a relieved sigh when the blast that followed was not near them.

Odd, wasn't it, how you never heard the blast when you were the target.

Her son was talking. "... when I walked inside, the foyer was intact, everything perfect, except for the sparrows that had flown in from the open roof above. They were sitting on the coat rack, and a lark was perched on that dragon table, singing when there was nothing to sing about."

She could hear him breathing, hear his breath catch a bit.

He sat down hard in the chair. "God ... but she loved that table."

What can I say to him? I can't make it go away. This

isn't like some scraped knee or a lost ball. All I can do is tell him what happened.

"What was it? What was worth her life and our child's?"

"I don't know. She ran in the kitchen. When I came around the corner, she was standing in front of the open icebox."

"The icebox? The icebox? Oh, God . . ." He lay his head on the bed next to her. A second later he was sobbing. It was an awful sound—the kind of crying that came from the deepest, darkest part of you, the kind of crying you heard with your heart, the kind of crying that broke it.

"I'm sorry, so sorry." She stroked his hair. The bed was shaking with his sobs, and he was saying something, but she couldn't understand him because his head was buried in his arms.

"Let it all go, my son. Let it go. I know it's such a waste."

"A waste?" he said bitterly, raising his head. Then he gave a hopeless laugh that sounded like glass breaking. "A *waste*? She died for the bloody fucking eggs."

"IT'S A BLUE WORLD"

It was little more than a week later that Skip was on the train back to Wellingham. He looked out the open window, above the dark blue blackout paint at a few inches of flashing colors: overcast sky, the dark green treetops and pitched roofs that melted together—

the world flying past him in a blur. It was an odd thing how in a time of war, life itself, the hours and minutes and days, all of it seemed to move at odd speeds, as if the world were in a nosedive spinning out of control.

It had been a mere eight days since he had buried his wife and unborn child in a quiet ceremony at Keighley. Eight nights that seemed like eight decades and eight days that seemed like eight seconds.

He'd brought back an aunt to stay with his mother until she could be released from the hospital, then spent two days and nights in a pub near Piccadilly. For hours he sat in a dark corner and stared at a red, black, and white *"My Good, My Guinness"* poster with a fat seal balancing a beer bottle on its nose while it served a foaming stout to a thirsty soldier.

Empty bottles of single-malt scotch lined up on the table like enlisted men while Skip knocked back glass after glass. He tried and failed to forget his vacuous existence, tried and failed to forget the obsequious platitudes people said to him, well-meant though they were.

Buck up, old chap. It will get better with time.

It's God's will, you know.

She's in a much better place.

You'll marry again.

That one was his favorite. It implied nothing except that people were like replacement parts on a motor. No problem, old chap, you go out and get another.

The brakes of the train squealed as they scraped metal, and the rail carriage came slowly to a stop. The engine spit a burst of steam, and it floated into his open window, condensed, and dripped down the glass of a small framed tobacco ad by Churchman's No. 1 with a pilot smoking and reminding you to recycle cardboard cigarette packets.

A female ticket collector in a grey woolen uniform with a slim skirt and fitted jacket—new styles that used less fabric—moved through the narrow aisle on low-heeled, sensible shoes created to conserve wood for the war effort.

She rang a small bell and called out, "Wellingham!"

The next moment he was stepping down from the train onto a wooden platform that was less than three miles from the airbase. The hard soles of his shoes made a hollow, empty sound as he walked with his musette bag slung over a shoulder, heading toward a base vehicle—an American-made Dodge WC12 half-ton that had been part of the Lend-Lease agreement from the Yanks. It was parked under an iron streetlamp seldom used anymore with the blackouts and bombing raids.

He tossed his bag in the back of the lorry and started to crawl inside, but froze when he looked up.

The men inside were all staring at him.

He hated that look on their faces, the one that said they didn't know what to say to him, looks that were awkward and pitying, but also tinged with a small edge of relief that it hadn't happened to them.

It was a long three miles back to base. A few of them tried to make inane conversation, then gave up and talked amongst themselves. Pilot Officer Mallory had the most kills. Eleven. He was now the squadron top ace.

The lorry drove through the gates and pulled to a stop in front of the pilots' quarters. No sooner was he out than the siren wailed and someone shouted, "Scramble! Scramble!"

Skip stiff-armed the barracks door; it slammed against the wooden wall. He ran toward his cot and tossed his bag on it, then jerked open his footlocker.

Within minutes he was zipped in a jumpsuit and leather jacket, strapped in flight gear, and pulling on his gloves as he ran across the grass for his Spit. Over half the squadron was already in the air, which smelled of high-octane plane fuel and an even higher level of anticipation. A tin-hatted ground crewman handed him a chute, while another checked the ammo supply. From the corner of his eye he saw that seven swastikas had been painted on the fuselage of his plane.

He tossed the chute in the cockpit as they shoved him onto the wing. He hopped inside and slid the canopy closed with one hand. The crew scattered like grouse while he strapped in and flicked a look at his gauges.

A second later he hit the switches. The Rolls-Royce Merlin engine rang up in vibrations through the control stick and into his palm, where it purred pure power. Boots on the rudder pedals, the sky overhead, and he was off down the field, bouncing over the jagged, wheel-churned ground of the grass airfield, the engine roaring toward takeoff speed, that sweet moment when he pulled back and left his stomach, his body weight, and the ground behind him.

And he was flying.

'ALL OR NOTHING AT ALL'

He broke the old squadron record of four kills in a day. He was rather surprised when he reflected on it as he flew back to base. It was quite easily done. Almost as if the enemy were flying into his sight. He'd pressed the button, tracers shot out, and he watched the planes spiral down in flames until they hit the Channel, disappearing and leaving no sign they had ever existed apart from a pale green patch in the water.

There were no chutes today. A Nazi bomb had ended his world. He would do what he had to to keep Nazi bombs from ending anyone else's. He merely kept firing until the planes exploded or fell apart.

The wheels of his Spit touched the field with a bounce, and he rolled over toward the maintenance hangars, then stopped. He shoved back the canopy and climbed out. The ground crew had made it a habit of waiting a few minutes after he landed before they came to work on the plane. The sergeant of the ground crew was a brittle old mechanic from Dorchester, a man with an understanding of pride, who gave him time to vomit.

Skip jumped down from the wing. He shoved an anchor brick against a front wheel, then slowly walked around the plane. He'd taken some hits in the wing from the dorsal gunner on a Heinkel. It wasn't too bad. Some holes in the starboard wing skin and a few chewed-up places on the tail.

Corporal Andrews came up to him. "Sorry, sir. No hits today."

"Five."

"What?" The kid turned and looked at him. "But, sir . . ."

"I didn't up jack my insides?" His laugh was biting. "I don't think I'll be having that problem any longer. I say, come here. Looks like one of them got the rear navigation light."

"Yes, sir."

The rest of the crew joined Andrews and began going over the plane. As Skip turned away, he saw the corporal lean over and whisper to another crewman. He didn't care what they were saying. He removed his fleece-lined gloves and strode towards the dispersal hut. He wanted some coffee.

Inside, he grabbed a sandwich from a plate and took a few bites as he poured himself a cup of strong black coffee. He leaned against the wall and crossed his boots at the ankle as he finished off the farmer's sandwich of cheddar and tomato, then ate another one that tasted like chicken salad. He wasn't certain what it was; he ate the whole thing in four bites. He was still chewing when his flight commander came in a few moments later.

"Good job, Inskip."

"Thanks."

Mallory came inside grousing about his sight being off. He hadn't a single kill. Skip sipped his coffee.

Soon the hut was filled with flyers all talking at once about the mission, the near hits and the damage, the one that got away. They hadn't lost a man that day. Eight sorties and no one pranged.

The CO tallied up the day's score. As he chalked up the squadron's kills, the talking in the room tapered off to almost nothing. Soon it was so quiet that all you could hear was the scratching of chalk on the blackboard.

After a moment the scratching stopped and the CO looked up.

There was no sound left in the room.

"We have a new squadron top ace." He turned and looked at Skip. "Flying Officer Inskip has twelve kills."

The room erupted in cheers, and he found himself smiling as they pounded him on the back and toasted his success with coffee and teacups and a few good bawdy jests.

He was top ace. The goal of every flyer.

The men all shook his hand, including Mallory, who swore he'd catch up with him the next day.

After Skip promised to meet a few of them in an hour for a celebratory beer, he left the hut and headed for the barracks. He walked into his quarters and began to remove his gear. He set his air jacket on the bunk, unbuckled his chute and let it fall. He took off his helmet and goggles, unstrapped his flight belt, and dumped his survival kit along with everything else into his footlocker, then kicked the lid closed. He was still in his flight suit, his gloves stuffed inside and hanging out of a pocket as he went into the WC and washed up. He bent over the basin and scrubbed the rubber smell of his oxygen mask off his cheeks and mouth, then straightened and rubbed a towel vigorously over his damp face.

He looked in the small round mirror above the basin.

Five kills.

And he felt nothing.

NORTH AFRICA

1941

Cassidy swore under his breath and wrenched open his side. His boots crunched on the rocks as he went back to the rear of the truck.

She scooted out the open door and swept his loose maps out with her. They brushed her leg, then crinkled to the ground.

As she stood up something small and hard bounced off the top of her foot. She bent down and felt around in the dry dirt, gathering the maps and refolding them. She kept brushing over the dirt, but she couldn't feel anything else but a bunch of dry twigs, and small stones.

She stood and stepped back. Her heel crunched down on something. She squatted down and swept her hand over the fine dirt until her fingers hit a round metal disc. She picked it up.

His compass? Probably. It also felt dented, but the glass was smooth and unbroken.

She straightened and walked toward the back of the truck, rubbing the compass clean on her skirt. "Captain Cassidy?"

"Just a minute." His aggravated voice came from deep inside the truck. "We have to get the gas out of here."

She rounded the corner and stopped at the tailgate.

"Dammit, Sabri! These are only twenty-liter cans."

"*Iya. Oui. Regardez. Bezzaf petrolkans.* There are many," Sabri told him. "*Soixante-cinq.*"

There was silence.

She leaned inside. "That's sixty-five."

"I speak five languages, Kincaid. I can count in seven."

"Sorry. Just trying to help."

"Well . . . don't."

Whoa . . . Not a good time to give him his dented compass. She shoved it into her pocket with the maps and waited while they slid gas cans to the edge of the truck with a metallic scraping noise that she felt in her back teeth. Rather like someone sawing a car in half.

Cassidy jumped down a moment later and took her arm with a blunt grip. "Okay. Look. This is going to take a while, since we get to fill it up five gallons at a time." He shoved the canteen into her hands. "Here. Take a drink."

She took the canteen and drank deeply. "Thanks, my mouth was dry as dust." She put the cap on and handed it back to him.

"You keep it. You might want more." He hesitated.

"What's wrong?"

"Nothing. I figure you might as well go do your business."

"Thank you."

"Listen, you about bit my head off earlier when I tried to help you walk safely out of sight. This time I'm going to be smarter and ask you first. Do you want help?"

"I can do it alone, if the terrain's not rocky."

"It's flat as an A cup." He grasped her shoulders and turned her. "Straight this way." He gave her a quick pat on the butt that barely passed for a nudge forward. "There's a small hill with some rocks in front of it about a hundred feet from here. A beeline. You'll have some privacy behind those rocks. The land's flatland all the way, sweetheart. Not a divot. Not a bush. Just dirt."

"I'm not your sweetheart." She started off toward the rocks.

He laughed, then called out. "You're not an A cup, either."

"NICE WORK IF YOU CAN GET IT"

J.R. left Sabri to finish filling the gas tank and went to the truck cab. He pulled the binoculars out of his pack and jogged off toward the rise a few hundred yards ahead of them. They had run out of gas at a dip in a ridge, part of an area of rippling valleys in between foothills. From his position back at the truck, he had barely been able to make out the top of the opposite ridge. According to Sabri, the rendezvous point was on the other side of the valley. Another hour, maybe less.

Now, standing at the crest of the rise, he could easily survey the crusty terrain below, which was covered with dry grass and desert brush. He raised the binoculars and scanned across the wide plain to the distant horizon, turning slowly so he wouldn't miss anything.

He'd been edgy. He couldn't guarantee that the Jerries who'd held Kincaid would head for the coast. The flat tire made him nervous; it gave them time to double back.

He adjusted the binoculars in sharper focus.

The hills were about thirty klicks away. He couldn't see much—a few more clusters of trees against the dusty color of the hillside. He scanned the area twice before he caught a glimmer of metal nestled at the base of a barren foothill to the north.

He adjusted the binoculars and held them completely still.

There it was: the dolphin nose of a C-47 transport. The plane was already there and waiting.

"Damn . . ." J.R. checked his watch, then looked off at the sun sliding down the sky. They had an hour of sunlight left, maybe a little more.

He cupped his hands over his mouth and hollered. "The plane's waiting. Sabri! Stop! That's enough gas. Start the truck." He turned toward the rocks. "Kincaid! Hurry up! Christ . . . How long does it take to squat behind a rock?"

It was a full minute before Kitty came stumbling out from behind the rock, brushing the skirt of her dress down.

Sabri had ditched the gas cans and was already in the truck cab. He slammed the door and started the engine. It sputtered to life.

J.R. signaled for him to go toward Kitty and pick her up first; then he shouted, "Can you hear me, Kincaid?"

"I'm blind, not deaf."

"Cute. Real cute. Just stay there . . . where you are. It'll be faster if the truck comes to you."

Sabri jammed into gear and turned the vehicle toward Kitty.

J.R. set off down the rise toward them.

The truck went about fifty feet. Sabri shifted into second and drove it another ten feet, and exploded in a ball of fire.

Jesus . . . J.R. blocked his eyes for a second, then lowered his arm and just stood there staring at what was left.

Sabri was gone. The truck was gone. Smoke spiraled

up from the black, burning ground. He glanced at Kitty.

She was okay, just standing there with her arms over her head.

He was so stunned it took a second for the cause of the explosion to register in his head.

"Cassidy?" Kitty straightened slowly, then dropped her arms. "My God . . . Cassidy? Are you there?" She took a step.

"Don't move!"

"What happened?" She was still walking.

"Stop, damn it! We're in a minefield!"

She went still as a rock. "Was that the truck?"

"Yes." He looked around.

"What about Sabri? Is he hurt? I don't hear anything."

"We can't help him."

"Wait. How do you know? Sabri!"

"There's nothing left of the truck. Nothing."

She made a painful sound and turned her head away for a moment.

J.R. had no idea how much of the land was mined. He looked around, but the whole area could have been mined for all he could tell.

"Cassidy?" Her voice was quiet.

"What?"

"Are we both in the minefield?"

"I know you're in it."

"So what do we do?" Her voice was higher, the way women's voices got when they were shaken.

"Stay calm. Stay still. I'm going to retrace my footsteps, then retrace yours. But you need to give me a minute, understand?"

"Okay."

He still had his equipment belt, just about the only thing besides the binoculars that he hadn't left in the truck. "First I need to fire a flare. A signal for the plane."

"Will they wait for us?"

"If they see the green flare they will." He pulled the flare gun, raised his arm, and pulled the trigger.

It clicked. Nothing.

He pulled out the cartridge and reloaded it, then fired again. Zilch . . . "Son of a bitch!"

"What happened?"

"The flare's a dud." He had to think. Fast.

"What are you going to do?"

Stick this flare gun in your mouth if you ask me another goddamn question.

"Are you still there?"

Hell . . . he'd forgotten she was blind and couldn't see him. "Give me a minute to think."

It was getting later. The sun was starting to go down; shadows were growing faint. The sky was turning rainbow colors.

He looked down. He had to be able to see their footsteps to retrace them. "I'm coming now." He began to walk. Step in each footstep. It seemed to take forever before he spotted a mine, then another one about five inches from a footprint. Damn. . . .

"Talk to me, Cassidy."

Fifty feet more. "Why?"

"Because I can't take the silence."

"Better silence than an explosion."

She didn't say a word.

"You're awfully quiet, Kincaid."

"I don't want to interfere with your concentration."

"Lucky for you, I'm good at what I do. Dying isn't part of my plan, sweetheart."

"I'm eternally grateful for your huge ego."

"Good. When this is all over, I'll have to come up with a way for you to repay me."

"You never stop, do you?"

"The Yankee in me likes the last word." He had made it back to his starting point. Now, he had to find her footprints. He studied the ground for a minute or two, then got real lucky. The distinct shape of the soles and heels of her shoes were easier to spot; they looked like fat exclamation points. The dirt was softer here and her footprints sank deeply.

But the mines were more difficult to spot. There was also the fact that if her foot had been only an inch or so away from a mine, his bigger boot could still trigger it.

"Where are you?"

"Halfway to you. This soft sandy dirt is a little trickier. You could always strip naked and give me a little more incentive."

"I'll give you incentive. I swear that if you get yourself blown to smithereens, I will hunt you down in the sweet hereafter and make your eternity absolute hell."

"When we die, sweetheart, I doubt you and I will be in the same place."

"True."

"Unless there's something lurid about your past you want to tell me."

"No."

"No, there's nothing lurid in your past?" A few more yards. "Or no, you don't want to tell me?"

"No. I'm not telling you anything."

"Too bad. But if you want to hunt me down, well then, that's fine with me. We can fan the flames of hell together."

"Your dream, my nightmare."

"Stay still." He held up his hand, then realized she couldn't see it so he let it drop. "I'm here, now . . . close, but don't move. Let me check the ground around us." There was a mine to her left, eight inches away and another a foot behind him at about three o'clock. The rest was clear.

He closed the distance between them and put his arms around her. "I gotcha."

She exhaled and sagged against his shoulder.

"You're safe."

"I know." She kept her arms around his neck.

"Are you crying? Don't turn into Wimpy on me, Kincaid."

"I feel like Wimpy," she said into his neck. "I'm scared."

"Enough slobbering. I won't let anything happen to you. But we need to move fast."

She dropped her hands from around his neck.

"The sun's setting. We have to get out of here so I can find a way to signal that plane."

"Okay, but couldn't we set off the mines? Wouldn't they see the explosions?"

"The signal is preplanned. A green flare. I'm going to carry you out on my back. I've turned around. My back's to you. I want you to lean into me and slide your arms around my neck." When she did, he said, "Now hang on." He grabbed the backs of her legs and pulled her onto his back. He walked a few steps. He could feel her heart beating fast and a slight quiver, as if she were shaking some. He took another step and said, "Nice, soft thighs you got there, Kincaid."

"I'd slap you for that, Cassidy, but my sense of self-preservation won't let me."

"I guess that means I can say what I want."

"As if anything would stop you."

"I don't see any point in asking permission."

"You're too busy giving orders."

He laughed. "I'm in the Army. Orders are everything. A few more yards and we're home free."

She held on to his neck more tightly.

It took less time to get back to the ridge, but it was late and quickly getting darker. He set her on her feet and took her hand. "We're okay here. No more mines. But I need you to walk a few steps down this embankment with me. Give me your other hand, and I'll lead you down."

At the edge of the ridge, he stopped. "I'm going to turn around. I want you to stay close and keep your hands on my shoulders. We'll use my body to keep you from falling."

"No. Wait." She shook her head. "Tell me how far we're going. I can count it off."

"Fifteen feet. But keep your hands on my shoulders as a guide. There's scrub and rocks." He was surprised how easy it was. She stayed right with him. Below, the valley was turning burnished gold from the setting sun.

"The sun is setting," she said.

"I thought you were blind."

"People aren't usually completely blind. I see shadows, silhouettes, some vague misty shades of color."

"I guess it's hard to miss that sunset."

The sky was a brilliant bright yellow and red.

"Stop here. I need to work on the flare gun." He pulled the flare out again and shoved it back hard, then tried the trigger a third time. Still nothing.

"It's so still and quiet here. I can't hear anything. No birds. No wind. Nothing." She had turned her face up as if she were looking at the air around her.

He jerked the cartridge out of the flare gun, then squatted down and broke it apart. The green powder poured out into a small pyre. He lit it, then moved back as green smoke spiraled up into the air.

He turned and looked off toward the distant foothills. *Come on, guys. Look over here.*

"Something's burning. What are you doing?"

"Lighting the flare powder."

"Oh."

He fanned the smoke upward and watched it.

"Cassidy?"

"Yeah?"

"Thank you."

"For what? Doing my job?"

"No. I couldn't help you at all in that minefield. I just had to stand there."

"Yeah, well, standing still in a minefield is a damn good idea."

"I don't like feeling helpless, but I would have never gotten out of that field alive. I was lucky to get across it in one piece the first time."

"We both were lucky." He straightened, pulled out his binoculars, and focused in the direction of the plane.

"Sabri wasn't lucky," she said in a vacant voice.

"No. He wasn't. I'd say he was pretty unlucky, with all that gasoline in the back. Those mines wouldn't have blown that truck to hell like it did. The gasoline was what sent it to Timbuktu."

"It could have been us."

"But it wasn't." He focused the binoculars again and slowly zeroed in on the landing site. "I don't deal with could-have-beens. One of the things you learn in the Army is to not try to understand why you make it and someone else doesn't. It would drive you nuts. It's just luck, Kincaid. Just luck."

"I thought it was your vast knowledge and huge ego."

"That too." He smiled and focused the binoculars in the direction of that far hillside. The sun glared at him and made it hard to see.

"Cassidy?"

He lowered the glasses and turned back to her. "What?"

"They didn't tell you I was blind, did they?"

"No." He looked back to the plane, adjusted the focus again.

"Is that because you wouldn't have taken the job if they had?"

"Don't go getting all mushy on me, now. I'm in the Army. This is my job. I do what they tell me."

"I'm trying to thank you."

"You know something, Kincaid?"

"What?"

"I'm thinking maybe it's a good thing you can't see."

She faced him, a little stunned. "Why?"

He turned the binoculars toward the sunset. "Because our ride home just flew away."

'MEIN VATER WAR EIN WANDERSMANN'

Rheinholdt's men had finished three long days of hard work under the blistering sun, burying over five hundred canisters of petrol and ammunition in the sand at mapped points along the routes of the Panzer Divisions. Now, miles away from the last emergency supply point, they had bivouacked in the deep fold of a desert wadi, where campfires and smoke would be hidden from enemy sight during the black, clear nights when fires could easily give away a unit's position.

Daylight hours here were different. The heat made the air wave and blur. There was natural camouflage in the desert that caused the human eye to see things that weren't there; a huge and distant lake that was only sand; a camel caravan that turned out to be a line of tall scrubs; smoke that was really sand blown upward by random wind funnels.

It had been a difficult twenty-four hours for everyone. The day before he had lost two men. His unit's latest assignment involved working close to the front. HQ had given them top priority and issued his men the new steel helmets that had just come from Berlin.

But the dark helmets stood out and shone in the sun, attracting gunfire twice. One soldier died, and the other had been seriously wounded and had to be sent back to the coast for medical treatment.

This from a piece of equipment that was supposed to protect them.

Rheinholdt stood with his hands clasped behind his back as he searched the broad horizon. Sunset looked to be two hours away. They were to wait in this vicinity for a rendezvous with the engineering corps before moving on to the next assignment. He turned back and observed the camp below from his position on a stony plateau just above them.

His men were listless. They lay like snakes baking in the sun. Desert war was a worse kind of hell. Logistically, a nightmare. After receiving no supplies or mail for over a month, the men were hungry for news, mail from home, and something decent to put in their stomachs.

But he could not blame this kind of lethargy solely on the heat, on days of blazing sun, on sand that stung your eyes or fleas that burrowed into your skin. Or on the fact that the supply convoy was more than a week late.

A comrade dies and death becomes suddenly concrete to every soldier in the unit. A hand with no lifeline right there before your eyes. The dead soldier could have been talking to you minutes before or joking around the fire the previous night, singing old beer-drinking songs along with a gramophone record and sharing a cigarette or a tin of fruit.

In one instant of war life can be gone. Standing face-to-face with mortality, a soldier must ask himself if the next bullet or scrap of shrapnel is marked for him. And when war becomes too real, confidence drops. Morale sinks faster than a rock in a cup of water.

Rheinholdt walked back down into the middle of the camp, unnoticed in the lassitude. He stood nearby and watched a soldier swat at flies while he used his bayonet to stab pieces of floating meat from a can of AM rations: the vile Italian meat packed in tins that were stamped "AM" for *Administrazione Militare.*

Rheinholdt tilted his field cap back and rubbed his chin. "So, Dietrich. How does it taste?"

He looked up, surprised. "I believe, Herr Leutnant, that AM stands for Alter Mann." He laughed at his own joke. "It tastes like old man."

"You could be right, yet I always believed that the AM stood for Alter Maulesel . . . old mule."

Every man within earshot laughed.

"Duce's men call it *asino morto.* Dead donkey," someone added.

He noticed that none of the men had stood to attention once they recognized him. He was their commanding officer, but military discipline faded on the front lines, where his concern was more about the well-being of his men, as well as their fighting preparedness . . . of which he saw little. It was time to remind them there was a war on.

Rheinholdt let them laugh, then nodded at the Kar98k lying beside Dietrich. "Hand me your rifle."

Dietrich sat straighter.

Rheinholdt examined the bolt-action weapon, then tossed it back on the ground. "Clean it." He turned to the others. "The rest of you. Put your weapons here." He gestured to the ground.

The men moved slowly, some of them groaning only because they had to sit up.

Five minutes later he had examined all the rifles, .08s, and two MP40s. "Every one of these weapons has sand in it."

They looked at him from eyes that held no emotion. Their faces were sunburned to a deep red, in spite of their already tanned but filthy skin. They all needed a shave almost as badly as they needed a bath.

"You are to stop this"—he waved his hand—"lazing about and remember where you are and why. You will clean those weapons every night. You will sleep with them. And when you wake up, you will clean them again."

They sat there like wooden ducks.

He wondered for a brief moment if they had even heard his order. *"Now."*

They scattered swiftly.

"Understand this . . ." he added, watching them and their expressions.

The men were annoyed and angry, but looked more alive than a few minutes ago.

"I will not send another man to the field hospital." He turned and walked straight toward the parked trucks, sidestepping a stack of rocks they used to anchor the tents against capricious desert winds.

He stopped behind the closest lorry and pulled back the canvas flap, checked the contents, then turned to one of his NCOs. "Distribute these cans of vehicle paint to the men. Have them use it on their helmets."

"Which color paint, Herr Leutnant? There are three colors."

"The mustard. The same one used on the half-track. While the paint is wet, they are to roll their helmets in sand. That should stop the glare and camouflage their heads in the trenches."

The man gave a sharp nod and sent five enlisted men to pull the paint cans from the lorry.

"The men have too much time on their hands. Make certain they have plenty to do before sunset."

"Jawohl, Herr Leutnant."

Rheinholdt walked over to his tent and went inside, where his personal belongings were sitting on a wooden cot. He began to unpack his canvas rucksack and settle in. He folded flat the empty sack and set it under the cot, then picked up a small shaving mirror and hung it on a wooden tent support.

From the mirror, a filthy, almost unrecognizable face stared back at him. Rings of grimy dirt were around his eyes in the shape of sand goggles, and his lips were swollen, cracked, and blistered. He looked like a badger. His overlong hair was stuck to his scalp in the shape of his field cap and was dusty gray on the ends from sand, dirt, and wind. He scratched his scalp with both hands for a full minute. A few of his men had used their razors to shave their heads—relief from the fleas.

He glanced down at his dull razor for a weak moment. He was filthy and ragged and as much out of uniform as most any soldier in the desert. He had cut the canvas tops of his high boots down to the ankle and allowed his men to do the same. He didn't wear his tunic daily; he settled for a shirt and shorts.

But he was still an officer. And by example, the leader of his men. He could take the fleas and the dirt and the itchy, scabbed scalp.

With a small cup of salty water from one of his canteens, he brushed his teeth, repeatedly scrubbing the brush against an almost nonexistent block of toothpowder. He rinsed his mouth, then used the same water to wash his face and hands before he dumped what was left into a canister for use in the vehicle radiators. He rewrapped a paper-thin piece of government-issue soap in old crinkled cellophane, then set it aside and sat down, unsnapping the flap on his shirt pocket before he pulled out an envelope.

It used to be ivory. Now it was smudged with dirt and fingerprints and spotted from where he'd spilled tea on it. The paper was torn, frayed from handling and rereading the letter inside every night. He blew into the open end and carefully pulled out the folded pages.

A photograph fell onto his knee.

His wife and children looked back at him as if he were the camera lens.

He picked up the photo and propped it against his mess tin atop an empty supply crate next to his bed. With the torn old envelope still in his hand, he rested his elbows on his knees for a moment and just looked at his family.

Hedwig wore a lace collar on a dark woolen dress with a narrow belt that made her waist look as small as that of his daughter, Marthe, who was only ten. She stood next to her mother with a wistful smile that was so like her mother's that he felt a wave of pity for the young man who would someday fall in love with his elder daughter. A man couldn't say no to a smile like that.

Standing on the other side of Heddy was Renate, their five year-old. She had an altogether different smile. She was grinning toothlessly. Inside the envelope was one of her front teeth she had sent him for good luck. He tapped the envelope against his palm and looked at the small ivory tooth. It was one of life's infamous ironies that a tooth could make him smile whenever he looked at it.

The thing he remembered most about his teeth as a child was that they were always loose. But his father's and mother's teeth had been loose, too, from malnourishment. One look at the photograph was enough to see that his own family looked healthy, with rosy cheeks, shining hair, and none of the pallor that hunger had given his own childhood and that of his brother and sister's.

Life had changed since the aftermath of the First World War, when he was very young and hungry and would dig in the fields with his father, searching for roots to cook because there was no food. After hours of combing their bare hands through dirt roads and barren fields for something—anything—to eat, they would come back to an icy-cold home with a few pieces of wood for a fire and filthy hands they had to wash in melted snow. On fortunate days, stuffed in their pockets were a few flower bulbs and a stub of a tree root for the soup pot.

He remembered the dead dogs in the streets and the sticklike bodies of the children who lived nearby, children who seldom played because if you were hungry, your head and belly ached too much to do anything but try to sleep it away. Two of those children, the boys in the next house—one, his friend Rudolph whose father had been killed on a battlefield in Belgium—died a few months apart. There had been many nights when Rheinholdt had fallen asleep to the cries of hungry babies and the churning of his own stomach.

Those were the days when Germany and her people almost cracked under the stifling inflation that made money in Germany worthless, the days of poverty, when they wore clothes made of ersatz cloth so paper-thin that it melted in rain and cracked in the freezing cold. It had been a time of no food or jobs or future, only poverty and despair.

Eventually, when Hitler had turned to propaganda to impress the outside world, most Germans, like Rheinholdt himself, accepted him because their own lives were now better. Things had changed.

His father did not like Adolf Hitler, and said he was only a fool trying to fool the world with his rows of cardboard tanks set up in city squares. In time, those long rows of military tanks made of cardboard and wood became real and were shown worldwide on German government-produced newsreels. Even when there was color in people's skin again, his father still did not trust the Nazis.

"You cannot join the Army, Frederich. You will be a Nazi."

"I will join the Wehrmacht, Father, not the Nazis."

"It is the same thing now."

"I do not think so. The Wehrmacht is Germany's army. But even if what you believe is true, is the Nazi army so terrible?"

"Ja!"

"It is only politics."

"You are wrong."

"But can you not see promise in what they say? We

will all have an automobile. The photos—long lines of Volkswagens—we subscribe and we will have cars. Every German. The cars are just waiting."

"I see no one getting these cars they promise. All I see are photographs of them. Like that nincompoop's rows of cardboard tanks."

"But the tanks are now real. And the government gave every German house a radio. You have one over there. Look. See? Soon you will have an automobile, too."

"I see. I see more than you do. They gave us radios to listen to their talk of power and strength, about their enemies and about their ideals, which are nothing but laws of absolutes. How can this be good for Germany? I tell you, you cannot trust these men."

"You said yourself that the men behind Hitler are the fanatics. They will not last."

"Nein. This is an ugly thing, Frederich."

"You were a soldier. It is a noble profession."

"Noble?" His father's fist slammed down on the table, and he stood up, looking down at him. "Can you be my son? How can you ignore what is happening? Do you not see the demonstrations? Do you not listen?"

"It is only propaganda . . . for the world to see, not for Germans."

"You believe this?"

"Ja."

"Your mother and I went to the theater last night. They kept the doors shut and guarded during the newsreels and during the Reich's films. Why do they lock the doors if this is not for Germans?"

Rheinholdt had only looked at his father.

"And tell me this, are Joseph and his father not Germans? Did the security police not come to the bank last month?"

"They came only to question them about some foreign accounts."

"And when they left, Joseph and his father were wearing the Jewish Star on their clothes. Joseph cannot remove it. Your friend. Your own sister's husband must wear this thing. What do you think will happen to her, to his family and their children?"

"Liesel is not Jewish. No one will harm Joseph or his father. The bank is too important to the city. Those foolish stars are only from Goebbels's bitterness. They mean nothing."

"You are young. You do not know. War is coming. I know what war is. I have seen it. I have been in a foxhole filled with my comrades' bodies. I have had the sun come up on a battlefield and looked down to see blood on my hands. War is young men ordered to kill strangers by strangers, for plots of land that matter little to those who kill and are killed. You, my son, will be part of war, perhaps part of creating it."

His father slumped down in his chair like a puppet with broken strings, which was unlike him. He was a strong, stubborn, and outspoken man. After a minute he covered his face with his hands and said quietly, "You will shame me."

Rheinholdt did not join.

His father died two years before the German Army invaded Poland. Four months before that, Rheinholdt was conscripted into the German Army, after the banking house he'd worked for became part of the government.

The army took him away from home, away from his daughters and wife. All he wanted, in truth, was for this war to be done and to go home alive. He also felt it was his own responsibility to see that his men went home to their families alive.

He put Renate's tooth back inside the envelope and set it near the photograph. For a few minutes he sat there, his elbows resting on his knees as he tried to remember what home looked like.

"Herr Leutnant?" The corporal was standing outside his tent.

"Come in."

"Here is the information you wanted for Fusilier Hoffman. He was from Bavaria, the town of Altomünster."

Rheinholdt took the address. "Thank you, Gefreiter."

The corporal left and Rheinholdt pulled his paybook from his back pocket and balanced it on his knees. He flipped it open and pulled some folded sheets of writing paper from the side pocket, then spread the paper out on a footlocker and took out a pen.

He had only written one other letter of condolence, before he came to North Africa. He rolled the pen in his fingers. The words seemed too difficult to find.

The paybook slipped; it fell through his legs, onto the ground. He dropped the pen on the footlocker, bent, and picked up the book, then set it next to the writing paper. The pages fanned open to the book's center. There, printed in bold letters, was the slogan:

The German Army Is Invincible!

He stared at it for a long time, then picked up the pen again.

Perhaps the Wehrmacht was invincible, but he had to write to the parents of an eighteen-year-old boy and tell them that that their son was not.

"SHOO SHOO BABY"

It was getting cold out. Once the sun went down, the air had cooled quickly. Kitty rubbed her arms, but kept moving alongside Cassidy, who didn't say much except to guide her around obstacles. Sharp, brittle weeds snagged her cotton stockings and her useless shoes—spectators with little holes along the seams and heels that sank. Her steps were constantly unsteady.

She stumbled again.

Cassidy's hand steadied her, and he said, "It's damned dark out here. I can't see my hand in front of my face."

"Me either."

She laughed when he said nothing else. "It's okay, Cassidy. You're not going to offend me if you laugh at my blind jokes. I've lived this way a long time. Stand still for a minute, please." She used his shoulder to brace herself and pulled off a shoe, then turned it upside-down and shook the dirt out of it. "My biggest problem is these shoes. They were good on the sandy slopes. The heels dug in and kept me from slipping down, but they're bad on this uneven ground."

"Give me your shoes."

She did, then heard a cracking snap. "What are you doing?"

"Here. Try this on."

She ran her hand over the shoe. The heel was gone. "Better?"

"I think so. Here's the other one."

She heard the same cracking sounds before he started talking again. "I don't want to stop until we get across this plain and into the cover of those trees."

"Thanks." She slid on the shoe. "I'm fine. Let's go."

"I'll take a drink from that canteen." He slipped it off her shoulder. After a moment he said, "All set."

"What about the canteen?"

"I'll carry it. You ready?"

"Sure, it's a walk in the park."

He laughed and they moved on.

The night air changed from a cool threat to cold and icy reality. For what felt like a few hours, they trudged across a giant plain of dirt that was hard or soft in turns, whenever you were just getting used to one or the other. The land was covered with brush that crackled like tumbleweeds and stones bigger than her feet.

Finally, she could feel the softness of grass underfoot instead of hard ground. Soon after, she inhaled the scent of pistachio trees. A blister on the side of her toe popped a few minutes later; she could feel the wetness and the sharp, burning pain of raw skin against shoe leather.

Please let him stop soon.

After about ten minutes more she was dragging that foot.

He stopped. "You're limping."

"I'm okay. Wait! Put me down."

"No."

"I'm blind, not lame."

"Don't argue."

"You can't carry me. Please, I want to walk."

"It's faster this way. And if you keep arguing with me about it, I'll just throw you over a shoulder."

"I would prefer to walk."

Silence. Long silence. So she locked her arms around his neck and let her tootsies enjoy the ride.

He carried her for a good half hour, and he wasn't even winded. She didn't know if that impressed her or annoyed her. He stopped. "This is far enough." He faced her. "Go ahead and sit down here. You're on soft grass. I need to check out something."

She heard him walking away, but then he stopped suddenly. "There's a tree at three o'clock. About six feet away."

"Thank you." She moved closer to the tree and sat down in the grass. She was freezing and took off her shoes and rubbed her cold feet, then chafed her arms.

He came back. "This looks like a good spot."

She could feel him looking at her.

"Cold?"

"Freezing." She shivered and stood up. "The ground is even colder than the air." She paced in front of the tree, because moving kept her warm.

"Give me a few minutes to get something to burn, and I'll make a fire. We're between dimples in the hills, so I'm not so worried about it being seen."

She stopped. "Don't we want to be seen? I thought you took the interior roads to lose Von Heidelmann."

"I'm not taking any chances. He might have enough

men to send in all directions. The sooner we're out of here, the better. Now I've just got to figure out how the hell we're going to do that."

"Why?"

"What do you mean 'why'?"

"Surely the plane will come back."

He laughed at her. "You're kidding, right?"

"No."

He laughed harder.

"I take it from your reaction the plane won't be coming back at the same time tomorrow."

"No."

"I don't understand. If we weren't there waiting for them as planned, then they have to know we're still here. Logic says we'd be waiting."

"Or dead."

She flinched.

"There aren't regular daily flights scheduled for planes used in covert operations." His tone was snide and officious.

She drew herself up and faced him. "Don't treat me like I'm stupid. I asked an honest question. I'm not an idiot. I just don't understand how these things work, okay?"

He was quiet and she knew he was looking at her. "You ask a lot of questions, Kincaid."

"Yes, I do. I had to learn to ask questions a long time ago. The things you take for granted, Cassidy, things like the trees and the grass and sky, I can't see." She could feel her voice rising, and she didn't like it. She sounded shrewish, so she stopped and took a deep breath. "Look, if I don't ask questions, I can't make adjustments."

"Okay. Okay. I get it. Truce. I don't know what it's like to be blind. You don't know anything about the Army."

"If the plane isn't coming back, what do we do?"

"We stay here tonight and then we keep walking."

"Keep walking where?"

"As far away from where you were as we can."

The man was a fount of information. She had six brothers who used that same tone of voice. Asking more questions would only get her more smart answers and no information other than the concrete knowledge that men could be horses' asses. She gave up and leaned against a tree. The trunk was warmer than the air and the ground.

"I wish the hell I could clearly remember the layout on those maps. Damn."

She reached into her pocket and pulled out the maps. "Here." She tossed them toward his voice.

He didn't say a word, but she heard his step and the crinkle of the maps when he picked them up and unfolded them.

"These shoes are killing me." She braced her palm against the tree trunk and reached down, then pulled off her left shoe. Half bent over, she touched the broken blisters with her finger and winced.

"These are my maps." He was looking at her. "How'd you get them?"

"I knocked them out of the truck when I slid across the seat to get out." She straightened and pulled out the bent compass. "This too." She held it out. "I stepped on it, but it doesn't feel broken."

He took the compass.

"I was going to give them back to you earlier, but you were busy in the back of the truck with the gas and were concerned about missing the plane. From the way you barked at me I decided it was more prudent to wait. Until you just mentioned them, I forgot I even had them."

"Sweetheart . . ." A second later he swept her into his arms and spun her around. "You might just have saved our necks. What a peach!"

"Put me down, you idiot." She had to laugh a little. "And for godsakes, don't mention food. I'm so hungry I could eat my hand."

He set her on her feet.

"Cassidy?"

"Yeah?"

"Are any nuts on those pistachio trees?"

He took a few steps. "Nope. Not a single one. But here." He moved closer, then took her hand and slapped something flat and rectangular into it. "It's a chocolate bar."

"Chocolate? Oh, God . . ." She lifted it to her nose and smelled it. "Thank you. And thank you, Mr. Hershey!" She tore off the wrappers, laughing. "In any normal situation I adore chocolate, but now, oh . . . this is heavenly." She stopped chewing and broke off another piece. "Here. Taste it."

"No, thanks."

She stopped cramming another piece into her mouth. "Wait a second. We are sharing."

"Nope."

"Oh, no, you don't."

"What?"

"You're not going to go and get all noble and give the whole thing to me. You've got to be as hungry as I am. Take this."

"I don't want any."

"I insist."

"No."

"I won't eat it if you don't."

"Look, I don't like chocolate."

"Sure." She snorted. "How can anyone in their right mind not like chocolate? Take it."

"I'm allergic to it."

"I don't believe you."

"I get these blisters on my tongue and my throat. My stomach burns, and soon it's hard for me to breathe. Not exactly a nice thing to go through, Kincaid. You eat it. I don't want it."

He was describing an allergic reaction to a T. Poor man, couldn't eat chocolate. She didn't want to laugh. She should sympathize. Really. She should. She swallowed. Lord above, it tasted good, so smooth and sweet. She hesitated before eating it all. Perhaps she should save the rest of it for later.

"Eat the damn thing. If I get hungry, I'll roast a squirrel."

"A squirrel?"

"I spotted a couple in those trees. Squirrel tastes pretty good. Like wild duck or pheasant . . . well, they taste that way when they're cooked. Raw they're a little tough to chew and the blood has this . . . metallic taste, but you get used to it after a few mouthfuls." He paused. "You want one? I'll set a snare."

"No . . . no. I'm fine with the chocolate."

"Good. I'm going to get some wood and start that fire."

She sat there holding the rest of the candy. Her stomach was somewhere near her throat. Her only image of squirrels had been furry little things that lived in the magnolia trees in Long Beach. She pulled her legs up and wrapped her skirt over them, then tucked under the hem. She tried to find that same mental image of them again.

He was cracking off tree branches. She finished off the candy, listening to the rustle of the leaves and the dull thud when he tossed branches on the ground. His footsteps moved away until they disappeared altogether.

She was alone. Completely alone. She locked her hands around her knees. She was cold, but extremely lucky she wasn't colder.

As in dead cold—a thought that was pretty grounding. One mere step could change your life; one misstep could end it.

"Hey, Kincaid!" Cassidy came walking back over the rise.

She looked up.

"We're all set." He dropped the wood on the ground in front of her. "These branches are green, but there's enough dry brush a few hundred yards out there. Give me a minute, and you'll have your fire."

"Good." She heard a click and snap. A lighter. She could smell the fluid and then the cloud of smoke from green leaves and branches. The brush crackled. "It's really cold."

"It won't be for long." His voice came from a lower angle. He was squatting on the other side of the fire.

She heard the crackle of the brush and the sharp

snapping of green wood as the fire caught. The air turned warmer.

After a few minutes he came over and sat next to her. "Better?"

"Much. Thank you."

He put his arm around her and pulled against his side. "You'll be warmer this way."

They sat there, alone in the quiet. It had been a long, long time since a man had put his arm around her. Her brothers did it all the time—something she had just taken for granted, until she was in a foreign country where you were crushed together like ants in the marketplaces, but no one ever touched you with affection. The fire snapped and popped and flared.

"There's not much of a moon tonight," he said.

"I know."

She could feel him looking at her.

"How do you know?"

"Gee, Captain, that question just brought you up a notch in my respect."

"Why? Because I was so low on the scale before? Nowhere to go but up?"

She laughed with him. "No. You find a different truth in human nature when you aren't like everyone else. People don't want to know about something that frightens them. They avoid it—and you, if you're blind. They don't know how to deal with you. They don't know what to say, so they say nothing. Some refer to you in the third person. Some shout at you, as if your loss of sight means you can't hear either."

"Like the American in Paris who can't speak French. They just yell their English louder."

"Exactly. The worst ones are those who treat you as if you've lost your brain instead of the ability to see clearly."

"You're a smart cookie. That was what I first noticed about you back at the Kasbah. You didn't panic. You didn't get hysterical. You used your head."

"Well, I suppose you have to factor in that I couldn't see the drop below, so hanging on that rope was probably easier for me than for a woman with full vision."

"Don't sell yourself short, sweetheart."

She smiled. "Thanks."

"You didn't answer my question."

"About what I can see?"

"Yeah."

"Not just a solid wall of black like people think. Me, for instance. I have macular problems. They aren't sure why. There are diseases that affect vision, like diabetes and Stargardt's. But they've ruled those out. My father believes it has something to do with the fact that I was born prematurely, a month early, but really, no one knows what happened, only that it happened.

"I see colors, shades and shadows, a smeared landscape; it's as if someone put Vaseline on my eyes. I can look into the sky and see the light and vague shapes. I'm lucky, really. I know what the moon looks like, because I could see until I was thirteen."

"Thirteen? You were just a kid. That must have been tough."

"It made me tough."

"I suppose it would."

She looked up at him. "Right now, when it's dark and the only light is from the fire, I can't see your face, only a fuzzy silhouette. I know it's there. In the daylight, I can see more. For example, I already know a lot about your physical traits. Just from the last twenty-four hours."

"Okay, go ahead. Spill the details."

"You're over six feet tall. Probably one ninety-five, give or take five pounds. Thirty-four inseam. Thirty-two waist. Size eleven shoe. Shirt size . . . sixteen and a half, thirty-four."

She could feel his reaction. "Surprised you, didn't I? What I can't see with my eyes, I see with my hands, with my ears, nose, and mouth, paying attention to things in ways sighted people don't need to."

"You're damned close there, sweetheart. Six-two. Thirty-three inseam and thirty-four waist. Two hundred and four, but I've probably lost five pounds in the last twenty-four hours."

She was laughing. "Life is so unfair. I couldn't lose five pounds if I stopped eating for a week."

"You're not supposed to. Women should be round and soft."

"Keep it up, Cassidy. You're moving up the scale."

"Men like something to hang on to."

"Oops, you dropped a half a notch."

"I was paying you a compliment."

"You were thinking about sex."

"There's nothing wrong with sex. Hell, that's why we're here. At least that's why I'm here."

She laughed. "I bet it is, and that all the women fall all over you in your dress uniform."

"I do okay." He shifted, drawing his legs up, then stood. She felt the cool air almost instantly, like when you first open the icebox door.

"I've got to put more wood on the fire. For light, so I can take a good look at those maps." He took a few steps, then hesitated. "You okay?"

She nodded. "Sure."

"Get some sleep. We'll start out before sunrise tomorrow."

She scooted closer to the fire and lay down on her side, curled into a tight ball; then she adjusted her skirt. She slid her arm under her head.

A moment later she heard him open the maps.

Right then, she wanted to go home in the worst way. Home felt so very far away. She rested her head on her bent arm and stared at the fire. The foggy light from the flames undulated across a field of night darkness.

She closed her eyes and she was thirteen again, the time when her sight had deteriorated so quickly. She was standing at the top of the staircase, staring out at a smudged world of colors with no edges or outlines to define what she was seeing. She took that first step and misjudged it, then moments later lay at the bottom of the stairs on the hardwood floor, bones ringing, stunned, then ashamed and angry. She hadn't known her head was bleeding all over the floorboards and would need stitches.

There was no air in her lungs. She couldn't even yell or cry. Her throat and chest were a vacuum. Her brothers stood above her, shouting at each other and her all at once, their voices panicked and louder than normal—which was somewhere in the decibel range of a train wreck.

But the worst part hadn't been her cracked head or her sore body. It hadn't been the humiliation or the fear in her brothers' arguing voices. The worst part was that she couldn't see their faces. There was nothing before her but a misty, flesh-toned blur with small spots of shadows she supposed were eyes and noses, the moving shadows mouths. Her blindness was suddenly real. It was the first time she had felt truly helpless.

"SUNRISE SERENADE"

Last night, if anyone had told Kitty she would be grateful for the cold, she'd have told them they were nuts. Now, however, she would have loved to be cold again. Cassidy got her up before dawn, when the air was still chilly. But they were quickly on the move, so she wasn't uncomfortable then at all.

They'd left the shelter of the treed foothills and moved across some low, rolling hills covered in thorny bushes and scattered rocks. At least two hours into the other side, Cassidy found some ripened dates on a palm near a small well, where they rested and drank water that tasted so metallic it almost came back up on the first swallow.

She thought they should stay there, and said as much, but Cassidy told her he had other plans. She didn't argue after she'd thought about it. A well in this lone area of the pre-Sahara didn't necessarily ensure that someone would find them. Or if they did, that that same someone wouldn't be big trouble for them. Yes, if they stayed at the well, they would have food and water, but no papers if the Vichy were to find them. And how would Cassidy explain his being there at all?

Now they had been walking for what felt like hours. She was soaked with sweat and limping. The sun was up and shining so intensely it felt to her as if it had grown ten times its size.

Her skin stung. He told her she was red as a Maine lobster and tried to give her his undershirt, but she told him to use it himself and took off her slip instead, then tied it around her head and the left side of her face. She stuffed her stockings into her pocket. Her girdle was miles behind her.

"You've been awfully quiet, Kincaid. Watch your step. There's a rock at nine o'clock."

"I was just thinking."

"I thought I heard a loud clunk back there."

"Funny."

"Yeah. It was."

She slowed down and felt his hand on the small of her back as he guided her in a slightly different direction.

"This way." He took a few more steps, then grasped her arm. "Stop for a minute."

"Why?"

"Here, take this." He grabbed her hand. "It's another salt pill. Here's the canteen."

She swallowed the pill with only a small sip of water. "Are you taking these tablets, too?"

"It wouldn't do us much good if I pass out. Sit here for a second. There's a large rock at six o'clock."

"You don't have to keep stopping for me. I'm okay."

"You're limping, and I need to look at the maps again."

She moved to the rock, which was hot, so she leaned

against it and untied the slip, then rubbed her wet hair. "You're staring at me."

"Yeah, I am."

"Is something wrong?"

"No. You're being quiet again."

"Is that a problem?"

"Throws me off when you're not hammering me with questions."

"If you think that's going to get a rise out of me, you're wrong. I'm stronger than you think. I'm not going to wilt like some fragile flower."

He just laughed quietly.

"What's so funny?"

"Never once have I thought of you as wilting, Kincaid."

"Thank you." She didn't say anything for a few minutes, before she admitted, "I was being quiet because I was thinking about college. I went to Stanford."

"Of course Arnan Kincaid's daughter would go to Stanford."

"That's not true."

"It isn't?"

"No. I could have gone to Harvard.

"So how about you? Tell me where you learned all those languages."

"English, no explanation there. Spanish from my grandmother, who was Castilian. French from my mother, whose parents were from the Loire Valley. Latin in high school. German in college."

"Which college?"

"West Point."

"I should have guessed."

"So how does the steppe of Morocco remind you of Stanford University? Seems like night and day to me."

"It is. I was thinking about the night before my graduation. A group of us were in the dorm, drinking rum and Coca-Cola—which I'd kill for right now—and there was this huge globe in our room which, from my perspective, was pretty worthless, except as a clothes hanger. That night my roommate Susan taped a pencil to the wooden arm that held the globe in place and we took turns spinning it, the idea being wherever it stopped would be the place of our destiny."

"No melodrama there."

"We were young."

"You still are."

"Okay, younger. We felt the world was calling us, opening its arms and saying come here. I had such dreams. Paris and Rome, Egypt and Singapore."

"So where'd it land when it was your turn?"

"Wait, you're jumping ahead. Susan's stopped on Copenhagen. Katie near Athens. Joyce in Tuscany and Nancy got Buenos Aires."

"And you?"

"Pocatello, Idaho."

He laughed with her. "They could have been lying to you."

"They were laughing too hard to be lying. I had the biggest dreams. Besides, they would never take advantage of my blindness. It would have been the last thing they would have done to me as a joke. Susan was a lit major whose dream was to be the next Willa Cather. She said she wanted to visit me there because Pocatello isn't all that far from Ketchum, where Hemingway has a place. She thought he was a brilliant writer. Anyway, as I was walking along, I was thinking this is certainly not Pocatello, Idaho."

"No, it's not."

"So." She straightened. "Where are we going, again?"

"There's a Vichy military camp marked here on the map. We should be able to steal a truck and get the hell out of here." He took her hand. "Eat some more of these dates."

She ate a few, then dropped the rest into her pocket and ran her hands down her cotton skirt. "How much farther is it?"

"If my calculations are right, I'd say just over that ridge."

"That ridge?" She laughed, pointing off in one direction. "Or the other ridge?" She turned and pointed in the opposite direction.

"I keep forgetting you can't see."

"I take that as a compliment."

"Good, then let's go." He took her arm and they walked straight into the sun.

It was hours later when they stood side by side on what Cassidy told her was an escarpment above the Vichy camp.

"Don't go any farther forward, Kincaid. We're close to the edge."

"Do you see anything?"

"Not much. This Vichy camp is only one stone building and—" Cassidy paused. "About a hundred yards past it is something that looks like a cross between a lean-to and a barn."

"No cars or trucks? Nothing?"

"There's something. One of everything. A car, a couple of tanks, some planes."

"Great!"

"The car is an ancient Fiat; it's resting on its bare axle behind the stone building. There's not a wheel or a tire in sight. The two tanks look like they're nothing but shells, and the planes are the kind that failed during the Spanish Civil War. Two of them are missing propellers."

"Why would they only have tank shells?"

"As decoys. This place is no longer an active army camp. The equipment isn't Vichy or German, but Italian."

Kitty touched his shoulder. "Do you hear that?"

"An engine just started."

"It sounds like a truck."

He turned away from her. "Yeah . . . there it is, coming out of the barn, a two-and-a-half-ton truck, and it's heading for the other building."

She listened to it rumble along, and moments later she heard the brakes squeal to a stop. A horn honked and there was a pause; then she heard men's voices and the sounds of them climbing inside the truck. The door slammed shut. The driver ground into gear and drove away. "Where are they heading?"

"Off toward the mountains in a cloud of dust."

"Is that good or bad?"

"They're not here, so I suppose that's good. But I won't know till I get down there and look around. If there's only a guard or two, then lady luck's with us. But if that truck was the only vehicle down there that runs—and that's how it looks right now—we're in trouble." He touched her forearm.

She noticed he did that more and more frequently, gave her a sign that he was there. Funny, how you could know some people for years and they'd never think to show you that one, small consideration.

"I need you to wait here while I go down and see what's there. I won't be long."

"Okay." She hesitated, then said, "Cassidy?"

"Yeah?"

"What if you get caught?"

"I won't."

"But suppose you do." She waited for his answer, but got none.

He'd already left.

She stood there for a few minutes, then sat down on the ground and stretched her legs out in front of her. Cassidy was interesting. He certainly didn't have a problem with confidence. Her impressions of him were mixed at first. Stubborn, aggressive, egocentric, all negatives in her mind at first, but were they negatives? Egocentric? Or courageous? Stubborn? Or determined? Aggressive? Or heroic?

He was a stranger who put his life on the line to get her safely home. He'd said he was just doing his job. His job was war. The business of war was not for the weak.

She felt weak, and it annoyed her to no end. To her, *weak* meant *needy*. She disliked needy people. She hated to admit that she couldn't do things. She'd learned to love her independence, to wear it like a wall surrounding her loss of sight.

But the truth was that she couldn't see her way out of a minefield.

She couldn't find a path out of the wilderness of the pre-Sahara.

She couldn't find food or build a fire, so if something happened to Cassidy, she didn't know what she would do.

Maybe twenty minutes passed before he came walking back over the ridge, whistling—of all things—"The Lullaby of Broadway."

"I take it from that happy little tune coming out of your mouth that you found something to get us out of here."

"Sure did." He took her arm. "Come on, Kitty. Let's make like a cat and scat."

She groaned, but let him tug her along. "There aren't any guards?"

"Just one. But he's all tied up right now."

"You know that puns are the lowest form of humor."

"Yeah, but they're damn funny. Come on." He steered her down to flatter terrain. He moved fast. To stay up with him she had to half run. The ground was hard as cement, but not rocky like most of the land they'd passed. He was running now, pulling her with him. "We're almost there."

The cool relief of a shadow crossed her face as they went inside a building that smelled of oil and gasoline and mechanics.

"Here it is. Our ticket home."

"What is it?"

"A Spanish-built biplane with a Fiat V-12 that purrs around six hundred horse power. It's the same thing as a CR-32."

"My eyes are glazing over."

He laughed. "You don't know much about planes."

"All I know is that everyone seems to refer to them by

letters and numbers I can't make much sense out of."

"It's called a Chirper, an HA-132-L Chirri. They were used in the Spanish Civil War. Stay here." He put her hands on what felt like a wing, then jumped up on it. "I'll have to help you up and into the seat. Give me your hand." He pulled her up and slipped his arm around her waist. "The upper wing is longer than the lower, so watch yourself. It's been converted into a two-seater. Lucky for you, bad for me."

"Why?"

"You won't have to sit on my lap."

"Thank God for small favors."

"Yeah, and after I tried to find a working engine in every single-seater out in that field."

"Cassidy . . ."

"What?"

"Don't start."

"The question is, will this engine start? Move back two feet and grab the wing support." He placed her hand on a metal rod. "Steady?"

She nodded.

"Good." He let go of her, then climbed up onto the fuselage. "Give me your hands and I'll pull you up and into the seat." He grabbed her wrists in a tight grip and dropped her into a small cockpit with a low seat.

"Shift your right hip. You're sitting on the belt."

She pushed his hands away. "I can get it." She buckled in.

"Pull your underwear off your head. I have a leather helmet you need to put on."

"It's my slip, not my underwear." She wadded the slip up and tucked it into her belt.

He slapped the helmet on her head.

She batted his hands away. "I can get it."

He tapped the right side of her helmet while she buckled the straps. "This ear cup is part of a Gosport tube, for communication between cockpits. If I need to talk to you, I'll shout through my mouthpiece and you'll hear it from this earpiece."

"How do I talk back to you?"

"You don't. It's only one-way communication."

"Ah . . . a male invention."

"You got it. Pretty ingenious. I talk. You listen. Worst comes to worst, lean forward and beat on the rim of the cockpit or kick the floor panels to get my attention." He reached inside and put something on the floor, then straightened. "I couldn't find any chutes, so you might want to say a quick prayer when we take off."

"You're doing this on purpose, aren't you?"

"What?"

"Never mind."

The plane rocked as he climbed into the front seat. He turned around. "The engine looks good on this little baby. As far as I can tell, it's not missing a single thing."

"As far as you can tell? Oh, God . . ."

"What's wrong?" He was facing her. "You afraid to fly?"

"Do you know what you're doing?"

"Sure." He turned back around. "I'm going to fly us out of here."

"I meant how much do you know about planes? How many flying hours do you have? Would you know if anything were missing?"

Her questions were immediately lost in the sound of

him trying to start the engine, which made a sick, whining sound that got louder and louder, then coughed into consumptive silence. A few minutes and several tries later, the engine was running, and stayed running.

Through the earpiece came the hollow sound of his voice. "Get ready, sweetheart. We're going to make like a bird and fly."

Perhaps praying was a good idea.

The plane rolled out into the daylight, which was no longer bright. The air was sticky. She could taste rain coming. The wind felt like it was coming out of the northwest. He turned the plane until the wind was at their back. The engine noise was such she barely heard his warning, "Here we go!"

They bounced and bobbed over the ground, the plane shimmying enough that she wondered if it were made of toothpicks. The engine was so loud she kept her head down and gripped the rim for all she was worth. On and on they went rolling toward a takeoff, faster and faster, until it felt like flying was the last thing this plane could do. She didn't know if that made her worried or relieved.

Then the plane lifted, taking her stomach up with it for a few feet, then bounced down hard on the ground, skipped back up in the air, and down again. The next time it lifted, she braced herself for the drop again, but they were in the air and climbing. Before long he banked the plane, then leveled out.

"We're heading northeast. I want to make certain we clear the mountains; then we'll circle back and fly this baby south along the coastline."

She couldn't say anything, because he couldn't hear

her. She just held on and prayed God was on her side. The wind blew hard against her face and the air was cooling off quickly. The plane skidded along the air currents, until it got bumpy.

"I'm going to take her up."

They were climbing again, and the air temperature was really dropping fast.

"There are clouds coming over those mountains. Looks like a storm. I'm going to take her up higher. But don't worry, Kincaid, we'll fly around this weather. Next stop, Gibraltar, and before you know it, you'll be home sweet home."

A moment later raindrops splattered onto her face.

"THERE'S SOMETHING IN THE AIR"

For over an hour, J.R. tried to fly around the storm, heading southeast at an altitude high enough to clear the mountains. But the storm was a doozy, and it overtook them with breakneck speed.

Next, he tried to go over it, but climbing in altitude meant being batted around. Something like a flea in a hurricane. Upstairs, the turbulence was hell.

He had no idea where they were. They were completely socked in by dark, roiling clouds, lashing rain, and wind that bounced them all over the place and made the plane skip like a dull needle on a scratched record.

"If you're okay back there, Kincaid, stomp on the floor panels!"

There was a loud *thump, thump, thump!*

"Good." They'd been communicating like this for a few hours. The engine noise was constant, loud, and exhaust came back at them whenever the wind changed. The plane bounced over the rough air, sometimes dropping a few hundred feet. He was doing his damned best to keep it together.

The plane dropped like a rock. He fought with the controls, pulling back on the stick, his feet on the rudders. "Hang on! Nothing to worry about!"

Thump! Thump! Thump! Thump! Thump! Thump!

Hell, she didn't buy it. She was too smart for his good.

They'd been in the air for a long time, lurching along and buffeted by wind and rain. He had no land or sun to get his bearings. Just dark clouds and a sky full of weather. Rain pelted his face and his eyes. He had to keep wiping them to see. His chest was aching from inhaling the exhaust. His head began to pound. The rain got worse, soaking him, lashing down. It was cold and wet and rough flying.

He liked his thrills, but this was more than he bargained for. He looked down. He saw nothing. His arms and hands were getting numb. The thigh muscle in his right leg had been cramping for a while. To top it off, it was getting darker.

The fuel gauge had read three-quarters full when he'd found the plane. He'd checked the tank before he'd gotten Kitty, and it had looked right to him. But he knew plane hadn't been maintained and the oil was old. He wasn't sure the gauges worked.

He could barely see the gauges in the rain. He wiped his eyes with his sleeve and looked again. "Jesus," he said aloud. "What the hell is wrong with these needles?"

Thump! Thump! Thump!

Crap . . . she'd heard him. He ignored her and watched the gauges.

Thump! Thump! Thump!

He still ignored her.

Thump! Thump! Thump!

He pretended everything was fine by lightly whistling.

Thump! Thump! Thump!

"Okay! Okay!" he shouted into the mouthpiece. "Stop hammering your feet, Kincaid. The needles on the gauges are all over the place. I don't know why, but don't worry; we'll just ride this storm out. Everything's fine. Relax."

Thump! Thump!

Yeah, he thought. It sounded like bullshit to him, too.

They bucked along for another half an hour or so. Then, amazingly, the rain stopped as quickly as it'd started. The wind softened to an easy drift. Smooth flying. The air grew warmer, and the clouds mistier; they changed from dark, to gray, to puffy cotton-white.

Just as suddenly, they flew out of the cotton and into a pink-and-blue sky. The sun cut into his eyes, orange and huge and blinding him for a moment.

He blinked. It was setting on his right, a huge fireball dropping down the sky.

Okay . . . that meant they were flying southeast.

He looked down, then shoved the stick forward and brought the plane a couple thousand feet lower, where the clouds were loose and scattered and he could see the ground below.

It was like looking into a hall of mirrors, seeing only the same thing again and again: a sea of orange sand, dune after rippling dune, the crests of them still damp and steaming from the rain.

He circled around twice, checked out the horizon. There were a few hills to the west, and there was one bruised mountain range turning purple from the sunset in the distance. In every other direction was just desert, the great, unending Sahara Desert.

He looked at the dials on the control panel; they were still shimmying all over the place.

Now what?

He didn't have a clue where the hell they were. He checked the fuel gauge. Three-quarters full. Same as takeoff. Yeah . . . right. He circled again.

"You okay back there?"

Thump!

"Good."

The hairs on his neck suddenly stood on end. Something was off. A slight miss in the engine, like the spark plugs were bad.

But the engine sounded fine. Felt fine. No glitch.

He questioned himself and wasn't certain if he heard it or if he'd felt it in the engine reverberation coming through the stick.

Maybe he'd just imagined it. He tightened his grip on the stick. Still nothing but the even hum of the engine against his hand. To his ears, the engine sounded loud but fine. Unfortunately, the exhaust was still his close friend.

Just stay in the air, baby. Just stay sweet.

He circled again, then headed north, thinking they might be close to the coast. He studied the horizon.

The engine missed, just one, minute sound—a chip in the hum of the motor. He glanced at the dials.

The engine stopped.

He swore and hit the starter.

Nothing.

"Oh, God, what happened!" she screamed.

"Stay calm, dammit!"

Hit it again.

Nothing.

"We're going to crash!"

"Shut up!" He tried to start it again. "Everything will be okay! A-okay! We're not going to crash. I can land it."

He had no choice . . . a dead-stick landing or they were dead ducks. He eased the control stick forward and hung his head out the side, watching the ground come up to meet him.

The sound of her muffled voice broke through his concentration. She was swearing like a stevedore.

He watched the dunes fly under them as the plane went lower and lower. He saw a level spot, short, but possible. He headed for it, down, down, where the plane slipped into a crevice between the dunes.

They hit hard.

Momentum sent him forward. The seat straps bit into his shoulders and hips.

He stood on the brakes, held the stick in both hands.

Skidding through the sand, it showered up around them, then over them. He couldn't see a thing.

The plane was slowing, slowing. He fought to keep it straight, sand in his face and eyes and then, in his mouth.

He started to choke, then cough. His foot slipped.

Damn!

The plane tipped forward, then tilted over the edge of a dune, where it hung, nose down, for one of those life-defining moments, then flipped over and slid down the other side.

'LET'S GET AWAY FROM IT ALL'

"Kincaid?"

"What?"

"You okay?"

"I don't know. Let me look."

"Funny."

"I can't see a thing."

"I take it from all these smart-ass remarks, you're not hurt."

"No. I'm just confused."

"Confused?"

"This doesn't feel like home, Captain. It feels like we're upside-down in a sand dune."

"We are." He released his seat belt, shrugged off the straps, and crawled out, sliding through the sand and under the broken W bracing on the right wing. The plane was tilted toward the down side of a sand dune that was a good twenty or thirty feet tall. "You're lucky you've still got your head attached."

"I ducked. My survival instinct kicked in."

"Quick thinking."

"Not really. I ducked down right after the engine stopped and you told me everything was going to be okay. 'A-okay.' Did you know that when you're lying, your voice gets this certain . . . don't-mess-with-me-I'm-trying-to-think tone?"

"I wasn't lying."

"Oh, sure. Everything's going to be okay. A-okay."

"You're alive. I'd leave it at that."

She didn't say anything for a full minute. "Do you think that God might have it in for one of us? First we're hanging off a tower while some Nazi smokes a cigarette at what . . . three A.M.? The truck has a flat tire. We run out of gas next to a minefield. Then Sabri drives over a mine and blows clear to Kingdom Come—God rest his poor soul—along with your military-hero stuff. . . ."

Military hero-stuff? She was lucky she couldn't see him right then.

". . . We're stuck in that same minefield. The signal flare doesn't work. We miss the rendezvous plane. We walk halfway to Cairo to steal a truck, and instead, find only a plane. We take off just as a storm blows in which promptly sends us off course. We fly out of the storm and what next? The engine quits and we crash in the desert."

"Are you through?"

"Yes."

"That was quite a speech."

"Don't you have anything to say about this mess we're in?"

"No. I'd say you covered it pretty well."

"I think serious prayer, confession, and groveling for forgiveness might be in order here."

"If you think it will help, go ahead. Pray yourself hoarse," he said.

"Me? I meant you." She was waiting.

She could wait all damn day. "You must drive your family nuts."

"I sure hope so. It's the only way one girl in a family of seven men can survive. I've stood in the middle of my six brothers and listened to them argue about what I should do, without, mind you, them ever once asking me what I think. My father is not that way, but it's been my experience that you men have a propensity for needing to tell us women what we should do . . . as if we are mindless creatures who can't think for ourselves."

"It's thinking that got you into this, sweetheart."

"No. My thinking got me stuck in a Moroccan Kasbah. Your thinking got me in the middle of God only knows where."

"We're in the desert."

"Thank you. I didn't know that."

She was working really hard to piss him off.

"You have nothing to say?"

"Why? You're doing a great job."

"I'm trying to pick a fight with you, Cassidy."

"It's not working."

"I know, which is even more maddening than that cool, calm voice of yours. How can you be so calm about this?"

"Probably because I'm already out of the plane."

"See? You do that on purpose."

"Do what?"

"Don't be obtuse. You know exactly what I'm talking about. Would you please get me out of here? The blood is rushing to my head."

"Give me a minute to look around and make sure everything's okay. A-okay."

"Ducky," she muttered. "I can't wait to see what goes wrong next."

"I thought you were so independent. Where's your sense of adventure, Kincaid?"

"I lost it somewhere between that minefield and this plane crash. Will you please get me out of here?"

"If you'll just be quiet for a minute, I'll be able to help you out."

"Is that an ultimatum? If I'm not quiet, you'll leave me here? I don't think so. I'm unbuckling this seat belt. I don't need your help, Cassidy."

"Don't! This is serious. I'm not playing some game with you. The plane's at a bad angle. Just let me figure out the best way to pull you out of there without dislodging it." He crawled under the wing, then turned over onto his back to see if the wing was even remotely secure.

The sand spilled out from under him. He started to slide and grabbed the wing.

A big mistake.

His weight pulled it back to the down side of the hill. He let go and rolled away.

The whole damn plane started to slide.

She screamed.

"Oh, God . . . Cassidy! I'm sorry, really. I'll be quiet. I promise. Just get me out of here!"

"Stay buckled in. Don't move. Don't panic."

The plane stopped sliding, but it was looking pretty unstable. It could go again anytime. The sand was fine and loose as salt.

Now what? He walked around the plane, studying its angles, then stopped. He scratched his itchy beard.

"The plane didn't shift when you got out. I think I should just try it."

"Wait. I've got an idea. I'm going to tilt the left wing back downhill and try to get its tip wedged into the sand. You stay still. Completely still. If the plane starts to slide again, just curl into a tight ball like you did before and let it take you down the sand dune. Okay?"

"Okay."

He walked around to the other side of the plane, then toward the tail. He climbed on, straddled it, and the plane slid down a few more feet.

She swore.

"Trust me and hold on a little longer." He gripped the tail wheel and used his weight to dig the vertical fin into the sand up to the stabilizers. Fifty-fifty it would hold.

"What are you doing?"

"I already did it."

He eased up the underside of the fuselage, then sat hard on the left wing.

The plane rocked downward. The wing tip slid into the sand, but the nose suddenly began a slow slip.

The plane rotated downward to ten o'clock.

He sat there on the wing, waiting. Nothing shifted. He looked down at the wing tip. The sand was still wet, which gave it some weight. He eased off the down side of the wing, dug down to wet sand, and shoved more of it against the wing tip. He stood, walked back around to the rear seat, squatted down, and looked at her.

She was bent over and hugging her knees.

"Sit up slow and easy."

She did. The plane didn't shift at all. She let out a long, relieved breath.

He reached in, unbuckled the seat belt, and hauled her out, then rolled away from the plane.

He'd misjudged the angle.

Momentum sent them rolling down the dune, twisted together, over and over to the sound of grunts and groans, the jabs and knocks of elbows and knees. They hit the bottom and stopped rolling. He was on top, pinning her down, her body smashed against his, her face in his neck, her leg between his and her knee against his balls.

He shook his head. Sand went everywhere. He glanced up. The plane was still in place, so he looked down at her.

She had sand all over her face, like she'd been rolled in flour. She coughed twice, then spit out a mouthful of swear words that turned the air blue.

He was impressed and half laughing by the time she finished. "You know, I've never heard two of those. I don't think a human being could do that first one. And if we men could do the other, we wouldn't need women."

She rubbed the sand off her face and scowled.

"You okay?"

"I will be when you get off me."

He stood, then grasped her hand and pulled her to her feet.

She had fine sand all over her. While she was brushing it off, he turned toward the plane. It was wedged wrong side up into the edge of the dune. Its right wing was broken. The plane looked like a toy, one of those, flimsy, balsa-wood five-and-dime planes you stick together, throw in the air, and they soar all of three feet before they tumble headlong into a bush.

He glanced up. The sky was a deep purple and gold. "The sun's going down."

"I have sand everywhere. I think it's in my pores." She dusted off her hands and faced him. "So what do we do now?"

"We walk." He grabbed her hand. "Come on. Let's get up the dune so I can get an idea of where we are."

"WHERE IN THE WORLD"

Kitty stood next to Cassidy on top of the dune. The sand was so soft that her feet sank to the ankle. "So. Any ideas where we are?"

"The middle of nowhere. Stay here. I've got to get something out of the plane, then we'll start walking."

She turned and could feel the setting sun on her face, which was raw and burned and tight feeling. She rubbed her hand over her cheek. Fine sand was all over her face and hands. She tried to dust it off, but it stuck. She stretched her arms up, took a deep breath, then twisted from side to side. Her muscles ached, and her neck was sore. She shoved her hair back out of her face. It felt gummy from sweating and gritty from the sand.

It wasn't extremely hot, just warm and humid, and the sand was damp around her ankles from the storm. A couple of flies buzzed annoyingly around her face.

His footsteps on the sand sounded strange, not like beach sand, where each step sounded gritty. Here you could hear the sound of the sand slipping away, a grainy whisper as if someone were saying, "Shhhh . . ."

"I'm back. You okay?"

She nodded.

"All right. Let's start. It looks like a long walk. I've got the compass. We'll set off to the north and hope the coast is somewhere over those hills in the distance. Give me your hand. The dunes are high, with long drops."

They started walking, which wasn't easy. Her feet sank deeply. In some places, it was like wading through sand and she'd start to lose her balance.

"Lean forward," he told her. "It's easier."

He was right.

The air was growing cooler pretty fast. "It's getting dark, isn't it?"

"The best time to walk in the desert."

"Do you have a plan?"

"I know dying here isn't an option."

"Where are we?"

"Lost in the desert on the continent of Africa."

"Wait." She stopped. "I have an idea."

"What?"

"If we know how long we were in the air, couldn't we calculate the time and airspeed and get some idea of the possible locations? A certain radius on the map?"

"With the storm and our fluctuating airspeed, I can't even come close to making a guess."

"So we walk?"

"Yeah, we walk north. The coast is north."

"How far is it to those mountains we're walking toward?"

"A couple of days, if we stay at a steady walk."

"Oh." A couple of *days*? "How much water do we have?"

"The canteen holds a liter. Are you thirsty?"

"Not thirsty enough to take a drink. I'll wait and save it for later."

She didn't say anything else but concentrated on walking, and walking. First up, then, after she fell twice, they slid down the sand dune, which sounded easy. She found out it wasn't.

Sand got into everything. Clothes, nails, eyes, and nose. It stuck to the skin. You couldn't wipe it off, you just moved it around. She walked until she was getting winded and then walked more.

Cassidy didn't talk much. He just kept going, like some robot.

The night air helped motivate her. It was cold, very cold, so she didn't want to stop moving.

They didn't hurry, didn't change pace, but stayed at a constant speed, resting a few minutes every hour, when they would talk a little about home, sip lightly on the water and split the last six dates as if each one were a full meal.

By sunrise, she was exhausted and bloated from the salt tablets. She could feel the twinges deep in her abdomen and realized she might have her period again. Stress, she thought.

Ducky. . . . Just ducky.

He stopped finally. "Let's take a rest."

"Thank God." She fell back down into the sand.

"Here's the canteen. And one more salt tablet."

"I don't want another salt pill."

"Take it."

"No."

"Look. It's going to be hot today. Feel that sun? It's barely up and you can already feel it on your skin."

"It feels good. I've been cold all night."

"Remember that in two hours."

"Okay, okay. Give me the damned pill." She washed it down with a swig of the canteen and corked it. "Here. That's enough." She held it out to him. "I'd rather have more later."

He didn't take it.

She waited.

"Cassidy? Take the canteen."

"Wait. I want you to hold real still."

"Why?"

"Don't argue with me. Give me your other hand, but do it slowly. No quick motions."

"Oh. God . . ." She slowly raised her hand.

His hand slid over hers to her wrist. He jerked her forward so violently he almost pulled her arm from its socket.

She screamed and they fell backwards. Again. Rolling down the opposite side of the dune like they had before. Grunts and groans. They lay there tangled together. Again.

She pulled the hard canteen out from between them, sat up, coughed, and spit the sand from her mouth.

"You shouldn't scream when you're rolling in the sand."

"Thank you for that advice." She picked the sand from her tongue, then asked, "What was it? A scorpion? I already know every desert insect on a first-name basis."

"No. A snake."

"A snake?" She got up quickly.

"Don't worry. It was on the other side of the dune. Damned thing came side-winding over the hill right behind you."

She moaned and rubbed the sudden chills on her arms.

"Look. You wait here. I'm going to go get it."

"Get it? What on earth for?"

He was already climbing back up the sand dune. "We have no food. We need something to eat. A snake is fresh meat."

"I'd rather have fried chicken, thank you."

"One of the first things you learn about survival, Kincaid, is to forget about those things that make life worth living, and concentrate on the things that make life possible."

There was nothing she could say to that; it made perfect sense. She turned toward his voice. "I just thought of something."

"What?"

"Are you certain that snake is still up there? What if it comes slithering around the other side? I can't see anything, remember?" She waited.

No answer.

"Hey! Am I safe here?"

"It can't come toward you without me seeing it."

"Oh. Good." She listened to the shh-shh of his feet walking farther and farther away. "Cassidy?"

"Now what?"

"What if it bites you?"

"Then bury me deep, so the vultures can't pick at me!" he called back down at her.

"You are such a comedian," she muttered, and plopped back down onto the hillside. She rubbed her feet as she waited. After a minute, she turned her face to the sun. It was hot and going to get hotter. She pulled her slip out of her belt and tied it on her head again, fanning the lace hem over her face.

She got a good whiff of herself. Soap and water would be really nice. She sat there, daydreaming about a hot bath with a huge bar of hard-milled soap, big fluffy white towels and starched sheets, clean underwear and cleaner hair.

Cassidy slid down the dune. "I'm back."

"With or without the snake?"

"What do you think?"

"Just keep it away from me."

"I cut the head off. It can't hurt you."

"How are you going to cook it? Drag it behind us and let the sunshine bake the heck out of it?"

"Not a bad idea, Kincaid."

"I was kidding."

"I know. Look, I think we can make it to harder ground if we go on for a few more hours. I could see scrub and flatland through the binoculars. Scrub burns pretty well. We'll rest there, make a fire, cook and eat this thing. We need food. We've got to get over those mountains."

She got up. "Okay, then. Let's go."

Three hours later he was true to his word. They'd

made it to harder ground, and when he finally stopped, she sat down and picked the fleas off of her. Her legs were raw from scratching at bites and as if that weren't enough, flies swarmed everywhere. They buzzed at her mouth and nose and lit on her face. They were relentless. She was miserable and tired and hot. And Cassidy said he was pulling up bushes to burn.

"I can't believe we're building a fire when it must be one hundred and ten degrees. Where was the scrub brush last night when we needed it?"

He was whistling and stopped. "You want to eat the snake raw, we can."

"Good grief, no." She drove a hand through her knotted hair and winced, scratching her scalp. "These fleas are everywhere."

"Fleas in the day. Mosquitoes at night. Flies all the time."

"You'd think it would be too blasted hot for them." She took a deep breath and almost swallowed a fly. She wiped her lips. "I always knew insects were stupid."

"The smoke from the fire should help repel 'em."

A few minutes later she heard the crackle of burning brush. The smoke came at her, so she moved to her right. Before long she heard a sizzle. She could smell the snake cooking. She tried to decide if she was hungry enough to eat a snake. She was awfully hungry. It actually smelled like food.

He came over to her and squatted down in front of her, "Here. Take it." He placed something crispy in her palm. "That's the skin on the bottom."

She winced.

"Pretend it's fish skin."

Snake was snake. Dead, cooked, or alive.

"It tastes like chicken. Try it."

"That's what my brother told me when he ordered frog legs for me one night at the Brown Derby." She picked at the cooked meat. It was stringy and warm. She raised it to her nose and smelled it. Not too bad.

"You didn't like the frog legs?"

"They didn't taste like chicken any more than the escargot he made me eat tasted like steak. Dessert was great, though. Baked Alaska. It tasted nothing like an igloo."

He laughed.

"Do you like frog legs?" She finally took a bite.

"Sure, and escargot. It's food. Good food. You have to think of it as the meal, not what it was when it was alive."

She ate some more. "I couldn't catch a fish and then eat it. Used to drive my family nuts."

"What's your favorite breakfast?"

"Hmmm. Scrambled eggs and a thick slice of ham."

"Chicken fetus and a pig leg."

"Oh. That's awful!" She groaned. "I'll never be able to eat breakfast again. Why did you do that?"

"Just trying to put things into perspective. Your problem is that you're a picky eater."

"I'm eating your snake, aren't I?"

"Yeah. You are. So, what's it taste like?"

"Burnt snake."

He laughed. "You know, Kincaid. You're a real doozy."

"I don't quite know how I should take that."

"It's a compliment, sweetheart." He got up again and

walked a few feet away; then she heard the fire crackle from fresh bushes he'd tossed on it. He stood there and he was whistling again. Amazingly, he sounded wide awake, and after they had been walking all night and half of the morning

"Don't you ever get tired?"

"Sure."

"Don't you ever get scared? On a mission like this?"

"Everyone gets scared. Fear keeps you alive. It's fear of the unknown that gets to you." A moment later he asked, "You want some more to eat?"

She shook her head. "No. Right now, all I want to do is sleep."

"Hand me the rest of that meat; then we'll fix you up a bed here in a minute."

She gave him the snake meat, wiped her hands on her skirt, and leaned back on her palms. She arched her back and groaned, "I'm sore everywhere. Sleeping on the ground isn't going to help any."

He walked around and stood behind her.

She turned and spoke up toward him. "What are you doing?"

"Making us comfortable." He sat down behind her, put his hands on her shoulders, and massaged them really hard.

"Oh, my. . . . I'll give you an hour to stop that."

He laughed and spread his legs on either side of her. "Lean back. You can sleep against me."

"What if there are more snakes around here?"

"Then we'll have our dinner."

She sighed tiredly. "You have an answer for everything."

"It's my job, Kincaid. Remember?"

"Is it? I thought you came to rescue me." She lay her head against his shoulder and closed her eyes.

"I did."

Every muscle in her body hurt. "I should thank you, I know, but I have a little problem."

"What's that?"

"I'm not sure how much more of your rescuing this poor body can take."

"HOCH AUF DEM GELBEN WAGEN"

The RAF planes stationed in Malta had managed with uncanny regularity to destroy German supply ships crossing the Mediterranean with fuel, food, munitions, and mail for the Afrika Korps. Estimates were that as much as fifty percent of the cargo lay at the bottom of the sea. This is what the supply officer told Rheinholdt when the lorries finally arrived, so many days late.

Inside his tent, not long after the supply trucks had driven away, he opened the last of his three letters and read it as he smoked a cigarette and walked toward his cot:

> *Dearest Frederich,*
> *I have only just sent you a letter, one I wrote yester-*
> *day. I must now write another. I have very bad news.*
> *Joseph's family is gone, everyone. The SS came and*

*took him, his father, his mother and sisters. They are
still in Berlin, but no one will say where. I have heard
that once anyone is on the trains to the camps, it is
impossible to get them released. There are terrible
rumors. I do not know if you have heard what they say
about the internment camps, but it is so horrible I
cannot write the words.*

*They did not take Liesel and the children. They
were not home at the time. But they have disappeared.
No one knows where they are. I wonder did they pick
them up on the street? We do not know and cannot
find out.*

*Frederich, I do not understand this. Your father
saw this coming. What kind of men do these things to
people, to Germans, to women and children?*

Rheinholdt read the last line of the letter and for a
moment did nothing. His jaw grew tight, and he
wadded the paper into his tight fist. He threw the cigarette on the ground and crushed it with his boot.

This letter should have been on one of the ships that
went down. It belonged on the ocean floor. He took
deep, long breaths to control the anger that made his
hands shake. He wanted to hit something.

His little sister and her beautiful children. His niece
and nephew were just four and two.

He sat down for a moment because he felt suddenly
empty. His friend Joseph, his brother by marriage. He
ached for the family that had been so much a part of his
life that he always thought of them as his good friends.
That they were Jewish did not matter. That anyone was
Jewish did not matter!

He felt a good million miles away and completely impotent.

His father had been right. He had become part of those politics. His feeling of shame was so intense his face grew hot. His hands still shook, his knuckles were white, his breath shallow. He turned, pulled his satchel out from under the cot, and dug furiously through it before he pulled out a bottle of schnapps, opened it, and took a long drink that burned down his throat.

He rested his head in his hand for a minute. There were tears in his eyes. He told himself they came from the schnapps. He took another drink, then put the cap back on the bottle and dropped it on his cot. He stood. He needed air and walked outside into the sun, which was setting and turning the sky a deep red that made everything look orange.

Hell must look like this, everything colored orange by the flames.

Somewhere in the camp, a gramophone was playing "Lili Marlene" and some of the men were singing along.

"Out of the land of my dreams, your loving lips
call to me . . . Lili Marlene."

The nightly fires were already burning. They dotted the campsite, and the men congregated around them in close-knit groups. Rheinholdt kept himself aloof; for an officer, that was important.

He sidestepped the wooden crates of mortar shells and new cans of ammunition just delivered by the supply caravan and walked around two lorries parked nearby. Nearby, a group of men were laughing.

Laughter. Why did it hurt to hear it? He listened to their banter and talk. At that moment he did not know if he would ever laugh again. As he watched them, he wondered if this was the way dead souls must feel when they watch those they've left behind—distant, useless, and perhaps with some envy.

Some of them were tearing open parcels from home as if it were Christmas. Shaving soap, magazines, and razor blades; cigarettes, chewing gum, baked goods, and candy. These were things sent from Germany and Austria, and in the fresh hygiene kits sent down from Berlin.

"Look here! In the Army they give us condoms for free!" A young private who was new to the unit held up the condom package as he rummaged through his kit.

"Ja, Rolf. But there are no women for five hundred miles!"

"I saw a female."

"Only in your dreams, my friend."

"I did!"

"When?"

"When we passed the caravan."

"Were you looking at the old woman or the camels?" They laughed again.

"That woman was eighty if a day!"

"Ja. And she needed the razor more than you do."

"Look!" Young Rolf held up a piece of white paper. "There is an important notice in my kit." He unfolded the paper. "It is from Generalmajor Mueller-Gebhard."

"The war must be almost over if the Generalmajor has nothing better to do than to send letters to privates."

"Read it, Rolf. Perhaps it will tell you where you can find a woman so you can use that condom."

The others all thought that was quite amusing.

Rolf skimmed the notice, then looked up and said, "Do not laugh. Listen to this: 'For members of the German Armed Forces, (officers excepted) only the brothel at Number Four Via Tassoni in Tripoli is available.'" He frowned and looked at the others. "Why is that?"

"It is staffed only with Italian women."

"It says here that 'use of other brothels, including those licensed to serve the Italian Armed Forces, is strictly forbidden. Attention is drawn to the penalty provision of the German Race Acts.'"

"That means the other brothels have Jews."

"With our luck, the first brothel we will find when we leave the desert will be Italian."

"The Italians have mobile brothels. They bring women to the soldiers."

"Ja, but the women who work in them are Syrian, French, Tunisian, and Jews."

"That would not stop me. A brothel's a brothel. The Generalmajor also says in this notice that we are to wear long trousers, a field tunic, shirt and tie, and belt. Or shorts with long socks and shirt and tie. Look at us! I have on a British shirt and Italian boots! You, Bernard, are wearing clothes from the South Africans. Tell me this. Who wears a tie when the temperature is a hundred and twenty degrees? What do I care for Berlin's silly orders? Let them come here in the desert and wear a tie for a day."

Veith stepped stiffly into the group. "If you have extramarital intercourse with a Jewish woman, you can be reported."

"It would not be illegal for me. I'm not married."

The men laughed.

"It is the duty of all of us to keep the German blood pure. The Jews, they soil us all. Have you forgotten who are our enemies? Germany must fight capitalist imperialism. We are here for the *Lebensraum*." Veith turned to Rolf, his manner bristling with Nazi choler. "You are a fool if you listen to these men. They will get you into trouble."

As Rheinholdt watched Veith, he was glad, for the first time in his life, that he had no son. A boy would be raised in Hitler's Youth and become what Veith was, a soldier with his mind soured and his humanity lost.

There was a loud rumble and raindrops splattered down. Everyone looked up at the sky.

Rheinholdt stepped into the group. "Move the camp to the high ground on the other side of the ridge. Do it quickly; you do not want to be here if this wash fills with water."

"Jawohl, Herr Leutnant." The men scattered quickly, but as young Rolf was moving away, a white piece of paper drifted behind him and to the ground.

Rheinholdt bent down to pick it up and saw the white condom envelope was also left on the ground. He retrieved them. On the condom wrapper was printed: *Tropenfest,* for "tropical-issue," and *Achtung!* "Attention," along with a warning to use with regard to the German Race Acts and its penalty provisions.

He glanced at the paper with orders from Berlin.

9. Do not buy anything from Jews. The non-Jewish shops are clearly marked.

The rain began to come down in huge splats, pelting his head and face and making the fire sizzle. Rheinholdt glanced at the fire and dropped the condom and the paper into the coals; then he stood there watching until the words burned into nothing.

In his mind's eye he saw Joseph laughing with him as they bought soft cheese and fresh bread for a picnic in the mountains one summer day, when they spent the afternoon canoeing their girlfriends—soon to be their wives—around an icy blue alpine lake with a hundred butterflies in the sweet air. He remembered riding bicycles to concerts in the square near the Biergarten, where he and Joseph laughed, drank, and sang. He remembered playing chess, both of them so equally matched that many times they were still playing when the sun came up.

Sweet was the memory of the day when Joseph's father shook his hand and gave him his job at the bank. Rheinholdt thought of his father, who he knew would point out the irony that, for years, Joseph's family banking business had been good enough for the German government accounts, in the days before the politics and the SS.

There were happy dinners in those days, and plays shared with the families; he remembered every one, but more than that, he could see so clearly the joyous look on Liesel's beautiful face when she married Joseph, a look that stayed with her for years.

He could not imagine what look was on her face now.

"WITH THE WIND AND THE RAIN IN YOUR HAIR"

Someone was calling his name.

"Cassidy. Wake up!"

Kincaid.

She shook his shoulder. "You sleep like a dead man."

He opened his eyes. "What's wrong?"

She was standing over him, one hand palm out. "It's raining."

A drop or two landed on his head.

"Feel it?"

He looked up. The sky was stone gray. Dark clouds obscured the distant mountaintops. All he could see was the bone-bare foothills. Rain sprinkled down, pattering the ground and his clothes with raindrops as big as half-dollars. By the time he stood up, the storm had broken loose. It was pouring.

"Is there any shelter nearby?" She was swiping at the rain, which flattened her hair and ran down her face.

"We need to get to higher ground," he told her as he grabbed her arm.

He took off, pulling her with him. Ahead of them were the lower foothills, crags of rock, gravel, and crusty dirt sitting at the base of the mountains.

They needed to move fast.

It was pouring so hard now that it was raining in torrents that turned the ground to a thick, pastelike mud; it was like running through quicksand—two steps and you sank past your ankle.

He dragged her up a rocky hill so crusty half of the ground crumbled away whenever they stepped on it. Water was beginning to form muddy rivers, and it rushed at his feet and down the hillside, taking the loose siltlike dirt with it.

"Wait!" she shouted and stopped. "Do you hear that?"

"I hear the rain."

"No. Listen. Is it thunder?"

There was a distant rumble, like thunder, but it wasn't coming from the sky; it was coming from the ground. He turned around in the direction of the fast-moving storm. It looked like the gray clouds were on the ground. He swore.

"What is it?"

"Flash flood! Run! Just run!" He almost dragged her up the hillside, climbing higher. The hillside was crumbling away from under them. He tried to find solid rock and scrambled up, pulling her with him, ridge after ridge.

He wedged his leg and hip between huge rocks just as the ground below them fell away.

She slipped with it and screamed his name.

"I've got you." He pulled her up by the wrists.

She was crying and almost fell again, but he grabbed her and shoved her in front of him. "Move your feet! Climb, Kincaid. Dammit, climb!" He shoved her up and over the edge of a jagged outcropping, then pulled himself up. "Crawl forward! Away from the edge!" He looked back. "Go! Here it comes!"

He pulled her against him and wedged in between two rocks, his feet braced against them. He locked his hands together and kept her pressed against him. "We'll make it, Kincaid! Hang on to me, brace your feet, and don't let go!"

You could hear the roar of water coming, loud, almost like ocean waves. The ground shook and rocks crumbled past them. He looked toward the sound just as a wall of brown water slammed into them.

Water rushed over his head against the rocks. She was choking.

All he could do was hold on to her, press his boots into the rock, and try to keep them from being swept away. The floodwater tore shallow-rooted bushes from the ground. They scratched at his cheeks, his face, but he forced her head down to keep her protected.

It felt like it lasted forever, waves of water that gave them a moment to catch a breath before hitting them again and slamming him against the rocks; it was like being beaten with boulders.

The water stopped, leveled out, and subsided, washing down the hills. But the rain didn't stop. The rocks gave them some shelter.

"You okay, Kincaid?"

She stirred, lifted her head, and pushed away from him. "Is it over?"

"I think we're okay."

"A-okay?"

"No. I'm not making that mistake again. We might have an earthquake next."

She gave a short laugh, but then stopped when the wind picked up and rain blew against them.

"Get comfortable, sweetheart. We're staying put."

They shifted positions so she was sitting between his legs again, her back against his chest. He locked his arms around her waist.

Cold, driving rain came down for the rest of the day and into the night. They stayed on the ledge, because it was the only place he felt the ground would hold. Water rushed over and around them, stung their faces when the wind turned bitterly wild.

They had to move positions twice for some kind of protection when the rain became gusts of water or drenching showers. Puddles formed around their bodies, and soon they were sleeping in a bed of sticky dark mud. He wondered if she were right, if perhaps someone did have it in for them.

Driving clouds obscured the sky, and little gusts of rain pattered against the rocks. The steady drumming of rain lulled you to sleep, only to be woken by the howling wind.

He woke up for the tenth time, checked his watch. It was 0300. Their bodies together gave off some welcome warmth, but his left leg was asleep. He shifted positions. She murmured something into his chest. He looked down at her and brushed the hair out of her face. Her breathing was even and her eyes were closed.

Even soaking wet, with her face sunburned and mud splattered over it, she was a looker. Her dress was soaked and melted against her thighs. She had great legs and all the right curves.

But then, so did a thousand women. And he had watched women all his life. Found them fascinating creatures. Walking, talking contradictions. So many of the ones who were knockouts used their looks like a Howitzer, blowing through platoons of men who never knew what hit 'em until it was too late.

But Kincaid was blind. Looks were no weapon with her. If there was anything she wielded, it was her damned honesty. And funny thing, he could respect that.

He was alone with a soft woman in his arms and he was thinking about her mind, instead of her tits. He stared at her for a full minute and felt a sudden rush of vitality, a high, a buzzing, like he'd drunk half a bottle of 100-proof Smirnoff.

Shit. . . . He had it bad.

"IN THE MIDDLE OF A KISS"

A sound woke her up. Kitty grabbed J.R.'s shoulders and shook the heck out of him. "Cassidy! Wake up! I hear a plane!"

He sat up, blinking, then shook his head. "What?"

"I hear a plane. Listen."

"A plane?" He shoved her aside and stood up.

"Can you see it?"

"No, but the sky's clear. Blue as all get-out. Damn, where are my binoculars? Shit, forget the binoculars."

"What's wrong?"

"Quick! Give me your slip." Before she could reach for it, he jerked it out of her belt. "Stay here. Don't move. I'm climbing up on the rocks so I can wave this at them."

She heard the scratching of his boots on the rocks; then his body blocked out some of the sun. "Can you see the plane yet?"

"No."

"I hear it from over there." She pointed.

"Yeah, there it is. It's coming from the west. It looks like they're not flying right over us. They're headed south and not close. Come on, you idiots! Look over here! Shit!" He paused. "Waving this at them won't work. Come here, Kincaid. Quick!"

She stepped toward his voice. He was squatting on the top of the rock. She felt his hand on her shoulder. She held out her hand for him, and he pulled her closer against the rock, which was almost as tall as she was. She heard the click of his lighter.

"Help me blow on it, Kincaid. To get it smoking. It's on this boulder at twelve o'clock about a foot away from your chin."

She could hear him huffing and puffing on it and leaned over and joined in.

"Come on! Harder, Kincaid. Harder! It's starting to smoke."

"I can smell it!" She kept blowing at it, and inhaling the smoke, so she had to turn her head away to inhale.

"Don't stop!"

She didn't. She blew and blew until she was getting light-headed and flashes of light swam before her blurred vision.

He swore again.

She kept blowing.

"You can stop now." She heard him exhale. He sounded disgusted. "It's too far away. They didn't see us."

"Are you sure?"

"They would have circled back."

She sagged against the boulder. "Seeing a plane must mean we're close to something."

"I hate to point this out to you, sweetheart, but we were in a plane and not close to anything but sand and desert and the damned flies."

"Could you tell what kind of plane it was?"

"I'm looking at it through the binoculars right now. It's flying into the sun. I can't tell what the hell it is."

She waited.

He jumped down from the rock. "It's gone."

"So now what?"

"We gather our stuff and climb over these mountains. I can see a pass ahead in the distance. It's not that far. We'll see where it leads. Maybe if we're lucky the coast will be on the other side of these mountains."

She couldn't smell the sea, but that didn't mean it wasn't there.

"The good news is, with all that rain we have a full canteen. You thirsty?"

She took a drink. It tasted so much better than that tinny, salty, well water. "That tastes so good. I swear that well water was like drinking the Pacific Ocean, during the red tide." She handed him the canteen and heard him take a drink.

"Water is water, but you're right. After the well water, this tastes almost as good as a beer."

"I'd love a beer. A cold, icy beer."

"When we get out of here, Kincaid, a beer's the first thing I'll buy you. All the beer you want."

"And a hot dog. With mustard, onions and sauerkraut."

"Why do you women talk about food all the time?"

"Women don't talk about food all the time."

"You were just talking about hot dogs. And then there's your reaction to that chocolate bar. It was a candy bar, not a Studebaker. Ever since I was a kid, whenever my mother and my aunts would get together in a room, all they could talk about was food."

"I'm certain they were only sharing recipes."

He laughed. "I doubt that. My mother has never cooked a day in her life."

"Really?"

"Really."

"Well, I like to fantasize. It gives me something to walk toward. Like the idea of a long bath. I'm going to sit in the tub until my skin is as wrinkled as a prune. How 'bout you? If you could be anywhere right now, doing anything at all, what would it be?"

"Me?" He turned back to her. "I'd be sailing in Naragansett Bay. Near Newport."

"I thought you had a Rhode Island accent."

"What ah you tahking about? We don't hahve ah ahccent."

She burst out laughing.

Four hours later, however, nothing was funny anymore. She was feeling the strain of the walk, the strain of everything. At the summit, there had been thick slabs of ice on the rocks, but the air wasn't unbearably cold, because the sun was out. However, the ice was melting and slick. She had trouble walking.

But the worst section to cross was the pass, where there were rocks everywhere. She knew she slowed him down. She'd slipped and stumbled almost every other step, until they figured out a routine. He would climb down the rock. She would slide down and into his arms and he'd set her on the next one.

Her arms were scratched, and she felt bruised all over, but her butt was the worst. Silently, she kept going, until she felt as if her legs were made of rubber and she had to say something. "Can we stop for a minute?"

"We can, but we're only about a hundred yards from the end of the pass. That's not much farther."

"Okay. Let's go on."

For the next five minutes he held on to her arm, at least until they left the rocks and hit more solid ground, which was muddy and sticky from last night's rain and sucked at her shoes.

"You can stop. We're on the other side."

"Can you see the coast? What do you see?"

He didn't say a word, and that was more telling than anything.

"Cassidy. Please. Tell me what you see."

"Desert. More goddamned desert. There's no coast in sight."

She swore.

"Before you give up, I'm using the binoculars."

"Do you see anything?"

"Yeah. I see something in the distance."

"What?"

"I don't know. I'm trying to focus. The terrain and the sun can play havoc with your eyes." He paused, then said, "Interesting."

"What?"

"I think I see a road." He faced her when he spoke. "Don't get too excited. It could be a mirage. We'll rest here and then move on. Here's the canteen."

She drank and handed it back. "I'm starving."

He laughed. "See? You bring up food."

"In case you haven't noticed, Cassidy, we're lost and close to starving. Even you have to be hungry."

"Yeah, I am. I'd guess you've changed your tune and that snake or a squirrel would taste pretty good right now."

"Anything would taste good right now. I swallowed a fly a little while ago and didn't even gag."

"If you keep walking with your mouth open, Kincaid, you might not be hungry anymore."

She groaned. "I'm not quite that desperate. Do you think there's any nutritional value in a fly?"

"Who knows? Maybe we'll get lucky and come across another snake."

"Never in my life did I think I'd be looking forward to coming face-to-face with a snake."

"You ready?"

"Sure." He took her hand and they did what they'd been doing for days. They walked across the desert in the hot sun and the great silence. They didn't talk much. She just concentrated on putting one foot in front of the other, and figured he was doing the same.

He stopped and handed her the canteen. "How you doing?"

"I'm okay."

He took the canteen back and clipped it to his belt. "Good, then let's pick it up. We're not that far away. From what I can see, it still looks like a road to me."

His steps picked up, and she stayed with him, until they were almost running. But the ground was hard and flat and she didn't care. "Can you see it?"

"Yeah. Come on." He pulled her with him; then a

few minutes later he stopped so suddenly she almost ran into him.

"What is it?"

He said nothing.

"Dammit, Cassidy. Tell me why you stopped."

"Here. Take about four steps." There was a smile in his voice. "Feel that." He placed her hand on a hot stone the size of a cantaloupe that was level with her waist.

"You know what that is?"

She brought her other hand over and felt up and down the pile of tall round rocks. "It's a marker?" She moved her hands over it quickly. There were smooth spots that felt like paint. "One of those desert road markers, the kind made of stones?"

"You got it, and it says, 'Cairo, four hundred twenty-three kilometers.' "

"Egypt? We're in Egypt?"

"Or near the Libyan border. The road looks like its headed northeast."

She started laughing. "We made it!"

"Yeah, Kincaid, it looks like we did." He grabbed her and spun her around again like he had before, but this time she didn't tell him to put her down. All she could do was hold on to his shoulders and laugh.

He stopped spinning with her and slowly set her onto the ground. "We've still got a long walk."

"I don't care. At least I know we're headed somewhere."

"We were headed somewhere before. We just didn't have a clue where."

She placed her hands on his scratchy, stubbled cheeks and stood on her toes and gave him a quick kiss on the mouth. "Thank you, Cassidy. Thank you, so much."

He didn't say anything. Next she felt his hand slide to the back of her head, his other hand around her waist. He kissed her, and not a quick smack on the lips.

She moved her hands to his shoulders, then one hand to his neck as he pulled her hard against him and separated her mouth with his tongue.

Is this crazy?

She didn't care. She just kissed him back, the two of them standing there together under the hot sun, hands everywhere, petting as if they were standing on a front porch back home.

She heard something, or thought she did, a distant sound, then one she recognized: the same rattle-slap noise she'd heard in the marketplace—rifles going from shoulder to hand.

"Achtung!"

Cassidy broke off the kiss and swore under his breath.

"Nicht bewegen!"

"Ja! You two. Do not move!"

"You know, Kincaid, looks like you might just get that hot dog . . . or at least the sauerkraut."

"MACHEN WIR'S DEN SCHWALBEN NACH"

Rheinholdt was examining the contents of a mortar crate when he heard a commotion. He straightened and turned to see three of his men leading a man and a woman toward him at gunpoint. They looked as if they had been in the desert for days.

"We found them while patrolling the road, Herr Leutnant. Engländers."

Rheinholdt faced the couple. "What is this? You are English?" He used their language.

"No. American." The man grasped the woman's hand. "My wife and I were in a small plane. We flew into a storm. The plane went down in the desert. Southwest of here. We've been walking for four days."

"They have no papers, Herr Leutnant," Dietrich said.

The man turned to Dietrich. "We barely got out of that plane."

Rheinholdt observed in silence. He saw that the woman stared at him with an oddly blank look in her pale eyes. She wasn't looking directly at him, but past him. He cast a quick glance over his shoulder.

"My wife is blind."

Rheinholdt turned back and studied the man who was looking at him so grimly. He had a thick dark beard, a few days old, and hair that was golden blond like his own. His skin was as burned by the sun as any one of them.

It was odd, because his clothes looked military-issue. However, he knew pilots wore jumpsuits and boots. The man wore no chain around his neck for military identification tags. The woman was quite pretty, with hair true black and light blue eyes. Her skin was uncomfortably red, and she was in a ragged, filthy dress that was the style Heddy would wear out to lunch. She wore broken shoes. But somehow she did not look broken.

He felt something like sorrow—he knew it wasn't pity—when he looked at her. It wasn't her affliction that made him feel something like compassion toward her. It wasn't even that she looked as if she'd been dragged here through miles of desert. There was something about the way she stood, this woman, in a place where you seldom saw women, that made him remember a courtesy too easily forgotten in a desert post comprised of men.

He walked over to her. "Please, Fräulein, sit down before you fall down." He turned to the husband. "I will have the men get you both something to eat and drink."

"Thank you," she said quietly. She raised her hand to her head and rubbed her forehead. She looked as if she might faint then and there. Her husband slid his arm around her, and she leaned against him.

Rheinholdt turned to Dietrich. "Get them some food and water."

There was something possessive about the way the man held her and led her to a stool a few feet away in the shade of a truck. Rheinholdt followed and watched them together for a moment, noticing that neither of them wore rings. "I am Feldleutnant Frederich Rheinholdt."

"James Cassidy," the man said, squatting in front of her. "And this is Kathryn."

"Yes, well, here comes Dietrich. You are fortunate. The supply caravan was here just days ago. We have bread and cheese and fresh water."

"Lieutenant?"

He faced the woman. "Yes, Fräulein?"

Her head was bent down and her hands clasped in her lap. "Thank you for sharing with us."

"Certainly. Please. Eat." Rheinholdt turned and moved toward the tent that housed the radio transmitter.

'AUF WIEDERSEHEN'

J.R. paced in front of Kitty.

"What do you think they're going to do?" she whispered.

"I don't know. The lieutenant was watching us very closely. I'm not certain what he was thinking. I don't think your buddy from the Kasbah could possibly be in touch with an army unit this far away. They're probably looking for us on the coast. This Rheinholdt really has no reason not to believe we are what I say we are." He stopped in front of her. "That was some performance, by the way."

"You liked that, huh?"

"Don't get too cocky, there, sweetheart. They have no reason to hold us, but that doesn't mean they can't.

We're outnumbered and outarmed. They moved us to this tent."

"He said he thought we were tired and wanted to rest and have some privacy."

J.R. snorted. "There's an armed guard outside."

"What time is it?"

"A little after six. Look's like the sun's going down."

"So what do we do?"

"Nothing."

"Why?"

"Because someone's coming."

The German lieutenant shoved aside the tent flap. "You are rested, Fräulein? Feeling better?"

"Yes, thank you." Her voice was so weak J.R. wondered if she were laying it on too thick.

"Good. You will both come with me, please."

"Where?" Kitty asked.

"It doesn't matter, Kathryn. Let's do what the lieutenant asks. Come. I'll help you up. You can hold on to me." J.R. took her hand and slid his arm around her and followed the German outside. It was dusk outside, and everything was cast in gold from the orange ball of the setting sun.

"This way, please." Rheinholdt crossed the edges of the camp and went around to the other side of a truck.

J.R. was trying to decide if he should take the guy on, but he noticed there was no armed guard. It was only the three of them.

The German walked over to an armored car and gestured to the seats. "Get in, please."

Kitty froze, but J.R. pushed her forward. "Get in, Kathryn."

He put her in the rear and got into the shotgun seat.

The lieutenant got in and started the car. He turned to J.R. "Some officials in Morocco are looking for a young blind American woman."

"What a coincidence," J.R. said, ready to reach for his throat.

"Yes, however, Germany is not at war with the United States."

"No."

"Why, I ask myself, would they want a blind American woman?"

"Perhaps because her father is important," J.R. said.

"Since she is not here, I do not have to worry about her. Women should not be part of war. Your wife looks tired. I cannot take you both to Cairo, but I can take you closer than you are." He shifted the car into gear and drove across the desert.

It was dark when he finally slowed the car. It was a rough, bumpy ride.

"I cannot drive on the road here or use the lights." They drove a few more miles, and he stopped the car and rested his arm on the back of the seat. "This is as far as I can take you. You see the lights to the west? There?"

"I see them."

"Those are the British lines. It is not too far to walk, I think."

"No. Not far." J. R. got out and helped Kincaid from the car.

"The road is to your right. You stay on the road. There are mines to the north."

"We will." J.R. faced the German, then leaned over the seat and held out his hand. "Thank you."

The lieutenant shook his hand. "You are welcome." He looked at Kitty. "I, too, have a wife, and daughters, Herr Cassidy. Good luck to you." Then he started the car, turned around, and drove back into the darkness.

"LULU'S BACK IN TOWN"

In the center of Cairo's hothouse atmosphere, the Swiss-owned, Shepheard's Hotel was Western sybaritism at its best: a marble lobby and huge potted palms, quality service that was obsequious to say the least, luxurious rooms with wide, lattice-paneled terraces, and sumptuous meals that were the talk of the town.

But it was the bathtub that made Kitty believe she had died and gone to heaven. With a blanket of bubbles clear up to her sunburned chin, she lay in the tepid water, squeaky clean, her skin pickling, eyes closed, listening to the soft ticking of the ceiling fan and the traffic noise of civilization coming up from the street below.

There was a light tapping on the bathroom door.

"Hekmet? Come in."

The door opened and she heard the quick padding steps of the personal maid supplied by the hotel. "The clothing from Cirurel's was delivered, *madame*. I have laid some of them out on the bed. Your linen and nightclothes are in the drawers of the dressing room as *madame* asked."

"Thank you. I'm going to stay in this bath a while longer. I won't need you for at least another hour."

"Yes, *madame*." And she left.

Kitty sat up and flicked on the warm water, then lay back again, ignoring the gurgling, sucking sound of the overflow spill. She wanted the water up to her neck. She closed her eyes and lay back again, soaking, her arms flung over the rim of the tub and the spicy-sweet scent of jasmine floating inside from the clay pots on the terrace.

The maid tapped again.

Service was uppermost at this hotel, but this was the third time the maid had bothered her in less than an hour. Kitty just wanted to loll around in the tub, without the sun beating on her, without having to walk anywhere, without fleas or flies or sand.

"Come in." The maid opened the door and Kitty started, "Thank you for looking after me so well, Hekmet. I really appreciate your help, but I don't need anything else right now." She paused, then added, "Well, perhaps a glass of water with ice would be nice before you leave. Then please don't come back for an hour. Take a break, a rest . . . something."

"I don't have any water, sweetheart. How about an icy cold beer and hot dog?"

"Cassidy? Dammit!" She grabbed a towel and draped it over the tub. "What are you doing in my room? My bathroom?"

"You said come in."

"Stay back."

He walked over to her. "Here." He put an ice-cold bottle of beer against her cheek.

"Good God, that's cold."

"Hold out your hand."

She huddled under the towel. "You're not going to leave, are you?"

"No."

"At this point I suppose any modesty on my part is a lost cause."

"You're a smart woman."

"Okay, then." She held her hand out over the top of the towel and heard the thin paper crinkle before she felt what it held. "That feels like a hot dog. It even smells like a hot dog."

"It is. Complete with mustard and sauerkraut."

"Where on earth did you get a hot dog in Cairo?" She lifted it to her nose, and her stomach growled.

"For the right price, you can get anything in Cairo."

"God, that smells good." She unwrapped it and took a bite. "It's wonderful," she said with her mouth full.

She heard him sit down on the dressing stool. "Did you get in touch with your family?"

She nodded and swallowed. "Not my father. He's in New Mexico, but I spoke with one of my brothers. He said they already received three wires that I was safe and sound and here in Cairo. The wire we sent, the British Army's wire, and the U.S. State Department's wire." She took a drink of the beer. "We were certainly burning up the telegraph services. My dad will call me here tomorrow."

"They're sending a transport out from Gibraltar sometime tomorrow to fly us back the next day."

She finished off the hot dog and washed it down with another swig of cold beer. "I don't think anything in my life has tasted as good as that just did."

"I'm glad. Are you still tired?"

"I shouldn't be. All I did yesterday was sleep in that

bed and wash my hair, seven times. I used a whole bottle of shampoo and I think I still have sand in it." She rubbed her scalp.

"What do you say we paint the town tonight? Celebrate our escape. Dinner, music, something?"

"This is Cairo, isn't it? Cabarets and exotic night life. I heard Rommel is only a few hundred miles away. Who knows when, if ever, I'll get back here."

"Do you have to talk yourself into this?"

She laughed. "No. I'd love to go out."

"Okay, then. I'll pick you up at seven-thirty." He stood and walked toward the door.

"Cassidy?"

"Yeah?"

"Thanks for the hot dog."

"Sure."

"And the beer."

"Okay. Anything else?"

"Well, yes. Please tell me the bubbles are some protection."

"Bubbles? What bubbles?" And he closed the door laughing.

I DOUBLE DARE YOU

"I can't find my key." Kitty was rummaging around in her small evening bag. "Oh, wait. Here it is. Look." She pulled out the key and held it up.

He took the key from her hand. "I'll do it."

"I bet you sure do do it," she murmured. Oops. She'd had too many gin fizzes.

"What did you say?"

"Nothing." She heard the click as he unlocked the door. "Well, I'd invite you inside, but I don't have a thing to drink." She moved past him and stood in the doorway, her hand on the jamb. "Dinner was wonderful, and I haven't danced like that . . . well, ever." She held out her hand. "Thank you for tonight."

He didn't take her hand.

She waited for him to do something. Anything. Kiss her, that was what she expected. What she wanted. What she had wanted all night.

His hand closed over hers and he shook it. "You're right. Tonight was fun."

She was so surprised she just stood there for a moment. What the heck was going on?

He didn't say anything more. He just dropped her hand. "Good night, Kincaid." He turned and walked down the hall toward his room, whistling.

She closed the door tightly before she leaned back against it and swore every word she knew. Thanks to her brothers, it took a few minutes.

Still annoyed, she shoved away from the door and crossed the room, tossing her bag and wrap in the vicinity of the sitting room sofa as she stalked into the dressing room and began to undress, mumbling to herself. "We're in the desert and he's sure full of innuendo. Mister hot-shot hero, with his glib tongue, which was, by the way, halfway down my throat when we found that road marker."

She tossed her shoes in the closet and put her satin

evening dress on a padded hanger, then hung it up. "We almost die together . . . minefields and airplane crashes and flash floods, and now, here we are, a perfect evening, and he doesn't take the bait." She put her hands on her hips. "And snakes! I forgot all about the snake."

She grabbed her silk robe off a hook and shrugged into it. "We walk through the desert together. We almost died together like . . . like Shakespearean lovers."

She yanked hard on the belt and pulled the pins and the hair pick from her hair. She turned and set them on the dressing table, then sat down and began to vigorously brush her hair. She stopped brushing and shook the brush in the air. "What is wrong with him?"

"Nothing's wrong with me."

"Cassidy?"

"You forgot your key."

She could just imagine him standing right there in the doorway, leaning against the jamb, probably holding up her key like some kind of prize.

Oh, God . . . How much had he heard? She spun around and threw her brush at him.

"Ouch! Damn."

She stood up and crossed the small room, her hand out until she found him standing there.

"You hit me in the head. How did you do that?"

"Blind luck."

"You know, Kincaid. That mouth of yours is going to get you in trouble."

"You think so?"

"I know so."

"Oh . . . I sure do hope so."

A heartbeat passed. One of those split-second strokes of time where you wonder where your nerve came from. She would have given anything to be able to see his face.

His hand touched her cheek, then, slowly slid to her jaw.

She tilted her head back. Just for a second she thought he wasn't going to kiss her. "Kiss me, Cassidy. Before I fall down."

"Oh, baby . . ." His mouth was on hers.

She grabbed his shirtfront in her fists and pulled him against her.

His hands slid down her to her bottom, and he lifted her up, deepening his kiss as he walked with her to the bed. He set her on her feet but kept his hands on her butt and slowly began to wad up the robe higher and higher and higher, until he could slide his hands over the bare skin of her bottom, squeezing it as he ate at her mouth.

The last time she'd kissed him he'd had a beard. She lifted her hand and drew it along his square jaw. She could smell the soap on his skin. It smelled clean and male and just wonderful.

She easily opened every button on his shirt, pushed it off his shoulders, and ran her hands over the muscles and bone and contours of his arms, drew a finger over the indentations, amazed at how they were sculpted.

So different from her. So hard. In the strength of those arms was the soldier, the man. She wanted to give him the gift of her body.

His fingers moved to the cleft of her buttocks, then inside, stroking her in places dark and forbidden. She moaned and rubbed against him, felt the robe split wide open, and her nipples rubbed against the thin cotton of his undershirt.

He was kissing her jaw.

She reached down and cupped him through his slacks.

His lips were on her ear, his tongue inside. "You're wearing too many clothes."

"Hmmm. Am I?"

"Yeah, baby."

She laughed and pulled at his belt. "Less than you."

His hands left her butt and tore at the robe; it fell off her shoulders. He jerked away the tie belt. "On the bed." He shoved her backward, out into the bedroom and then onto the bed. "Now."

She heard the sound of his belt, then his zipper, the thud of his shoes. She lay there naked, exposed to him.

He wasn't moving.

She could hear his breathing. "What are you doing?"

"Looking at you."

"Not fair. I have to use my hands to see you."

"Yeah, and you were doing such a good job of it, you were about to see more than you planned."

"Like what?"

"Me losing my pride and shooting off like I was fifteen."

"I wouldn't care."

"I would."

She lay there, wondering how long before he touched her again. "I want your hands on me, Cassidy. Please . . . ."

He stood between her legs, which were bent and hanging down from the bed; he pushed them apart. His hands stroked her inner thighs, and she sucked in a deep breath.

"God, but you're beautiful . . ." His finger separated her; the air was cold on her.

She was so wet it was embarrassing. She made a noise when he rubbed her. "Wait."

"Shhhh." He knelt down and put her legs over his shoulders. He grabbed her bottom and pulled her toward him, open, exposed, his head between her thighs. Just the barest tip of his tongue flicked her.

She moaned and quivered. "No, don't. Please."

His only answer was to lick her again. Then he blew on her.

"Please . . ."

"Please what?"

"Please don't."

"Please don't what?"

"Please don't . . . stop."

"I'M IN THE MOOD FOR LOVE"

He'd never had a virgin. Always thought of virginity as a nuisance. He was wrong. She was all over him, with an innocence he found refreshingly fun.

Four times. Hell, maybe he was a hero.

They lay sideways in the bed, the sheets somewhere on the floor, her legs tangled in his and her head resting on his chest as she combed her fingers through his chest hair and he played with her hard nipple. The window was open, but the air was warm and the room still steamy and smelling like sex. It made him want her again.

A car horn honked in the distance. A taxi boy blew his whistle at the taxi queue downstairs. He could hear people walking and talking outside, milling around in front of the hotel. Laughter drifted up into the room. Every so often, there was a lull in the street noise and he could hear the faint sound of music from a distant nightclub.

From just across the hall came the soft whish of the hydraulic brakes on the elevator. The cage gate creaked open. The elevator operator clicked his castanet, and the door closed.

Footsteps. A man laughing. A woman's sigh. A door closed down the hall.

She shifted a little. "What time is it?"

"Late." He reached for his watch on the nightstand, flicked on the table lamp. "Three."

"Ummm." She took a deep breath and put her leg over his hip. Her pussy was wet. She moved her mouth to his chest and began to kiss him.

He reached toward the night table. "This is the last condom."

"Oh." She sounded so disappointed he almost laughed.

"Don't worry about it." He lifted her onto his prick, then rubbed his hands up her bent thighs. "There are other things we can do, sweetheart."

She slid down him and he wanted like crazy to jerk off the condom and really feel her inside. Yeah, next time. He could always pull out.

"Other things?" She shifted her hips. "Like what, Cassidy?"

He lay back and closed his eyes. So hot . . . She was so hot inside. "Later. Ride me, baby. Just ride me."

She was doing it slow and easy. He waited and waited, then gripped her hips, wanting it harder and faster. She moved like silk around him, warm and wet and soft.

He looked at her.

Her head was back, her lips swollen and pink, her mouth open and moist. It drove him crazy. Her breasts jiggled as she moved. The nipples were hard and pink. He rose up and sucked one into his mouth, rolled his tongue over it as she slid down him. He felt her little clit against the base of his dick. He thrust up three times fast. She throbbed, and he came like crazy.

She fell asleep first, while he lay there watching her in the curve of his arm. He edged out from under her, slipped out of the bed, and pulled on his pants, buttoning the fly as he left the bedroom.

In the sitting room, he picked up the black telephone, dialed out, and moved toward the terrace doors with the phone in his hand, stepping around the cord. He had to wait a good half hour for the call to go through all the various operators.

"Hey there, Pistonbrain. Yeah, I know it's two A.M. there, but this is an emergency. I need your help."

Jake Wells, the head mechanic at the Army airbase in Gibraltar, had been stationed on a base with him not long after he graduated from West Point.

"Look, buddy. You know that C-33 transport that is supposed to fly out here tomorrow? Yeah, that's it. There's five hundred bucks in it for you if you can delay it for a couple of days."

J.R. held the phone away from his ear for a moment. "I know it's a top priority flight. No. I don't care how. That's your job, old buddy. Just make sure that plane can't take off until Thursday. Is it a deal?"

He waited patiently while Jake called him a few good names before he agreed. "Good. Thanks. What? No." J.R. laughed. "A brunette. A long-legged, smart-mouthed, brunette. Yeah, I know I'm lucky. Even luckier than you think, buddy. Sheer blind luck." He smiled. "Sure thing, and Jake? Thanks. I owe you one." He hung up.

Smiling, he dropped the phone back on the table and went into the bedroom. Light from the moon shone through the latticework and spilled lacelike shadows over the bed and her bare skin. Odd, but he found he could stand there and watch her, not wanting to leave. He didn't think of another woman, at another time, in another place. Instead he felt something like heart-pounding pleasure coursing through him.

He took off his pants, walked around the bed, and picked up the linen sheet, then lay back down and covered them both. He eased his arm under her head and closed his eyes.

Two hours later he woke up from a helluva great dream, to find reality even sweeter still. Her mouth was on him, sucking lightly. Her hair spread over his thighs, her breasts pressed between his legs.

Hell, he might have to marry this girl.

'I MARRIED AN ANGEL'

The little green Sunbeam taxi careened around a corner and fishtailed. Kitty tightened her grip on the strap near the rear window.

"Christ," Cassidy muttered.

"What?"

"He almost ran over a donkey cart filled with chickens and ducks."

She'd heard the quacking and squawking.

He took another sharp turn that slammed her into Cassidy's ribs. She was struck by the absurdly real thought that the gods of irony could easily strike and kill her in a Cairo cab after she had survived all those ordeals in the desert. "Does he have to drive so fast?"

"It'll only be worse if I ask him to slow down. He'll speed up." Cassidy put his arm around her. "It's not much farther."

She nodded.

The cabdriver slammed on the brakes, and the car skidded into another one. The crunch of metal wasn't half as loud as the Arabic curses their driver was shouting. Trolleys rang past and beasts of burden, donkeys and camels, snorted and bawled.

Someone was praying. It should have been her.

The driver didn't get out. He merely jammed the car into reverse, backed up at about thirty miles per hour, then took off again through the loud, honking traffic of Cairo. He didn't hit the brakes again until they were at the docks, where the taxi skidded for a good minute before it finally stopped.

Seemingly unfazed, Cassidy helped her out of the car and paid the driver, who floored it and took off. After the exhaust dissipated, she could smell the brine of the water and hear the birds calling out as they circled overhead. She straightened her hat and tugged down on the short, net hat-veil that dipped down just enough to cover her forehead and brows. She placed her hand gently on Cassidy's arm. "Are we crazy?"

"Yeah. But I like you crazy." She could hear his smile. "I don't think I'd have it any other way." He pulled her into his arms and kissed her quickly, then stopped suddenly, and he grew very still.

She could feel him looking down at her. "What's wrong?"

"Do you want out? We don't have to do this if you've changed your mind."

"No. I haven't changed my mind. Have you changed your mind?"

"No. Not on your life."

She relaxed against him, her head on his shoulder for however long it took for her to take a deep, relieved breath. "Good." She stepped back and slid her arm through his and held it tightly to her side. "Because if you had said yes, I'd have had to kill you. Or call that cabdriver back. Getting into that cab again would be suicide."

He laughed, then leaned down and gave her a quick kiss on the nose. "Okay, Kincaid. This is it. You ready?"

"I'm ready. I think I've been waiting forever for this."

A gust of warm wind came up suddenly, whipped around her head, and she reached up to hold down her hat. The thin silk of her knife-pleated skirt pressed against her legs as they walked with two British junior officers who escorted them up a gangplank, where the ship's captain was waiting. Ten minutes later, in the middle of the River Nile, on a bright and breezy day, he married them.

U.S.

1941–1942

"REMEMBER ME"

SANTA FE, NEW MEXICO, 1941

The front of F.W. Woolworth's in Santa Fe Plaza was deep vermilion red, but it was the only place around where you could buy a wooden spool of Coats and Clark thread in Forget-Me-Not Blue, a sapphire blue bottle of Evening in Paris perfume, and a sky-blue parakeet you could teach to say "Blueboy!"

The store manager was a native son named Harold Blue, who drove a sky blue Studebaker and always wore a midnight blue bow tie clipped on a shirt so bright you could tell it was washed with bluing. He married Emily Morgan, who had bright blue eyes and lived on Cerulean Road. When she gave birth to his daughter, they named her Azure. Now Emily was pregnant again, and bets were going around town that if it was a boy, the poor kid would be stuck with the name of Royal.

Like most folks, Charley wore some shade of blue when she knew she was going to the local five-and-dime, because Mr. Blue might just take a few cents off of your purchase.

Since junior high school, when she and her pop had made New Mexico their permanent home, Woolworth's had been Charley's favorite place to wander. In those days all the kids in town gathered at the fountain counter after school to have cherry Cokes or clay-thick chocolate shakes served in tall metal canisters so cold you had to use a paper napkin to hold them in your hands.

Woolworth's lunch counter fed almost every person in town at least one day a week. It was a well-known national fact in every small town, in every city, that the luncheonettes had the best-flavored Cokes, Hires root beer floats, and Squeeze orangeade anywhere around.

Here in Santa Fe, it was no different. They served up bacon, lettuce, and tomato sandwiches on toast, fountain drinks, and every bit of news and gossip in town.

Charley strolled down the center aisle, under a low cork ceiling where the old iron circular fans rotated slowly, but didn't send a whiff of air onto anything below.

She grabbed a pair of pale blue terry-cloth house slippers and a small red box of Gem razor blades, then tossed them into her basket next to two flat cards of hair and bobby pins and a glass jar of wave-setting lotion. She also bought a gold Helena Rubenstein powder compact and a brown mascara that, according to the display, you could wet with a stubby brush and apply to the pale tips of your eyelashes to make them look as long as Claudette Colbert's.

A few minutes later she paid for everything with her father's metal charge plate. Even with a job as a flight instructor and a decent income in an economy that was moving upward again, she was a single woman. It was a rarity when a single woman could get credit without a man co-signing on the account—a father, a brother, an uncle.

Charley walked toward the glass door, her hand on the metal handle to push it open and leave. Her stomach growled. She had no willpower whatsoever.

She turned on her heel and marched back to the lunch counter, accepting the fact that she would not lose ten pounds this month. She sat down on a red swivel stool, ordered a bacon and tomato sandwich and cherry fountain Coke.

She ate the sandwich and the long dill pickle, but passed on the fried onions. Instead she sat there, stirring the thick red syrup off the bottom of a classic-shaped Coca-Cola glass with her paper straw and ignoring the rattling of the crushed ice.

She took a drink. Some things just tasted better when you were home.

"Hey, Charley!"

She looked up.

A small blonde in a form-fitting cotton sundress with a wide halter top waved at her from down the counter a ways.

Dorothy Ledbetter.

Dot and her sister, Patti Marie, a busty blonde who looked like Betty Grable, got up and came over to sit down on either side of her. Dot asked the counter girl to bring their meals over there when they were ready, then spun around on her swivel stool and faced Charley. "I didn't know you were back in town. It's been a long time since you've been home."

"I got back yesterday. I'm here to visit Pop for a couple of weeks."

The blonde on her other side leaned closer to Charley. Patti Marie smelled of carnations and vanilla, like Blue

Waltz perfume. "Did you fly your plane here?"

"Of course she flew, Patti Marie. Charley is a *pilot*."

"Well, I know that. But just because she flies planes all over the country doesn't mean she can't get in a car and drive once in a while."

"I'm not flying all over the country much anymore." Charley took a drink of her Coke.

"Why not?"

"I'm working as a flight instructor."

"You're teaching people how to fly?" Patti perked up a bit.

Charley nodded. "For the last ten months, thanks to the Civil Training Act." She cast a quick glance at the look on Patti Marie's face. The girl had grown suddenly pensive. "They take one woman for every ten men. Are you interested in flight training? You could join. You're in college, right?"

"I sure am. Baylor," she said with a proud nod.

"What's your major?"

"Men," Dot said dryly.

"That's not true."

"Okay . . . Okay . . ." Dot held up her hands. "I was wrong. You're not majoring in men."

"Thank you. That was completely unfair, sis."

Dot faced Charley. "She's majoring in doctors."

There was a meaningful pause, then they all laughed, even Patti.

"Don't let her bamboozle you, Charley." Dot was still laughing. "She figured if she went to a college that had a med school, she could hook a doctor for a husband."

Patti Marie ignored her sister and grasped Charley's

arm with two hands, then leaned closer. "I'm dating this wonderful premed dreamboat named Montgomery Wilson. His family's from San Antonio. Monty has a friend who's real tall, Charley. Six foot six. He has blond hair and green eyes and the longest eyelashes you've ever seen. He wants to be a gynecologist. I can set you up."

Charley shook her head. "No, thanks. I'm here to see Pop." She exchanged a smile with Dot. It was Patti Marie's sole goal in life to make certain every woman had a man. In school, Charley had never dated much. The only person taller than she was, was the captain of the basketball team, and he'd dated a girl who was five feet two and looked like a china doll.

"See, Patti. I told you no woman in her right mind wants to date a man whose professional goal is to be a gynecologist."

Patti started to argue, but the counter girl set a meat-loaf sandwich in front of her.

"Eat," her older sister said. "And stop playing match-maker. You're worse than an old aunt." Dot looked back at Charley. "Did that tall fella with the Texas drawl ever find you?"

Charley finished swallowing a gulp of Coke. "What? Someone was looking for me?"

"Uh-huh. He came through here, oh, maybe four months ago or so." She paused thoughtfully. "I'm not certain when.... Wait, I do remember. It was around last Thanksgiving, because there were turkey cookies in the bakery window and I had been at the Millinery with Mother, looking for a new hat for the holidays. He was driving a dusty old Ford truck and had the brightest wavy red hair you've ever seen. A great smile and a drawl so slow and sweet that it could make your toes melt. He stopped at the filling station when I was putting gas in mother's car."

The only person she knew who matched that description was Red Walker. "Was he about twenty or so?"

"Looked like it. John Lawson at the feed store was there and gave him directions to your dad's place."

Charley smiled to herself. Whenever there was a storm, she thought about Red Walker. A few times she'd wondered if he'd followed her suggestion about trading some mechanical work for flying lessons. Nowadays few people had to pay for flight instruction. The war in Europe had spurred the government into giving lessons for free in the hopes of luring pilots into the Air Corps. She drank some more Coke, then frowned. "You know, it's odd that Pop didn't say a word about him. I wonder what happened?" Her voice trailed off.

"Well, I saw him drive off toward your place. He wrote down the directions. I remember because I loaned him a pencil. What a cutie pie he was. Just as polite as all get-out."

They talked for a few more minutes, small-town gossip about who was seeing whom, who was getting married and having babies, who was in the doghouse for coming home with lipstick on his collar.

Charley finished the last of her drink. "Well, I'd better run." She stood. "I'll be around for a week or so." She turned to Patti Marie. "If you change your mind about those lessons, let me know. Waco isn't that far from Dallas."

"Patti in a plane?" Dot laughed it off. "I don't think so."

But Charley caught something in Patti's expression. She'd have been willing to bet that Patti Marie Ledbetter wanted to fly as badly as she wanted to marry a doctor, and even more than she wanted to matchmake all the Southwest.

"I'm in Odessa now," Charley told her, paying the bill with a quarter. "But I'll be moving to Whiting Field in a few months." She looked Patti Marie in the eye. "Just in case you want to know." She picked up her shopper, then smiled and left.

"SOUTH OF THE BORDER"

Less than an hour later Charley turned the wide steering wheel of her pop's '36 Ford wood-paneled station wagon onto a private drive and under an arched iron sign that read: *"Casa del Cielo."* Her mind was elsewhere, until she glanced in the rearview mirror and saw the dry dust of the road billowing up behind the car in a pumpkin-colored cloud. Like desert smoke signals, the dust always told you when someone was coming up the road. She glanced at the speedometer; she was still traveling at about forty miles per hour, so she let off the pedal.

The private road to *Casa del Cielo* had been carved easily out of rolling waves of New Mexican land brindled with piñon and juniper, bushes of sagebrush and clumps of high desert grasses that after May turned the yellow color of a corn tortilla. In the distance, past the nearby foothills, stood the Sangre de Cristo Mountains, covered in ponderosa pine and looking incredibly green against the bleached, brittle colors of high desert that spread out for miles below. Midway between the two, like angels standing between life and death, were lacy aspen-covered foothills that shimmered silver in the afternoon sunshine and never ceased to remind Charley that this was home.

Another mile and she rounded a turn where the dirt road changed to gravel that crunched under the wagon's tires. One more sharp turn and the road was suddenly flanked by two rows of tall juniper trees that led the way to a peach stucco, hacienda-style house that was built into the north side of a mountain. She parked and got out.

There were wrought-iron entrance gates that always squeaked when you opened them and a Mexican-tiled courtyard with a huge lion's head fountain that you had to walk around to reach the heavily carved front doors.

She closed the doors behind her, turned, and tossed her bag onto a nearby Spanish oak bench, then paused and listened. There was music playing from the radio in the kitchen. Unmistakable music: the jazzy sounds of Tommy Dorsey. She hunched down to look into a low, dark-framed mirror on the creamy plaster wall, humming and jiving a bit as she unpinned her straw hat.

She put the hat on her shopping bag. She turned and sashayed her way into the kitchen, singing, "Let's catch a tuna, way out in Laguna. Let's get away from it all . . ."

The room was empty, no sounds in the place but her humming and the voices of that new crooner Frankie

Sinatra and the Pied Pipers singing from the wooden Zenith on the sink. She turned down the music. "Pop?"

"I'm in the den!"

She waited a second, expecting him to ask her for a beer. When he didn't, she shrugged, flicked the volume back up, and crossed the tiled floor. She grabbed the handle on the white Frigidaire and danced the swing with it.

"Charley?"

She stopped. "Yeah?"

"Bring me a beer, will you?"

"Sure!" She smiled to herself, already bent over, her head half inside the open door of the fridge.

It was always amazing to her how good her voice sounded in hollow places like the refrigerator and the shower. Sometimes, when she was flying high in the clouds with the cool clean air in her hair, looking out at that blue, blue sky above her or down at the green mosaic pattern of the land below, she would sing as loud as she could, sing her heart out, sing up toward heaven just to let them know she was almost there.

"Let's get away from it all . . ." She shoved aside a bottle of thick buttermilk and a jar of even thicker golden honey, then took out two long-necked icy cold beers, spun around, and closed the door with a Carmen Miranda flick of her hip. She pried up the teeth of the metal beer caps with a bottle opener on the corner of the Fridge, then left through the arched hallway toward the back of the house.

She stood against the open doorway to the den. It smelled of the rum pipe tobacco her father smoked, a scent that she had always loved. When she was a little girl, they had a ritual. He would let her fill his pipe and taught her how to pack the tobacco tightly. She would sit and wait until he lit it before she ran off to play in some aircraft hangar or in the brittle grass of the land used as an airfield, which was usually next to a place they used as their temporary home. Her childhood could have been as colorless as the places they lived in, as vacuous as that of those poor, ragged children who followed their parents from town to town after the fall in 1929.

But it wasn't. Looking back on her childhood with older, wiser eyes, she realized she could easily have disappeared. Among local children who had bonded together in a classroom for year after year, the ones who'd played together and grew up together, she could have gone unnoticed, like faded white paint on the walls of a place you see day after day. It's there, but who cares?

Instead, she was the girl who flew in airplanes, the one with the father everyone liked and accepted and who would fly right over the schoolhouse at lunchtime and wave his wings. On Fridays, without fail, he would give three of her classmates an airplane ride. So for a time, the kids would try to get to know her, until she flew off to a new place, a new classroom filled with new faces.

Eventually they had settled down in Santa Fe, and her father swiftly built an aircraft business and eventually this home, where the den also served as his office. Here, there were photographs of aircraft and air races, of celebrities and famous clients, displayed everywhere, on the walls, the tables, and the huge double-sided mahogany desk.

In a display case on the west wall were brightly

painted models of her father's modified Lilienthal aircraft, nicknamed Ottos. At Charley's suggestion, he had named his company after Otto Lilienthal, a German scientist who made thousands of glider flights and whose experiments in flight gave both inspiration and airfoil data to the Wright brothers.

The room was thoroughly masculine, with plastered walls, thick dark wood moldings and beams, and the same tiles that covered all the floors of the house. The expensive handmade rug that dominated the center of the room was a hundred years old and the rich red color of bordeaux wine. Dark velvet draperies framed the wide wood-and-glass doors that opened out to a patio, and the leather furniture was a similar oxblood color with deep tufts and nailhead trim.

The room was like her dad. Large and bold, yet comfortably warm.

"Hey, Pop." She crossed the room.

Her father looked up and smiled at her from his leather chair behind the desk.

She handed him the beer.

"Thanks, kiddo." He took a long swig. "How was town?"

"The same."

"The same?"

"Durable."

He laughed. "You must have been in the Five-and-Dime."

"You know me too well." She slid her arms over his shoulders from behind and gave him a quick hug.

"Not really. You're wearing blue."

"Sure am. Saved you a nickel, too."

He laughed, then turned his head slightly so he could look at her. "So town disappointed you, did it?"

"It's the same. Not just similar, but exactly the same."

"Yes, it is. They work hard to keep things the way they like them here."

"I didn't mean anything derogatory. You know that. But I do wonder how a town, in this day and age, can feel so completely unchanged?"

"What happened to, 'Oh, Pop, are we *ever* going to have a *real* hometown? Someplace cozy and warm, like *real* people?' "

"I was twelve."

"You were Joan Crawford."

She laughed and walked around the desk. "You are awful, you know that? Besides, we were barely staying in one place for more than a couple of months. I was a sensitive child," she said airily, waving a hand in the air. "One who needed stability."

"Stability? I guess that's why now you're flying all over the country."

"I inherited your wanderlust."

"You've lived in eight places in the last three years."

"Little girls *do* grow up." She paused, then grinned. "Unlike Santa Fe, people change."

"I think I know one little girl who has gotten too big for her britches."

"I'm six foot one. I've always been too big for my britches."

He gave a shake of his silvery head and relented. In those years when her life had been so migratory, there hadn't been time to form close friendships with other children. But she had Pop.

Now they were like twin legs on a compass. He could go off in one direction, she on to another, but they always came back together again. They were joined by something stronger than their mutual love of flying, something different than the love between father and daughter, different than blood ties or family or all of those naturally accepted bonds.

They genuinely liked and respected each other. He was her best friend.

She hitched her hip on the corner of the desk and glanced down at the papers scattered all over the tooled-leather blotter she'd bought him last Christmas. "Whatcha-doing?"

"Reading this letter from Maggie."

"Maggie Caldwell?" Margaret Caldwell was an infamous flyer, an attractive blonde with sharp eyes to the future, a woman who felt strongly that she should be Amelia Earhart's successor.

Maggie was one of those people whom you knew, the moment you met them, would someday make their mark in the world. Charley had met Maggie through her dad, on a trip to Florida. At the time, Maggie had just broken Howard Hughes's New York to Miami speed record and had already twice won the Bendix Trophy, the top American air race. She also had several Harmon International Trophies to her credit, distinguishing Maggie Caldwell as the outstanding woman aviator in the world. The amazing thing was, she had only been flying for five years. "So. How is Maggie?"

"Fine. Busy. She has her usual five irons in the fire. But she's now Mrs. Cooper Crosby."

"She and Coop got married? Good."

"You sound relieved. Afraid she might have been your stepmother?"

"Let's just say Maggie is a woman who knows her mind, and expects you to know it, too." Charley took a drink of her beer.

She knew her father liked Maggie's spunk and drive. She was a strong, forceful woman. Pop and Maggie had become friends from the first time they'd met, at an air race in California where one of his modified racing planes was performing, outperforming actually, and ultimately won. Pop had mentioned Maggie often enough that Charley thought perhaps he might have finally found a woman to share his life.

But any hope her father might have had for some kind of relationship with Maggie was all fairy tale. She already had a man in her life. Cooper Crosby was a wealthy financier, a man who gave his first wife Bonwit Teller as a divorce settlement. He adored Maggie.

Charley looked at her father for a moment. His expression was a little empty, as if he had lost something. She instantly felt bad about what she'd just said. He could be in love with Maggie and completely heartbroken. "Are you truly sorry, Pop?"

"Sorry that Maggie and Coop got married? No."

"Actually, I was thinking that you might be sorry that Coop found her first." She paused. "Don't look at me that way."

"Which way?"

"With your forehead all scrunched up and your mouth in such a thin line it looks like a landing strip from ten thousand feet. I know that look. It means you think I'm out of line."

"What it means is I think you need a man to keep you busy so you'll stop meddling in my life."

"I can keep myself busy without a man, thank you."

He gave her one of those parental looks, the kind that made you feel as if you were six and had just told a huge lie.

"Men don't find me attractive."

"Then they must be blind . . . or you are."

"Spoken like a true doting father."

He just looked at her.

"Look, Pop, it's okay. I'm happy the way things are. Really. I am. Most men want petite little women they can throw around the dance floor. It's part of their masculine psyche. Men want women who make them feel big and strong and protective."

"So find a little guy who needs you to protect him."

Charley burst out laughing. "You are funny. Now, since we're speaking of men . . . I ran into the Ledbetter sisters in town. Dot said there was someone who came through here looking for me and they gave him directions here."

"Him? Have you been keeping someone secret from your old pop?"

"No."

"Who was it?"

"I think it was Red Walker."

"Who is Red Walker?"

"I told you about him. The nice young man from the Texaco station."

"The tornado watcher?"

She nodded. "That's him."

"No one came by here that I know of. When was this?"

"Dot said she thought it was before Thanksgiving."

"I wasn't home in November. We took the planes to the races in Arizona. If he came by here then, there wouldn't have been anyone here."

So Pop had been gone. For a moment she felt a stab of disappointment. She wondered what Red had wanted. If he wanted to learn to fly, she could teach him in Odessa or even in Dallas when she moved there.

"Do you think it was important?"

She shook her head. "Probably not, or else he'd have come back or contacted you by now." She walked around the desk, then leaned down and rested her arms on her father's shoulder, reading the letter from Maggie, figuring it was just a chatty letter between two old friends . . . until she spotted her name. "She's talking about me in this letter."

"Yep."

"Let me see that, you old devil." She straightened and held out her hand.

He handed her the letter over his shoulder, and Charley began to read as she paced the room.

Dear Bob,

I hope this finds you healthy and happily flying those Ottos of yours all over the Southwest. Coop and I got hitched a while back. He sends his best. As you probably know, he was a major contributor in the Roosevelt campaign, which means that we frequent the social events at the White House, where I have been on a new campaign of my own. And now the most wonderful thing has happened. Eleanor Roosevelt has given my plan her complete support.

We are campaigning for a women's air corps, Bob.

A separate women's air corps. I feel so strongly that women pilots can handle noncombat jobs and free up the men for duties overseas. Coop is certain we will be at war before the year is out. I suspect you know that as well.

A few months back, Eleanor told the nation about my plan on her My Day radio broadcast. Did you by chance hear it? The response has been overwhelming.

The best news is now General Arnold is on my side, too. But things in DC are at a standstill, stuck in the bureaucratic BS that is Washington these days.

However, on the General's recommendation, I have written to the head of Britain's Air Transit Auxiliary, Lord Beaverbrook. The British are using women, as test pilots, for ferrying planes and airmarking.

Charley read the next paragraph and she couldn't believe what she was reading. "Pop . . ." she looked up. "Did you read this?"

He nodded.

With Charley's experience and her qualifications, I feel strongly that she should have the opportunity to join a small test group of American women who I hope will be working with the ATA in Great Britain. If she's interested . . .

"If I'm interested?" She laughed. "I don't know a female pilot who wouldn't be."

Please have her fill out the enclosed application. In all truth, it might be months before I hear back from Lord Beaverbrook and the answer could be a resounding no. But General Arnold sent a recommendation and notice of his support. So just in case it isn't, tell her to make certain her passport is updated and ready.

"Is my passport still in the safe?"

"I take it that's a *yes*. You want to go?"

"Of course it's a yes. Where's the application?"

He handed her a few sheets of paper. She snatched them up and began to read them as she crossed the room, then opened a door that revealed a wall safe. She opened it, rummaged through, and took out her passport, then locked the safe and checked the passport expiration date. "It's still good for three more years."

"You want me to get up so you can sit down and fill those out now? She says she needs it back in a month."

She cast a glance over her shoulder. "Are you being sarcastic?" But then she caught that emptiness in his expression again. She had a sudden, sick feeling that she was the cause. "Pop? What's wrong?"

"There is a war on."

"Yes, there is."

"People are dying over there."

"Would that stop you from going?"

"You know it wouldn't."

She crossed the room and set her passport and the application papers on the desk, then squatted down and rested her arms on the rim of the desk and her chin on her arms. She looked her father in the eye. "You have never stopped me from doing anything, Pop. You always said there wasn't a thing in this world I couldn't do if I set my mind to it. You've never once treated me differently because I'm a woman. In fact, you're the one who taught me to go after what I want."

He didn't say anything.

"Tell me something, Pop. If I were a man, your son instead of your daughter, and I wanted to join the Army or better yet, say, the Army Air Corps, would you try to stop me?"

He was quiet for a long time. Finally he said quietly, "I would still worry."

"That wasn't what I asked you."

"Do you know that when you look at me like that you look just like your mother."

"Stop changing the subject."

"Hell . . ." he grumbled. "I'd join up myself if I wasn't so damn old."

"Fifty-three isn't old. It's seasoned." She paused, then went in for the kill. "Surely you aren't being like this because I'm a woman."

"If I were, I would never admit it to you. I'd have to run for cover."

She laughed softly. "I always said you were the smartest man I know."

"I don't know how smart it is to let you wrap me around your little finger."

"Pop, look here." She pointed to a paragraph of Maggie's letter. "It says we'll be air-mapping for the British—which I've already done—and ferrying planes and pilots."

"In a country that's being barraged with bombs and under attack from the Luftwaffe."

"I'll duck first if I see any MEs, okay?"

He gave her a hard look.

"I don't mean to be flip. I just want you to know I will be so very careful. I swear I will."

"Part of me understands why you want to do this, kiddo, but you're all I've got. For a few minutes let me be a normal father."

"You've never been a normal father in your life, and please don't start now. It's one of the things I love most about you."

Even he had to laugh.

Her childhood had been anything but normal. Despite the fact that they'd settled in Santa Fe, he had still taken Charley to air races and on business trips, where she met people like Lindbergh and Earhart. One sunny afternoon when she was about fourteen, she had come home to find Will Rogers sitting in this very room, and for her birthday one year, Pop took her on a special flight to Dayton, where they visited Hawthorne Hill and had dinner with Orville Wright.

She took the pipe away from him that he'd just picked up and reached for the humidor herself. "Tell you what. I promise that if I see a German plane, I'll land or fly out of sight. Okay?" She filled the pipe before she held it out to him rather like a peace offering.

He glanced at it, then looked into her face with a distant and warm expression on his. It was one of those rare moments when things become apparently simple; they were just a father and daughter again, as if fifteen years hadn't passed by at all. She struck a match, held it up for him, and sat there, waiting.

He took the pipe from her and put it between his teeth.

She shook out the first burning match and lit a fresh one.

"Afraid you'll get your fingers burned?"

"No, Pop. You are."

It didn't take him long to get her meaning. He took the match from her, lit his pipe with a few deep puffs, his forehead wrinkling as if it were difficult to light, but she knew that frown was because he had no good rebuttal argument. He shook out the match and tossed it in a copper ashtray with a beanbag base.

When he looked up at her, his expression softened. He drew on the pipe and exhaled the smoke. "Okay, kiddo. You win."

"Nothing is going to happen."

"Well, I suppose I'll have to think like you do. Besides, you'd do it anyway with or without my support."

"I knew if you looked at it from my perspective, logically, that you'd come around."

"You mean because I have no choice in the matter?"

"No, because you know when I'm right."

"How did I raise such a persistent child?"

"I'm just like you." Laughing, she jumped up and gave him another hug.

He patted her hands clasped across his chest. "I can't help feeling protective."

"I understand, Pop."

"Do you?"

"Of course I do. You love me."

"Actually, I was thinking more about what you said."

She didn't understand and peered over his shoulder to look at him. His face told her nothing. "And what was that exactly?"

"Well, kiddo, based on your insight into universal male motive," he said dryly, "I can't help feeling protective. It's part of my masculine psyche."

"PRACTICE MAKES PERFECT"

It was barely eleven o'clock in the morning, and the air in the flight-training room was already hot and thick and ebullient with the fumes of stale cigarette smoke and too much Tabu perfume. In the corner, an empty glass water jug in a wobbly metal stand crouched over a brown trash can spilling a trail of crushed paper cups and stubbed cigarette butts, both marked with different shades of red lipstick. Diagrams of Mustangs, Tiger Moths, Mosquitoes, and other aircraft covered the murky walls, and a huge dusty chalkboard marked with navigation data dominated one side of the room. An old, yellowed meteorology chart the size of a door hung at a cockeyed angle and was pinned with ads for everything from airplane parts and local jobs to a full-color Latin travel poster claiming the newly streamlined Douglas Aircraft Pan Am Clippers could get you from New York to Rio in only thirty hours. Some comedienne among the ATA candidates had taken an eyebrow pencil and drawn a dark mustache and thick eyebrows on Carmen Miranda's face. At first glance she looked like Groucho Marx beckoning you to South America's white-sand beaches. But no one was going to South America now, not since the Japanese had bombed Pearl Harbor.

Charley sat sprawled out on a hard wooden chair, her long legs propped on a metal electric heater that she was sure was about as useful in this part of Texas as wings on an ostrich. Right then, the thermometer was hovering around ninety-five degrees and the humidity felt to be about ninety percent. She was sweating—a permanent state since she'd arrived here—while she studied the tech manual for a P-51A.

Called Mustangs by the British, the planes were single-seat fighters contracted by the British Purchasing Commission in a deal struck with North American Aviation. The plane was said to handle beautifully thanks to its semi-laminar-flow airfoil wing. The Allison V-1710 engine had 1150 horsepower and a maximum cruising speed at fifteen thousand feet of three hundred miles per hour. It was a plane she'd been wanting to fly from the first moment she'd heard of it, because once inside, she would have her first glimpse of a fighter pilot's world.

But before the American women could be approved to leave with Maggie Caldwell for the Air Transit Authority positions in Great Britain, they each had to be checked out in certain types of planes. Official testing and certification was required by the ATA. If the instructor failed her, the applicant would be tossed out of the program. They had started with forty women, and now there were only twenty-seven left, assigned in small groups at three different airfields.

Charlie focused again on the plane's manual. She had a lot riding on this last training flight.

Rosalie Allen came rushing through the door. "Scuttlebutt has it that we're leaving for London before the week's out."

"That soon?" Joan Harting groaned. "I almost failed the test flights yesterday. Rafferty was on his high horse again."

"When isn't he on his high horse?" Dolores Salazar said with a wry laugh.

"High horse has nothing to do with Bill Rafferty."

They all turned and looked at Connie Bellows as if she were nuts for defending him.

"It's the low end of the horse . . ." she went on. "The horse's ass."

They all got a good laugh out of that. Their flight instructor was unreasonably difficult, one of those damned-if-you-do, damned-if-you-don't kinds of people.

Joan set her books aside and poured another cup of black coffee, then leaned against a filing cabinet and took a long sip. She scowled into the cup. "Good God, that's strong. Who made it, Caffeine Connie?"

Joan was a tea drinker, but since there was no tea available, she had to settle for coffee. Connie usually got up early to make coffee the way she liked it: thick as syrup and darker than engine sludge. But Connie could drink a whole pot of it and then settle in for a long nap. They had all learned early that caffeine didn't affect her.

"I don't understand it," Joan said.

"The coffee?"

"No. That's easy to understand. Connie was born without taste buds. What I don't understand is why someone would send Rafferty, the misogynist, to supervise the flight training for a handful of women. Maggie Caldwell had to fight pigheaded men like Bill Rafferty every step of the way to get these contracts accepted.

Why on earth is someone like him in charge of our instruction?"

"I don't understand, either." Rosalie sank into a chair in the corner. "I swear he was trying to get me to wash out all last week. You'd think Maggie would want someone who had some stake in seeing us succeed."

"Maggie had nothing to do with it," Charley told them. "She had no choice about who would control the flight testing. He was sent down here from the Atlantic Ferry Office in Montreal as part of the contract agreements."

"He wants us to fail. I heard him talking. The pilots in Canada were grousing about sending women at all, especially Yanks. Most of them believe it's only a stunt. I think Rafferty's from that camp. He had already decided before he ever got here to make it as difficult as possible for us to succeed."

"So he came here with that chip already on his shoulder," Dolores said.

"Sure did."

"I'm not giving him the satisfaction of washing me out," Charley said. "This is my last qualifier and then I'm home free."

But by three o'clock that afternoon, she was beginning to wonder if she would receive her assignment today at all. She was still waiting. They were behind schedule, and Rafferty was having a fit.

When her call finally came, she ran out of the flight room and toward the P-51, feeling both anxious and nervous, but sense told her it was good old American knowhow that made the aircraft. The P-51 was designed, built, and made ready to fly in only a hundred-and-twenty-odd days. Now if she could just do her stuff in it for about a hundred-and-twenty-odd minutes, she'd be guaranteed a trip to London, something she wanted badly. She would be part of the first team of American women to fly for the war effort, a part of history doing something she lived and breathed for: flying.

She climbed onto the wing and got a good look at the cockpit for the first time. It was so small that with all her flight gear on it was going to be a tight squeeze to get inside and get strapped into the flight seat.

How the hell were men supposed to fly this thing?

This wasn't the first time she wished she was five foot four and a hundred and thirty pounds. "I wonder if Rafferty thought I would fit inside it at all," she muttered as she placed her hand on the rim of the cockpit opening and climbed inside. She gripped the rim of the cockpit with one hand and leaned back so she could slide down into the seat without hitting her chin. She got about halfway down when she stopped sliding and felt her chute straps bite into her shoulders and groin.

"Dammit." Her chute was caught on the seat back.

She twisted and pulled herself back up. It took a few moments to get untangled, which was like trying to dance the Lindy in a telephone booth. She closed the cockpit, then locked and checked the safety latch and pins. Even though she had spent the morning going over the technical manual, she still had to spend time familiarizing herself with the actual plane. She checked the boost and supercharger controls, fuel and oil switches . . . where was the fuel-booster pump?

Rafferty's gravelly voice came over the radio. "What the hell is taking so long, Morrison? Just because you're trying to go to England doesn't make this mother-frigging teatime. Get that machine in the air. *Now!*"

She covered the mike on her radio headset with her hand and quietly suggested he put the machine in the same place his head was.

"Did you say something, Morrison?"

"Just a prayer, sir." Charley flicked the switches. The engine coughed to a start. She checked her gauges, then talked to the tower on the radio. She powered up and took off.

This was an amazing machine. She was upstairs a few minutes later, learning and loving what the plane could do. She wanted to take her up, way up, to dive, to loop and spin, to take her up to full speed, but if she did, she'd be washed out.

Her job was to ferry planes, not dogfight over the Channel . . . if she ever got there. No, when she got there. She would show Rafferty she could control this plane. She was going to England.

There were two main runways at Whiting. One which ran north and south and was used most often, but today that runway was closed, which was why they were behind, so she was told she had to use the east-west runway for her touchdowns and takeoffs, which meant at this time of day she was going to be landing into the setting sun.

She spent the next hour doing the required testing and learning the feel of the plane. But after a while, what she actually felt she was testing was her own skill as a pilot. The haze around the field was growing thicker by the minute. As the sun began to go down, landing was getting tricky, especially on a shorter runway. The P-51 could easily overshoot it.

She had Rafferty to contend with. But she was going to Britain. Period.

Whiting Field was not the best in normal weather, but in the sun haze, well, she was landing almost blind. To compensate, she memorized all the hazards over the end of the short field. There were power poles with crossbars at the end of the runway, not to mention the houses and businesses and telephone poles that were all clustered nearby.

To help her land as the visibility grew worse and worse, she would count off the hazards, "one telephone pole, two telephone pole, three telephone pole, one power pole . . . Jackson Avenue . . . two power pole . . ." until she knew she was right over the edge of the runway; then she would drop down for what was pretty much a blind landing.

They were required to take off and land a certain number of times to be officially checked out. Some instructors would give you some slack on that, but not Rafferty.

She checked her logs. She had one takeoff and landing left to qualify. The sun was getting lower, but she felt there was still enough time.

She taxied around again and prepared for her last takeoff.

"You're not going to make it, Morrison." Rafferty was talking to her from the tower.

The bastard was smiling. She could hear it in his voice through the earphones in her headset.

"You have one landing left to qualify. Too bad, Morrison. I can't qualify you. They're closing the airport because of the haze. Bring that plane to the west hangar."

She tapped the mike with her finger to make some static noise, then blew into it a few times as she turned the plane for another takeoff. "Sorry, sir, but I can barely understand you."

"I said bring the plane in!"

"You're cutting out," she lied.

"Turn that goddamn plane around!"

"Cannot copy. Can you repeat, sir?"

"I said . . . do not take off!"

"Roger, I'm taking off as ordered. Over." And up she went.

"OH, LOOK AT ME NOW"

Red pulled his truck into the lot across the street from the airfield and parked. He opened the door and stood alongside his dusty black truck, one foot on the running board and his arm resting on the truck cab.

In front of him was a big, old brown-brick building with a flat roof and four floors—each one cut with white, wooden-framed windows that ran across the side like dominoes spread out on a parlor table. Two skimpy trees stood in the front, and there was a gravel walkway that led to the door. Off to the south in a vacant side yard, the lawn was brown and burnt, with round, scabby patches of dirt showing through the grass that made it look as if it had skinned its knees. Above that was a good hundred feet or more of clothesline strung in Zs. He'd never seen so much female underwear in his life, bras, panties, and slips, all of it bleached to a crisp, blinding white, except one lacy brassiere that was red enough to fire up a bull.

He'd been told that the women were assigned to quarters near the field, in an old Sears and Roebuck building. One look at that clothesline was enough. He'd found it.

He crossed to the front door and rapped on it.

Nothing.

From an open window on the third floor, he could hear the thin, scratchy sound of radio music and the distant chattering of women talking and laughing. He knocked again, louder, then searched for a bell to ring.

There was none.

He stepped back and looked up at the closest open window; it was up on the third floor and had a flimsy-looking flowered curtain drifting out of it. Since the air was still as a rock, the only thing that could make that curtain drift would be a fan in the room.

"*Hel*-lo!" He waited.

Nothing.

"*Hello!*" Still nothing.

He cupped his hands around his mouth and hollered, "Is anybody in there?"

A pert looking brunette with full lips and a head full of pin curls swiped aside the curtains and stuck her head outside the window, scowling.

"Hello, ma'am." He slipped off his service cap and nodded to her.

Her expression changed on a dime. She hitched her hip on the window frame and grinned down at him. "Well, well . . . hello to you, soldier."

"I'm looking for Charley Morrison."

"Lucky Charley."

That was why he liked Charley. She didn't embarrass him the way this girl did. He looked down for a moment, away from her come-on look, and stared at the field cap in his hands.

"Who are you talking to, Rosalie?" Another girl wedged her head out between Rosalie and the window frame.

"Charley's beau."

"Charley has a beau?"

"No." He shook his head. "I'm just a friend."

"Uh-huh, sure," the new girl said. She gave a sharp nod toward the airfield. "She's at the field. Ask over there and someone can tell you where she is."

"Thank you, ma'am. I—" He stopped.

She hadn't waited for him to finish. She was gone as quickly as she had appeared. But not Rosalie, who was still sitting in that window, languid as a cat full of buttermilk on a warm summer day. "Oh, don't you mind her, sugar. She's always like that. But I'm not. No, siree. Not me. I *like* men."

He just wanted to leave, but he didn't want to be rude to her.

She laughed and waved a hand at him. "Go on. Find Charley. But if she's busy, you come on back here and I'll be happy to keep you company."

"Yes, ma'am." Red put his hat back on and turned, then flatfooted it across the dirt lot, heading off toward the airfield.

For the next twenty minutes he wandered around, asking for Charley. Everyone had seen her, but no one knew where she was. He had two places left to look, one was the tower and he doubted she was there, and the other was a big Lockheed Aircraft hangar out on the west end.

Red rounded the corner of the hangar, out of the relentless heat and sun into a sanctum of shade. Across the hangar, past a small trainer and the maintenance area, where a mechanic was working on a Lodestar transport, he spotted a man with a crop of white hair and sporting grease-stained coveralls.

Red moved closer, close enough to see the man was sitting at a workbench, talking excitedly into a radio mike.

"Five-niner-three. Can you hear me, now? Come in?"

Static crackled back from the ham radio.

Red stood just behind him and the old-timer glanced up at him, then held up a hand, frowning as he repeated, "This is Whiting Airfield. Hangar B. Come in again if you can hear me. Over."

More static.

"Damn and hell . . . I can't get it." Scratching his jaw, he turned to Red. "Caught a distress call from a plane out there somewhere. Sounded like big trouble."

"Who is it?"

"I don't know. I was repairing this here radio when out of the clear blue this panicked voice comes through."

"Why isn't the pilot talking to the tower?"

"She said she couldn't get their frequency."

"She?"

"I think it's one of those ATA gals."

"I DON'T WANT TO SET THE WORLD ON FIRE"

Charley counted off the hazards. "Three telephone pole ... Jackson Avenue ... Two power pole...." *One more to go.* She knew she should clear it by about ten feet. She checked her gauges, the needles looked off.

Rafferty's voice bellowed into her earphones. "Morrison!"

Suddenly the plane clipped the last pole. There was a horrific crunch. She swore and grabbed the controls with both hands.

The nose shot up. The plane started to roll.

Oh, God....

She jerked on the controls, hard, gave the plane full power. It vibrated violently. There was a loud, high-pitched whining sound, like a human screaming. She jerked up the gear and tried to straighten the plane, both at the same time.

It bucked like a bronco. "Come in, Whiting Tower. Tower? Come in." Nothing on the radio.

Damn ... damn ... damn ....

The plane lifted a bit and leveled out. She wasn't rolling anymore. The plane began to shudder and pulled against her hand controls. She glanced at the instruments, but the plane was vibrating so much she couldn't read them.

The engine stopped screaming so sharply she froze for an instant.

This is it.

She pulled the emergency release handle on the cockpit so she wouldn't be trapped inside, then waited for the engine to stall, then for that inevitable drop that would follow.

But it was the oddest thing. The drop didn't come. The engine was still running, rough, but running.

She looked down.

The plane was in the air, flying low over the runway. But bad for her: over the end of the runway, and heading straight for an airplane hangar. The huge hangar door was open. She could see a trainer and a C-57 transport parked inside.

Some men were waving their arms at her. The letters on the hangar—"Lockheed Aircraft"—grew bigger and closer. Way too close.

She tried to get the plane up. Gunned it. Pulled on the controls, trying to get it up. She needed some altitude.

Come on baby . . . come on . . .

Now she could read the gasoline advertising sign that hung on the front of the hangar. It had a logo of a huge clipper plane on it, one that seemed to be coming at her.

Desperate, she punched the engine to full power, not knowing what it would do.

Get up there!

The P-51 sluggishly responded. It was flying barely above a stall.

The hangar was right there. In front of her. A huge metal coffin.

She gave it full throttle. "Dear God," she whispered. "Please. Just let me get over it." She gritted her teeth, then closed her eyes.

It was one of those moments when everything stopped. Suspended. The world outside the cockpit just ceased to exist.

The seconds slowed. Charley waited to die.

One breath . . .

Two . . .

Three . . .

She opened her eyes. The hangar roof was beneath her as she passed over it, barely. Some kind of low sound came out of her, from deep inside her, and she wasn't sure if it was a curse or a prayer. She inhaled, took two quick, deep breaths.

For as long as she lived—if she got out of this alive—she didn't want to ever know by how much she had just cleared that hangar.

Okay. You're still flying. That's good. Think, now. God, somehow I have to get to a higher altitude.

After a minute at full throttle, the plane was actually gaining altitude again, a fact that made her racing heart slow down a little. She didn't dare move a thing, just fought to hold the controls right where they were and to keep the plane up and level.

Think. Think.

She could hear an eerie, clanging sound coming from starboard, as if a piece of the plane were banging against the hull. Or the angels were knocking on her door.

She looked at the left wing. No angels there. She would have rather seen an angel. Hell, she would have rather seen a devil. Part of the wing was missing.

She took a quick glance back at the tail.

Half the elevator was gone. She glanced back again. It looked at if it had been eaten. She stared out at the sky around her and realized she was high enough now to bail out.

Okay . . . she was going to live. She looked down below her for a second.

The plane was flying well enough to gain altitude, and she had it under control, even though it was awkward.

Do I really want to scuttle this plane?

She thought she could try working with it a little, try to get the gear down and see if maybe she could land.

Chewing on her lip, she glanced down again. No matter what, bail or give it a go, she had to get away from this populated area. And fast.

Fighting like crazy to keep the plane straight, she headed away from the airport, north of town, where there was nothing around and if she went down . . . well, then it would only be her.

'SO HELP ME'

"Where the hell is she going?"

"Sweet Jesus. . . . I can't believe she's still in the air."

"Well, you can believe it," Red said to the two men standing at the glass window of the tower. "The Charley Morrison I know doesn't give up." He crossed over to the radio, picked up the mike, sat down, and dialed an outside frequency. "Charley? Come in. This is Red Walker. Over."

He paused, then played with another frequency, one close to the ham radio operator's.

"Charley? Can you hear me? Over."

"Whiting Tower—" Her crackling voice spliced through, then there was nothing.

"Charley!" He adjusted the dial. "Come in. We can hear you! This is Red Walker. Over."

"Red?" There was a pause. "Texaco Red?"

He laughed a little. "Sounds like you're in some trouble. Over." There was silence, and he wasn't sure if he'd lost her or not.

"I'm struggling up here." Her voice came through, only cutting out a little.

"Repeat."

"The engine noise is really something awful and the instrument panel's vibrating like crazy. I can barely read it. I don't dare take my hand off the controls."

One of the men grabbed the mike from Red's hand. "Morrison? This is Rafferty. Turn that goddamn plane around and get your ass back here! You hear me?"

There was no response.

Red wanted to wrap the mike around this Rafferty's thick neck.

"Morrison!"

"Give me back the mike." Red held out his hand. He stood about four inches taller than Rafferty, but the guy tried to bull-dog him. Rafferty took a step closer and looked up at him, chin out like his granddaddy's old mule, ready to have it out.

"Look." Red nodded in the direction of the plane. "She's up there now on nothing more than a wing and a prayer. Screaming at her like some drill sergeant is only going to make it worse."

"I'm responsible for those ATA women and for that plane. She knocked out the frigging airport power pole. Last we saw of that plane, half the wing and tail were gone. Hell, I couldn't see her goddamn landing gear." He drove a hand through his hair. "Shit! What a mess!"

"Exactly. You yell at her. You shake her up, and she'll crash that plane in the middle of a civilian neighborhood."

"He's right, Bill. Give him the mike. Maybe he can sweet-talk her down."

Sweet-talk? Obviously neither of these men knew Charley. But Rafferty backed off and handed him the mike.

"Charley. It's me again, Red. Tell me what's happening. Can you turn the plane? Over."

"This is one sick puppy. I'm holding hard left rudder and right stick to make it fly straight."

"Jesus . . ." the other man muttered.

"I'm thinking I should try to head out of town and then bail out. Over."

Rafferty swore viciously.

Red looked at him.

He glared back. "That plane costs a fortune!"

"Red?" Her voice sounded too quiet.

"I'm here."

There was a pause; then she said, "I hate to destroy the plane when I can still fly it straight."

He wondered if she'd heard Rafferty in the background. "It's getting dark. You don't want to land it in the dark."

"I know . . . I know . . . but let me try something first."

"What?"

"Just a minute."

The engine noise in the background of her transmissions suddenly disappeared.

Red didn't know if they'd lost communication or if the engine had stopped. He waited for her voice. *God, don't let her crash.*

A moment later her voice came over the radio loud and clear. "It worked! Red, it worked! I throttled back and raised the nose. I think I can do this. I think I can control her enough to land."

"How much fuel have you got?"

"Not much. Maybe enough to get back to the field." She paused. "If I can find it."

"There are no lights on the field." Rafferty's voice was snide. "She knocked out the power."

Red turned to the other man. "What about smudge pots?"

"They were shipped to Fort Worth by mistake. We've been trying to get them back here for months."

Red turned back to the mike. "There's a problem on this end. We have no lights for you, Charley."

Another voice crackled into the radio. "Five-niner-three. This is Ed Hunter in Hangar B."

It was the ham radio operator.

"We're moving the trucks out of maintenance and onto the runway. Their headlights will light the field for you. They're already moving. Give us two minutes."

"Charley? Did you hear that?" Red asked.

"Roger. I heard." Her voice sounded as if she were crying.

From the tower they could hear the drone of her engine. "We can hear you, but can't see your landing lights. Can you see the runway?"

"I'm not sure. There are streetlights all over. I can't even be certain where the field is."

"Take a chance. Pass over it once. Over."

"Roger. I can't read the gauges. I have to be flying on fumes. Wait! I think I see you!"

"We can't see you."

"I need to be certain where my landing light switch is. Ask Bill Rafferty where the toggle switch is for the landing lights. I don't want to flip the wrong switch."

Rafferty grabbed the mike and barked out the answer.

"There she is!"

Red turned and could see the dim lights of the plane about a quarter of a mile out. Silently, the three men watched her approach.

Red spoke into the mike, "I can see your wheels down, Charley. Looks good."

"Thank God . . . I think I just spotted the runway." She paused. "Yes! That's it!"

"Good girl."

"Red?"

"I'm here."

"I swear I won't hit the gas pumps."

Joking at a moment like this. "Hell, Charley, they're not Texaco pumps. You can clip 'em if you want to."

"I think I've clipped enough things for one day."

Red watched her approach, the plane weaving in the air. He could imagine what she was doing to control the plane. Alone. "You can do this, Charley."

"I guess we'll find out now. Here goes . . ."

The plane turned and now was headed for a radio transmission tower.

"Charley! The radio tower!"

"I see it! But I'm already at full throttle. I can't get her up!"

Red's heart stopped.

"Oh, God . . ."

At the sound of her voice, they all shifted closer to the glass. It was so quiet, you could have heard a feather float.

She was having trouble controlling the plane. It slipped up, then down and struggled. He expected to see it dive down any moment. Suddenly, the nose shot up. He could hear the engine rev up. She missed the tower.

"God . . . She's got an angel on her shoulder."

The nose of the plane tilted down. She was heading down and for the runway, but so slowly that the wings of the plane were waving as if the plane were bouncing on air. At her slow speed, it was a struggle just to stay up in the air.

Closer to the ground . . . closer, then closer. She landed the thing like a rock, just dropped heavily onto the ground, because she had so little speed left.

"I'll be a son of a bitch. She made it." Rafferty was shaking his head.

Red dropped the mike and ran down the tower stairs. He heard the others on his heels. He shoved the doors open so hard they slammed against the walls; then he ran across the field, through the glaring line of head-lights.

She taxied the plane toward a hangar. By the time Red got to her, there was a crowd surrounding the plane. She hadn't moved. Her head was face down on her arms, which were resting on the control panel.

Red shoved his way through the crowd.

She lifted her head and turned as if she knew he was there; then she smiled and gave him a weak wave and shook her head as if she couldn't believe she'd made it either.

He jumped up on what was left of the wing, squatted so he was eye level with her. "Charley?"

She took off her headset, unstrapped her helmet, and looked at him. "I don't think I can get out of here. I'm shaking so bad."

Her hands were trembling.

"It's really cramped in here." Now her teeth were chattering.

She was in shock, and he didn't blame her one bit.

"You need help?" someone called out.

"No. I got her." He pulled her out, then just held her. She was so limp that she clung to him, her face in his shoulder, and he could feel her take in deep breaths. "It's okay." He rubbed her back. "You did it. I don't know how in blazes you did it, but you landed this plane with half a wing gone, part of the tail ripped off, and the belly split like a gutted catfish."

Some of the mechanics were walking around the plane, talking among themselves and looking at the damage, shaking their heads.

She turned back toward the plane. "My God. Look at that. One of the propeller blades is half-melted."

He kept his hand on her shoulder to steady her. She was still shaking.

"It must have melted from the power lines."

He turned her back toward him and looked down at her stunned face. "That was some flying."

She closed her eyes and looked down, like she was going to cry.

"Especially for a woman."

Funny thing, then. Her head shot up.

He gave her a wink.

She gave him a weak smile, but it looked like her tears were gone. "Help me down, will you?"

He didn't let go of her shoulders. "You're sure you're okay? I'll wait if you need me to hold you up a bit longer."

"I'm okay. Right now all I want is to feel the ground under my feet."

He jumped down, then turned and half-caught her when she slid down from the wing. A group of women pilots, all of them talking at once, closed in around them, hugging her, two of them were crying. Over her head he watched as Rafferty came forward and put his hand on her shoulder.

Charley turned around and saw who it was. Her smile melted like that propeller, and she stiffened, almost as if she were waiting for a blow. The other women grew suddenly quiet, all of them looking at Rafferty, then at her, then back to Rafferty.

"Good job, Morrison."

Her jaw dropped open when he took and shook her hand.

Rafferty said nothing else, but didn't move.

She recovered quickly. "Thank you, sir." Then the

women took her hands and swept her along with them, chattering and heading for the outbuildings.

Red turned when he saw Rafferty walk away and join the group of men who were looking over the plane.

"Can't believe she landed it."

"Amazing. For a dame."

"Yeah. That was some flying." One of them whistled. "Did you see her almost clip that radio tower? Jeez . . ."

"You'll have to pass her, Rafferty. She's a damn good pilot."

"Yeah, anyone else would have probably bailed or ended up dead."

"Hell," Rafferty said. "I don't give a rat's ass if the bitch goes and kills herself. I just don't want her doing it when I'm in charge." Rafferty spun around.

And Red knocked him out cold.

"I WAS LUCKY"

Three hours later, when the last of the ATA gals and a few of the airfield employees finally left, Charley and Red were alone at a table in a nearby bar. A local band called Joe Corn and His Five Cobs was performing on a makeshift pinewood stage in a dimly lit corner. The bandleader, a great trumpet player named Guy Jay, had just announced they were ending the set with a special arrangement of "Deep Purple."

Charley set down her whiskey sour and began to pick

out the chili-coated pecans from a snack dish shaped like a longhorn steer.

"Those women are something." Red shook his head. "They all talk at once."

She laughed. "We've become good friends. It's been hard. So many have been washing out because of Rafferty." She swallowed, then looked Red in the eye. "I haven't had a chance to thank you for what you did."

"There's nothing to thank me for. I didn't do anything. You did it, not me."

"I was so scared I just reacted by instinct." She paused, looking into her drink and remembering how scared she had really been. She looked up and admitted, "It was easier to think more clearly once I heard your voice. I guess what I'm trying to say is that thanks to you, I didn't feel as if I was alone anymore."

"I wouldn't have wanted to try to land that plane for all the oil in Texas. Most pilots would have bailed."

"Rafferty would have killed me if I'd ditched that plane."

"You don't have to worry about Rafferty anymore."

"I can't believe he qualified me."

Red popped a handful of nuts into his mouth and chewed on them for a bit. "When do you leave for England?"

"They haven't told us. Rumor is within the week. How long's your leave?"

"Four more days. I need to be back to the base by Sunday at oh-nine-hundred."

She smiled and pointed to his Army Air Corps jacket with flying cadet insignia, silver wings, and sergeant stripes. "I like the uniform."

She reached out and touched his insignia. "I don't understand your ranking. Sergeant Pilot? I didn't know there was such a thing."

"Neither do some of the MPs. I've been stopped a few times and told to take off my pilot's wings. When I refused, they hog-tied me good and took me in. A few phone calls later they let me go, wings intact. One of us was clubbed in Houston when he refused to take his wings off. Now they call us Flight Officers, but there's still no official insignia. It's kind of a hinterland between enlisted men and commissioned officers."

She took another drink. "So, when did you join up?"

"Not too long after you left. I signed up first for airplane mechanics training; then after that I could apply for pilot training." He grinned and popped some more nuts into his mouth. "They were desperate for pilots, so they let me in."

"They must have been." She laughed when he threw a nut at her. It hit the back of the chair and bounced off her shoulder. "What a lousy shot. Good thing you weren't going to gunnery school." She brushed the chili powder off her shoulder.

"I was aiming for the back of the chair."

"Sure you were." She moved the nut dish closer to her and took another sip of her drink. She set the glass down and looked up at him again. "Seriously, what made you decide to leave the gas station?"

"You. And my sister. Nettie pointed out that even as a kid I was always dreaming of someplace else—any-place but where I was. She says wanderlust is in my blood and that I couldn't stop it any more than I could stop breathing."

"You listen to your sister."

"Listen to Nettie?" He laughed. "She doesn't give you any other choice. My sister, the riveter. She gets something into her head and she won't let it go. She just kept at me. 'You don't belong in that gas station, Red. Go follow your dreams and stop trying to be something you're not.'"

She laughed at his high, mimicking voice, complete with Southern drawl. "I think I would like Nettie."

"Most likely you would. She's even more stubborn and pigheaded than I am, maybe even more than you." He took a swig of his beer, then grinned when she punched him in the arm. "She was right and I should have left earlier."

"Why didn't you?"

He looked into his beer as if the answer were written in there. "I kept trying to be like my daddy, I guess, probably because I didn't want to be like Mama. Until one day I realized I didn't want to spend my life like he spent his: living inside his gas station, afraid—ashamed because he was afraid—his only world inside an engine and his dreams wrapped up in a woman who couldn't have stayed with him even if she wanted to."

"Your mother left."

He nodded. "When I was twelve."

"I'm sorry, Red."

He shrugged, not looking her in the eye. "It was a long time ago. And it doesn't matter. What does matter is a few months after you left, I woke up one morning and it was all so clear. I knew I wanted more. I have you to thank for that." He looked at her then, a look she'd seen before—like she hung the moon.

"You didn't look all too thankful when I landed that day." She reached out and squeezed his arm, laughing, because she needed to make a joke to keep things from being too serious.

He just said, "You were living my dream. I watched you fly away and this bell went off in my head, like some kind of alarm or something. There was another whole world outside of that Texaco station in Acme, Texas. But I was just too afraid to walk out into it."

"Red," she laughed. "Anyone who sits on a rickety old water tower during a storm so he can watch tornadoes go by already has the courage and heart to do anything he sets his mind to."

"I wanted to fly." He rolled the beer bottle between his palms. "Since the day I set eyes on my first airplane, I've always wanted to fly."

For a moment neither of them said anything, lost in feelings only people who've flown a plane can understand. She knew what it was like to hold that control stick in her hand. The speed and power of the engine in front of you, feeling it all the way into your hands and feet. That moment when you lift and leave your belly and the world below behind you. You're in the air— suddenly a human cloud—flying a machine that gives you wings, and you are in a sudden and reverent awe of the sheer wonder of aerodynamics.

The band stopped playing and took a break. The clinking sound of glasses came from behind them where the bartender was dishwashing. Overhead smoke drifted in long foglike fingers up in the beamed ceiling, and a few people were talking in low tones from the cocktail tables huddled in dark corners. Charley fiddled with the napkin under her drink, tearing the corners and folding it into the shape of an airplane. "What were you doing down in Santa Fe last Thanksgiving?"

He laughed and looked down as if he were embarrassed. "You heard about that."

"I'm sorry I wasn't there. And Pop was at an air race in Arizona."

"I was coming through and thought I'd see if I could track you down through your daddy. I had just finished flight school. I was riding pretty high that week. It had been tough getting there."

"Through flight school?"

He nodded.

"Why?"

"There was a lot of hazing. I don't think I'd slept much more than ten hours a week. I was afraid I'd wash out. They worked us hard and tore us down, testing our tolerance points. The military does that."

"Rafferty gave us a pretty hard time. Does the Air Corps do it because they want you to fail in the same way he wanted us to fail?"

"I don't think so. It isn't prejudice. It's the Army's way. They figure it's better to fail here than on the battlefield, when other lives are at stake."

She nodded. "I wish that had been Rafferty's reasoning."

"Some things were pretty harmless. For the first three weeks we could only sit on the first three inches of our chairs. They had us marching so much on the parade grounds that we were up all night studying; then we'd go up the next day with a flight instructor who would crack our knees with the stick if we did something that wasn't done the way he liked it. I can remember being so tired I had trouble remembering where I was, in the air or on the ground. I'd wake up at night thinking I was landing a BT-13. They came in on inspections at all hours. You'd just fall asleep and the lights would come on and they'd rip apart your locker.

"You needed every ounce of stubbornness you could grab onto. Pretty soon, it's just you against them. You're damn well not going to fail just to spite them." He paused and took a swig of his beer. "You never knew what was going to happen, so you stayed on your guard. One time, some joker removed the bolts in my flight seat, so when I took off, I suddenly found myself lying on my back and staring up through the canopy at the wild blue yonder."

She started giggling, and couldn't stop, then held her hand out. "I'm sorry. It's not funny, I know."

"It's funny, Charley. I know it is. After I was able to sit up and get control again, I cursed the air bluer than that sky, but I had to laugh. It was pretty inventive. I can imagine what my face must have looked like. One minute I'm staring out ahead of me and the next, I'm flat on my back. Stop your giggling, girl."

"I'm sorry." She couldn't stop and bit her lip, then decided sipping on her drink would help. She took a giant gulp.

"Are you through?" Even he was having trouble keeping a straight face.

"Yes, thank you."

"Good. I expect you would have been right there with those guys standing along the runway and laughing like jackasses when I landed.

"None of that matters now. I'm a pilot. And every lost minute of sleep, every sore foot and bloody blister, every humiliating joke and embarrassing moment, was all worth it the day I graduated."

She reached out and clasped his hand. "I'm glad, Red. Really. I'm happy for you. You'll make a wonderful pilot."

His neck flushed the color of his hair, and he looked down at her hand, so she let go and wrapped her hands around her drink. "Where are you stationed?"

"San Antone. I've a got a four-day pass before I start bombardment courses at Randolph Field."

"Bombers? You're going to train to fly bombers?"

He nodded.

"I'm so envious. I'd give anything to fly a bomber."

"After what I saw tonight, I expect you could fly a tin can."

"Thanks." She took another drink, then ate some of the ice from a glass of ice water at her elbow.

The music started again, the soft sweet notes of "And the Angels Sing."

Charley listened for a moment, then said, "I swear. Look. It's ten o'clock at night and still a hundred degrees." She pressed the glass to her forehead and sighed. "This feels so good. I'd like to take a bath in a huge vat of ice."

He looked at her for a second. "Let's get out of here." He stood up and paid the bill. "Come on." He put his hat on and pulled her off the stool, then threaded her arm through his. "I know someplace much cooler."

"THE MOON GOT IN MY EYES"

Charley looked out the windshield of Red's truck and saw nothing but a black night sky and below it, in dark relief, the features of the landscape. "Why are we stopping here?"

"You'll see." Red stepped out of the truck, came around, and helped her out.

"But I don't see anything."

"You will." He slammed the door. "Follow me." He grabbed her hand and pulled her along with him over a clump of land and down toward a gully, where a dark cluster of sprawling trees were filled with the assonant purr of locusts and the grass was so softly moist it didn't crunch like hay under her feet.

She could smell the red Texas dirt; it had a smell like no other place she'd ever been. Texas dirt smelled like what was grown in it: wheat and cotton. You breathed in Texas dirt once or twice and it became a part of your memory, so when you put your hands in a bowl of flour or ironed a clean shirt, you found yourself drifting back to a place so flat and broad the horizons looked like the very edges of the world.

Red pulled her along through a few rustling bushes that had soft waxy leaves but no thorns or burrs. She could taste the moistness of water in the air before they came out of the bushes. There, before her, lay a large

pond that turned silver as the moon crawled out from
behind a drift of gauzy clouds. Squat dandelions and
limp bluebonnets grew in a tangled cluster near some
rocks where a frog croaked, then plopped into the water.

At the pond's edge, he released her hand and sat
down on the ground, untied his shoes, then peeled off
his socks. He glanced up at her over a shoulder. "Well?"

"Red, this is wonderful!" Charley laughed. After
those tense weeks at Whiting, the sound of her laughter
seemed light and distant in that sudden cradle of silence.
It carried up above her, floating up there as if it had come
from someone she didn't know. She sat down in the soft
grass and took off her flight boots and socks, then rolled
the legs of her jumpsuit up to her knees and slid her pale
feet and calves into the cool water.

A second later she flopped back, her arms over her
eyes as she kicked her feet in the water and groaned, "It
feels just like heaven."

Something dropped on the ground next to her. The
wind from it brushed her face. She lifted her arm and
looked up at Red.

He was shirtless and busy unbuckling his belt.

She sat up. "What are you doing?"

"I'm going swimming. That's why I brought you
here." He stepped out of his pants and dropped them on
the ground. He climbed onto a nearby rock and dove in
with hardly a splash, just a concentric ring of ripples. He
surfaced and slicked the hair and water back from his
grinning face. "What are you waiting for?"

"A bathing suit."

Laughing, he swam a few feet closer and faced her
again. "I thought you were hot."

"I am." She didn't move, but glanced up at the sky. The moon was slipping across that broad Texas sky. The air was like the inside of an oven, the pond secluded; the water was simply there, waiting. For a minute she didn't do a single thing; then she stood and grabbed the lapels of her flight suit and in one motion pulled open all the front snaps. She fought with the heavy metal zipper that always stuck, then managed to slip it down. She let the jumpsuit drop, stepped out of it quickly, and headed straight into the water until she was in knee-deep.

It was so incredibly freeing, doing something like this, leaving her clothes and maybe her sense behind, wading out in that island of water. But then today had been one of those kinds of days that almost squeezed all the life out of you. There were rare events in your life that time could never make stale, moments that ached just as much years later as they did when you lived through them. She had the feeling this was going to be one of those kinds of "real memory" days.

She took a deep breath of warm summer air, then arched with her arms high and dove down, swimming along the murky bottom of the pond. There, she didn't have to qualify to live her dreams. There, she didn't have to prove herself. There, she could just move in the water and feel as if she had become a part of it.

She kicked out and flipped over, then pushed through the cool silk of the water, looking up above her. Everything was black, an opaque cocoon, except for the circle of silver-green, a glowing rime of the moon and its light that made the softly fluent water almost transparent and lit a path to the surface. She swam upward. When she burst through and gasped for air, she felt as if there was fresh blood inside of her, in her heart, her limbs and her mind.

She treaded water for a moment, looking around the pond.

Red swam over to her.

"This is too wonderful for words."

"I figured a cool swim was just what you needed."

"How did you know about this place?" She floated onto her back.

He turned over and floated beside her out into the middle of the pond. "My granddaddy had a small farm about ten miles from here. My mama used to bring Nettie and me there." He paused. "Whenever she needed to get away from Daddy, she'd leave us with Granddaddy Ross."

For too many years Charley had missed having her mother there for her. It was one of those things that girls without mothers thought about . . . the moments when you missed your mother so badly that you felt as if you were only half a person. But she understood something then, from what Red had just said. She knew that it was better to lose your mother to death than to apathy.

That he was a kind man said something about his strength of character. The truth was, she liked him, as much for his quick smile and openness as she did for his honest words.

"I learned to swim in this pond," he said.

"You did?"

"Yep. On my sixth birthday."

"Whoever taught you to swim did a darn fine job, Red Walker. You're a good swimmer."

"Taught me?" He laughed. "No one taught me. My

granddaddy just threw me in, then sat down on that patch of grass right over there and said, 'Move your arms and feet, boy. Else you're gonna sink like a rock.' "

"That's horrible!"

"No. It was his way. He did things the only way he knew how. His daddy and his Uncle Buddy taught him to swim by throwing him in the Red River, and when he'd struggle and cry and then crawl out, they'd throw him in again, and again, and again, until he finally figured out how to swim his way out. He told me they threw him in a good ten times before he caught on. It was his fourth birthday. He told me I was fifty percent older than he had been." Red laughed quietly. "He figured he was giving me a real kindness because he told me to move my arms and legs, which was more than he got told."

What kind of person does that to a child?

He looked at her. "You stopped swimming."

She couldn't hide the horror she felt from her expression.

"It's okay, Charley. Granddaddy was a good man. He taught me all the things young boys need to know: how to tell the weather by the moon and the sky; how to find your way home by a star; how to shoot a dove off a fence with a single shot and to bait a fishhook. He taught me to understand the land and the soil and when the time was right to plant wheat, maize, or cotton. We spent a lot of days chopping cotton side by side.

"And those times, when I had a hoe in my hand and sweat and dirt covering every part of me, well, that was when that old man taught me the truly important things: to take a man for who he was, not how he looked or spoke. That it was okay to be alone in the world.

"Sometimes I wonder if he saw my future like some gypsy. He understood his daughter, my mama, the way simple men can see into the real heart of things—clear as looking through glass in a window. He didn't judge her. I don't think he judged anyone. He figured each one of us is on this earth for his own reason, with his own unique view of his world, and what he thinks he wants from it."

"You loved him a lot, didn't you?"

"Yep. Respected him, too. Granddaddy used to say that you can't understand a man and his decisions until you've walked in his shoes. He was the only man I ever knew who really lived by the words he preached. Every single day for fifty years." He stopped speaking for a moment. "Fifty years," he repeated as he shook his head. "Then one hot, summer day, he just up and dropped dead behind his plow horse."

"Oh, Red. I'm sorry."

He looked over at her, searched her face for something, then said, "He'd have loved you."

"Me? Why?"

"You could look him in the eye. Granddaddy would have liked a woman who could look him in the eye."

"Well, that's not much. I could have looked him in the eye at thirteen. I was almost six feet tall then."

"I bet you were something else."

"Oh, I was something else, all right, something big and gawky." There it was. She'd said it. She wasn't comfortable with her size; she'd learned to accept her height years ago. She knew she couldn't change it unless she wanted to cut off her legs, and somehow, even at thirteen, that seemed a bit drastic.

But accepting it didn't stop her from longing for things smaller women took for granted: looking up into a man's face instead of at the crooked part in his hair, having a man swing you into his arms and carry you laughing into a room, dancing something fast and swinging. Accepting that she was bigger than man-sized didn't mean she felt good when she walked into a room and towered over every woman and most of the men there.

"You know, Charley. Here in Texas we like big things. Big ranches. Big cattle with big horns. Hell, look up at that big ol' Texas sky. Granddaddy always said that everything's big in Texas." Then Red flipped over and swam alongside her, stroke for stroke. He was a beautiful swimmer, each stroke of his arm a precise motion. He didn't swim through the water like she did—splashing this way and that—he glided over the pond's surface the way a sharpened knife slices through butter.

"Look at this. Out here in the water, it doesn't matter how tall you are. All that shows is your head." He treaded water next to her. "See? Neither of us can touch the bottom. That makes us equal."

She treaded water next to him.

"Admit it. Here and now. Does it matter if you're five foot two or six foot two?"

She looked from him to her position in the water with their heads just bobbing above the surface. "No, I guess it doesn't matter here."

"Well, then, every time you walk into a room and feel taller than everyone else, you got to pretend you're out here treading water. Now, come on, girl, I'll race you to the rocks."

"Oh, no you don't. I need a handicap."

"I'll give you ten strokes. Go."

They cut across the center of the pond in a race that she lost even with a head start. She snuck up on him and dunked him under. When she was in shallow water, standing there and trying to find him in the darkness, he swam under her and stood up, catching her on his shoulders and vaulting her into the water, arms and legs flailing. And when she came up sputtering, he told her half the pond was gone. They played like children, free and easy. Then she rested against the rocks, letting her feet float up to the surface, wiggling her toes and staring at the way they were getting water-wrinkled, while he swam laps with all the energy of a retriever.

She closed her eyes and let the world fall away until she almost fell asleep, propped there with her head back and her eyes closed. When she opened them, she was looking up at the moon, moving across the sky, passing time and making it later and later. After a few minutes of the luxury of doing absolutely nothing, including sweating, she pushed off from the rocks and moved toward the water's edge and their forgotten clothes.

Red cut across the pond and caught up with her. Without a question, he waded out when she did, water dripping from their thin cotton underwear that stuck to the skin and didn't hide much if you looked where you shouldn't.

She picked up her clothes, holding them in front of her. "I hate to end this, Red, but I need to be back to the house before midnight. We have a curfew."

"Sure." He turned away and put his pants on.

She shrugged into her flight suit, then struggled with the sticky zipper.

"Here." He brushed her hands away and zipped it up almost too easily, as if the stubborn thing worked for Red because it liked him better.

Her gaze followed the zipper up, and when it stopped at the vee in her lapels, neither of them was looking at it. She saw his feelings there in his light eyes as surely as if he wore them on his sleeve. But she didn't look away or laugh them off or even step away this time.

She leaned a little closer.

His hand slipped behind her neck and he pulled her to his mouth. "Charley."

Then Red kissed her.

She had invited this and wanted it without thinking why. It was a sweet kiss, a soft touch of the lips, guileless, innocent, then youthfully eager as he slid his hands down over her back and stroked her lips with his tongue. He hadn't put his shirt on yet, and the water from his chest hair soaked through her suit and made her spine weak and her skin break out in goose bumps.

The kiss grew deeper and he pulled her closer against him, hip to hip, and stroked her jaw with his fingers. He tasted her for the longest time, never moving his hands to other, more private places like most men. This was just kissing. Just holding.

She liked it, too much, and finally had to step back and away, surprised that she felt something more elemental than she wanted to. She licked her lips and took a deep breath. "You make me late, and all we went through today will be for nothing."

He waited a second, then gave her a reluctant grin. "The carriage turns into a pumpkin." He bent down and picked up his shirt, slid into it, and sat down on the ground by their shoes. He picked hers up and held them out to her. "Here, Cinderella. Put on your glass slippers so I can take you home."

She sat down next to him, and they put their shoes back on together, sitting hip by hip, shoulder by shoulder; then he finished and helped her up.

He didn't let go of her hand.

They faced each other in the sultry night, standing at the edge of the pond and teetering on the edge of something that felt half-lit and shadowy, like the moon slipping behind another soft cloud, out of human reach and control.

Neither of them said anything. Perhaps they knew that words could too easily spoil moments of the heart, moments that hung between two people in the infancy of a relationship with no clear definition—not lovers, not friends, but something in between the two that only time and emotion would ever define.

Yet twenty minutes later, they were standing the same way, facing each other at the front door of the old Sears building. From the upper floors, a few lights cast long, boxes of dim light onto the dry lawn.

He took off his hat and stood there, turning it in his hands before he said, "Have dinner with me tomorrow night."

"I'd love to have dinner with you."

"Seven o'clock?"

"Seven o'clock."

"Barbecue?"

"Barbecue."

His smile could have lit the front yard.

She leaned over and kissed him gently. "Good night, Texaco Red."

He put his hat back on his head, giving it a tug. "Good night, Cinderella."

Laughing softly, she closed the door and ran up the stairs to her room. An hour later, when the fan was blowing the hot air around that stuffy room with its cracked walls, lopsided pictures, and old cork floors, she lay her head down on the pillow, but as she closed her eyes, she realized she was still smiling.

"A RENDEZVOUS WITH A DREAM"

"I'm sorry, but he hasn't been back since you called an hour ago. All of your messages are still in his box, Miss Morrison."

"Can you see if you can find him? This is really important."

"I'm sorry, but the YMCA is filled with military men. I'll make certain Sergeant Pilot Walker gets the messages when he checks back in with us. I will personally hand him all five of them, miss."

"You did check his room?"

"Yes." The man's voice was clipped.

"Oh . . . well, thank you." Charley hung up the telephone's bell-shaped earpiece and sagged back against the downstairs wall in frustration. "Oh, Red, where are you?" she whispered up at the veined ceiling.

On the floor overhead, women were rushing to get

packed, running around the halls like a bunch of loose marbles.

"Connie? Have you seen my coat?"

"Hell's bells, Rosalie. Who needs a coat in Texas in July?"

"It's cold in London."

"Look under your bed ... next to your mink mittens."

The ATA orders had come through late that morning, the way things with the government always did: with little warning and no time to spare. They were leaving today. The women were to pack up and report at the airfield at two o'clock. It was already one-thirty.

"Charley?"

She pushed away from the wall and walked to the base of the stairs.

Dolores was standing at the top landing, leaning over the iron railing. "I can't get my suitcase closed. Would you come sit on it for me?"

"Sure." Charley went up the stairs.

"You still couldn't reach him?" Dolores walked with her down the long narrow hallway to the room they shared.

"No. No one knows where he is."

"Well, if he shows up and we're all gone, he'll figure it out. Do you know where he's stationed?"

"Randolph Field."

"You can always write to him there."

"I suppose. It's probably for the best anyway. We're leaving and who knows how long we'll be in England."

"You know, Charley, this is a time that tests friendships. Most of the women I know are writing to their sweethearts because they're apart. We're all scattered all over the country. If we enter the war like they're predicting, we'll be scattered all over the world. The days of dating the boy next door are gone."

Dolores was probably right.

"You like him, don't you?"

"He's a nice guy." Charley hesitated to say much more; then she looked at her friend. "Do you think our ages are a problem?"

Dolores laughed. "Oh, my, yes. You are *so* old. I'm certain people will look at the two of you and think, how shameful! Look at that gray-haired old hag with the little soldier boy. She ought to be ashamed of herself."

Dolores ducked quickly as a feather pillow flew past her.

Charley had to laugh then. "Okay, so it's only a few years."

"How old is he?"

She gave a small groan. "I haven't asked. I don't want to know." She bounced a little on the suitcase. "Is it closing now?"

"Almost. Bounce again like you just did." She laughed then. "You should have eaten that piece of chocolate cake the other night."

"Very funny. I have plenty of backside." She bounced a little harder. "Have you ever dated anyone younger?"

"Me?" Dolores looked up and shrugged. "Only my little brother's crib playmate."

"I'm serious."

"I think you are serious." Dolores finally snapped the last closure on her suitcase. "There. You can get up now. It's closed."

Charley stood, then reached down and straightened

out her white slip and snug tweed skirt. Styles of clothing had become so formfitting. Less fabric for skirts, more fabric for planes and trucks and uniforms. The new styles were pretty unforgiving. One dessert could make your skirt bunch up.

Dolores leaned into the mirror and freshened her lipstick, then licked her finger and twisted the loose hair above her eyes around her finger and held it there as she turned back around. "I think you like Red Walker, and there's no doubt about how he feels about you. What I've done, what anyone else has done, doesn't matter, does it?"

"No."

Dolores unwrapped the curl, eyed it a second, then spun around. "Besides, I would love to have a man look at me like he looks at you. I don't know a girl who wouldn't." She grabbed the leather handles on her suitcase with two hands and dragged it off the bed, then moved toward the door. "Come on. We need to get our stuff downstairs. Are you all packed?"

Charley nodded. "I learned at a young age to travel pretty light."

"Not like Connie, huh?"

"Four bags?"

"Six."

"Good God . . . ." Charley picked up her flight bag, then put her crocodile purse inside and zipped it closed. She paused and looked around the room, not because she felt like it was home, but because this room was where she'd spent her last night in the States.

"Charley? You coming? The truck's out front and waiting."

"Be right there!" She picked up her suitcase and

flight bag, then left the room and went downstairs with the rest of the women flyers. As she walked past the black boxy wall phone, she paused, and felt an ache for something that almost was; then she shook her head and walked outside.

Half an hour later she was inside the transport plane, buckled in her seat and waiting for takeoff. The seats were more comfortable than most. The plane had been a Pan Am commercial liner before becoming a private charter that Maggie had Coop contract to fly the women into Canada, where they would sign the final ATA papers and then fly on to London to meet Maggie Caldwell Cooper and become the first American women to fly for the war effort. History. In a few days Charley was going to be a part of history.

The noise level in the plane was something else. The women were all talking at once, excited and happy and scared, laughing and giggling, because this was finally it—all they had worked for.

"Charley!" Dolores was hanging over her seat. "Look outside. Quick!"

Charley leaned forward and looked out the oval window.

A dusty black truck sped through the gates of the airfield and raced down the maintenance road heading toward the north runway. The plane's engines were running, but the door was still open, the metal stairs still wedged against it.

She unbuckled and moved to the aisle.

"Run, Charley, or you'll miss him!"

Charley went out the door and ran down the stairs. She glanced over a shoulder. They were still loading the luggage into the belly of the plane. She ran forward, across the asphalt toward Red, but a ten-foot-tall chicken-wire fence was between the maintenance road and the runway.

Red braked the truck and was out the door as she reached the gate.

"You made it!" she said, out of breath.

"I didn't even try to call. I just read the first message and drove like hell to get here."

"I'm sorry about dinner."

"I'll take a rain check."

She gripped the fence tightly with her hands.

He reached out and covered her white knuckles with his long freckled fingers. "Take care of yourself."

"You, too."

He nodded.

"I'll write you and let you know where we end up."

"Sure."

"When you're up in those B-17s, think of me drinking tea and eating crumpets."

"And ferrying airplanes. Don't forget the best part. But I hear those RAF boys are all spit and polish, full of boast and bull crap. You watch out for them."

She laughed. "I will."

"You're a damn fine looking woman, Charley Morrison."

"Red . . ." She couldn't seem to find the right words. His name hung in the air between them before she finally said, "I have to go."

"I know."

"Bye, Red. Take care."

"Bye, Cinderella. Be sure to duck."

"I will." She turned and ran for the plane and up the stairs. At the doorway, she paused and looked back, one hand on the edge of the doorway. A breeze from the starboard engine whipped her hair into her face, and she brushed it aside.

Red was still standing at the fence, looking tall and slim and handsome in his OD uniform.

She waved.

He waved back, then stuck his hands in the pockets of his loose slacks and didn't budge from that same spot. She wondered what he was thinking and when she would see him again. If she would ever see him again.

She ducked down and went inside, walked along the rows, and sat down in her seat, then strapped in. They closed the door. As the plane began to taxi, she leaned forward, peering out the window.

She waved her fingers at him again, that tall red-haired man with a heart as big as Texas, a man who was good and fun and who kissed her like she was a real woman instead of a strange and foreign land to be conquered.

He had moved and was standing at the open door of his truck, watching the plane take off. He slipped his hat off his head and waved it high in the air.

The plane sped past and took off.

She kept looking out the plane window for the longest time. Her breath fogged the window and she swiped it clear with her fingers, still looking back, looking back, until Red and his truck were nothing but small, dark spots on the long, flat miles of clay-colored ground.

GREAT BRITAIN

1942

"I GET ALONG WITHOUT YOU VERY WELL"

A reporter for the London *Times* wanted to interview him. When he balked, his commander suggested it was good for the RAF and for the country's morale. The number of kills credited to a flying ace was newsworthy. Let his countrymen cheer No. 77 Squadron's victories the same way the men in the squadron cheered his rise and continued success as top ace for more than a year.

But Skip suspected this interview wasn't about morale but a search for altruism. He didn't care to discuss his duty. There was no glory in it for him, and he didn't want some stranger asking him his motive or digging into his private life so the prime details could be plastered all over the newspapers. What "inspired" him was no one's bloody business but his own.

There were, however, some distinct advantages to being your country's top pilot, other than a quick rise through the official ranks. He'd received another commission a few days before. Thank God and country there were no more promotion exams.

He was now Lieutenant Commander and would be taking over the squad when Henderson, his flight commander, moved on to Biggin Hill. Along with Skip's exalted position of hero came some modicum of power. There was something about British nature that made them cater to those with an elitist attitude, whether deserved or not.

When it served his purpose, Skip used his image as paragon of the skies. This morning it served his purpose. He paid Mallory, who had three fewer kills, to sit in for him with the reporter, and Skip took an unplanned leave home to Keighley.

To get there, he drove a Riley 9 open tourer that belonged to Hemmings and had one of those stubborn crash gearboxes instead of the synchromesh gears fitted onto later models. After an hour, he had mastered a shift that was so smooth only the rev of the engine gave away a gear change.

Out in the countryside the air was cool, and the car moved along sportingly. It was somewhat surreal, driving past the barrage balloons in towns and villages and the blackened places where bombs had blown out huge holes in fields near airplane and munitions factories. Before long, he was passing only the occasional hay wagon with a plodding team or a farmer's tractor. Then it was as if the war were a lifetime away.

He entered the estate road through stone gates and parked in front of the house, a three-story stone manor that would comfortably billet his entire squadron in classic, English-country-house style. But he didn't go up the stone stairs and inside the huge front doors. Instead, he walked around the west wing, then stood there with his hands buried in his trouser pockets as he looked out at the lands before him, at rolling green hills with clumps of ancient elm trees, at the woods thick with oak trees and streams that ran clear all year, then off into the distance at the purple haze of hills.

Time seemed to stand still for him, those past decades of his life spent here. As a lad, he had been too young to understand his ties to Keighley because he seldom left it, and when he did, it was only to go to another family home—the house in Town or his great-uncle's grand estate in the Cotswolds.

It had been when he first went away to school that he understood how Keighley had silently seeped into his pores, until it was buried so deeply under his skin it became the meat and bone of him. Before long Greer was just as much a part of home to him, so whenever he came back here with her, he saw this place as his beginning, their beginning.

Human joy colored what you viewed in blindingly bright rainbows. When he was in love, he had looked out on his lands with a great sense of peace. Greer's death changed everything. Afterward, he saw it all in shadows, grays and darks that mirrored his broken soul the way the images turn nightmarish in the negative of a photograph, so horrible that you can almost not bear to look at it.

But those days felt as if they had passed, the days when his anger at her death was fresh and he dared not look to the east. He could look now and see the neighboring estate that belonged to her family, and in between their lands sat the lake, blue and calm. Nearby, a slab of hard, gray stone marked the spot where they had first met.

Memories were what destroyed those who loved and were left behind. He had learned that the hard way when he once made the mistake of staying in the somewhat repaired townhouse while on an overnight to

London. Sitting in the old study, he had glanced up expecting to see her. It shook him to the bone.

Later he had walked down the stairs and stopped, when he thought he saw a flash of color: a bit of a floral skirt disappearing into another room. In the middle of the night, he awoke to the smell of Ma Griffe. In the morning, he awoke crying and calling her name. Those bleak moments took his breath from him, stopped his heart, and stole a minute or two of his life, before reminding him all over again that he had none.

But now he could look to the east, yes, he could, in the way a dead man's eyes look into nothingness after being disembodied from his rising soul. Numb, he moved along the walk, almost forgetting why he'd come, until he caught sight of a figure through one of the long first-floor windows and stopped where he was.

His mother was sitting in the music room, her silhouette visible through the fine lace curtain that would be covered with blackout cloth in a few hours. She looked china-fragile, the woman with a spine of steel who never shied from anything, especially if it meant a good fight. Audrey Cecile Benton Inskip loved to do battle. She claimed it was in her blood, since her family dated back to Hastings.

Ah, Mother, the devils we must face.

His aunt had written to him. Audrey refused to do much of anything now, Aunt Eleanore told him, but sit in the house day in and day out and stare at nothing. She would not let anyone read to her. She would not let anyone assist her with meals. She wanted to bathe and dress herself and be left completely alone. She balked at help of any kind, even from the servants. Imagine . . . this from the woman to whom servants were always as much a necessity of life as daily bread and who had never even run her own bath.

But last month his mother had tried to pension off all the household help. She refused to pull the call bell. She flooded her bath and dressing room. One day last week, she fell trying to get down the stairs alone. Luck was on her side, and she only managed to badly sprain her ankle as opposed to cracking open her stubborn head.

It was this final act that had precipitated his aunt's wire asking him to come home. According to Eleanore, his mother had been difficult enough to handle before the fall, but now, with her ankle the size of a melon, her whole manner had reversed. She was not fighting everyone any longer, but instead slipping into a deep and silent depression.

He went into the house, quietly closed the doors, and stood in the hall outside the music room, looking inside where sunlight spilled through the curtains. Oddly enough, the finely wrought lace cast almost monstrously distorted shadows on his mother's ageless face. He was stunned at her pallor and the way she seemed to have shrunk into a tiny creature that was huddled in an overstuffed chair and looked like a porcelain doll from fifty years ago.

She faced him, sitting up a bit and with a surprising suddenness looking more like herself, except her eyes were flat and opaque. "George?"

"Do I walk that loudly?"

She gave a slight laugh that almost sounded like her. "No, dear."

"Did someone tell you I was home?"

She shook her head and held out her hand. "Come and talk to me. Tell me what you are doing here."

"I took a leave to come see you." He placed a hand on her shoulder and leaned down and dropped a kiss on her cheek. "All too long since I've been home, you know."

"Eleanore contacted you, didn't she? The woman is a snitch."

"She's your younger sister and she cares about you."

"She was put on this earth to drive me mad. It was horrid enough when we were girls, but now . . . " She sniffed. "She is intolerably bossy, you know."

"I cannot imagine where she gets it."

"I am determined, not bossy. There is a difference. I am also older than she is. I should be watching over her, not the other way around."

He dared not mention that a blind woman looking after someone might present a bit of a dilemma. And after seeing his mother through the window, when she thought no one was looking, he was most glad to see any emotion, even anger, in her. "If you say so, Mother."

"Did you come home merely to patronize me, or are you going to get on with it and scold me like Eleanore?"

"I heard you took a fall."

"No doubt she wired you about it. I was absolutely right. She *is* a snitch."

"Your ankle looks quite bruised."

"No more bruised, I suppose, than my pride . . . which, I might add, no one around here appreciates."

"I see there is a cane by your chair. Have you been able to use it to take the weight off that ankle?"

"Yes. They wanted Peters to carry me from room to

room. Can you imagine? They treat me like an invalid, George. I cannot abide it one single moment longer."

He knelt beside her chair and picked up her hand, then rubbed over it with his own. "I will steal you away for a spin about the gardens. The sun is shining and I would like to have you all to myself for a bit."

"I'd like that."

"Let me help you up."

She gripped his hand tightly, and he pulled her up. "Now you understand this. I only let you help me—not, mind you, because I cannot do it by myself—but because it is proper for a son to assist his mother. Good manners and all."

"Of course you can stand by yourself. I never doubted it for a moment."

"You are a good son."

"Here's the walking stick." He placed its silver handle against her palm.

She braced her weight onto it.

"Take my arm so I don't outrun you." He threaded her hand through his arm and turned her slightly so they could move unencumbered to the doorway. "We pilots have acquired the habit of running everywhere. It's been difficult to separate a call to scramble from merely going to mess. Seems we are always rushing about, everyone of us trying to squeeze into the door at once. You should see us all gather at the train station near to the base, Mother. One minute we're all slacking about, mooning away time; the next, the train pulls in and it's a damned race for it."

"I can keep up with you." She shuffled along with his

steps, which he slowed. She seemed to be concentrating terribly hard to make each step look effortless.

"You get along quite well, Mother."

"That is exactly what I have been trying to make everyone understand," she grumbled.

Peters was in the entry hall already waiting when their shoes tapped across the marble floor. The butler opened the door.

As they moved slowly towards it, Skip looked down and saw she was doing her damnedest not to hobble. Out of the corner of his eye he caught a flash of green and glanced up at the staircase.

His aunt was coming downstairs. She spotted them and stopped halfway, quickly holding a finger up to her lips.

He nodded in agreement and continued on towards the front door as if he hadn't seen her.

As they walked through the entrance, his mother said imperiously, "Thank you, Peters." Then she tugged on Skip's arm to stop him. "Wait." She turned and over her shoulder said, "Good afternoon, Eleanore. Please continue down the stairs."

So much for that deception.

Eleanore rolled her eyes at him.

"I'm blind, not deaf, sister. And I shan't need you, you know." She turned, her head regally tilted, and took another step. "I am going for a walk in the gardens with my son."

"MY SISTER AND I"

Skip rested his elbows on his knees and held a glass of scotch between his hands. He stared down at a deep blue, two-hundred-year-old Aubusson rug. When he was seven or eight, his dogs had bounded into the room while he was studying and spilled a pot of ink on that rug. The old black stain was still there; it stared back at him from the center of a wine-colored rose. He covered it with his foot . . . old habit.

His mother was upstairs in her rooms, resting before dinner. The long walk they took in the gardens completely exhausted her. "She looks bloody horrible, Eleanore."

"I thought you should see for yourself." His aunt sat across from him on one of the two davenports. A fire blazed in the huge Adam fireplace and sucked up the same old draft that slipped through the garden doors and always chilled the edges of the room.

"My first reaction when I saw her was she looked as if she were disappearing." He took a long drink. God, that he could do the same. To merely . . . disappear.

"In the last six months she has sent three private nurses packing. She refuses to learn Braille or take any blind training. She called Reverend Eisings a damned prig. She can't even be civil to Bromley, who has been with her so long the poor woman's almost part of the family. You saw your mother's behavior to Peters. She threatened to pension him off if he tried to ever carry her anywhere again. The poor man was quite baffled." Eleanore leaned back against the cushions and sipped a Gordon's and tonic water, then after a minute looked up at him and shook her head. "It rips me apart to see her like this."

"I'll ring up the doctor first thing tomorrow. I tried before I left, but I couldn't reach him from the base."

"I've spoken to him."

"Does he have any answers?"

"He suggested that she might need companionship. Someone who isn't family."

He crossed a leg across his knee and gripped his ankle. "From your tone, I'd say you don't agree."

"I can't see her being receptive or cordial to anyone who comes to try to help her."

"Based on what I saw today, I suppose you're right. Do you have any ideas?"

"You mean other than cutting out her tongue?"

Skip laughed out loud. "I'm sorry for laughing, Eleanore. I know she's a handful. We could run through a list of her friends, see if anyone could bring her spirits up a bit."

"I already have. I've racked my head for the right person, but there's no one I dislike enough to call." She took a sip of her drink.

"Eleanore," he said quietly.

She glanced back up at him.

"You've been here for over a year. Certainly long enough, I'd say. I'll try to make other arrangements."

She raised her hand. "No, no, don't." She took a deep

breath and sagged back against the pillows again. "I'm merely frustrated. I know it must be terrible for her. I can barely imagine what it must be like to find yourself suddenly living in a world that's only darkness." She looked into her glass. "She's my only sister, George. I want to be here. Your Uncle Gerald's duties with the War Office keep him gone for months at a time. Helen has been assigned as a driver for some American military advisor, and Richard is off studying in the States. Neither will be home until Christmas, if then. I'd rather be here with Audrey than rattling around those drafty old rooms at Brookstead."

"You have been a saint to stay as long as you have."

"I know. Bucking for sainthood would bother the stuffing out of her." She handed him her empty glass. "Don't mind me. Humor is my only defense, dear. It keeps everything in perspective when I want to give her a smack."

The ormolu clock on the mantel chimed Beethoven. Eleanore stood and walked over to the windows, systematically pulling down the blackout cloths.

He stood and followed her.

"I have it," she said over a shoulder. "Such a nuisance, those horrid Huns."

He laughed and drew one of the shades down anyway.

She pulled down the last cloth and faced him. "Seriously, George. Thank you for coming. Perhaps a visit from you was all she needed for now. She has livened up a bit."

He felt a jab of guilt for not coming home. He started to speak.

She held up a hand. "Don't say anything. You have your hands full—single-handedly saving the country and all. It's quite difficult to believe our top ace is the same lad in short pants who crawled around under the dining table pretending to be Haversham's favorite hunting spaniel. Your mother was quite horrified at your sniffing his lordship's boots."

"Ah, well, I was preparing myself for a career in military service."

Now she was laughing. She patted his cheek. "You're a good lad. Although I suppose you aren't much of a lad anymore. Look at this. My nose is scarcely level with your lapel." She threaded her arm through his. "Coming home now, for even this short time, is enough, George. You needn't feel torn between your duty and your mother's needs. Your mother understands your duty. And that is why I'm here. You should know we all are extremely proud of you. Now, that being said, come along; dinner will be ready soon. I should go up to check on Audrey." She leaned over and gave him a kiss on the cheek.

"I'll go with you." He pulled away and set his glass down on a bar tray, then walked with her towards the doors.

They made it as far as the hall when there was an enormous crash from the upper floors.

"Good God . . . . Audrey!" His aunt stopped.

He raced ahead, taking the stairs two at a time.

"Hurry, George. Dear God, hurry." Eleanore was coming up behind.

He ran down the hallway and jerked open the doors to his mother's rooms. "Mother!" He went inside. "Mother?"

Crying, soft, muted and pitiable, came from the next rooms. He ran to her dressing room, then on through to the WC.

She lay on the hard, black-and-white marble floor in a sea of shattered perfume bottles, glass cosmetic jars, and the remnants of her dressing table mirror. The table was overturned, its chintz skirt up and the thin spindled legs showing. The small upholstered chair was lying on top of his mother's hips and legs. It wasn't pinning her down, but he could see from her position she hadn't moved much at all.

Her black hair covered her face as she lay there, sobbing into her arms. The palm of one hand was open and bleeding. He could see bloody handprints on the floor from glass cuts when she had tried to push herself upright.

"Mother." He crossed over to her, his shoes crunching on the glass. He pulled the chair off of her and knelt down, then placed a hand gently on her shoulder. From behind him he heard the tap of running feet, heard his aunt tell Bromley, his mother's maid, to stay back and let him take care of her.

His mother's crying slowed and then stopped, but she still lay there, face in her bent arm, spots of blood speckling the floor.

"Mother, please. Let me help you."

Slowly, she lifted her head and looked up at them. Her face was wet and strained, her expression so bitter it hurt to look at it. Fresh lipstick was smeared across her mouth in the way of some kind of grotesque clown.

The silence became noticeable, almost as if another person—someone entirely inappropriate—had entered the room. His mother's embarrassment was almost palpable; her pride had to be as shattered as all that glass.

She had closed her eyes—a reflex of shame or terror. He watched the tears drip down her high, pale cheekbones, down to her jaw, onto her arm. She took a long wavering breath and turned, then stared blankly up at all of them. "One of the best things about being blind, you know, is that I can't see the pity on your faces."

"THERE'S A LULL IN MY LIFE"

Skip buttoned his coat as he left the New Public Offices, and walked down to Whitehall, past the pillboxes and sandbags along the entrances, then ran up the stone steps into War Offices. The halls were dismal and stuffy; they smelled like ancient wood panelling and cigarette smoke older than the Great War. The heels of his shoes clicked briskly on the marble floor and echoed back as he went along the hallway, where war posters lined the paint-chipped walls.

Keep A Pig. Start A Pig Club.
'We could do with thousands like you.' Join the Women's
Land Army.
'Arf A Mo!' National Service Needs You.
Be Like Dad. Keep Mum!

He pressed the lift button and waited till it came to a stop. A woman ran to make it on. Skip removed his hat and tucked it under one arm as the lift went up. She stood beside him, kept glancing at him while the lift clattered upward. He hadn't bothered to look at her face when she got on. Her perfume smelled like incense. He hated incense.

The lift stopped on the top floor. He took his hat out from under his arm and held the door for her.

"Thank you." She was a Yank.

He said nothing.

She took a few steps, stopped, and glanced back at him.

For a single heartbeat of a second he saw Greer in her expression; then the image faded and he was looking at a tall stranger with blonde hair. He spun on his heel and walked quickly away, settling his hat on his head.

A few seconds later he stood in the doorway of his uncle's office.

Eleanore's husband was leaning against his desk, his back to the room, as he looked out the long window behind his desk.

"I say there. It's good to see they're not working you too hard."

"George." His uncle turned and straightened. "I didn't think you'd be here for another half hour or so. By God, it's good to see you." He stepped around the desk and crossed the room, hand extended. "Come in. Come in."

"Uncle Gerald." Skip clasped his hand while his uncle slapped him on the shoulder.

Gerald pulled him towards a winged chair, one of two. "Sit, my boy."

Skip sat, tossed his cap on the desk, crossed his ankle

on one knee and leaned back in the chair as his uncle sat down.

"Tell me. How's your mother?"

"Giving Aunt Eleanore fits. Your wife is a saint."

"I thank God that I found that woman twenty-five years ago. Snatched her right out from under Bennington's nose, you know. At a point-to-point . . . I think it was at Crawley's place in Dorset. Yes, that was it." He laughed and shook his head. "Twenty-five years. Sometimes it feels as if I've spent twenty of them right here in this office." He looked up. "How is the old girl? Haven't been home in weeks."

"She looks well. She told me Helen has been driving some of those Yank advisors."

"The girl was driving Major General Bradley—some crony of Eisenhower's—until last week when the general went back to Washington. She's been transferred to a civilian VIP from the States, but there was some kind of delay, so she's free all this week. I asked her to meet us for dinner. Didn't think you'd mind."

"No. Of course not. The last time I saw Helen—" He stopped because in his mind he saw her dressed in black, as the rest of them had been. His cousin had the same hair color as Greer. He remembered glancing up at the grave site, seeing only her hat and veil and her light hair. For just one moment, he had thought the coffin in front of him was, in truth, only a bad dream.

His uncle's hand squeezed his shoulder.

He hadn't realised Gerald had stood and come over to him. His throat grew tight. He started to sweat—that same clammy feeling he'd get whenever he awoke from a nightmare. When he was overly tired, he would dream the same thing: him in his plane, spinning to his death, round and round . . . the world out of control, the absurdity that all he could do in his last moment on earth was sweat.

Your last instant of life condensed down to nothing but a few drops of wasted moisture.

"George?"

"Don't mind me." Skip swiped the sweat from his hairline and shook his head, looked down a bit. The RAF emblem on his cap stared back at him. "I was thinking about something."

Gerald kept his hand on his shoulder. "She was a lovely young woman, George. We all miss her. This war is a nasty thing."

"Yes. Nasty."

"How are you getting on?"

"Well enough. The Luftwaffe's been going at us a bit more lately."

"You don't have to go on every mission."

"No, that's true. I always have the option of being paraded before the public for the sake of the war effort. 'Look here, chaps! A real live hero!' Did you know, Uncle, they give me a new blue uniform every time they send me out? Want me to look crisp as bacon when I stand up there encouraging the people of London to buy war stamps." His tone was so bitter he could taste the words on his tongue.

"The country needs heroes." Gerald walked back around the desk and faced him, still standing. "We need men like you because the people need to know that we're not taking this horrid hammering from those Huns lying down."

Skip slouched back in the chair and stared down at nothing. He didn't want to be needed. He didn't want to be a walking, breathing poster for his countrymen. Someone might as well stamp the war slogan *"Seeing It Through"* on his forehead. He drove a hand through his damp hair again. "I know. I understand morale. I have to for the sake of the men who fly with me every mission. But I despise feeling as if the public owns a piece of me."

"When you choose the Royal Air Force for a career, everyone owns a piece of you."

Skip knew that. He was wearing a government-issued uniform, shirt, trousers, belt, jacket, medals, emblems, cap, shoes; even his bloody underwear was given to him by the government. "True." He looked up at his uncle. "But I don't have to like it."

"Are you sorry you joined the Air Force?"

"I love to fly."

"Do you want to transfer out? You did some test piloting before all hell broke loose. With your record you can take your pick of positions."

"I haven't really thought about it."

"Perhaps you're tired of the No. 77."

Skip could hear a woman laughing in the outer office. He turned and looked at the closed door. She sounded like Greer.

"Is something wrong?"

Skip turned back. "Sorry. It was nothing important. I suppose it's merely the new reporters that bother me. I don't like their prying questions."

"We have the same problem around here. Walk out the door and they're dogging your every step." Gerald relaxed back in his chair. "So tell me what you've been up to."

"I was at Keighley until two days ago. I'd borrowed another chap's automobile, and the bloody thing broke down outside of Kettering. Some kind of rubber hose problem, so any kind of repair was out of the question. Took me forever to get to the nearest train station. I had to wait for the one-forty. By the time I got back to the base, I'd missed the afternoon briefing. Nothing much to do but read the reports that came in while I was gone. Most of the men were at the local pub, so I grabbed a cheese sandwich, went over the leave roster, and turned in early. Nothing different, really."

"Sounds as if you have established a routine."

He nodded. "I have."

His uncle leaned forward and rested his arms on the desktop. "You need to let go, George."

"Of my routine?"

"Don't dance around me, my boy. You know what I'm talking about. I don't mean to sound like a Dutch uncle—"

"Then don't."

"Your father's gone. Your mother has her own troubles. Someone has to talk to you. You've separated yourself from almost everyone and everything. Have you been out to dinner? Dancing? Gone to the cinema?"

His tight-lipped silence was enough of an answer.

"You need a girl."

"Despite what the government believes, we human beings are not interchangeable. You can't replace people the way you replace parts on those broken Spits. Crash and smash and put them together and you have another."

"No, of course it is not the same thing. But I'll tell you

this, you're trying awfully bloody hard to prove to everyone around you that you don't need anything or anyone. That in itself shouts out to the world that you haven't let Greer go. Let her go, George. You must let her go."

He waited a long time before he spoke and when he did, he looked directly at his uncle. "Can you tell me how exactly I'm supposed to do that? Tell me how to let go of her and I will. You think I want to see her in every woman's face? I can barely look at women. What no one seems to remember is that I have lived more years of my lifetime *with* Greer than without her."

"I understand it must be difficult for you, but—"

"It's not difficult. It's bloody impossible." He stood and braced his hands on the desk, gripping the carving on its edge until he could feel it press into his palms. "Does a man lose his leg and ever really forget what it was like to walk on two feet? How do you make a piece of yourself suddenly go away?"

"You move on. You let go because it doesn't do any good not to."

He closed his eyes. "I can't."

"You can. You have to."

Skip began to pace.

"Tell me this. What advice would you give one of your men if he were in your situation?"

He stopped in front of the desk again and faced his uncle. "I would tell him if he needed to talk he could come to me."

"I believe I told you the same a year ago."

Skip was silent as a stone.

"So let's say he didn't come to you, then what?"

"I don't know. I can't make that kind of decision without thinking it through and judging the man himself."

"Could you remove how you personally feel from that decision and do what was best for the man?"

"I don't know. I'm not arrogant enough to think I know what would be good for him."

"Then you shouldn't be an officer if you haven't learned to take your own experience and use it to make yourself and your men better soldiers."

That cut to the quick. Sliced right through his pride as a soldier. A damned good one, too. "You're saying I'm a bad officer."

"You are risking the lives of your men."

"We risk our lives from the moment we lift off the ground. We're pilots in the RAF. You find one of them who doesn't carry the same feeling of fatalism."

"When a man keeps everything troublesome inside of him like you are, George, it's difficult to think on your feet."

"I would never willingly risk their lives. You should know that."

"I do, but you cannot keep holing yourself up in your quarters, never going out on the town. You've seen it in your men. You said so yourself. Your men were at the local pub, and I wager they're in town as often as they can get away from the field. Soldiers blow off steam. They must after so much time spent in the air. But you, you're a kettle ready to blow. I'm not telling you anything you don't already know. You might not want to hear it, but you can't continue this way."

"I take leave."

"One in five months?"

"Two, and just who have you been talking to?"

"Henderson, and a few others."

"They had no right to come to you and tell you anything about me."

"They didn't come to me. I went to them."

"You went to them?" Skip frowned. "Why?"

"For the very reason I called you here." He leaned back and looked at him directly, his hand rubbing his whiskered jaw.

"I thought you called me here for dinner. Now I see. You must do the dirty deed," he said sharply. "You called me here to tell me I'm relieved of my command. What is it? You all feel sorry for the man who lost his wife. 'The sod loved her so much he won't forget her. So sad, really. Must be mad. Can't let the chap jeopardize his men, now can we?' So the kind uncle breaks the news to the poor fellow?"

"No. This is nothing of the sort. Your superior officers and your men have the most remarkable respect for you. They claim there is no one they would rather fly with. Those men have nothing but the best to say, George."

He didn't understand. "Then why did you call me here?"

Gerald steepled his hands, resting his chin on them for a brief pause.

Skip wondered what decision his uncle was making and whether he had dismally failed some important test.

"I brought you here to show you this." He picked up a folder, reached across the desk, and handed it to him.

Skip leaned forward and flipped it open.

Inside were aerial reconnaissance photographs. Written at the top of the first group of photos was "Bruneval," on the coast of France. The series of shots showed German radar defenses. The second, also titled "Bruneval," showed only the remains of destroyed radar towers and bunkers.

The next group was identified as "Fish Oil Factories—Vagsoy," an island off the Norwegian coast. The German-occupied herring and cod oil factories produced glycerin, which was extremely valuable for its use in the manufacture of explosives. The after photos showed the burning factories and the storage tanks destroyed, with spilled fish oil sending clouds of dark smoke toward the camera.

"This damage wasn't from aerial bombing."

Gerald shook his head. "No. It wasn't. It's from Mountbatten's Combined Operations—special forces units comprised of men from the Navy, Army, and Air Force. *Commando* units."

"I don't want to fly photo-recon."

"I'm not asking you to. We're short of pilots."

"For parachutists?"

"No. For butcher-and-bolt raids. It's hazardous duty and long hours."

Skip laughed. "Worse than the Battle of Britain?"

"I supposed I deserved that."

"I want the job."

"You'll have to be ready to go at a moment's notice."

"You just finished pointing out to me that I had no life. I'd say that should work in my favor."

"Not really, but we'll talk about that in a moment. I need to make you aware of the risks."

"I don't care what the risks are. Every time I take off, I'm at risk. Hell, you can be walking down the street and be at risk. I still want it."

"You'll be giving up your squadron, and won't billet with a unit. You'll be given an allowance and be responsible for your own food and lodging, that is, if you're accepted."

"If I'm accepted?"

"Yes."

"This is conditional? On what?"

"You'll need my signature of approval. And, George, I feel rather strongly that this duty takes a certain type of soldier—a man who plays as hard as he fights."

"I want the position."

"Fine." His uncle leaned back in his chair. "Then I have a proposition for you."

'HE WEARS A PAIR OF SILVER WINGS"

"Watch your step, Helen." Skip pulled his cousin away from some building debris scattered in the dark street. "And for godsakes, keep the light aimed at the ground. Every time you say something, you wave the blasted torch all over the place."

"Well, *someone* has to say something. You've hardly said a thing since we left Father."

"I'm quiet because I'm trying to decide if this was a conspiracy."

"What? Are you so terribly caught up in yourself that you think everyone is sneaking around behind your back?"

"If not, then you had perfectly rotten timing, Helen."

"Well . . . not that I need to justify anything, but I had already made plans to go out when Father asked me to join you for dinner. I'd be some kind of fool to pass up a free meal at the Embassy Club. My flatmate and I had a small gathering last weekend and completely depleted both our ration booklets. I've have been living on jam and toast for a week."

"Not very sensible a move. Was it worth it?"

"Yes, and I've never been sensible. Why should I start now?" She looked up at him. "Regarding dinner, I didn't see you backing away from that huge steak, or the wine, or the cognac."

"Military food has about as much flavor as the stove they cook it on. You're never quite certain what it is they're dishing out. Every bloody damned meal looks the same. It doesn't matter what they call it. I seldom bother to read the menu board. Unless they're serving fish and chips, which they haven't yet figured a way to make into a dashed mess, at least not yet."

"Well, it would have been quite rude of me to stand up and leave without inviting you along."

"I would have been happier."

"Happy? You? Ha! You've been in the doldrums for so long your manner is nothing but morose. You seldom laugh and never smile. And how was I to know that Father is in the process of coercing you off your golden pedestal?"

"You have a smart mouth, Miss Clever."

"Yes . . . I do, don't I?"

"You needn't sound so pleased. It wasn't meant as a compliment."

"I know. However, you can't be held responsible for your lack of insight into what makes a woman interesting. What could you know? You've been out of society for too long. Socially you should be in shambles, but amazingly your absence seems to have added to your heroic mystique."

He groaned.

"Tonight will be such fun, Skip. And your conversation and social graces are most likely getting quite rusted, hanging about with no one but mechanics and flyers. Don't look daggers at me like that or sink into one of your sulks."

"How can you tell how I'm looking at you? It's dark."

"Well, I could do this." She shone the light in his face.

"Damn and blast it, Helen." He batted it away. "Give me that before you blind me." He reached for the torchlight, but she tucked it close to her and danced away a few steps.

"I've got it. My eyes are adjusted. I can see your face without it."

"After that blast in the face I can't see a thing." He squinted. Flashes of bright light were spotting all over his line of vision.

"It wouldn't matter if I couldn't see you, because believe me, Skip, when you're angry at someone, they know it. Your anger is there in your manner and in your voice."

"I'm not angry at you. Or at least I wasn't until you stuck that torch in my face."

"I know because you're never truly angry with me. But you are angry with Father and you're sulking about it. He is right, you know. You need a life and, lucky you, I'm just the person to find it for you."

"What if I don't want a life?"

"You have no choice in the matter. Your family is taking charge. I don't know what Father's using to blackmail you, but whatever it is, you must want it badly. Now stop dragging your boot heels and come along. There's always quite the crowd at the canteen door."

"You mean I have to queue up to do this?"

"Mostly likely not. They'll recognize you at the door, and if not, I shall shout your name and infamous Spit number for all to hear, and then no one will leave you alone all night."

He looked heavenward. "What am I doing here?"

"You're here to accompany your favorite cousin."

"The question you might consider asking yourself is exactly how long you will remain my favorite."

"I've always been your favorite, just as you've been my favorite. Now look. Just there. Around the corner." She pulled him along with her. "Come along."

"Watch yourself! The walk is cracked. Come this way so you don't get your heel caught."

"I know they try to clean the streets, but with so much bombing going about, it's a bloody mess on these back streets."

They walked along in companionable silence, passing quite a few people. The cars and cabs moved slowly with their lights blacked out. There were more people pedaling around on bicycles than driving in automobiles. It was dark, with no searchlights crisscrossing the sky, no sirens, no hum of plane engines, no whining bombs.

"I shall be quite the spectacle tonight," she said. "Coming in on the arm of the illustrious and elusive Pilot Commander Inskip. Only my close friends know we're related. Every woman in the room will be positively green."

"You're really enjoying yourself, aren't you?"

"Quite. And you needn't worry. Just walking into the room will be enough to set the place on its ear."

"I would rather face Goering himself."

"Stop your grousing and try to pretend you're enjoying yourself. The orchestra is usually quite good. Drink a whiskey or two. Stand around in that stunningly fitted blue uniform, with those silver wings and medals, looking like the dashing RAF ace that you are."

"Helen, for a bright girl, you are a remarkable pain in the ass."

"I adore you, too." She stopped walking and faced him, shaking her finger under his nose. "Now you must remember your promise. Five dances. One with me. One with my friend, and the others can be with partners of your own choosing."

"How magnanimous of you."

"Yes. I'm feeling quite the thing, you know. Must be the company." She hugged his arm affectionately. "Look, there it is. See?"

At mid-block stood a group of multi-uniformed men and women, mixed with many other young gadabouts in all sorts of evening dress. They were queued up three deep in front of the place, chattering, laughing, and smoking. There was a golden glow from a half-opened doorway that spilled onto the bottom stairs.

He could hear the band inside. They were playing "Pennsylvania 6-5000." He let Helen drag him along, the whole time thinking—*I don't want to do this.*

"BEAT ME, DADDY, EIGHT TO THE BAR"

By a quarter to midnight, Charley had counted forty-three women in the room who had used eyebrow pencil to draw seams on their bare legs, thirty-two who didn't wear a brassiere, twenty-eight men who could look her in the eye—four who were actually taller than she, none of whom had asked her to dance—and the band had played "In the Mood" and "It's Only a Paper Moon" eight times.

She left her quiet corner and edged her way through the crowd toward the bar, where she would order one last drink to usher in midnight, with high hopes that she could convince the other ATA women to leave.

Someone pinched her on the backside. "Ouch!" She turned around to see three men grinning up at her.

She ignored them and moved on. She should have gone to the movies instead, but the previous night she'd spent nerve-racking hours in the Underground, packed together with most of London. The stalwart Londoners calmly drank tea, made jests about Hitler, and played cards as the bombs and incendiaries rained down for hours.

But Charley had sat on a cot, flinching and shaking

for most of the time, unable to think about anything but the sound above and the intense fear of feeling like a sitting duck.

So tonight, she'd thought she needed to do something active and fun. There was a choking haze of smoke above everyone's heads, and the band was louder here than in her corner. Everyone was talking at once and laughing or shouting.

About five feet from the bar was as close as she could get. She spent a couple of long minutes trying to get the bartender's attention, then spotted an opening and wedged between two groups of soldiers with their backs to her. The groups closed in around her and she was stuck.

She cupped her hands around her mouth. "Bartender!"

Nothing.

She waved at him.

Still nothing.

"How can he not see me? I have to be head and shoulders above most of these guys." She stood on her toes. "Sir? Sir? Mister Bartender!"

Nothing. The guy had selective vision.

She lifted her hand again to wave at him, and someone grabbed it from behind. "What the—?"

Holding on to her wrist was a familiar-looking, black-haired RAF pilot with pale blue eyes and a darkly serious look. "Try this." He slipped a pound note into her hand.

She just stared at him, trying to identify that face, beyond the fact that it was so drop-dead gorgeous it should have been on a Brylcreem billboard.

He was still holding her wrist, so he waved it for her. *Do I know him?*

He released her hand and nodded toward the bar. "The bartender wants to know what you want."

"Oh. A whiskey sour, please."

"A whiskey sour and a double scotch!" he shouted.

"I forgot. With a cherry."

"She forgot her cherry!"

There was a sudden break of quiet; the band had stopped playing. People seemed to have all stopped talking at once.

His words just hung there; then everyone around them started laughing.

She could feel her face turning flushed. With her stomach near her ankles she looked at him, expecting to see a smart-alecky soldier grin, like the ones on the guys who'd pinched her.

To her surprise, he seemed embarrassed, too.

"Sorry about that." He looked her squarely in the eye. All night long men had either been looking up at her or looking straight ahead at her chest.

"It's okay . . ." She glanced at his uniform. "Commander."

"Pilot Commander George Inskip, of His Majesty's Royal Air Force. I'd take my hat off and make you a bow, but there's no room. And call me Skip."

"Hello, Skip. I'm Charlotte Morrison." She held out her hand, but hadn't realized she still held his money. "Sorry. This is yours."

He took it, then took her hand.

"From all that decoration on your uniform, I'd guess you are quite the war hero."

He gave a long and serious look, then said quietly, "I'm no hero."

"Hey there! Here are your drinks!"

They both turned toward the bartender. She began to open her purse.

"Don't." Skip stopped her. "I'll get it." He moved past her and grabbed their drinks, then handed her a slim glass with a red cherry in the bottom.

"Thank you."

He merely studied her for a moment, then frowned.

When he continued to say nothing for a full minute, she spoke up. "Well. Thank you again, for the drink." She pointed a thumb over her shoulder. "I'll just work my way back to the corner." She turned.

"Wait!" He touched her shoulder, then quickly pulled his hand back.

She faced him. "What's wrong?"

"You're the girl from the elevator. At the War Office today."

"Oh." She laughed. "That's where I saw you. I couldn't remember. I only knew you looked familiar."

The band began to play "Paper Moon."

"Again?" He looked at the band, then looked at her. "They've played that song nine times tonight."

"I know. It's rivaled only by 'In the Mood.'"

"I say there, looks as if we've both had nothing better to do than count songs."

She smiled and nodded. "I guess so."

"Tell me something, Charlotte Morrison. Is it quiet over in that corner of yours?"

"Quieter than it is here."

"Good. My ears are ringing from the noise levels in

here. Makes a dogfight sound docile. Would you mind if I join you?"

"Of course not. I don't mind at all." She grabbed his hand. "Come along." She pulled him through the crowd, and a few minutes later they were sitting at a small table in a shadowed corner at the opposite side of the room.

He took out a pack of Player's and offered her one.

"No, thanks."

He took a cigarette out and tapped the ends on the back of his hand, then lit it and leaned back in his chair. "So tell me what brings a pretty Yank named Charlotte to London."

"Everyone calls me Charley, and I'm out of uniform." She cupped her drink in her hands and turned it absently. "I'm a pilot with the ATA."

"Air Transport Auxiliary? So you're one of the Yanks who ferry planes all over the countryside."

She laughed. "You don't have to sound so surprised. That was not very politic of you, you know. Don't burst my bubble and tell me you're one of those arrogant pilots who would prefer that women not be in the air at all."

He held up his hands. "Never. We need those planes. I'm glad my men don't have to leave the skies to do the job the ATA is doing." He took a drink. "I was only surprised because we're both pilots."

"My father was a barnstormer. I grew up in airplanes. Now he designs and manufactures them. In fact, that's why I was at the War Office today. Pop was supposed to be there, but he's been delayed back in the States. I didn't find out until I got there."

"Morrison. As in Robert Morrison? Your father makes the Lilienthal?"

She nodded.

He whistled. "I daresay you did grow up in an airplane."

She took a drink and glanced at the stage. The female band singer, a small brunette, left through a back curtain, and the musicians struck up a new song.

After a few beats, Skip looked at her. "Hear that?"

She nodded. "'Flying Home.' They haven't played that before."

He stubbed out his cigarette and stood up. "Seems to me that two pilots ought to be out there dancing to this. Come on, Charley." He held out a hand.

They moved out onto the crowded dance floor. As he swung her into his arms, she realized that a night could change from bad to good in a matter of minutes. The song was short, but he kept her out on the dance floor when he grabbed her hand and pulled her into a conga line that grew and grew until it wrapped around the room in a ribbon of drumbeat motion. A good fifteen minutes of sheer fun, and when it was over, they danced close to "Star Dust."

When it was over, everyone on the floor stood there applauding the music—the band was truly good—and when the band singer came back onstage, she had two other women in tow. They smiled and turned. Soldiers began to whistle and call out. The trumpet player stood, lifted his horn, and played those reveille notes from "Boogie Woogie Bugle Boy."

Charley turned to leave.

Skip pulled her back. "Where are you going?"

"Back to the table."

"Why?"

"This is a swing tune."

"I know. Take my hand. We'll show them how it's done."

"To this?" She laughed. "I don't dance the swing."

"I'll teach you."

She shook her head. "No. You don't understand. You don't have to teach me. I know how. Doorknobs make great dance partners."

"Then why don't you dance?"

"Skip." She laughed. "You can look me in the eye and really ask that?"

He didn't answer her. He pulled her against him, placed his hand on her lower back, and off they went. The next thing she knew he was twirling her out onto the dance floor and pulling her back, spinning her and slipping in beside her to match steps.

Maybe it was because they both could fly and they understood motion and air; maybe it was because they both knew how to control a powerful machine that could so lightly defy gravity and skim the clouds; and maybe it was because they were the same size and could read the moves in each other's eyes. But whatever it was, they danced together in perfect sync. A step, a twirl, slide, side-by-side cross steps, bending down and hand-slapping their knees, then crossing foot over foot, step over step and together again. They were so perfectly even that the crowd fell away, and a few minutes later he flipped her in the air and, God bless him, he caught her.

For some crazy reason, she couldn't stop laughing.

"DOUBLE TROUBLE"

ACHNACARRY CASTLE,

SCOTLAND, 1942

When the President of the United States asks you to do a favor for him, you don't say no. Sure you're aware that your life has changed, because you have a wife now and you'd rather chase her around the house than chase a bunch of enemy soldiers around the front lines. But your country's at war, so when the President sits in his wheelchair and uses words like "for your country," you find that your values, your ego, and your sense of patriotism get all mixed up together.

You think, yeah! Hooyah!

Then you get the details from your father, a Major General, and his crony, another Major General named Eisenhower, and General Marshall, who all explain to you how valuable you can be as a "candidate" in a combined special forces intelligence experiment. You completely forget that "candidate" is just another word for "volunteer," which is just another word for "guinea pig"—something you never want to be in the military.

Then, weeks later, you're thousands of miles away from your wife, who needs chasing. You're lying face down in a ravine full of mud—a seventy-pound field pack on your back—after you've fallen twenty feet off a log ladder. There's a captain from the Black Watch, a real son of a bitch who is the commando instructor, standing over you and hollering for you to get your buggering ass up and run fifteen miles . . . again.

At that moment things are pretty clear. You think back to your choices and you ask yourself . . . do you know how to spell "dumb shit"?

Not that long ago, some people had called J.R. a wild son of a bitch. He had thought he was, too. But during the past eleven weeks at the Commando Training Depot here in Scotland, he had been with thirty of the wildest sons of bitches anyone would ever think to see.

There were handfuls of men from the U.S., Canada, Britain, France, Greece, Czechoslovakia, Russia, and Poland. And they were here to learn from the experienced British SAS crack commando units. The ultimate goal: to create small teams of highly trained men for guerrilla hit-and-run action behind enemy lines.

Together they had slogged through bogs, forded rivers, rappelled cliffs, and jumped out of planes into pitch blackness. They could survive in the wilds for a lifetime if they wanted, and could swim across a lake, then come out running and march for twenty miles. Every single one of them could derail a train or blow up a bridge with the smallest possible charge.

But here today during the last week of training, J.R. was racing over the assault course against his teammate, George Inskip, a Brit who was an RAF ace from the Battle of Britain. At stake was twenty pounds, a fifty-year-old bottle of scotch, and a thick steak taken from a box marked for Lord Mountbatten when the supply truck had stopped at the camp mess kitchen that morning.

J.R. clambered down the roof of a smoking house filled with smudge pots, then hit the ground running with full field pack and weapons. Skip was right beside him when he ran up a twenty-foot ladder of logs, then jumped down into the mud and came up ready to fire. He moved carefully over a slender log bridge. If one of his feet slipped, which had happened twice last week, he would fall into a gully of barbed wire.

He jumped off the end of the bridge with Inskip only a few lengths behind him. They ran for the final exercise. The men dubbed it the Achnacarry Death Ride. Each man doubled his toggle rope over a fifty-foot cable and swung like Johnny Weismuller across a river of icy water.

But Tarzan had it easy. He swung through the movie-made jungles, and there weren't live demolition charges going off under him.

Inskip had caught up with him. They both flung their toggles over the cable. They both missed. J.R. got it on the second toss, looped the rope, and launched off the cliff.

"Bye, bye, buddy!" he yelled.

Skip was barely a second or two behind him.

J.R. watched the other side of the ravine coming toward him and laughed. Then his hand slipped and he slammed into the ground with a loud grunt.

Skip landed on his feet and trotted past him. "Tally ho!" Then he turned backward as he ran and waved at him.

Groaning, J.R. sat up, then rested his hands on his knees as he watched Skip disappear toward the barracks. He shook his head and spelled, "D-u-m-b-s-h-i-t."

"EAST OF THE SUN"

To everyone's utter surprise, there came a few days of flawlessly perfect weather, with cloudless blue skies and hardly a breath of wind. The enemy bombing raids were at night and concentrated on London. On days like this it felt like the war was far, far away and the goal of every single pilot was to be up there flying around in that big blue sky.

It was a Tuesday, and most of the ferrying pilots had taken to the air with the crack of dawn, but Charley was left bored and alone in the commons room on a Priority-One Wait, which meant she had to stay put and wait for her plane. Once it arrived, she was to fly it to its destination. Pronto.

At the sound of plane engines she got up and looked out the window. Two taxi planes landed on the grass about three minutes apart. They were bringing back some of the pool's ferrying pilots. Before long, the women came through the doors as they always did, gear hanging about them, chattering, dropping their chutes and vests, and making straight for a tea cart. It was loaded daily with wonderfully delicious sandwiches—the English made a sandwich better than anyone in the world—and sweet, freshly baked cakes brought to them by the generous local women, who drew lots for the days of the week they would supply the pilots and airfield workers.

Around the base they were known as Miss Judith Wednesday, cheese and cucumber sandwiches and strawberry cake, Mrs. Flora Tuesday, salmon, cream cheese, and pudding, and Mrs. Mary Friday, who had a farm, so she often brought egg salad and nut bread with cinnamon.

"Hey there, Charley." Dolores poured a cup of tea. "You're back early."

"I haven't left yet. I drew a P-one-W and have been sitting here half the day."

"It's your punishment for capturing the attention of the most eligible bachelor in all of Great Britain." Paulette, one of the British pilots, sat down across from her with a full plate.

Charley groaned. *Not this again.*

"You are so lucky. What a dreamboat!"

"I go all gooey for a man with dark hair and blue eyes."

All of them, the three British pilots and the American women, were looking at her expectantly. "I've told you this before. We only danced together for a few dances. That was all."

"Oh, right." Lois laughed. "He called here twice for you."

"But you weren't here." Joan said. "I told him I was available, Charley, but he'd already hung up."

"That was weeks and weeks ago. The last I saw of Pilot Commander Inskip was the wave of his hand and the back of his dark head when he walked out the door of the dance, with his cousin . . . if she even was his cousin."

"Oh, she's his cousin all right. We checked for you,

sweetie." Dolores patted her shoulder as she walked past. "Apparently he hasn't dated anyone since his wife was killed. You're it."

"There's nothing going on between us. There's not going to *be* anything going on. He danced with me. Period."

"I don't know, Charley. You two looked like a smooth couple on that dance floor."

"We were a couple. There were two of us."

"You know what I meant."

"Where's he from, anyway?"

"Didn't Connie say something about the family estate in the Uplands?"

"Whoa." Dolores raised her hand. "Stop right there. Don't listen to Connie. She's not too good with geography. Back at training school in Texas, when Rosalie came in and told us the Japanese had bombed Pearl Harbor, Connie looked up with all seriousness—I swear this is true—and asked, 'Who's Pearl Harbor?' "

Paulette, Joan, and Lois, the British pilots, who hadn't heard the story before, began to laugh pretty hard.

"Did I hear the words 'Pearl Harbor'?" Connie came in and closed the door behind her. "Are you telling that horrid little story again? Such silly old news."

"Maybe, but you're never going to live it down." Dolores said, laughing.

"No. I'm not. Thanks to most of you. You'll probably still be telling it when my grandchildren are alive."

"Well, you have to admit it was pretty funny. We *were* in navigation classes."

"I'm from Vermont. I've never been to the Hawaiian

Islands. One of you needs to do something really stupid and save me from Dolores's big mouth."

Before anyone could respond, the door burst open and Rosalie came storming inside. She tossed her brown leather helmet on an empty chair. "You are not going to believe this!"

Dolores handed her a cup of black tea. "What?"

"Thanks." Rosalie took a sip. "I had a Hurricane to deliver to East Anglia, and someone from chain watch thought I was a bogie, so they ordered up three more aircraft to investigate me."

"That happened to me last month."

"Well, it gets better. Those planes, too, were designated as bogies, so the next thing you know, half the fighter command is in the air, flying around to investigate themselves and me."

Everyone was laughing.

"It could have been worse." Dolores poured her own tea. "They might have classified you as a bandit instead of merely unidentified aircraft."

"That's right," Connie said. "Someone might have shot you down."

"Oh, wait." Rosalie held up her hand. "I'm not done. We're going over the Thames at about five thousand feet, and Ops tells us to circle until they can figure out what to do with all of us. So, get this. Every time we pass over the ack-ack batteries, they open fire on us."

Dolores was laughing so hard she was snorting and holding herself up with one hand on the tea cart.

"We didn't dare break orders, so we tried to edge off course a little each time we passed the guns."

"Good God . . ." someone muttered.

"Ops finally makes a decision—there is a God—and sends us to Hornchurch. Well, get this . . . when we land, the CO gets on the phone and tracks down the battery commander, who tells him he is 'frightfully sorry, but his chaps have been on alert for a long time and were getting rather rusty, so when we all came along, it gave them the chance for some real target practice.'"

"Lord, but I do so love the British way of dealing with mistakes," Dolores said.

"He then pointed out, with this twisted bit of logic, that the very fact that they hadn't hit any of us just proved how badly they needed the practice." She set her tea down and grabbed a sandwich, then flopped down in a morris chair, disgusted. She pulled her hair ribbon out of her curly dark hair and tied it around her wrist. "I swear, I am never flying over Sheppey again."

Paddy the dispatcher stuck his head in the door. "Morrison. Your plane's here. It's that Lysander II the crew's fueling up."

Charley grabbed her gear. "See you later!" She walked outside, spotted the plane, and began to run across the grass toward it.

Paddy caught up with her. "Here's the paperwork." He shoved it in her hand. "Good luck!" He turned around and made off for the base office.

She climbed into the pilot's seat with the help of one of the crew, who were just removing the fuel hose. She did her checks quickly, then fired her up. Soon she was in the air.

A half an hour into her flight Charley stared down below her wing at the coast drifting by. From above, the land below looked human: a spine of a railroad track;

the green hills, patches of farmland, and small villages formed the vital organs and the muscles that made it strong; the rivers, truly the veins of the land.

She veered southeast and met a cloud or two, then watched the ribbon of English coastline thread along the deep blue water as time and the miles passed by.

She landed the plane at a small field on the south coast. The sky was turning dusky pink and violet-gray when she taxied along the grass toward the ground activity, and someone with a torchlight waved her over toward a group of dark-uniformed soldiers. She parked the plane, and before she could unbuckle, a tall man with black on his face jumped up on the wing.

"We've been waiting. Ten more minutes and we'd have had to abort."

There was a moment's pause.

"Charlotte?"

She didn't recognize the man's face through the face-black. She looked closer. "Skip?"

"Say, I'm glad it's you. Will you help us out and taxi over to those petrol pumps? We're running late."

"Sure. No problem."

He gave her the okay sign.

She moved the plane to the pumps, then got out quickly and tossed her chute and flight bag on the grass. The ground crew had already begun fueling.

Skip was followed by a blond man about their same height. He was smearing on face-black as he ran. He handed his gear to a crew member to stow onboard. He gave Charley a long, assessing look, then climbed on the wing, where Skip handed him a heavy canvas bag and a small black suitcase. The man on the wing tossed the gear in back and turned around. He looked at her, then at Skip.

He rattled off something in German.

Charley stiffened, then looked at him uneasily.

"You're not amusing, Cassidy. Get your Yank ass inside the damned plane."

Thank God, a Yank, not a Nazi.

"Yeah. Sure." Cassidy winked at her. "There's all kinds of Yank ass around here." He crawled into the passenger seat.

She burst out laughing.

Skip turned back around. "Sorry. Ignore him."

"It's okay. Really. Are you the one who's flying this plane out?"

"Yes."

"Will you sign this delivery chit for me?"

He took it and scribbled his name across, then handed it back to her. "I rang you up a couple of times."

"I know."

"I can't call you for a while."

"I understand. Duty calls."

He was searching her face for something, but she didn't know why.

"What's wrong? A wart on my nose? Lipstick on my teeth?"

"No. I forgot something that night."

"What?"

He grabbed her by her shoulders and gave her a long, deep kiss that seemed to go on forever.

"Inskip." Cassidy called down from the plane.

Skip pulled back and looked at her, ignoring Cassidy. She smiled at him.

"Hey, there, you two. It's seventeen-hundred."

They both turned and looked at Cassidy, who was holding up his wrist and tapping his watch.

"I've got to go."

She nodded, and he released her shoulders and jumped onto the wing. She watched him jump up and crawl inside the plane, then buckle in.

He looked at her and gave a quick salute.

"Good-bye, Skip."

He leaned out of the plane. "No. Not good-bye." Then he gave it throttle, and a few minutes later he was in the air.

She stood there for a long time after the plane had taken off and banked toward the Channel, stood there watching until it was only a speck in the quickly darkening sky. She touched her mouth and smiled, but when she pulled her fingers away, they were covered in greasy, black face paint. She wiped her mouth with her sleeve and laughed as she walked to find a ride to the train station.

Later, she sat in the train unable to see anything outside the painted windows, so she stared at a brightly colored *"Dig For Victory"* poster and wondered where Skip was. If he was safe. He'd only said he couldn't call her for a while and this wasn't good-bye. That was all he'd said, and she hadn't asked more. Loose lips, keeping mum, and all that.

But she thought about him and little else for the long train ride back. She conjured up a hundred clandestine scenarios until they became a little outlandish; only then did she let herself think about the kiss, and she wondered if she would ever see him again.

"THIS IS WORTH FIGHTING FOR"

Saboteurs, like spies, go out when the moon is high. That's what somebody said once. Somebody was a liar. Since working on covert missions in tandem with British Special Air Service, the SAS, J.R. had yet to go out in a single clear night. He'd been in a cramped sub, only to then silently row a small rubber boat through a cold, solid bank of silent fog where even your breathing could carry enough sound to alert the enemy. There was a seaplane in thick cloud cover. He'd parachuted out of a C-47 transport in a snowstorm—his personal favorite mission—or, there was tonight's adventure, facing torrential rain as they flew to Alsace, deep in France.

The plane bounced along the unpredictable currents, then dropped like concrete about a hundred feet.

"Jesus! It was clear as vodka when we left."

"Not here, it isn't." Inskip had both hands on the controls.

The plane fell again . . . a few hundred feet; then they hit turbulence that was so strong it almost pulled the yoke out of Inskip's hands. "Damn . . . ." He throttled up. "This weather's soggy as hell. Can't see a thing."

J.R. sat forward and looked over Inskip's shoulder to his white knuckles on the yoke and his intense gaze that was locked on the instruments. J.R. glanced at the gauges.

They were flying low. Real low. He turned and looked outside.

Rain poured in thick sheets down the windshield, blurring everything from view with a film of drenching water. He thought of Kitty.

Now that he was married to her, he found there were plenty of moments like this, when he would catch a glimpse of her world. It always humbled him a little, knowing he was outclassed by her ability to be the person she was: stronger, smarter, and more of an enigma to him than most women he'd known, women who had perfect sight. He was damned proud of her.

Pigheaded, obstinate, smart-mouthed, that was Kincaid. What she did to him with that mouth . . . well, that was something else. God, he missed her. Leave time, whether forty-eight hours or seventy-two, was nothing special for him here. When he got away from the war, what he wanted to do was lose himself inside of her, not inside a local pub, drinking and throwing darts at a board or sitting in a movie house alone or with men he saw day in and day out.

Funny thing, J.R. had never needed anyone before. He'd relied solely on himself. But now there were some nights when he needed her so much he ached for any small reminder of her, something tangible. They'd all talked about it. During war you needed something personal to remind you that all the destruction and killing, the blood and death, was for something invaluable and not just mankind run amok.

Sure, he'd have liked to believe that he was a patriot as he was bouncing around over enemy territory in this goddamn plane, and that merely a salute to the flag would keep him focused on his duty. But it would have been a lie. A salute, the flag and what it symbolized, well, it wasn't enough. Not now. Instead, at night, he would hold her letters to his nose and breathe them in, because she was home, she was that something that was worth fighting for.

"Look to the west, Cassidy. Can you see anything?"

J.R. looked down. The rain had let up, just scattered drops on the window. "Looks like trees." He snapped open his lighter and scanned the maps. "The grass field is only a few miles from the train station. Just beyond the hills."

"We had to come in low and from the south to stay undetected. Wait. There. I see something at ten o'clock."

"That's it."

"Yeah. I see the torches at the ends of the field." He pulled out his binoculars. "Circle once."

Skip flew the plane low and around.

"It looks good. I see the *maquis*. Jean-Luc and the others."

"Okay. We're going in." Skip took the plane down.

J.R. checked the gear and pulled his knit cap down over his head.

Half an hour later he was following a couple of members of the French Resistance slogging through the mud to a train depot, teeming with both *Wehrmacht* troops and a few *SS*.

They had to wait three hours. The train was delayed by the weather and flooding on the tracks.

Jean-Luc elbowed J.R. in the side. "Here comes the train." He used his stolen Mauser rifle to point at a curl of pale smoke slipping over a rise toward the west.

A few minutes later you could hear the chugging of engine as the troop and supply train rounded the bend and pulled to a stop at the station. The steam had barely settled before the soldiers began to load equipment and men into the cars.

By the time the engine pulled out, heading toward Frankfurt and then on to Prague, J.R., Skip, and *maquis* officer Jean-Luc were lying on top of the second-to-the-last railroad car. The train wound its way out of eastern France and into Germany over a broad bridge that spanned the Rhine and past their objective, an *SS* operation headquarters tucked away in a well-fortified castle. Blowing up the bridge? Well, that bit of fireworks would come afterward.

'I'M SHOOTING HIGH'

LUTON AIR BASE

Red was in the briefing room with the other crews of the 17th Bombardment Group. The men sat in their small, hard chairs; some slouched down and others tapped out the notes to songs on their knees or chewed gum nervously, waiting—wordless—a sense of tension and anticipation keeping them from talking to one another. Scuttlebutt had been circling around the aerodrome for days that this was the big one—HQ's most important and largest air operation to date.

The door opened. Everyone turned as the intelligence officer walked down the aisle toward the front of the room, where he paused, then pulled away a dark cloth covering the wall map. The man next to Red let out a low, long whistle. A bright string pinned on the map marked their route, a line from their B-17 base in England to somewhere in southern Germany.

"Your primary target is here." The IO tapped a pointer against the map. "This, gentlemen, is the largest center for the manufacture and assembly of the ME 109. You destroy it and you destroy thirty percent of Goering's fighter production." He faced them. "I expect you know exactly what that means to all of you on a personal level."

There were a few laughs. What it meant was lives to the Allies, lives to men sitting inside that room.

After a long and intense briefing, Red filed out of the room early, while most of the others stayed there discussing the mission. They were wound up tight as springs. This was their first mission into Germany.

Once outside, Red stood with his hands in the pockets of his leather flight jacket, and stared up at the night sky. Overhead the stars were dimly visible through the mist covering the blacked-out bomber field. He was a long way from Acme, Texas.

He was in Britain and he hadn't been to London, yet. Almost two years ago he had upped and left Acme, Texas, to go out into the wide open world, only to find his own shrunk down to the confining cockpit of a B-17 bomber.

He laughed at the irony of it. Charley ... Charley. She would laugh when he told her that. Whenever he looked up at the stars, he thought about her, thought about a cool pond in Texas, and a hot night that changed him forever.

She was here in England. They had written to each other. But her base wasn't nearby. The ATA bases were scattered all over the place. His group had been here for three months, and he'd had almost no time off. They flew mission after mission, and when they weren't flying around at twenty thousand feet, they were waiting to fly around at twenty thousand feet.

He'd had no time to track her down. But he would. Soon.

Back at Randolph Field, when there had been nothing to do at night but think, he would lie there in his cot, his hands folded behind his head, and look out the open louvered window above him at the clear Texas sky and a thousand stars. He'd played a game, telling himself that maybe she was looking at them, too. That was what carried him through those empty nights alone with only the men in the unit, times when home and the memory of a girl were all you had to hang on to.

The mist grew thicker, colder, condensed and dripped off his hat. The English weather; the damp air here seeped clear into your bones. He tugged down on the bill of his cap and made his way to the Ops office to check out his Fortress assignment. Once inside, he skimmed the crew sheet on the bulletin board. It listed the lead, low, and high squadrons. He was listed for a copilot's seat in the lead group. The first ones to run the target.

Someone clapped him on the shoulder. Red turned.

Squadron Commander O'Malley was an Irishman from Hoboken who was well-liked and had a reputation for steady-nerved flying. "Hey, Walker. You on the *Canterbury Mary* tomorrow?"

"No, sir. Looks like I'm on the *U.S.O. Flo*. With Lambert."

O'Malley turned to the operations officer. "Sid! Come here, will ya? And bring your pencil."

A couple of minutes later, with a few strokes of an eraser, Red was moved to high squadron as copilot on O'Malley's *Mary*.

At five-thirty the next morning Red sat with the crew underneath the sinister shadow of their crouching B-17 as they waited for the weather to clear. The postponement ratcheted up tension about tenfold. For something to do, he checked over his gear—Mae West, oxygen mask, and parachute. He made certain his escape kit was pinned securely to the knee pocket of his flight suit, checked his .45 pistol, ammo, and slid a hunting knife between his shoe and flying boot.

O'Malley calmly walked around the plane, running a hand over the cool metal skin, giving it a pat here and there, checking oxygen and ammo, bomb bay and tires. The gunners field-stripped their .50-calibers again and oiled the bolts. The turret gunner lay on the damp grass, his head resting on his chute and canvas pack, eerily quiet and sweat beading on his face. He'd been worried all week. This was his thirteenth mission.

By seven-thirty that morning Red was in the *Mary*'s copilot's seat, watching the other B-17s below him break like huge silver bullets through the white cloud deck, their glass noses aimed upward for the long climb to twenty thousand feet.

Red looked at his logs: "FT—Flight Time 6:45, ET—

Time over Enemy Territory 3:35, Altitude—24K, Bomb Load, 10,500 # of HE—High Explosive." He checked the dials, then played with the heating units on his gloves. The temperature gauge read minus 23 degrees.

They circled for over an hour above the weather in the clear blue sky, until the arrowhead formations, a thousand feet apart, followed the lead group away from the south of England and out over the blue-green waters of the Channel, then on to the golden, sun-glittered surface of the North Sea.

Red looked out to see a smattering of blue smoke ahead from the gunners testing their guns while they still had the chance. He tightened his oxygen mask and watched the glass tube on the instrument panel; the ball inside it moved up and down with each breath he took, exactly the way it was supposed to, like a life monitor, a heartbeat.

Fifteen minutes later the first flak blossom exploded in the sky from the batteries along the north coast; it was too low and inaccurate. He barely felt the kick of it when it exploded in the air well below them.

They flew on toward the target, three formations of Flying Fortresses all loaded for bear. Along the way they released bundles of metal paper and foil to muck up the enemy radar. Subsequent flak was low and off enough that the paper must have worked.

Red made a note on his logs.

More than an hour into the flight, the tail gunner got the bends. You could hear him yelling in the earphones and destroying communications until one of the crew ᴐlled him into the plane's belly and took his position. ᴛ flak grew solid and accurate as they flew over the eastern edges of France, over the Rhine, and into southern Germany.

He checked the temperature gauge. It was minus 41 degrees. The heaters were working, but he was still cold as hell. The closer they got to the target, the worse the flak. Concussion drove the plane down. Antiaircraft fire exploded near the engine. The ship shook.

Number two engine went bad. They feathered it. He heard someone swear. A gunner called out, "Fighters at two o'clock low!"

Two FW-190s dove into the front formation. They fired, tracers flashing. Almost as suddenly they peeled away in half rolls, then sped low over Red's group. One fighter flashed by, its yellow nose smoking.

The *Mary*'s turret gunner blasted it. Pieces of plane flew past. A yellow German chute opened below. More fighters came in. Within seconds all the *Mary*'s gunners were firing. The smell of burnt cordite filled the cockpit. Now he was sweating.

Ahead, he could see smoke trailing from three B-17s that were hit, but still keeping formation toward the target. One of them had lost an engine. A piece of the tail was missing from another.

Flak exploded around them and shook the plane, rattled his teeth; they struggled with the controls, the reality of war around them, in front of them, and shaking the hell out of them.

A new squad of MEs came soaring in.

You could hear the shouts, "Bandits! Three o'clock!" "Look out! Twelve o'clock high!"

The navigator gave Red the coordinates. He contacted the bombardier.

"Two minutes to target."

Ahead of them the forts began dropping their loads. The flak was so thick you could walk on it. The gunners worked hard and furiously. Tracers were everywhere, green and fiery.

Two ships broke up, and they counted the chutes, eight from one, five from the other. The fighters were still around, soon the air was full of smoke and plenty of parachutes, German and Allied. Then it got bad. Real bad.

Red watched the *Flo* in the front formation take a direct hit from a blazing ME and break in half, flaming as it spiraled down and then exploded.

There were no chutes.

No chutes. He took deep breaths from his oxygen. The smell of flak blasts came through with the oxygen. He felt sick, like he might vomit in the mask. He turned and met O'Malley's sharp-eyed gaze, but neither of them said anything. Red turned back and stared ahead. He owed his life to the man next to him and to an eraser on the end of a pencil.

The blasts kept coming. The noise inside, the sheer cacophony of it, was the true sound of war. He kept his eyes ahead, then watched the lead formation, stunned motionless, as the bomb load from one fort dropped through the wings of another ship.

"Shit!" O'Malley saw it. "Look. It's the *Lucky 13*."

"My God . . . he's still flying."

The plane was in the air. Together, except for part of the wing. No sign of chutes; it struggled to stay in formation in a sky ablaze with smoke and tracers and planes.

"Damn . . . look at that. He's holding his own."

Just then an ME came at them, guns blazing. They took a hit in the wing. Number three engine quit, the oil line severed. Red watched the dials, shouting readings.

The bombardier dropped their load. They flew another two minutes. A blast from starboard sent the ship down. Number four engine was on fire.

Another enemy fighter was on them. The tail gunner was screaming and firing.

Like angels from heaven their own fighter escort finally came speeding in from out of the sun, dropped their belly tanks, and went to work, dogfights breaking out all over the skies, the Allied fighters shooting past to the whistles of the crew, and the Luftwaffe diving into the bomber formations to avoid fire from the P-47s.

There was a huge noise, then the sickening sound of chunks of steel ripping into the ship. Men screamed. Smoke was everywhere inside. The navigator went back with some of the crew; they were working to put out the flames. When they did, there was a huge hole in the ship and it was vibrating like it was going to break up.

"Walker!" O'Malley pulled one hand away from his side. He was bleeding.

Red took over, struggling to hold the plane. Ten more minutes and they were losing altitude. It was more and more difficult to stay with the group. Finally they dropped and dropped, the plane shuddering. O'Malley couldn't bail. Red refused to. The plane dropped again.

He couldn't get her up, so he headed for a grass field. Down and down. They hit hard, with a horrible sound, and he gripped the controls with everything he had. The plane was sliding. There was a horrible cracking sound. It broke in half and the front spun around, the tail catching the nose and the windows blew out.

The plane stopped spinning. Smoke was everywhere. It took Red a minute to realize he was alive.

O'Malley was swearing.

"Shit! Fucking shit!"

Everyone was swearing.

Some of the men were wounded and bleeding, screaming names and voices answering as they tried to find everyone.

"Get out! Get out fast!"

Red grabbed O'Malley and pulled him toward the hole. The ball gunner dropped down, blood covering his right eye, but he helped drag O'Malley, and they all tumbled out onto the soaking wet ground, sinking into mud so thick and deep it was like quicksand. It was the mud that probably saved them, slowing the plane's momentum.

Rounds of rifle fire shot into the air.

The bombardier dropped, his thigh bleeding.

"Achtung! Hände hoch!"

Then silence.

"Surrender!" Someone shouted in accented English. "Come out! Now! Hands up!"

Red looked at the men. Dolan, the navigator, had passed out, and the tail gunner looked dead.

Another shot came in from the left.

Red ducked and pulled O'Malley back and under the protection of part of the fuselage and wing. Two of the crew crawled over.

"Stay here," Red told them. "Watch the commander."

"What are you doing?"

"Surrender and you will live!"

Of the *Mary*'s crew: three wounded, one possibly dead, and three others beside Red.

"Lieutenant?"

Red turned back.

"They're going to shoot us if we don't give up."

"From what I hear, they might shoot us if we do. Besides, I'm not going to let them take me that easily, and not O'Malley either. This is war we're here for. Let's damn well fight it." Red pulled his .45.

O'Malley fumbled to find his gun, winced, then pulled it out. Dolan already had his pistol drawn.

A second later a bullet took Dolan out with a shoulder wound. Red crawled under the wing, moving toward the nose. He drew no fire, so his position must not have been visible. He picked up a broken tree branch and squatted there a moment, took off his flight helmet and slipped it on the branch, then slowly raised it into view.

A bullet cut right through the branch; the helmet went flying.

Whoa . . . that was some shooting.

Another shot rang out from the trees across from them. They were moving in from east and west, trying to get them in cross fire.

Red shifted back and found a space between the plane, a crack that was about six inches of open view. He took aim and waited for the sure shot, the way his granddaddy had taught him.

He watched for the glint of the rifle in the trees

beyond, watched until he saw it, fired, and moved on to another spot before he heard the man fall.

Two rifles fired back from similar positions. "Surrender! Or we will shoot you. All of you."

Red picked off another one and rolled away, then another, and another. Shots began coming from all over the woods.

Crap . . . How many of them are there?

The crew members who could were exchanging fire. Pistols versus rifles gave the enemy the edge.

Red took aim, then heard a rifle report about a hundred feet away. A bullet slammed through the metal of the plane, a few inches from his head. He ducked away into the brush, pulled his knife from his boot, and waited, then slowly got up and moved through the trees.

A few minutes later, there was one less enemy. He had a German rifle along with a few rounds of Mauser ammo.

Things had evened up a bit: a handful of us and twenty some-odd of them? Hell, it was a cakewalk.

'PRAISE THE LORD AND PASS THE AMMUNITION'

Skip secured the explosive pack on the train car and set the timers. He looked over to the next railcar at Cassidy, who gave him the okay sign. His charges were set, too. They had been in Germany for almost sixty hours and were now just outside the last bend in the track near the train station where they had started.

Jean-Luc came up from his position near the engine and signaled to jump now. Skip stood as the train rattled down the tracks. Out of the corner of his eye he saw Cassidy do the same. The train whistled as it turned the bend. All three jumped off the railroad cars simultaneously.

Skip hit hard, tucked and rolled down the embankment, over some hard rocks and into a ravine. He lay there as still as the stone that gouged him.

The train sped past. Not a shot was fired.

He stood and brushed off the grass and leaves as Cassidy came to his side, limping.

Skip glanced at his leg. "Are you hurt?"

"No. I pulled a muscle. I'm okay."

"Too much time on your duff, old chap. We'll fix you up fine. Just send you back to Achnacarry for a solid week on the assault course."

Cassidy gave a low groan. "No. Please. . . . Shoot off my balls instead. It's gotta be less painful."

Jean-Luc climbed out of a clump of bushes nearby. He slung his gun strap over his shoulder and gave a sharp nod of his head. "Come. This way."

They followed him down and out of the ravine, across an icy cold stream, and into the woods that sloped downward and covered a steep hillside thick with spindle-like birch that cracked and broke if you hit them wrong. It was a tricky exercise to get through quietly.

After a few hundred yards of damp, shoulder-high brush, they came to the edge of an open meadow, where the Frenchman stopped, crouched down, surveyed the area, then sat, leaning his rifle against a tree trunk. "It is not safe to cross. We will wait here." He took out a knife, picked up a broken piece of a branch, and began to skin the bark off with his knife.

A quarter of an hour later they heard the distant, faint blasts of the charges they had planted on the train.

Cassidy checked his watch. "Right on time."

Skip nodded, and from then on, all they did was wait. For two hours. He checked his watch about half as often as Cassidy did. After a while, even Jean-Luc was becoming edgy.

Then the Frenchman froze. Skip had heard it, too. The breaking of a twig from the west. Cassidy had crouched down and pulled his gun.

There was the quiet call of a loon; the notes wavered in the air. Jean-Luc held up his hand, then made a similar sound. Like ciphers, three dark-clothed Frenchmen came out of the trees.

One was Jean-Luc's youngest brother, Eduard. "There is trouble. The Germans found your plane and have tripled their patrols in the area. We were afraid to come here until we were certain they had gone past. But now they have moved to another target."

"What target?" Jean-Luc asked.

"A bomber went down in the fields outside of the village."

Skip looked at him. "An Allied bomber?"

Eduard nodded. "A B-17."

Cassidy swore.

"Show us. *Vite, vite.*"

They took off, running through more woods and down another hillside. Before long they could hear the distant gunfire. It grew louder and sharper the closer they got.

Still hidden by the trees, Eduard and Jean-Luc slowed, then signaled and stopped. Skip and the others took positions about a hundred feet away from the open field.

The bomber sat cracked apart in the middle of the field. But the crew was returning fire at the enemy hidden in another cluster of trees. There were shots from three positions. From the sound, he was certain one was a rifle and the other two were pistol fire.

Skip spotted some motion to the south. Two enemy soldiers were stealthily moving into position, maybe a hundred feet from sparks of fire coming from a spot under the plane's belly.

Skip took aim. Cassidy did, too.

But a deadly shot dropped one man like a broken puppet before Skip could pull the trigger on his revolver. Two seconds later, the other enemy soldier went down.

Neither he nor Cassidy nor the Frenchman had fired a shot.

"Holy shit . . . That's some shooting." Cassidy scanned the perimeter, then nodded. "Over there. Near that rock. To the west of the tail. See?"

Skip saw the movement. Four, maybe five enemy soldiers.

"Looks like they're bringing in a machine gun." He grinned at Skip. "Let's give those bomber boys some help."

The rifleman under the bomber crawled a few feet, then inside the broken plane.

Jean-Luc and his men faded further back into the trees and began to circle around, while Skip and Cassidy crawled forward into better range.

The enemy never got that gun mounted.

From inside the bomber, the rifleman took out five men in less than a minute.

"So much for helping him out. Come on. Let's let him know we're here." Cassidy started to move forward.

"Wait. I don't fancy getting myself shot," Skip told him.

Cassidy hesitated, then began to whistle "Buffalo Gals, Won't You Come Out Tonight."

There was one of those long, drawn-out moments; then someone near the downed plane began to whistle the same tune back.

The enemy, however, was firing straight at them.

A few minutes later Skip, Cassidy, and Jean-Luc were inside the bomber returning fire next to two crewmen and a pilot manned with a rifle and a sharpshooter's dead-on aim. He was good. Awfully bloody good.

An hour later they were secure in a cellar room under a local barn used by the French Resistance. A local doctor had seen to the crew's wounds and just left. The rest of them were eating some hot soup, cheese, and bread Eduard had brought them.

One man had died. The other crew members were okay. The pilot, a man named O'Malley, was wounded in the side and wasn't mobile, but the doctor had tended the wounds and told them he could travel without danger.

Lieutenant Walker, the shooter, got up to check on O'Malley, then came back to sit down near Skip.

"That was some shooting." Cassidy handed him a tin cup of hot coffee.

Walker shrugged and replied, "Didn't see that I had much of a choice, Major. I was damned glad to see you, though. The IOs always advise us to seek out the Resistance if we're downed. The problem was, none of us ever quite knew how to go about it." He laughed and took a long drink of his coffee.

"Where the hell did you learn to shoot like that?"

"Texas."

Cassidy laughed. "There's a joke in that somewhere, but I'll be damned if I can think if it."

The trapdoor opened and Jean-Luc came down the ladder. "We'll move you out in an hour. There's a barge that will take you down the river and then on to the coast. We've let them know you are coming. It will take two days. We have to be careful. They have check-points on the river." He smiled. "But we know how to get by them. You will be picked up by your navy. You should all be safe." He nodded at O'Malley. "Even the wounded."

Two hours later, when they were safely on the barge, Cassidy came over and sat down next to Skip. "What do you think about that kid?"

"Walker?"

He nodded.

"I think he could shoot dead center into the eye of a needle."

"Yeah. That's what I thought. I'm going to talk to him. Think I'll see if I can persuade him to transfer to something more . . . individual."

Skip nodded. "Have at him, old boy."

"You help me out if I need it. I'm depending on you to tell him how much fun we have."

Skip laughed. "I got it. You want me to lie."

"Yeah. Like he's the fucking *SS.*"

Skip lit a cigarette he'd gotten from Eduard and listened as Cassidy started on Walker.

"Yeah, it's only for a special few," Cassidy was saying. "But I can cut through the red tape."

Walker asked him something.

"Good? Yeah. You'll love it. More like a frigging fairy tale than the Army. You see, there's this castle in Scotland . . ."

'SING, SING, SING (WITH A SWING)'

It was a great day for Charley, one she wasn't going to forget. She drew her first Spit, fresh from the factory and gleaming in the bright, warm sunlight. Radios were most often installed after delivery, so ferrying pilots had to fly with a map, a compass, and a prayer. Sometimes they didn't even have gyros.

But not today; this Spit had everything, including the radio. She took her plane upstairs, then played with the radio frequency until she had dialed in some great flying music.

The swing beat of Benny Goodman and the perfect handling of a Supermarine Spitfire. The two went together like rum and Coca-Cola.

The cockpit was tight, with its bubble canopy, but she didn't feel claustrophobic as she tested the machine. It didn't take long for her to see why this plane was so loved. It truly did move with her, like an extension of her body.

And man-oh-man, was it fun!

"Sing, sing, sing, sing . . ." She took the plane up again, flying high to the song's drum solo, then came the trumpets, and she flew through a billowing, cotton-white cloud, slipping and sliding, her wings rocking to the beat of the song.

They were told specifically not to do any aerobatics. But heck . . . it was just her and the sky and the sweetest plane she'd ever flown. She didn't think there was a pilot in the world that could pass this up.

As the music spun, she put the ailerons over on one side and did a slow roll.

Perfect!

She leveled out, then rolled into another, and another, and another, coming out of it to swing her wings to the beat of the trumpet, and sing, sing, sing, singing, "Da-da-dahhh-da . . ."

She turned the music up and climbed as the notes climbed higher, slipped into the air currents to the beat of the drums and rolled the moment the trumpets blared.

She and that Spit just danced across the sky like bobby-soxers at a school dance. The music and fighter . . . well, they played together, flew together, danced together, until the final notes, and she did a double roll, singing at the top of her lungs.

Something metallic flashed past her face.

Oh, crap! Did she break something?

It flew past as she turned over again.

It was gold. She searched the panel. Nothing on the plane was gold.

An instant later she recognized it.

Her Helena Rubinstein powder compact flew past her nose and hit the canopy. The compact popped open.

Ivory Pearl face powder went everywhere.

"Oh, double crap!"

A pinkish cloud filled the cockpit. She coughed and waved it away.

The powder stuck to the canopy, stuck to her face and mouth. There were clouds of it around her, settling as she tried and failed over and over again to wave it all away.

She didn't think there could possibly be so blasted much powder in that case! A few minutes later, the whole canopy looked like milk glass. Powder was on the instruments, on the switches and the knobs.

Squinting, she reached out and tried to wipe the windshield clean. It smeared like a paste from the natural moisture. It was a warm day.

But she kept rubbing and smearing, rubbing and smearing, until she managed to clean enough of a spot for her to see. She landed half an hour later and taxied in and parked.

Now what? She sat there, then unbuckled and opened the canopy. She took a deep breath of air that didn't smell like the face powder, which had dusted everything inside the plane.

A mechanic came running over and spotted her, then turned around and ran back toward the command hut calling like crazy for an ambulance.

She sat there and watched him, completely stunned, then looked down at her powdered skin and hands.

Does he think I'm burned? Damn . . .

She closed her eyes. She had some explaining to do, and sure as shooting, she had some cleaning to do, too. "Well, this ought to top Connie's Pearl Harbor story."

She started to climb out, but stopped when she spotted her metal compact on the floor. She bent down to get it, snapped it closed, and carefully sat up, wiping her dry mouth with her sleeve, which also had powder all over it.

"What a mess!" She turned to get out.

Skip was leaning on the fuselage. He looked at her, frowning, "Charley?"

She groaned.

"Are you okay?"

"Yes." She held up the compact and shrugged. Then all she heard was his laughter.

"YOU CAN'T STOP ME FROM DREAMING"

Their first date was dinner at a small village pub whose owner didn't mind that she was dusted in pale powder and wore a flight jumpsuit. Their second date was at another dance club, where they danced all night until the band played "Auld Lang Syne." The third date was during a two-day leave in London, where they met at the train station and went to the cinema.

They sat in the plush ruby velvet seats of the loge so

Skip could smoke, and watched two war documentaries, a Melodyland cartoon, and an episode of the *Jungle Girl* serial before they laughed through the silliness of *Buck Privates,* starring Abbott and Costello.

They were walking down a dark side street toward a pub when the air-raid sirens went off. Charley turned to look at the sky at the same time Skip did.

Searchlights crisscrossed the sky in moving trails of white light.

"I hate this," she said quietly.

"Come along." He grabbed her hand. "The Underground's too far away. There should be a shelter close by." They walked quite a distance, the sirens whining; then he was moving faster, almost running and holding her hand.

They reached a corner in a block of commercial buildings, and Skip stopped suddenly and swore. "Hurry."

She could hear the plane engines overhead. There was no telling if they were theirs or the Germans'.

He pulled her behind him down the next dark block. "There's an Anderson shelter."

She saw the low mound of sandbags as they made for it. He pulled open the door and pushed her inside. It was empty and darker inside than outside. Blindly she ran down the few steps, and he closed the door, flicked on his lighter, and followed her. He lit an oil lamp sitting on a battered table in the corner.

There was one old fold-up cot, three chairs, a jug of water, and some thin woolen blankets stacked in the corner. The shelter looked as if it hadn't been used much. Most people made straight for the Underground, where there was usually food, room, and light.

"Better settle in. Who knows how long this will last."

She walked over, spread a blanket on the fold-up, and sat down, resting her chin in her hands, her elbows on her knees. She had little experience with bomb raids. London and the south of England got the worst of it. Her base was well north of London, and since they had been there, they'd had only one raid, where no bombs fell. She had been in two in London and found them unsettling because she felt like a sitting duck. Charley was someone who took action; to merely sit there and leave her fate to chance went against her natural instincts.

"I think I'd rather be in the air than here. I feel as if I have a target on my head."

He laughed softly. He thought she was joking.

The bombs began to fall, exploding and making the ground vibrate. She looked at him. He was standing stiffly across from her.

They hit hard. It was all she could do not to jump. She clasped her hands so tightly they went numb.

The bombs hit again. Louder. The room shook, and sand spilled from some of the sandbags. She began to rub her arm. They didn't speak. There was no sound but the bombs hitting. She looked from corner to corner to corner, to see if the sandbags would hold. "They're close."

He looked at her with an expression of surprise, as if he had forgotten her. He crossed over and sat down next to her. He put his arm around her the same way he had at the movies.

His body was hard and warm. "Thank you." She leaned her head on his shoulder.

A bomb hit so close the sandbags shimmied and dirt and dust hit her arms and face.

He tightened his hold on her. The bombs came whistling down, one after another, almost every minute, shattering things aboveground and shattering her nerves along with them.

"They sound like banshees." She was shaking.

He tightened his hold on her. "Take it easy. I'm here."

She looked up.

A bomb hit. Dust went everywhere.

She cried out and clung to him.

Then he was kissing her and she was kissing him back. He pulled at her clothes and she at his. His hands were everywhere, on her breasts, her thighs, pulling up her dress. She wanted his touch, even in bare, moist places that no one saw but her, because feeling meant she was alive.

He pushed her back down on the cot and unbuckled his belt at the same time. He opened all the buttons on the back of her dress and pulled it down to her waist, then off.

The bombs were screaming and blasting around them. They touched and kissed as if they couldn't get close enough.

The cot shook and her clothes were on the floor. Skip was pressing his hips between her legs, and her hands were gripping his tight bare buttocks, pulling him closer. He plunged inside and she cried out.

Bombs blasted, hard and furiously. His hips pushed into her as deeply as he could, over and over, as if each stroke could block out the blasts, the crumbling dirt, and the shaking walls and ground. The smell of smoke and incendiaries.

He raised his head mid-stroke and looked down at her. "Charley." He hesitated. "It's you." He touched the tears on her cheeks with one hand. The other was under her. "I'm sorry. I couldn't stop. I'm sorry."

"Just love me, Skip." She grabbed at his bottom, gripped it, and pressed him down into her, even though it hurt. She wanted him deeper. She wanted to see all of what this mysterious thing called sex was. She wanted it to be him in her, like he was in her dreams every night. "Do it, please. I want this with you."

He shifted and put his hands under her and gave her what she wanted, while the bombs fell all night and London burned.

"TAKE THE 'A' TRAIN"

The train pulled into Victoria Station and ground to a stop in a cloud of white steam. Skip pushed away from the wall, his hat under his arm. Charley was supposed to be on the four-forty. He checked his watch. The train was late.

He couldn't see her with the blacked-out windows, but she'd missed only one date, because of a change in her ferrying schedule. Two weeks afterward, he'd flown to meet her when he came back from an assignment in France involving a Nazi rocket-bomb launching device set up on the coast. For the last three months, they'd been planning and coordinating their leave time to be together.

His uncle was happy. Skip had a girl.

She must have spotted him before he saw her, because she tapped him on the shoulder from behind. "Hey, there."

He spun around.

She tossed her head. Her honey-colored hair brushed her shoulders. She didn't often wear hats. She would wear a ribbon that matched whatever she was wearing. He liked that about her, found her sense of freedom refreshing. Perhaps working with Cassidy made him accustomed to that casual, open manner of the Yanks.

She leaned back and slowly slid the long narrow tweed skirt of her suit up past her knee. "Want to have a good time, soldier?"

"I don't know." He gave her a long, studied look. "How much do you charge?"

A pair of older women were passing by and heard. They starched up and clucked their tongues before they hurried past.

Charley burst out laughing. "You've turned me into a shameless hussy."

"I've always been keen on shameless hussies. Which one are you again?"

Laughing, she tucked her arm into his, and they walked together toward the exit.

"How is your mother?"

"Overbearing, unreasonable, and stubborn."

"Ah, I wondered where you got those traits."

"You are quite badly disciplined, you know. I must speak with your father about the ill manner in which you were raised."

She laughed, hugging his arm closer. "He'll be here

soon enough. But I'm afraid he'll agree with you. I've always been strong-willed. You two can commiserate together over my failure to be quiet and demure. It should break the ice. Now, you must tell me what I need to do to hit it off with your mother. From everything you've been telling me, I'm half terrified of her."

He covered her hand with his. "Truthfully, be yourself. She's really quite a wonderful woman . . . when she wants to be."

"It must be difficult for her. And you."

"Eleanore takes the brunt of it, but I do believe good fortune has smiled on us. I think I have found the answer to handling Mother. You met Cassidy—the Yank I was with in the Lysander that day?"

"He's rather hard to forget. Quick mind, bawdy sense of humor, and damn good looking."

"His face was blacked."

"Hmmm, so was yours."

"Look. Are you hungry? We can stop here for tea."

"I'm famished."

He opened the door for her, and a few minutes later they were seated at a small, quiet table.

"So, I interrupted your story. Tell me about your mother and Cassidy."

He shook his head. "We've worked together for months. I had no idea until the other day when we were talking over a drink. His wife is a blind teacher. Wait. I didn't say that right. She teaches the blind how to get on. Exactly what we tried to hire for Mother, exactly what she needs but is too stubborn to admit it or accept it."

"That's amazing. Can she help her? I mean, didn't she send the others running?"

"Yes, but we have let Mother have her way for a while now. Kitty Cassidy is blind herself. Apparently she understands what Mother's going through. Cassidy's trying to pull some strings to get her over here. We shall find out soon enough."

She was quiet as they brought tea. She ate a bit of sandwich, then said, "Pop didn't want me to come here at first. He felt I'd be too close to the war for him to feel comfortable about my safety. In fact, I expect that's one of the reasons he's coming. Business is certainly part of it, but I know him well enough to bet he jumped at the opportunity to check up on me."

"He sounds like a man of high intelligence."

"Funny. My point is, how will her family feel about her being over here?"

"I did ask about that. She's from California, and Cassidy said he didn't figure after Pearl Harbor that she would be any more at risk here than on the West Coast. He laughed and said it wouldn't matter anyway. No one in her family, including him, would dare make the mistake of telling her what to do. Then he told me how they met. Apparently she was living in Morocco with the family of a college friend. They were in the diplomatic corps and had two blind children. When the war broke out, they left, but her papers were delayed. Got herself in some kind of fix. They sent him in to get her out of it."

"Oh, good," she said, grinning. "I think I like her already."

"Of course you do. I'm surrounded by contrary females. I'm counting on Mother to react the same way."

"We wouldn't want you to grow complacent and bored. National heroes need a little humbling."

"You sound like Helen." He signaled for the bill.

"I adore Helen. We've met twice since you introduced us."

"An action I will live to regret, no doubt."

They left arm in arm and wound their way along the London streets, which were filled with people in uniform—olive drab, nut brown, crisp white, and deep blue. They walked in the park and had a photograph taken near the Serpentine, then went to Oxford Street and stopped at Selfridges, where she bought a new red ribbon and a small box of tea-olive soap for one of her ferry chums.

On the way out of the store they passed a fragrance counter that showed the effects of the war. The few bottles of fine perfume there were dearly priced and locked away in a glass case. The fragrances that were on the counter were plain vials of cheap scent. A salesclerk stopped her and sprayed a small amount of cologne made from rose oil and alcohol on her wrist.

Charley sniffed it and raised her wrist for him to smell.

"It smells like a sot fell in a rose garden."

She laughed and put the bottle down.

"Show us that one." Skip pointed to the glass doors.

The salesclerk perked up, took a silver key from her belt, and unlocked the cabinet. "Skip?" Charley put her hand on his arm.

"It's for my mother."

"Oh."

The salesclerk set the bottle on the counter. "You'll have to sniff the stopper. I can't let you sample this one. There are only three bottles left."

Charley held up a hand. "No. I don't need to try it. It's for his mother."

"See if you like it."

Charley looked at him, frowning.

"Go on."

She sniffed the glass cap, and she smiled softly, then handed it back to the salesclerk. "It's just lovely."

"I'll take it." Skip paid for it and he watched Charley while the salesclerk wrapped up the bottle of perfume.

Charley was smelling the cheap bottles and frowning with each one.

The salesclerk handed him the box and they left. The wind picked up from a dark and roiling storm blowing in from the distance. The temperature had dropped while they were inside, and the rain began to fall in fat drops.

"We'd best head for the hotel." He put his arm around her shoulders, and they ran the few blocks to their hotel.

Once inside the lobby, he handed her the box. "This is for you."

She stopped walking. "You said it was for your mother."

"I lied."

"I can't accept this."

"It's done. Be gracious and accept my gift."

"Skip. This is *Ma Griffe*. It's terribly expensive."

"I can afford it."

"That's not the point."

"I didn't get you a Christmas gift."

"We didn't know each other at Christmas."

"When is your birthday?"

She stood there, stubbornly silent, her lips thin as a pencil line.

"Fine, I'll ask your father when he arrives next week."

"Okay, fine. It's July fourth."

"Your Independence Day?"

She nodded.

"No wonder you're so stubborn. You were born on the day those colonial anarchists rose up against the Mother Country."

She was still laughing when he pulled her along with him toward the lift and walked her inside, blocking her with his body before he leaned down and whispered in her ear. "Think of it as a gift for me. As soon as we get to the room, you can dab that scent on all the soft spots I'm going to suck."

He could see the moment she gave in. She leaned her head into his shoulder. All he could see was the part in her hair.

"Thank you. I love your exorbitant gift."

A few minutes later he unlocked the door and they went inside. Her bag had been delivered from the station and was sitting in the dressing room, but the last thing he wanted on her was more clothes. The useless ones she was wearing ended up on the floor. They went straight to bed and stayed there.

He awoke sometime in the early morning. There had been no raid that night. The weather had turned terribly bad. He smoked a cigarette and stood near the bed, watching her sleep, listening to the soft sound of her even breathing and thinking about what was beginning between them.

She'd made the mistake of falling in love with him. He had seen it on her face that night and the last time they had been together. He took a deep drag off the cigarette. Some decent part of him wanted to warn her, to tell her the women he loved were killed or blinded, that loving him was suicide for the heart and perhaps the spirit.

But he couldn't tell her. He wanted her to love him, even though he couldn't love her back.

He stubbed out the cigarette in a marble ashtray and moved closer to the bed.

He had lost his sense of honor, ironically, because of war—where honor, duty, and valor were supposed to be what made fighting men. None of those things motivated him. He asked himself if his lack of them made him a coward.

It was an odd thing to him that of late, and with regularity, he thought that he did not want to die, which . . . wasn't exactly the same thing as wanting to live.

He wondered if there was a God. If there was purity after death. Or did we just exist only to die and there was nothing more to life and death than that? He stood there in a dark room with a woman he craved, with unsettling emotions he didn't understand, in a world he couldn't control.

The wind outside whispered through the curtains in time and meter with her soft, easy breathing. He felt nothing of ease; he felt awkward, out of place; he had a sudden sense of lost time. Her perfume was in the air, light and familiar, but it didn't make him any more comfortable. He looked across the room.

A huge mirror hung on the opposite wall above a

clothes chest, and he could see his silhouette reflected in it. No features. Nothing familiar, merely the dark outlines of a man who appeared to be a stranger. Then he realized that perhaps it wasn't time he had lost, but himself.

'WHITE CLIFFS OF DOVER'

It was June in southern California, that time of year when mornings were gray and overcast, but by noon the sun would come through and burn your nose to a crisp if you forgot to wear a hat. Kitty sat on the front porch swing, idly pushing it back and forth with her bare toes as the seagulls called out from overhead, the breeze made the palm tree fronds sway in whispers, and the waves drummed deeply on the beach across the street.

A phone rang in the distance, irritatingly brash and loud. The swing creaked; it needed oiling. The breeze swept by, ruffled her hair, and smelled like salt and seaweed and hot dogs from the Pike down the beach.

The beginnings of summer were in the air on days like today, lazy days, lonely days, empty days. Kitty could not have cared less if it was summer or winter. She was waiting for the mailman, waiting for some word from her husband.

The screen door squeaked open. "Kitty! Come quick! J.R.'s on the telephone!"

"The telephone? Where is he?" She stood so quickly the swing hit on the backs of her knees.

"England, I guess. I didn't ask him. Come on."

Two steps away from the swing and Dennis, her sixteen-year-old brother, grabbed her hand and pulled her inside, shoving her through the house toward the phone on the kitchen wall.

She held the earpiece to her ear. "Cassidy?"

His wonderful deep voice crackled through the static on the line.

"Hi. Yes. I can hear fine. Are you okay? Where are you? What? England, not Scotland? Oh. I'm glad you're busy. It's smart of them to keep you out of trouble. Yeah, well. I'm the only person you can get into that kind of trouble with." She laughed. "What? Nothing. Absolutely nothing. I'm bored witless. No job yet. They think soon, but I've been waiting for months now. Why?"

She listened as he told her about Audrey Inskip, the blind mother of a buddy of his, who needed her skills very badly. "Do I want the job? There, near you? No, of course not. Why on earth would I want to be near my husband? You fool. Of course I want to come." She pulled away from the phone.

Her brother was hovering nearby. Listening. He had opened the icebox and was drinking buttermilk—she could smell it—most likely right out of the milk bottle.

"Dennis, get something and write this down for me, please." She repeated the mailing address and telephone number of the Inskip estate called Keighley. "Yes, we got it. When do I go and how?" She stood there unable to speak for an instant. "Did you say tomorrow? No . . . no. If that's the only transport you can get me on, then I'll be there. Yes, I'll fly. I don't care how cold it is. I'll bring blankets, coats, mittens. Okay. I understand. Take care. Yes . . . me, too. Bye."

She hung up the phone and said, "I'm going to

England. I'm going to England!" She reached out and grabbed her brother. "Call Daddy for me, please."

"Sure, sis." He moved to the phone.

"Tell him J.R. found me a position near him, and I'm flying out tomorrow. I've got to pack." She ran out of the room and was halfway up the stairs when she heard the mail slot scrape closed.

"The heck with the mail!" She kept running, around the corner and into her room. She didn't need to wait for letters her brother would read to her. She pulled her suitcase down from the closet shelf and a hatbox tumbled onto the floor. She didn't care. She tossed her suitcase on the bed and snapped it open. Then she sat down for a second because her heart was beating so fast.

"Pocatello, Idaho, my fanny!" She threw back her head and laughed. In three days, she would see Cassidy. Three days!

Two days, sixteen hours, and twenty-five minutes later she stood at the open door of the airplane as J.R. ran up the metal steps, swept her into those wonderful arms of his, and gave her a kiss that could melt the seams in her only pair of stockings.

She held on to her hat and broke off the kiss. The small bit of netting on her hat was scraping her eyebrow.

He brushed it aside. His face was mere inches away. She could taste his breath. She could smell the soap he used to shave, his hair oil, the starch in his uniform. Their bodies fit perfectly, his hand on her hip, his knee brushing her thigh.

She was wearing short gloves, but her hand still rested on his chest. She could feel his heart beating. "Hello, Cassidy."

"Hello, Kincaid."

"I missed you."

"Me too, sweetheart. I didn't have anyone to give me a hard time."

She laughed. "Don't worry. I'll make up for it."

He helped her down the metal steps to the asphalt. "That's what I'm hoping. We have a lot of things to make up for. The good news is we have plenty of time. Just you and me. We don't have to go to Keighley until the weekend."

"What day is this?"

"Tuesday. Long flight, isn't it?"

"I don't care. I would have flown on the back of a duck to get here."

"Stay here. Let me grab your suitcases. They're unloading now."

She stood and waited. The stench of fuel was in the air, which was brisk and a little damp, as if it were foggy or getting ready to rain.

He took her hand, folded her fingers between his, and they walked to a car. He helped her into the backseat, then put her luggage in the trunk and climbed in beside her. "Take us to the Connaught."

He drew her into his arms and kissed her long and deeply, his hands touching her body until their breathing was fast and her skin warm and flushed. She broke off the kiss and touched his lips with her gloved fingers. "Wait, my darling. Please."

He kissed her fingers. "Okay, sweetheart, but once we're in the room, look out."

"Look out? I can't look out. I'm blind in one eye and can't see out of the other."

"You know, Kincaid, I think it's that smart mouth of yours that first made me notice you."

"Somehow I doubt that, considering your constant references to my cup size. Now let's stop this. You can tell me all you know about Skip's mother."

"He doesn't want us to tell her why you're there."

"That might be wise if she isn't going to be accepting. You implied she's a handful."

"So he tells me."

"It's a fine line to walk. Pride and pain and pity, all mixed up at once. You fight to prove to the world that you don't need them, that you want desperately to show you can be like everyone else. At the same time you are consumed with shame and self-doubt because you know you aren't going to, and never can, be like everyone else."

He slid his arm around her. "You are a brilliant woman, you know that?"

"Sure. I married you, didn't I? Is there anything else I should know about Audrey?"

"Skip thinks she shouldn't know you're blind."

"Okay. I've done that one before. More times than you can count. It works with the stubborn ones. So what's our story?"

"You're my wife and will be welcome to stay there. As a houseguest. The place is huge, I take it. We won't be the only ones there this weekend. There's Skip's girl, Charley."

"Charley?"

"Charlotte. She's an ATA pilot. Tall, over six feet, blond, and gorgeous. Legs that go on forever."

"Don't start, Cassidy."

He laughed. "You are so easy."

She punched him in the arm with her bony knuckles.

"Okay. Truce. Her father is Bob Morrison. He designs and manufactures planes. He's here on business with the government, and Skip asked him along. His aunt stays there, along with the staff. So there will be a houseful of us. But then, the English like it that way. They're very open and warm. I think you'll feel right at home."

"I'm just glad to be here."

The car stopped and J.R. helped her out, then gave the porter the luggage, and they followed him up to the room. As they were riding up in the lift, he slid his hand onto her butt and squeezed it, then slid a little lower and snapped her garter.

She jabbed him in the ribs with her elbow and whispered, "Behave."

She had to smile when he opened the hotel room door, took the suitcases from the poor porter, and handed him some money, saying. "Thanks, I've got it."

He closed the door, turned around. For a few moments he didn't say anything; then quietly, he said, "You're wearing too many clothes, Kincaid."

"So are you, Cassidy." She took off her hat and tossed it away.

"How do you know I'm not naked?"

"I can hear the change jangling in your pockets."

He was behind her, and he unzipped her dress, pushed it off her shoulders, and it fell to her feet. He did the same thing with her slip; then he knelt in front of her and unhooked her garters, one by one, rolling down her stockings and kissing her calves, the backs of her knees, her lower thighs. He rolled down her girdle. He pressed his lips against the front of her panties, and she gripped his head and held it there.

His hands held her hips; then he drew down her panties. She stepped out of the pool of her clothes, and he slowly pushed her back a couple of steps.

He put his hand flat on her belly and gently pushed her backward.

She went down on the bed. He went down on her.

"LADY IN RED"

Red Walker's actions in France had earned him a Distinguished Flying Cross and a captain's silver bars. But finishing those twelve weeks of training at Achnacarry Castle was what made him into a different kind of soldier, maybe even a different man.

He wasn't just one of the select few who had completed commando training and were given a green beret. He'd learned to shoot accurately while running and to kill silently with a knife or a garrot.

Marching fifteen miles? He did it in the required two and a quarter hours, repeatedly. He could climb a mountain, scale a cliff, or cross a river with a few lengths of rope, a wooden toggle, and a loop, and from somewhere deep inside of him, he found the confidence, ability, and attitude to fight and survive on misty moors, sheer cliffs, or wide, boulder-edged lakes, all while under fire from live ammo.

He'd surprised himself and had wondered at first where all this came from. On one of those nights when there was nothing to do but lie on a cot, his hands folded behind his head, he realized that maybe, just maybe, he had his parents to thank.

Growing up in a house no bigger than a latrine, with walls so thin he could hear his parents' angry quarrels, his mother's bitter voice unrestrained by the alcohol she loved and needed, was war to a kid. He figured it was kind of like growing up on the front lines. And it served him well.

Sure, he felt something that might have been fear. He figured every soldier felt that. There were plenty of times when he held his breath to the point of bursting, when danger was what scared the hell out of him. But it was also what made him jump up and run toward an enemy machine-gun nest with a grenade pin between his teeth.

He'd been on his first two assignments, both with Cassidy, now a Lieutenant Colonel, and Commander Inskip. One to Belgium. One back to France. They quickly melded into the best of what the instructors at Achnacarry called "butcher-and-bolt teams."

He liked and respected the men he worked with. They'd fought together, slipped past the enemy's lines, and drank together at the local pubs. They had invited him along with them this weekend, but Red felt out of place without a date and decided to put his leave to good use.

The train pulled into the station. The engine was one of those old locomotives with a cow-catcher that the U.S. had sent to England at the outset of the war. It was a strange sight to him, the lush peaceful English countryside, spotted with silver barrage balloons—miniature Hindenburgs—and a train engine that looked like it came out of the *Great Train Robbery*.

He disembarked and walked around the station, then down the dirt road, where he hitched a ride on a hay wagon to Branton Manor, the housing quarters for the No. 2 Ferry Pool. The wagon was driven by two Land Girls in their knickers and headscarves, who liked the looks of his uniform and decorations, gave him an apple, and cheerfully flirted with him. They dropped him off near the gates, where he showed his ID, then walked up the long gravel drive to the huge front doors.

He rang the bell.

A pretty blond British woman in a flight suit opened the door.

"Is Charlotte Morrison here?"

"Charley?" She smiled. "Come in. Please. You may wait for her in here. Have a seat. I know she was here earlier." She left the room.

He stood there, his hat in his hands.

"Tell Charley someone's waiting for her downstairs!" he heard the blonde tell someone on the stairs.

He walked over to the fireplace. There was a mirror over the mantel, and he looked in it, stuck his hat under his arm, licked his hand, and slicked back his hair.

A minute later someone came running down the stairs. He turned when he heard the quick tapping of a woman's heels on the marble of the entry.

"You're early, you cad! Don't you know—" Charley stopped speaking the moment she saw him. "Red?" She hesitated, the skirt of her dress floating softly around her legs.

He took it all in, all that beautiful woman.

"Red!" She crossed the room, holding her hands out to him. "It's you!"

He laughed, taking her hands. "Yes, Charley-girl. It's me."

"Red. I can't believe it." She stepped back, still holding on to him, and continued to stare at him, then shook her head. "I'm sorry. I'm just so surprised to see you. Come, sit down." She pulled him over to a small sofa. "When did you get here? What's going on with you? Where are you stationed? Look at you," she rattled on, then sat back. "My God . . . that's a DFC pinned to your jacket. You're a war hero! For petesakes, why didn't you write? Tell me everything."

"I thought if you're free, I'd fill you in during dinner. You owe me a date. Although the chances of us finding barbeque are not likely."

Her smile froze, then melted away. "I can't, Red."

"Okay. Another night. I know I just showed up without any notice. I'm sorry, but—"

She held up her hand and shook her head. "It's not that. Who at this time in the world makes plans?"

"Maybe next week then."

"Red." She took a deep breath and stared at him with a pained look that made his gut turn over. "I can't see you. I mean, I can't date you. I'm sorry. I don't know what to say."

"I guess you don't have to say anything, Charley. You just said it all."

She put her hand on his arm.

He looked down at her hand. Her nails were painted red to match the dress. He glanced up. He hated the pity he saw in her expression. It made him feel foolish and out of place. His dreams, well, they weren't hers.

She took his hand. "Red . . . We missed what might have been. With the war. The ATA. Things changed. Everything is so different. Everything changes so fast."

He stared down at their hands. She was still holding his, and it felt and looked too big, especially next to hers.

"I've met a man, and I'm just nuts about him."

He could only look at the face he saw every night when he closed his eyes and at the same time listen to the words from her that broke his heart.

She watched him so intently.

"Lucky guy." He gave a short laugh and tried to smile.

The door chimed loudly, and they both turned as someone ran down the stairs and opened the front door. A tall, distinguished, older man stepped into the foyer.

"Charley?"

"Pop!" Charley stood and ran to him. He had gray hair and a familiar square jaw and a broad, easy smile. He hugged her. She turned and pulled him over toward Red. "Pop, this is my friend Red Walker."

He held out his hand. "Hello, young man."

"Mr. Morrison." Red shook his hand.

"It's good to finally meet you. I heard you taught my daughter a thing or two about tornadoes."

"Yes, sir. I believe she was about to fly into one."

Charley laughed. "I was not. I was aiming for your gas pumps, and you know it."

Red could tell she was nervous. "I've been trying to get her to admit that for the longest time."

"She doesn't admit she's wrong."

"You two can stop talking about me as if I'm not here."

"Who's not here?" Skip came walking into the room. Cassidy was right on his heels with a beautiful woman, pin-up material, with fine features, coal-black hair and pale blue eyes.

Red straightened and saluted him. "Commander." Then Cassidy. "Colonel."

"Walker?" Inskip frowned.

"Hey there, Red," Cassidy said. "What are you doing here?"

"We're old friends," Charley said nervously, then she moved toward Skip and took his arm. "How do you all know each other?"

With a feeling of dread Red saw plainly the gist of things, even before Skip put his arm around Charley and gave her a kiss. The breath Red took felt airless. He tried to keep his expression blank. He had no idea if he was successful.

"We work together." Inskip was eyeing him differently. He didn't let go of her.

"Captain Red Walker. This is my wife, Kitty."

"Ma'am," Red, said stiffly. He didn't mean to sound so sharp.

Kitty Cassidy held out her hand, but looked right past him with those light, unseeing eyes. "Captain. J.R. has told me all about you. I understand you are quite the marksman."

"Yes, ma'am." Red took her hand. She was blind. He'd had no idea. Cassidy never said a word.

"The team sharpshooter? That's you?" Charley looked from Skip to Red. "Oh, my God." She faced him. "I never knew you could shoot."

Red shrugged. "Most Texans can shoot."

She looked at his DFC medal and the other badges on his uniform, then up at his face. He could see she didn't know what to say, and Inskip was all too quiet. The room was quiet. Red had made the mistake of telling Skip there was a special girl he wanted to track down this weekend.

"Well," he said, spinning his hat in his hands. "I should be leaving. Charley." He nodded in her direction. "It was good to see you again." He turned. "Mr. Morrison."

"Captain."

"Commander." Red nodded at Skip and to the other couple. "Colonel. Mrs. Cassidy. It was good to meet you."

"Thank you," Kitty said quietly. "You stay at J.R.'s back, will you? I want my husband to come home when this is all over."

"Yes, ma'am." Red headed for the door.

"Red, wait. Please." Charley reached out to him.

Red stopped, even though he wanted out of there. Fast. But he couldn't ignore her, and turned.

She stepped away from Skip and gave him a light kiss on the cheek. "Take care of yourself."

"You, too." Red left, and put his hat on his head as he walked down the front steps, heading for someplace, anyplace as long as it was away from there.

He walked down the drive without looking back. His shoes crunched on the gravel. Crunch, crunch, crunch, like bones cracking in two. Or maybe it was his heart. He was angry . . . at himself. He wanted to hit something. He just walked on, past the gates, down the road.

A few minutes later the car that had been parked in front of the manor came through the gates. He stopped and watched it drive off in the opposite direction.

He was hurting so deep inside it was as if he had an open wound in a place no one could find to heal. He knew this feeling. He remembered standing under that Texaco star and watching a Ford V8 disappear down a lonely Texas road.

He stood there for a long time. He didn't know how long. When he turned to walk on, he looked up. The sky was gray and cloudy; that English mist was slowly rolling in. He stared down as he walked. The green grass was damp. The soil was dark, but the ground of the road was solid.

He needed to remember to keep his feet there.

He walked for miles, then, unaware of time passing. The thick mist moved in completely and crawled across the ground in front of him. It was white and eerie. He kept walking until he felt it condense and drip down his face. Funny thing. His face was already wet.

"OH MAMA"

Audrey stood silently in the foyer, waiting, her hands clasped in front of her, a pose she hoped looked calm. The true reason she held on to her hands was that if she didn't she might unconsciously begin to wring them.

George came up the steps, greeting Peters as he came through the doors. His friends were behind him. She heard car doors close. There were voices and footsteps, light chattering, the higher sound of women's heels tapping up the stone front steps.

She listened to them with a hunger that filled an emptiness inside of her she hadn't known existed. The voices she heard, all excited and talking at once, reminded her that she was really still alive. They made her feel the same way she felt when she walked outside and down through her gardens.

A woman laughed. There was a joyous sound to it that she hadn't heard in so long. One of the American men had a deep, resonant voice.

She wondered how she looked. Was her hair parted the way she'd always worn it? On the left, not the right. She had forgotten to check it. She wondered how much gray she was getting. Her gray hair had started showing a year before the war. A hair here and there.

Was her slip showing? Were the seams on her hosiery straight? This relying on others for her appearance made her feel like an invalid, some toddler or someone so feeble she couldn't dress herself. She despised feeling that way. But no more than she despised herself for the stubborn pride that kept her from saying the words: I need help.

No one asked to help her anymore. She deserved that. She had made them all miserable for ever asking. And even at her weakest moments, she still couldn't bear to ask them.

"Mother!" George grabbed her shoulders and kissed her cheek. "You look ravishing."

"My, but that is good to hear. I say that means Eleanore and Bromley aren't lying to me."

"Why would they do that?"

"I am not the easiest person in the world to live with. I'm certain there are days when they wish I had lost my voice in the Blitz." She clung a bit to his arm. "Now tell me, dear. What am I wearing?"

"Blue lace that matches your eyes."

She smiled. "You are a good son. Should I mention that it's been too long since you've been home?"

"No, you shouldn't."

"I suppose not. This is terribly exciting. We haven't entertained since before the war. This old house needs some fresh voices echoing off those high ceilings, and God knows we could all use some laughter around here. Did you know that my sister has no sense of humor?"

"That's odd, Mother. She says the same about you."

Audrey laughed, and she heard Eleanore laughing, too. Gerald was coming down to join them the next day. Her sister's husband hadn't visited in more than a year. She wasn't certain Eleanore had seen him in more than a year. The war separated families in terrible ways.

She stood there and met all of George's friends, listening to each of their voices, measuring their height compared to hers as they stood before her, the touch of their hands, the things that gave some idea of who they were when you couldn't look into their eyes. You learned some things out of necessity.

But she wanted badly to see their faces.

George then introduced them to Eleanore, while Audrey tried to take the measure of the woman her son had brought to Keighley. Charlotte. The girl was standing in front of her and was terribly nervous.

She could understand that all too well as she held out her hand. "Charlotte. Welcome to Keighley."

"Thank you for having me. Your home is lovely and the grounds are breathtaking."

"You like the out-of-doors? Splendid. You and I shall have to take a walk in the gardens later." She leaned closer and patted her hand. "I promise I won't eat you alive. Now relax, my dear, I'm truly pleased you are here."

"Thank you. That is so kind of you," Charlotte said quietly. "This is my father, Bob Morrison. Come closer, Pop."

"Mrs. Inskip." There was that deep voice. He was very tall, and his presence seemed to take up a large space in front of her.

He took her hand in his.

It was a hard hand. Callused.

"My name is Audrey. Please. And I shall call you Bob."

"Thank you for opening your lovely home to us. I can't tell you how relieved I am to get out of London for a few days. Haven't had much chance to see your country since I got here. If your home and the grounds are anything to go by, then I have certainly missed some beautiful country."

"Yes, well, it is particularly nice when we aren't at war," she said dryly. "My son tells me you draw planes."

She said it at a lull in the conversations, and for a moment there was complete silence.

"Not draw, Mother. Bob is an aerocraft designer."

"Well, if he designs them, George dear, he must have to draw them on something. Isn't that right, Bob?"

She could hear his smile when he replied, "Well, Audrey, I'd say you're right about that. I draw 'em, build 'em, and fly 'em. How about I take you up in one sometime? Ever been in a plane?"

"Good God, no."

"Your son's a pilot."

"It doesn't run in the family."

"You might like it."

She didn't say anything for a moment because her first reaction was to laugh at the mere thought of climbing into an aeroplane. But she didn't laugh. Instead she remembered a photo she had seen years before in the newspapers of Amy Johnson, standing by her plane and smiling. The woman looked free and happy. "You think I would like it?"

"You seem to me to be the kind of woman who would like the power of it, Audrey. There's a great feeling of satisfaction in doing something that seems impossible. I think you would enjoy it. I hear you are a woman who likes a challenge."

Did she? Perhaps she used to be that kind of woman. The person she was now didn't want to face any more challenges. She shook her head. "I don't think so. Not me. George did tell me that you knew the Wright brothers?"

Before he could answer, she heard George laugh loud and hard and honestly.

Audrey turned suddenly toward the sound of it, a sound she hadn't heard in a long, long time.

"Charley," her son warned his friend, still laughing at something she'd said. "You are looking for trouble, my girl."

Her son was really laughing. There was no bitterness to the sound at all.

She hadn't meant to ignore Charlotte's father. She could feel Bob looking at her.

He leaned down and said quietly, "Are you all right? You look haunted."

"Perhaps I am," she said quietly. "I just heard something I thought had died."

"MASQUERADE IS OVER"

For the next day and a half, Keighley was a different place for Audrey. The young people were so full of fun. And she liked Bob Morrison. Gerald, Eleanore, Bob, and she played cards in the evening. It was great fun. Kitty Cassidy would be staying at Keighley, and Eleanore was going with Gerald to London for a few weeks. Everything had been going well until breakfast, when Charley almost bit Skip's head off and they had a small row.

She gave the girl time to cool down and then asked where she was. Peters told her Miss Charlotte was in the small parlor reading.

Audrey stood in the doorway. "I was wondering if you would help me, dear. I would like to go for a walk. They say it's lovely outside."

"Of course." Charlotte walked over to her.

Audrey put her arm around the girl's waist. "My, you are tall."

"Yes, I know. Luckily I don't have to duck through doorways and I can reach things on the top shelves. But let me tell you, those little blue tea chairs in the parlor are a long way down."

They laughed and walked outside arm in arm.

"I heard you and George this morning."

"I'm sorry you had to hear." The tone of her voice said that she was still very upset.

"Would you like to talk about it? I love my son, dear, but I was married for a long time. Men can be quite foolish."

"I'm just . . . I don't know. I feel terrible. Skip and I had a lovely day in London a few weeks ago. He bought me a bottle of *Ma Griffe*. Actually, he lied to me and said he was buying it for you because he knew I wouldn't accept it. He tricked me. But this morning I heard one of the servants talking. One of them said it was strange because I smelled like Greer."

"Yes, well, my son is an ass."

"I believe that was what I called him."

"You know, Charlotte. It smells quite lovely on you."

"Thank you, but it doesn't feel right. Wearing his dead wife's perfume?"

"Did you know that scents react to the individual? To the skin? Perfumes smell differently on each person. I can tell you, while the scent might be familiar, it doesn't smell the way it did on Greer."

"I would like to believe that."

"I wouldn't lie about it. If you smelled like her, I'd tell you to give the bottle away. In your shoes, I might have thrown it at him."

They walked through the path in the rose garden and Audrey said, "I can smell the roses here this time of year. The pink ones have the strongest and sweetest scent."

"They're beautiful."

"Each type of rose has a different scent. Rather like women."

"That was subtle."

"I'm not known for my subtlety, but for my directness."

"I appreciate it, Audrey. Thank you."

They made their way down the gravel pathway that the gardeners had added so she could walk safely to the stone bench set near the edge of the lake. She liked to sit there on sunny days.

"I love the gardens and the lake," Charlotte told her. "Everything is so green here. I feel as if I'm a million miles away from the war."

"Good. You should. The bench is nearby?"

"Yes. It's only a foot away from us. To the right a bit. Not too far from the gravestone."

"That is Greer's."

"I thought it might be." She hesitated. "I've never asked Skip about her. I didn't want to open old wounds for him, but I would like to know about her."

"Of course you would. I have an idea. You must promise to come here whenever you can, my dear. I'd welcome your visit. The house is open to you anytime. Whenever they're not flying you all over the countryside. You will most likely want to see Kitty. We can have a grand time together, all of us. And I promise I'll tell you about Greer, and about George when he was a boy."

"I'd like that."

"Of course you would. A woman who is in love with a man should know all about his past, his accomplishments, and his faults." She took the girl's hand and patted it. "I understand that he made a mistake when he bought the perfume, but I'm certain it was well meant. I believe he wanted to give you a gift. He wouldn't purposely hurt you."

"I think I know that now. And I will come back and we'll talk." She cut off what she was going to say.

Someone was coming.

Charlotte turned away from her for a second. "Hey, Pop!"

"Hello, ladies." Bob's footsteps crunched on the gravel walk. "It's a lovely day. Sunshine and blue skies." He paused. "How's my girl feeling?"

"I'm better. Audrey and I talked."

"And what did you two decide?"

"Men are stupid." Charlotte laughed.

"I'm outnumbered, so I won't argue for our cause."

"Good."

"Charlotte, why don't you find my son and talk to him."

"Perhaps I should. I wasn't very nice to him earlier."

"You run along, then."

Charley leaned down and kissed her on the cheek. "Thank you. Bye, Pop!" Then there was only the sound of footsteps running up the path.

Neither Audrey nor Bob spoke for a minute.

"I don't know what you said to my daughter, but whatever it was, it seems to have helped."

"She's a good girl."

"Yes. She is. She was pretty upset this morning."

"My son would not knowingly hurt her. He did something without thinking."

"That's why we need you women around to point out

our shortcomings to us. Keep us on the straight and nar-row."

"Surely, you aren't being sarcastic, Bob."

"Me? Never. I'm used to having all my faults pointed out to me. Charley has never hesitated to tell me when she thinks I'm wrong."

"When she thinks you're wrong or when you *are* wrong?"

"Both." He was quiet for a moment. "Here. Take my arm and let's walk."

They moved toward the house, through the garden. They talked about the flowers and she told him which roses were which. She hadn't realized she knew them by their fragrances.

He talked about his planes and his home in the desert of New Mexico. They reached the house and went into the study. She sat in a chair by the garden doors where the sun shone in while he made them both a drink.

A few minutes later he crossed the room and handed it to her.

"Thank you."

She heard him take a drink. *These Yanks and their ice.*

"You seem like an honest woman."

"More like blunt to a fault, I'd say. My husband used to tell me, 'Audrey, old girl, you wield your opinions like a weapon—a cannon right to the face.' "

They both laughed.

"The reason I mentioned it is because I think there's something you ought to know," Bob said.

"What?"

"Kitty Cassidy is blind."

She froze instantly, her drink halfway to her mouth.

"Charley told me that Skip didn't want you to know. Kitty is a very well-accomplished teacher for the blind."

"Damn," she said under her breath, feeling that same old pride rise to cover her humiliation. "Now I understand all the questions she's been asking." She thought about it, then added, "And that terribly odd conversation at dinner last night."

"They were more obvious than I believe they thought they were. I felt you should know the truth."

She felt so stiff that she thought if she moved she might shatter into a thousand pieces.

"You're upset. I can see that. I felt they were doing such a piss-poor job of subterfuge that you would figure it all out soon enough and then probably be mad as hell."

"I am mad as hell." Her voice was clipped. She couldn't help it. She didn't want to be this way, not in front of Bob. She liked him, but she was terribly embarrassed.

"I understand."

"Do you?" She set her drink down. "Do you know what it's like to suddenly wake up in a world where there is no color, or blue skies, no green grass, a place where you can't see the look on your son's face?"

"No. I don't know what that's like."

"No, you don't. You should keep to your own business."

"I probably should. But I hate to see a good woman wasted."

"You think I'm wasted?"

"I don't know what you were like before. I only know what I see now. You are a beautiful woman, Audrey, with half of your life still ahead of you."

"A life where I cannot see anything?"

"Kitty is smart and amazingly independent. I've watched her. She has a freedom that is surprising for someone who is blind. She has what we Yanks call gumption. But so do you."

She didn't say a word.

"I noticed that when she needs help, she asks for it."

She turned and faced him. "And I don't."

"Not in the same way and not often enough. You sit and let the world rush by you. You asked me about Orville and Wilbur Wright. Orville talks quite a bit about how his brother felt about flying. People thought they were crazy. People said they would never do it and probably would kill themselves trying. Why do it? people asked them repeatedly. But I remember him telling me something Wilbur said once. 'If you are looking for perfect safety, you will do well to sit on a fence and merely watch the birds; but if you really wish to learn, you must mount a machine and become acquainted with its tricks by actual trial.' It seems to me you should think about what you want to do for the next forty years. Do you want to sit on the fence or do you want to fly?"

She couldn't answer him. She was crying. She heard him walking away, and it about killed her. She raised her hand. "Bob! Wait!"

"I'm here," he said from a distance, near the doorway.

She took a deep breath and stood, then took a few steps, then a few more. She held out her hands to him. "Will you help me? Please. I want to fly."

"THIS IS IT"

For two weeks Red had managed to avoid his team. Nothing was going on. It was one of those times when there was nothing to do but sit around and do nothing. Rumor was: the big one was in the works. Eisenhower and Montgomery together in a combined Allied Forces invasion of North Africa.

Before the invasion, they would send in as many teams as they could to muck up things for the enemy. So his team was on alert. They'd all been called in to wait for briefing.

Red spent the afternoon getting some target practice. He knelt at the line, raised his weapon, sighted, and pulled the trigger, again and again and again. Every shot was dead center. He spent an hour firing, until all five targets looked chewed up in the middle and the sergeant in charge told him to get the hell out of there. He left the range still feeling antsy.

He walked back and took a shower, then shaved, checked his overseas pack, and finally went to get something to eat. It was dinnertime, and most of the men from the teams were in the mess.

Red sat down at a table. Inskip was at the opposite end, reading the newspaper. He looked up when Red sat down but didn't say anything. Cassidy was nowhere to be seen.

Red ate silently while the others talked, occasionally asking him or Inskip a question. Some of the men finished and left to go to the rec room and throw some darts. Finally Skip put down the paper and lit a cigarette.

It was just the two of them, and until now, the last time they'd seen each other was at Branton Manor, where Charley was billeted.

"It's hard to believe that of all the women out there, you and I find the same one." Skip was watching him intently.

"Yeah."

"She told me how you met."

Red didn't say anything.

"Sorry, old chap. I guess I beat you to the punch."

Red looked up at him. "What do you want me to say? Congratulations?"

"Bloody hell . . . This is stupid!" Skip stubbed out his cigarette and stood up.

Red stood up, too. "Nothing about Charley is stupid."

"She's mine, Walker. Remember that."

Red closed the distance between them. "I'm not going to forget it. Just don't rub my fucking nose in it. Charley loves you. I accept that. Don't hurt her."

"You think I'm going to hurt her?" Skip was obviously ticked off. His voice was loud.

"I'm just telling you not to." Red started to turn away, but he was pissed off and muttered, "Limey asshole."

Skip spun him around and grabbed him by the shirt, then jerked him forward.

Red drew back his fist.

"Hey, you two." J.R. broke them apart. "What the hell is this?"

There was silence. Red would be damned if he was going to say anything. He just wished he could have hit him before Cassidy came in.

"Nothing." Skip turned away.

"It had better be nothing. Save that for the Jerries. I just heard. . . . It's a go. We have to report to the briefing room. Come on." Cassidy moved toward the door.

Red and Skip followed him, walking a good distance apart.

NORTH AFRICA

1942

LIBYAN DESERT

They waited in a truck that was parked out of sight in a ravine about twenty feet from a sharp curve in the road. Walker was on a bluff with a set of field glasses, watching the road for the enemy truck convoy. Their job was to get into that convoy and travel with it to the compound. Inside the truck was a team of SIG, Special Interrogation Group, a bogus title for a handful of German Jews from Palestine dressed as Afrika Korps, whose mission was to get inside and eliminate the key officers. They had information from one source that Rommel was at the compound.

A squad from the Long Range Desert Group attached to the British Special Air Service would already be in position near the compound. The LRDG's job was to blow the petrol and ammo dumps.

Inskip was to take out the airfield. He carried enough explosives to blow them all back to Britain. Walker would take care of the supply bunkers. And J.R.? His job was to steal as much intelligence information as he could.

Walker came sliding down the bluff. "They're coming."

J.R. made for the truck and Skip put out his cigarette and followed.

"You ready?" J.R. asked everyone. "Remember. We let eleven trucks go by. Before Number Twelve comes around the curve, we fall into line."

"Wouldn't it be better if we were the last truck?" one of the SIG asked.

J.R. shook his head. "If I were commanding that convoy, I'd make certain the last truck knew they were the last truck. For that very reason. This way Number Eleven truck will think we're Number Twelve and Number Twelve truck will think we're Number Eleven.

"About a mile from the gates there's another bend in the road. We'll break down there, block the last truck, and take it out. Then the SIG can drive into the compound as Number Twelve, and we'll take our positions at the perimeters."

"I hear 'em coming, sir."

"Okay. Start the engine. You in back. Pull that camouflage net over you."

J.R. was the last inside.

Dimmed driving lights from the first truck came into view and rumbled past. Then another and another.

J.R. counted them off. "That was eleven! Go!"

The truck shot out from the ravine and slid easily into the convoy. The enemy never knew there were thirteen sets of headlights.

EASTERN PERIMETER

There was no sleep for the wicked.

Certainly not tonight. Skip checked his watch, then moved silently along a narrow dip between the road and the perimeter cross-stakes. He needed to find the airfield.

The wooden cross-stakes tangled with barbed wire were positioned lower than the dunes, blocking the view, so he headed for a rise about a hundred yards away. He crawled over the edge and scanned the horizon. He spotted the shadow of a pole with a windsleeve.

Housey, housey. There she is!

He picked up his explosive pack and crept under the fence and over the dunes, sliding down the opposite side feetfirst. Before him was a ten-foot-high revetment made from a pile of logs, rock, and empty oil barrels. He moved along the shadows, hidden by the height of the wall. When he reached the end, he edged around slowly.

The airfield spread below. Over a dozen planes were parked at the perimeter of the small field: Stukas, MEs, and a few bombers—Heinkels and a single JU88 that was parked away from the others. He counted fifteen.

With their usual attention to order, the Jadgwaffe had lined the planes up in groups of three, wings less than a foot apart. He checked out the area and saw a repair hut at the opposite end of the field, along with two trucks, an armored half-track, and some tanks set at angles facing the surrounding dunes.

There was a building about a hundred feet away. Light shone from inside, and he could hear voices and the sounds of a kitchen through the open windows. He suspected it was the pilots' quarters.

He moved along the building, low, ducking down past the windows, and heard men arguing over music. Then a record began to play, and the music followed him as he ran out onto the field.

It was Wagner. He'd have preferred Beethoven.

They made his job too easy for him, parking the planes in neat sets of three. Because of their proximity, he could set his explosives on the middle plane, near its fuel tank, and blow up all three with a single charge, which left him plenty of explosives for the tanks.

Some days things just went your way. Skip dropped his bag on the ground, crouched under the first group of planes, and began to set the charges while the notes of Wagner played from a scratchy phonograph.

COMMAND BUNKER

Rheinholdt left the commons room. Too many of the men were smoking inside, and the cigarettes swallowed up all the air. He felt as if he could not breathe, so he took his cup of ersatz coffee, something brown that tasted like strong tea mixed with machine oil, and walked outside.

He stood there for a moment, adjusting to the cold night air before he crossed over to the middle of the compound, where the light was softer and he could see the stars overhead. It was cold out, but he was dressed in new long underwear and one of the wool uniforms he'd purchased on leave in Tripoli.

While there, he had a spot of luck and was able to speak to his wife, his daughters, and mother. They were still in their Berlin apartment, but the building next door had been bombed the week before. They were moving to the mountains soon, with Heddy's cousin, if the bombings continued.

He told them not to wait. To go now. Rumors of Allied invasion of France were all about, although the point of the invasion changed from day to day. Still, information indicated that the Allies were readying for an offensive. He felt the bombings would get worse before they got better.

Like so many other officers, he had not been home in over two years. For some officers on the Russian front it had been even longer. The Wehrmacht did not let them go home. The voices of his family, even for a few minutes, were a gift for him to hear.

He'd also received information on his sister. Liesel and her children were thankfully alive in Hamburg. His niece and nephew were being hidden in one of the many brothels in the Reeperbahn, while Liesel worked as a cook, laundress, and maid for the prostitutes there. There had been no trouble as yet, and they expected none, since the woman who owned the brothel was a sympathizer with connections so high in the *SS,* they never searched her place.

But his Heddy was working with Alfred Goebbels, who, unlike his brother, Joseph, was helping save people marked for the camps. Alfred had been instrumental in getting many families out of Nazi-occupied areas and to safety in the neutral countries of Switzerland and Spain.

There was no word on Joseph and his family. No one

knew where they were. His friend was gone, and no one could seem to find out anything. Not Goebbels as yet. Not anyone.

Rheinholdt wanted to go home more than anything else. He wanted to hold his daughters and his wife and drink beer. He wanted to toast Joseph with a beer and song, and to laugh. He wanted life to be the way it had been before, before Poland, before France. Before war.

He was not alone in his feelings. Morale was low. His leave on the coast didn't boost his spirits even though he had slept and bathed and lived without fleas for a time. The men were tired, and supplies were cut off more often than not by the Allied planes and navy in the Mediterranean. The desert took more from a soldier here than it gave. It took a man's juice and then boiled him in it.

They were on equal footing, the Allies and the Axis, but the Italians were giving up by the dozens. Word was that Rommel was matched by Montgomery and the Allies were better supplied. The engineers had only last week finished building the fuel tanks here, and now trucks came by convoy from the coast with fuel to fill them.

He took one last look up at the night sky, then walked back toward the bunker. He rounded the corner and came face to face with the enemy.

For a heartbeat, they stared at each other.

He dropped his cup and reached for his Lüger.

The man carried a submachine gun.

I'm dead, he thought as he pulled his pistol; it caught on the holster.

But the man didn't fire his gun. He stared at him. "I know you. . . . *Drop the gun!*"

"Your wife is blind." Rheinholdt recognized him through the black smeared on his face.

"I said drop the gun."

Rheinholdt looked at the pistol in his hand.

"Halt!" someone shouted in the distance.

The place exploded in gunfire. Cassidy came at him. Lights flooded the area. He was blinded for an instant, then, all he saw was the butt of the submachine gun. It caught his chin. White light and pain flashed before his eyes for a mere instant, then there was nothing but blackness.

SUPPLY BUNKER

Red watched the officer in the center of the compound. He just stood there drinking coffee and looking up at the sky. As long as he was there, Red had to stay put. He checked his watch. He couldn't shoot him without jeopardizing the whole mission, so he leaned against the wall holding his BAR. Waiting.

"Halt!"

He didn't move. The order was distant, as if it came from the truck depot. He heard the enemy running. A lot of enemy.

He scrambled up and bolted out into the open, his BAR firing toward the depot, which lit up suddenly like Texas sunshine.

Bullets spit back at him. The enemy came out from everywhere. He fired rounds, running until he made it to the shelter of a metal shed.

The SIG trucks were surrounded. What gave them away? Machine guns were going off from all four corners of the compound. Bullets hacked into the flimsy shed walls, popping through the metal and past his ears and head.

He ducked down, jammed in more ammo. His BAR was smoking. The steel barrel was so hot from firing that it was a purple-red.

One of them came around the corner.

Red raised his gun and fired.

Click. Nothing. It jammed.

He swung and smacked the guy in the face with the red-hot barrel. It sent him down screaming.

Red grabbed the soldier's MP40 and took off across the compound, firing at the enemy near the SIG trucks and watching them fall. The crossfire was deafening. Bullets shadowed him, tearing up the ground.

Tracers flashed from the LRDG position, then a petrol tank blew up black and orange like Halloween. Hot air and smoke hit him in the face. The blast rattled through his teeth; he could feel it in his fillings and eardrums.

For an instant there was no other sound. Deafening silence, something more frightening than enfilade noise.

He checked his watch. Bingo . . .

The supply building blew, shattered by his charges. Concrete flew like shrapnel through the air. Pieces slammed into his helmet. He went down, head ringing, but he crawled for cover behind a pile of crates, pulled himself up, trying to focus, shook his head, then got to his feet.

He heard the dull pop of a bazooka. Ten feet away a truck blew up. That blast sent him flying. He hit the ground hard on his back. He couldn't breathe for a moment. He couldn't move. Someone could shoot him. The air was gone from his chest. He was terrified.

Then just as suddenly he caught his breath, swore, and rolled, came up running, firing the submachine gun like it was an extension of his arm.

An LRDG vehicle roared up from behind him, rear mounted machine gun firing, the bearded Brits inside shouting. He couldn't hear what.

This was war. It sounded like war.

The Brits shouted at him again. They were waving at him to hop on.

"No!" he shouted, and shook his head. He wasn't leaving his team.

They disappeared over the dunes.

He ran between the fences and saw the airfield burning. He turned.

Coming at him was a JU88. Enemy bomber. An enemy armored car came careening around the corner and sped under the plane's wing.

Red stepped back, crouched down in the shadows, checked his ammo, and waited for them to get closer. The car pulled in front of the taxiing plane.

Suddenly the tail went up in the air. The plane's nose lowered, leveled. The 20mm cannon started blazing. The Junkers shot the hell out of the armored car.

Red stood frozen, confused. He looked up at the cockpit.

Inskip was in the pilot's seat.

Red ran for the plane.

WESTERN EDGES OF PERIMETER

J.R. dragged the unconscious lieutenant away from the bunker and into a ditch near the dunes. He moved his way back around the corner of the bunker again and spotted the firing exchange with SIG, near the truck-fueling area.

He had to get to the airfield. Stuffed into his uniform were the most recent code books, diagrams for two planned combined Panzer operations, and a list of Afrika Korps officers along with their units and positions—a treasure of information that could help ensure the success of a combined Allied invasion of North Africa.

All hell broke loose. He took off running, his Tommy firing.

A second later the fuel blew and flames went high into the sky. The LRDG did their job. He kept running, around a burning truck and over a low wall of crates. He stopped and looked at them.

Guns and ammo. He checked his watch. He was already late. *What the hell . . .*

He went down on one knee and pulled out a charge, set it and took off again. A minute later he heard it go off.

Bingo!

For the next three minutes it was him against them. One after another came at him. Then there was nothing but the noise.

He made it to the eastern edge of the compound, went over the fence, and fell on his ass.

He turned over.

A JU88 turned and was coming past him. He raised his gun and pulled the trigger.

It didn't fire. He swore and tossed it away, scanning the ground. He spotted the barrel of an MP40 and pulled it out from under the dead soldier. Ready to give 'em hell, he looked up.

Red was hanging out of the cockpit. "Cassidy!"

Three enemy came at him from the south. J.R. fired until there was no one firing back.

He heard a car, and the Desert Rats flew out of the compound and disappeared over the dunes as if they had been a mirage.

He turned back toward the plane. It was on the road and moving away. They were going to take off. He just might make it.

J.R. took off running.

He was close, then closer.

He pumped his arms and legs.

"Run, Colonel! Run!" Walker was hanging out the plane door, gripping the side of the belly door, his hand extended.

He was still a few feet away from it.

Faster! Faster! Faster! I can make it! I can!

Bullets suddenly ate the ground behind him.

Pop! Pop! Pop! Pop! Pop!

That's what bullets sounded like. Like popcorn. Firecrackers. Cap guns. They never sounded real. They never sounded like they could kill you.

He looked back.

A car with a mounted machine gun was chasing after him.

Pop! Pop! Pop!

Eyes ahead, he turned it on, ratcheted up. Boots pounding the road.

Inches away, he reached for Red's hand.

"Come on! Come on!" Red shouted.

Pop! Pop! Pop!

Red's hand closed over his wrist.

J.R. grabbed the door frame with his free hand. Then he was lying on the cold belly of the plane, his breath gone.

For just a moment, he closed his eyes. He could hear the German gunner still firing at them. *How the hell did they miss me?*

Red crawled over him and headed for the rear gun.

J.R. took a breath. He rolled over and moved toward Red, who was seated at the gun mount, taking aim.

J.R. looked over Red's shoulder.

The German armored car was a mere few feet away. The gunner was that same German lieutenant.

J.R. reached up and shoved the gun handle down. Red fired, and the bullets went into the air.

"What the hell?" Red turned.

The plane lifted off the ground.

"Just leave it," J.R. said.

Red looked at him strangely.

J.R. shrugged. "Don't ask. It would take more breath than I have to explain."

Red climbed down from the gunner seat and clapped him on the shoulder. "You made it, sir!"

"Only because you were late."

"Inskip had some trouble."

"Let's go." J.R. moved toward the cockpit and climbed up. He settled into the copilot's seat as they flew over the desert, heading for the coast. "You were late," he said to Skip.

"Walker had a gun to my head."

J.R. studied Skip to see if he was kidding. He wasn't.

Red was sitting with his back against the rear wall, his long legs out in front of him. He shrugged when J.R. looked at him. "Seemed like a good idea at the time."

J.R. laughed loud and hard. "You dumb fuck. That'll get you court-martialed."

"What the hell. I figured you're the only thing keeping the two of us from killing each other."

J.R. looked down as they crossed the coast and flew out over the Mediterranean. He turned to Skip. "Where are we headed?"

"From the fuel gauges, I'd say we can get to Gibraltar." Skip nodded at the radio near Red. "But one of you had better start playing with that radio. Let them know who's in this plane."

Red put on the headset and began working the radio. A few minutes later he turned and said, "I can't get anything. It's dead."

"Keep trying," J.R. said.

"I'm going to take her up out of range," Skip said, and the plane began a slow climb.

The first shell hit the wingtip.

"Get the chutes!"

The plane shuddered.

The second shell took out the engine and part of the fuselage.

"Jump! Go!"

The plane stalled. Smoke and flames filled it, then it began to fall.

Two chutes opened as it spun down toward the sea.
The third shell hit, the plane exploded.

"UNTIL TODAY"

Charley jerked open the hospital doors and pulled Kitty
inside with her. The place was bedlam. There had
been incendiary bombing the night before. People were
lined up three deep at the information station near the
front entrance. "It's packed like sardines in here. Come this
way. I'm taking you down the hall and out of the crowd.
What did they say when they telephoned again?"

"A plane was shot down. They said I was listed as
J.R.'s next of kin and to come down here right away.
They didn't tell me anything else. Even if he's
alive . . . nothing. I think I'm going to vomit."

Charley slowed down, then stopped and looked at
Kitty. Her face was gray-green. "Here. Sit. Put your
head down on your knees for a second."

"No, I need J.R."

"Just for a moment. You look like you're going to
faint. Take deep breaths. Now think. Did they give you
a name? Who called?"

"All that registered in my head after I heard the
words 'next of kin' was the name of the hospital. I'm not
even certain if it was the hospital or the Army who was
calling. It was a man."

"Okay, well, that isn't going to help us. Feeling
better?"

"Yes." She sat up slowly. "We have to find him, Charley . . . please. I'm really scared."

With Kitty in tow, Charley moved down two more hallways and into an open area. She went to the desk. A man in a doctor's smock with a stethoscope was standing there, thumbing through a patient's chart. Charley put her arm around Kitty's shoulders. "This is Mrs. Cassidy. Her husband is Lt. Col. J.R. Cassidy, U.S. Army."

"He's actually assigned to the Office of Strategic Services, here in conjunction with the SAS," Kitty said, driving a hand through her tangled black hair. "I wasn't supposed to tell anyone that."

"I don't think that matters, Kitty," Charley said, turning to the man. "He's here somewhere, we think. Someone called her but didn't leave a name. Please. Can you help? They told her to come right away."

He looked from her to Kitty, then said, "Wait here for a moment, please." He walked over and talked to a nurse, who looked back at them.

Charley had a sinking feeling in her gut.

"What's happening, Charley?"

She tried to make her voice sound normal for Kitty's sake. "He's talking to someone. Wait. He just waved us toward another door. Come." She grabbed Kitty's hand.

He pushed open a set of doors. "His doctor is down this corridor. You'll have to speak with him. It's the third door past the stairs. On the left."

"Oh, Charley. This sounds bad." She hesitated for a moment, then quietly added, "They don't tell you anything when they're dead."

"Don't do that to yourself, Kitty. J.R. is okay. I don't think they tell you anything when they're alive, either.

There have been too many mistakes made over who is missing and who's dead. You know that."

"I know. I'm just so scared."

"Here we are." Charley stopped in front of a door that was half frosted glass. She could see the shadow of someone inside and knocked. "Damn . . . We didn't ask the doctor's name."

The door opened and he looked from Charley to Kitty, then said, "Mrs. Cassidy?"

"Yes, that's me."

"I'm Dr. Lansdowne. Come in." He picked up on Kitty's situation immediately. "Please, Mrs. Cassidy. Over here, sit down." He took her hand and kindly helped her to a chair in front of his desk.

"Charley?" Kitty asked.

"I'm here."

"Come sit with me. Doctor, this is my friend, Miss Morrison."

"Hello." He shook her hand and waited until Charley was in the chair next to Kitty.

"Please, Doctor. Tell me he is okay," Kitty said.

"He is alive and very lucky."

Kitty crumpled into the chair. She began to cry and take breaths at the same time. Charley leaned over and put her arm around her.

"He's one lucky man. He has over twenty bullet wounds in him and not one in a vital organ. He's lost a lot of blood and is in shock, but he'll make it."

"Can I see him?"

"Certainly." He stood up. "He's resting and might still be sedated. You can stay as long as you like."

Charley stood as he helped Kitty up. "We'll make

arrangements for you to stay with him if that's what you want."

"Yes," Kitty said forcefully. "I'm not leaving until I can talk to him. I have to hear his voice. I have to touch him."

"I understand," Lansdowne said.

Charley and Kitty walked with him down a hall that was much quieter. There was no doubt this was the intensive-care ward.

"Do you know what happened?" Charley asked the doctor.

"He was shot down over the Mediterranean. They said it was a mistake. A terrible mistake. He was in a Luftwaffe plane. They were shot down by our own guns. Some naval gunner kept shooting at him. The fellow was only sixteen. Too young." He shook his head. "We see it all the time. This war sends children out on the battlefields. The lad saw the enemy plane, shot it down, then saw the parachutes and kept firing like the gun was a toy." The doctor stopped outside of a room. Ward C, Room 7. "He's in here." He opened the door.

Charley helped Kitty inside. The doctor followed them in and closed the door.

"How bad is it?" Kitty asked in a hoarse whisper.

Charley thought he looked like hell, but she wasn't going to tell her that. "He's bandaged up pretty much, arms, one hand, shoulder, chest, and head. He's sleeping. Come here, three steps. There's a chair by the bed."

"I can do it." Kitty reached out and ran her hand along the bed. "I don't want to touch him where he's wounded and hurt him."

Charley placed Kitty's hand on a spot of J.R.'s bare shoulder.

Kitty touched him lightly, then moved her hand up his neck to his cheek. She laughed nervously. "He needs a shave." Then she covered her mouth with one hand and started crying. She sat in the chair, then took a sobering breath and ran her hands softly over his bandaged arm. Then her fingers closed over his hand. Still crying, she leaned her head against the edge of the bed for the longest time. Then she stopped, raised her head, and said, "I'm sorry."

"It's okay, Kitty. My God. It's okay."

"I'm going to stay. I don't care how long it takes for him to wake up. I'll be okay."

"Sure. I understand."

"Thank you, Charley." She sounded as if she wanted to say more but couldn't find the words.

Charley patted her shoulder. "I know." She followed the doctor out of the room.

He closed the door. She knew Skip and J.R. worked together often and lately Red and two other men were on the same team. "How can I find out if there was anyone else on that plane?"

"I'd start with the War Office."

"Thank you." Charley turned. There had been a maze of hallways from the front doors to this ward. "Where's the nearest exit? Do I have to go all the way back through to the front entrance?"

"No. Go through those doors and you'll see an exit at the end of the hallway."

"Thank you." She turned and left through a set of swinging doors.

"REMEMBER ME"

He stepped out of the cab. The air smelled of smoke from the bombings the night before. Fires were still burning that morning in the warehouses on the wharves. He paid the cabbie and walked inside the hospital, spoke to a nurse and got the directions to Cassidy's room, before he moved down corridors that smelled like antiseptic, sulfur, and heroism.

In the C Ward, he found the room number and quietly opened the door.

Cassidy's wife was sitting by the bed talking softly.

He waited for her to finish, then asked, "How is he?"

She turned when he spoke. Her face was red and wet from crying.

"I hurt like hell," Cassidy rasped, and opened his eyes. "How come that kid hit me so damn many times and missed you?"

"Clean living. Have you seen Charley?"

"She was just here a minute ago," Kitty said to him. "She walked outside with the doctor."

"Excuse me . . . I have to find her."

Cassidy looked at him.

He met that look for a fraction of a second, then wordlessly left the room.

A doctor came out of the next room and turned, looking down at a chart. He started to make notes.

"I'm looking for a woman."

The doctor looked up.

"Tall, blonde."

"Miss Morrison?"

"Yes. Have you seen her?"

"She left. Through those doors and toward the exit. If you hurry you should be able to catch her."

"Thanks." He ran past the doctor and through the swinging doors.

She was at the other end of the hall, her hand on the exit door.

"Charley!"

She turned and looked at him. "Oh! I'm so glad you're here. I thought you might have been with J.R."

He didn't stop running until he was in front of her. "I'm glad I caught you." He paused, looking at her face and trying to find the words. "Let's go sit down and talk."

"What? Why?" For a mere second she looked confused, then her expression changed suddenly. "Oh, God. No . . ." She put her hand out, palm toward him. "Red? Where's Skip?" She was looking into his eyes with a pleading look. "He wasn't with Cassidy."

"He didn't make it, Charley. They shot the plane down before he could get out."

"Oh, my God . . . Oh, my God . . ." There was such a harrowing look of human pain on her face that keeping his own void of emotion almost killed him.

She reached out toward him, then suddenly pulled back, shaking her head, her hand still out almost warding him off. "No . . ." She looked unsteady, teetering like someone old and disoriented.

He wasn't certain if he should reach out and steady her or hold her. He wanted to do something. Instead he did nothing but stand there.

She put her hand on the wall, straight-armed, as if it were all that was holding her up. She was staring down at the ground, her breathing labored, then she just melted onto the floor, huddled there, pulling her legs to herself. The sound she made was the worst thing he'd ever heard.

He sat down with her, beside her, wrapped his arms around her and pulled her against him, rocking her. "I'm sorry . . ."

Her fists hit his shoulders, not hard, but with each whispered "No . . . No . . . No . . ."

He rested his chin on her head and held her even tighter. "I'm sorry . . . Charley, I'm so sorry."

"ALONE"

TWO MONTHS LATER

She was down by the lake at Keighley near the broad and ancient elm trees that had survived generations of wars and politics. The wild ducks were noisy, but the swans wonderfully quiet. Charley was sitting on the grass, cross-legged, as she watched those swans glide over the lake. She liked the way they moved, smooth and effortlessly, like a plane in the sky on a clear, aquamarine day.

They were black swans. Somehow black swans, like black roses, were right for this place. Not because they were the color of mourning. They were the color of his hair.

She picked up a basket of freshly cut flowers, bright yellow and red, and filled the grave next to his. Graves without flowers looked sorrowful, lost, or even worse . . . they looked forgotten.

Isn't that the reason for a marker? It's not so you know where someone's buried in the ground. After all, the soul, the thing that matters, well, it isn't there anymore. It's out there somewhere in "the Grand Scheme of Things." Perhaps that place is called Heaven. Perhaps that place is called Hell. Or perhaps, the soul is like a hundred fireflies on a summer night, scattering light, just small bits of it, here and there in the memory and the hearts of the ones left behind.

The reason you mark the earth with a gravestone is to say: this person was here.

Charley adjusted the black roses. She needed them to look perfect. Fussy. She was being fussy. She glanced up. Audrey stood at the garden doors. For a moment Charley thought she might walk down the path.

Kitty had been Skip's answer for his mother. Everyone who mattered understood that for Audrey, losing her eyesight was like a raindrop in a hurricane compared to losing her son. Her suffering was deeply horrific.

So many mothers' sons were dead on the front lines, or worse yet, buried beneath blank white crosses, their parents never knowing where they were, the sons now only a name typed in black ink on a list in some government office.

Why was it that people didn't know what to say to those left behind? Their voices, their choice of words, always felt grating, like a record played on the wrong speed. All the words in all the human languages in all the world were too trivial to comfort a loss that was so deeply personal.

But she and Audrey walked together sometimes, feeling an unspoken closeness in their shared grief and love of the same man. The sounds here by the lake and in the gardens, the life outside, free and open, helped Audrey exist in a world where mothers outlived their sons.

The doors opened wider and her father came outside to stand beside Audrey. He smiled and waved to her. She waved back and watched him lean down to speak to Audrey, before they went inside.

Charley stood and dusted the grass and dirt from her skirt, then moved over to sit down on a bench setting in the sunshine, surrounded by flower beds, a sundial, and stone birdbath; it was the kind of place where grandmothers let children sit on their laps.

She heard the crunch of steps on the gravel path behind her and turned around.

Red stopped with a suddenness that said he was afraid to come closer.

"Hi." She smiled. "Come here. The sunshine is wonderful."

Red walked toward her in that loose-limbed, Southern walk of his, hands and feet moving different ways all at once. "I just wanted to see how you're doing."

She scooted over and patted the stone seat. "Sit."

He sat down and stretched out his legs, his hands resting between them.

She turned her face upward. "The sun feels good."

He looked up, then she could feel him looking at her.

"Kitty told Audrey about this wonderful quote from Helen Keller. She said, 'Turn your face toward the sunshine and you'll never see the shadow.'"

"Does it work?"

"Sometimes."

Red seemed to understand. He sat there quietly, companionably. A mallard took off, and three others followed. A breeze ruffled past, and she wiped the hair away from her face.

"Charley?"

"Hmm?"

"I need to ask you something."

"Go ahead. Ask away."

"I want you to marry me." He blurted it out awkwardly.

She turned away from the sunshine and looked at him. "That wasn't a question."

"I didn't do that the right way." He sounded disgusted with himself.

"Someone told you I'm pregnant."

"I would marry you in a heartbeat, baby or no baby."

"Let me guess who it was. J.R., right?"

"Listen to me. Please. I would love your child. I'd be a good father."

"Oh, Red, you are a good man, and I know you would be a great father to any child." She placed her hand on his arm. "I love you for what you just asked, and even more for what you are willing to give up for me and my baby."

"I'm not giving up anything."

"I loved Skip. I still love him." She kissed his cheek. "Thank you, but I can't do that."

He didn't say anything for a long time. "I thought you might say that." He took a deep breath and exhaled. "I still had to ask."

They sat there shoulder to shoulder in the bright sunshine. Friends, perhaps more than friends.

"I might be nuts to do this," she said in a half-laugh. "I sure don't know anything about raising a child alone."

"You're not alone." He put his arm around her shoulders. "No matter what happens, you'll never be alone."

"COME FLY WITH ME"

OCTOBER 11, 1968

I am my father's son, not merely in name but in nature, or so they tell me. I never knew my father. He exists for me only as a character in a thousand stories—tales that are quite possibly taller than the man—and in a few faded black-and-white photographs.

But I see him in the mirror when I shave in the morning. Every so often I catch a glimpse of him that has nothing to do with muscle and blood and bone, only a fleeting bittersweet look in my mother's eyes. It was years before I understood that look for what it was: just one small second in a lifetime of hours, days, weeks, months, and years, where I have done something that instantly reminds her of him.

With my grandmother it's different. For her, my mother says I have replaced him, that losing him was more than even a strong woman like Audrey could accept. I, too, am called Skip, and lately, sometimes she forgets which one she's talking to.

When I was a child, she was my favorite person in the world. She always recognized my footsteps. No matter what else was going on around her, she knew when I was in the room. She was a young woman, not even fifty when I was born. She is blind. The blast from a bomb during the Blitz took her eyesight, but I have always been amazed at what she, a woman who has lost her sight, can see.

We had a deal, she and I, for the times when I would visit her. She loves the outdoors, breathing in the fragrance of her complex English gardens or the arid, stark simplicity of the New Mexican desert. I was probably only four or five when we decided that I would be her eyes for those long walks in the English country or the Southwest, those moments when it was only the two of us. She, in turn, passed on to me the stories of my father's life he was not there to tell, stories as stark as white chalk against the blank paternal slate of my child's mind. It was my grandmother who gave me the strongest sense of both the boy and the man my father was.

Audrey is my only grandmother, both paternal and maternal. Yes, that's right. My father's mother married my mother's father. My grandfather claims that she did so just to create confusion for a future generation, for some poor bored relative with an interest in genealogy, whose purpose in life will be to document where we all have come from in the hope of finding out who they are.

My grandfather is Robert Morrison, a legend in aviation design, a man who knows exactly what he wants and has never been afraid to go after it. He showed me this impossible world is full of possibilities. "Who," he always says, "would have thought a man could fly?"

I look at my watch. The hands are dragging. By now a crowd of VIPs are gathering in bleachers to watch. My mother will be among them, standing head and shoulders above every woman there, and above every woman I have ever met in my life. She complains to me about never seeing any grandchildren, and I tell her when I meet a girl like her, I'll marry her in a heartbeat. And I will, too.

My dad is there. My stepdad. When I was a boy, he taught me how to tell the weather by the moon and the sky; how to find my way home by a star; how to shoot a dove off a fence with a single shot and to bait a fish hook. He taught me to understand the land and the soil and the truly important things: to take a man for who he was, not how he looked or spoke. That it was okay to be alone in the world. Dad taught me all the things a man should know, the things his granddaddy taught him, the things my mother says make you into a good man.

The men in my family are good men. My best friend is a good man. He isn't here. He can't be. Jim is somewhere in the jungles of Viet Nam. But the General and his wife Kitty wouldn't miss this. They are his father and mother and my parents' closest friends. They started out as strangers, over a quarter of a century ago, but were brought together by war, kept together by the bonds of its experience, their lives irrevocably entwined even until today, even in the generation after them.

The call comes. Nothing complex, simply a statically rasping voice over an intercom and the flash of a green light on a pale wall in the waiting area filled with orange Naugahyde furniture and brown tweed carpet.

I walk down the halls, into an elevator, out on the boarding ramp, then inside the cockpit, my crew walking along with me. I'm the pilot, a boy's dream come true after a lot of hard work.

Thank you, Grandfather.

I take my seat and buckle in. Before I begin system checks I pat my chest pocket for luck. Inside is a small hunk of smooth turquoise over seventy years old that has seen the farm fields of Texas and the battlefields of war. Also there are the photographs I needed to bring with me today: an old shot of a dashing RAF pilot in uniform standing next to a Spitfire, his expression serious, and a newer one of a tall red-haired man looking out from the cockpit of a twin-engine Cessna with a grin as big as Texas; the man who gave me life, and the man who taught me how to live it.

I am about to live this life like few men can. For the next interminable minutes my time belongs to others. I do my job, checking and rechecking the systems, doing the work I've trained for.

And then it is time. I close my eyes. I feel the speed like no other aircraft on earth; it consumes my body. In my earphones I hear "Houston. We have liftoff."

My special thanks to the following:

Scott Olitsky, M.D., Associate Professor of Ophthalmology, State University of New York at Buffalo, Chief of Ophthalmology, The Children's Hospital of Buffalo, for his insight and invaluable assistance on macular degeneration, and for his kindness in answering all of my "what if" questions no matter how odd.

Captain Tom Adams, pilot, Northwest Airlines, retired, for his help with the details of aeronautics, the flight sequences, and scene problems that arose in this book. His knowledge and kind advice made the flight scenes plausible. Any mistakes made in those sections of the book are mine alone.

Angel Fernandez, MA3, U. S. Navy, for kindly guiding both me and my characters through their missions and for his technical advice on weapons, vehicles, strategy, and what it's like to jump out of a plane, because I would never try it!

Linda and **Peter Crone,** for their German expertise, for the stories of the war, and most of all for a treasured friendship that has lasted over forty years.

Joyce Boren, for the wonderful gift of her cousin's poignant letters home.

John Robertson, for his expertise on anything with an engine, and for his friendship for thirty-four years.

Lillian Schoppa, for scouring the dusty depths of Larry McMurtry's antiquarian bookstore and finding the treasures of information I needed. And for just being one of the finest ladies I've ever known.

Lu Barnett and **Jan Barnett,** for their vibrant memories.

Pocket Books, everyone past and present, for their support since 1988. In particular, Gina Centrello for starting this, Linda Marrow for the years of creative freedom, Judith Curr for believing in the idea, and Maggie Crawford for her incredibly wise editorial insight, her time and patience, and her magic pencil.

Marcy Posner, for her faith, her persistence, and her friendship. So much of this belongs to you.

Kim Fisk, my assistant, for her hard work and for actually being able to find my notes in any language, on any size slip of paper, in the black hole that is my desk. You are amazing.

Kristin Hannah, for her constant and unflagging support over the years of our friendship, and in particular over the twenty-two months it took for the creation of this book—there really are no words.

And my favorite person in the world, my daughter, who understands my creative mind, accepts my writer's life as normal, even with all its pratfalls and rainbow moments.

**Visit the Simon & Schuster
romance Web site:**

www.SimonSaysLove.com

**and sign up for our
romance e-mail updates!**

Keep up on the latest
new romance releases,
author appearances, news, chats,
special offers, and more!
We'll deliver the information
right to your inbox—if it's new,
you'll know about it.

POCKET BOOKS

2800.02

Visit
❖ Pocket Books ❖
online at

www.SimonSays.com

Keep up on the latest new releases from your favorite authors, as well as author appearances, news, chats, special offers and more.

2381-01